Hao, by contrast, looked extremely pleased with himself, and grinned at Gita on his way by.

Tu Winston and Raj Peche, Trackers who were among the best in the empire, followed in the gunrunner's wake, and Emmory came into the room behind them. He paused a moment to speak with Gita, nodding and gripping her shoulder briefly before closing the door behind her.

Sinking back into my seat seemed the best option. I crossed my legs and leaned back, raising an eyebrow at Hao. He bared his teeth at me in a wicked grin and shoved Bial to the floor.

"Your Imperial Majesty." Hao's bow was ridiculously extravagant.

"A gift, Hao? It's not even my birthday."

Praise for

THE INDRANAN WAR

BEHIND THE THRONE

"This debut ranks among the best political SF novels in years, largely because of the indomitable, prickly Hail... [a] fast-paced, twisty space opera."   —*Library Journal* (starred review)

"Taut suspense, strong characterization, and dark, rapid-fire humor are the highlights of this excellent SF adventure debut."
—*Publishers Weekly* (starred review)

"Full of fast-paced action and brutal palace intrigue, starring the fiercest princess this side of Westeros."
—*B&N Sci-Fi & Fantasy Blog*

AFTER THE CROWN

"*Crown* is fast paced, and its focus on a female action heroine defined by her decisions rather than romance is refreshing and fun."   —*Washington Post*

"Craving a galactic adventure? K. B. Wagers's second Indranan War novel is just the ticket."   —*Bookish*

"Two books in, this series has exemplified political plotting as compelling as the badass heroine at its center."
—*B&N Sci-Fi & Fantasy Blog*

By K. B. Wagers

THE INDRANAN WAR
Behind the Throne
After the Crown
Beyond the Empire

BEYOND THE EMPIRE

THE INDRANAN WAR: BOOK 3

K. B. WAGERS

www.orbitbooks.net

Copyright © 2017 by Katy B. Wagers
Excerpt from *There Before the Chaos* copyright © 2017 by Katy B. Wagers

Author photograph by Donald Branum
Cover design by Lauren Panepinto
Cover images by Shutterstock and Arcangel Images
Cover copyright © 2017 by Hachette Book Group, Inc.

Orbit
Hachette Book Group
1290 Avenue of the Americas
New York, NY 10104
orbitbooks.net

First Edition: November 2017

Orbit is an imprint of Hachette Book Group.
The Orbit name and logo are trademarks of Little, Brown Book Group Limited.

The publisher is not responsible for websites (or their content)
that are not owned by the publisher.

The Hachette Speakers Bureau provides a wide range of authors for speaking events. To find out more, go to www.hachettespeakersbureau.com or call (866) 376-6591.

Library of Congress Cataloging-in-Publication Data

Names: Wagers, K. B., author.
Title: Beyond the empire / K.B. Wagers.
Description: First edition. | New York : Orbit, 2017. | Series:
The Indranan War ; book 3
Identifiers: LCCN 2017012251| ISBN 9780316308649 (trade pbk.) |
ISBN 9780316308656 (ebook (open)) | ISBN 9781478923473
(audio book (downloadable))
Subjects: LCSH: Space colonies—Fiction. | GSAFD: Science fiction. |
Adventure fiction. | Suspense fiction.
Classification: LCC PS3623.A35245 B49 2017 | DDC 813/.6—dc23
LC record available at https://lccn.loc.gov/2017012251

ISBNs: 978-0-316-30864-9 (trade paperback), 978-0-316-30865-6 (ebook)

Printed in the United States of America

LSC-C

10 9 8 7 6 5 4 3 2 1

Dear Carrie Fisher,

*I never got to tell you
what an honor it was
to have Hail
compared to Leia
or how much
your strength
meant to me.*

Thank You

BEYOND THE EMPIRE

1

The impact of fist to bag echoed up through my arm. It was a rhythmic shock—*one, one, two, backhand, two, elbow*—in time with the beating of my broken heart.

Sweat dripped into my eyes, burning them. The sting wasn't enough to erase the image of Clara Desai's lifeless body sliding to the floor.

A matriarch of the empire. The head of the council; a woman who'd been there for my whole childhood and had welcomed me back home without the slightest hesitation. There had been no concern from Clara, of either my right or my ability to rule. Unlike so many others, she'd planted herself at my side and defended me.

She had defended me to the end and been loyal to me and to Indrana, even as she was slaughtered in front of my eyes by the same man who was responsible for the death of my whole family.

Wilson.

I snarled and slammed my fist into the bag again.

Wilson had engineered it all: from the assassination of my father more than twenty years ago, to the deaths of my sisters, my niece, and my mother.

A week ago he'd looked me in the eye and told me he wouldn't stop the killing until everyone I cared about was dead.

Then he'd shot Clara.

One, one, two. Backhand, two, elbow. Elbow. I grabbed the bag and rammed my knee into it twice with a snarl of rage, only backing off to wipe the sweat from my face before I surged forward again.

The worst thing was I still didn't know why. I didn't know what my family had done to this man to engender such vicious fury in our direction.

Wilson was a ghost: a man with no real name, no real face, no real past. What was I? Gunrunner, Empress of Indrana; none of it seemed to matter. I was losing a game directed by a madman. Cressen Stone wouldn't have let this happen. She would have stopped at nothing to exact justice, or get revenge. I was fast becoming a pale shadow of my former self, the best parts of me disappearing like ash in a stiff breeze.

I welcomed the pain as I slammed the side of my fist into the bag.

"How long has she been at that?" Zin asked the audience who sat a safe distance away from me.

"About an hour," Cas replied.

"She looks ready to drop. Why haven't you stopped her?"

"Emmory wouldn't."

"Don't look at me," Iza said. "I don't want to get punched today."

"Her Majesty's care and feeding isn't my area," Hao replied, but the laughter in my former mentor's voice was edged with the slightest hint of concern.

He was right to be concerned. Clara's death had hit us all hard, drowning out our euphoria from our victory over the

Saxon forces at Canafey and sending us into a depression we'd yet to recover from.

I spun, my bare heel slamming into the bag, knocking it loose from its mooring, and my Guards fell silent when it crashed to the floor.

"Hail."

I swung at Zin, my fist coming around in what would have been a brutal haymaker had it connected. As per usual, my BodyGuard leaned out of the way of my punch with an exhalation. He caught my wrist on its way by, guiding it past his expressionless face.

Fool that I was, I tried to hit him with my other hand as I sailed by him, but Zin was already gone, his grip on my wrist a fading memory. I spun, fists raised, and came at him again.

Zin stepped to the side, easily avoiding my punch. His hands were up, palms open and facing me. "You know I'm not going to fight you," he said. His voice was too gentle, teasing aside the anger in my gut to get at the pain underneath. "Stop it."

I stared at him and sucked in a lungful of air before I replied, "I can't."

If I stop I'll fall apart.

A sad smile flickered over his face. "I know, ma'am. Keep moving. Don't stop. You'll break apart in front of everyone and be no use at all. I know. I did just that when you needed me most. I failed you, ma'am. I know it. You know it. Emmory knows it. I chose him over you. His loyalty is endless. Mine, apparently, is not."

"Damn it, Zin, we've been over this—"

He shook his head, and I swallowed back my words. I'd ordered him to stay with Emmory when my *Ekam* had been shot—killed, if we were being honest. The only reason Emmory was alive was because Fasé had brought him back to life. Without the Farian's strange abilities, I'd be down not just one but two more of my BodyGuards. The thought made me ill.

Zin had done what I told him to do, but the cost to my BodyGuard's confidence was written all over his face.

I dropped my hands, fists uncurling in surrender—or exhaustion, it was hard to tell.

"Majesty," Zin said, his voice more formal. "Your *Ekam* would like to see you."

I took the out he handed me along with the towel Hao passed over. I didn't have the energy to fight with my Body-Guard and we both knew it. Zin could take me down even at my best, anyway, and right now I was far from my best. But I filed away the look in his eyes to bring up with Emmory later. We still had some downtime, and it was time best spent healing—for all of us.

The others formed up around us and the two Royal Marines inside the door of the gym snapped to attention, opening the doors as we approached.

My rock star status had gone through the roof since the battle of Canafey, and only someone truly insane would make an attempt on my life right now. That didn't stop my *Ekam* from being excessively cautious.

Rumors swirled about my part in the fight on Darshan Station, despite my best attempts to downplay my involvement and turn the attention to Admiral Hassan and the real heroes of the fight. The "Gunrunner Empress" of Indrana was on everyone's lips, and if Hao was to be believed, in everyone's hearts.

However, no matter how suicidal an assassination attempt might be, my enemies had already proven their disregard for human life. Wilson would mow down a thousand of my people for the chance to kill me. Emmory wasn't about to take any chances, and I couldn't blame him for his caution.

He'd been startled by my lack of protest over the decision to move the command center to the planet, but it wasn't much of an argument in my mind. Ships I could do, those at least moved around. But a space station was just a gigantic box in the sky—immobile and vulnerable. Darshan Station was even more so because of the damage from the fight to retake the system.

I needed the fresh air planetside.

Thankfully, it was springtime in the capital of Canafey Major. The mild weather was a blessing after frozen Pashati and the blackness of space, especially now that my customary nightmares had made their reappearance in the early-morning hours. Portis, Jet, Clara—there were far too many lives on my conscience. Too many people I hadn't been able to save.

Most of the rubble in the governor's mansion on Canafey Major had been cleaned up by the Saxons after their attack, and the surrender of the majority of the troops on the ground had happened without additional damage to the old structure. Saxon guerillas would test the palace defenses and lob ordnance in our direction every chance they got. It had made for a nerve-racking situation the first few days, but now it seemed like one more annoyance to deal with before I left.

I walked through the spotless corridors, the ghosts of paintings visible only in their absence on the walls and the empty cases with shattered glass panels telling the story of their missing contents.

"Majesty." Stasia met me at the door of my temporary rooms. I'd refused to stay in Governor Phillus's now-vacant quarters and so we were in the wing for visiting guests instead.

"Stasia. How is Fasé this morning?"

"Better, I think, ma'am. I haven't seen her yet today, but Major Morri said she ate without a fuss." Grief flickered for an instant in my maid's smile, but it was gone as quick as a flame in the vacuum of space.

I'd almost lost Fasé, too. Bringing Emmory back to life violated a religious code of her people, and the crisis of faith nearly drove Fasé to suicide. My intervention had stopped her, but the repercussions likely went deeper than any of us could guess. She'd been unresponsive since the incident on Admiral Hassan's ship, but the fact that she was eating was a good sign.

"Zin said you were coming, ma'am. I started a shower for you."

Steam filled the bathroom. I stripped, and covered my hair before I stepped under the water because if I got it wet it would take us an extra hour to make it presentable.

In the safety of the shower, I queued up the playback of Clara's death and watched it. I let the tears fall where the water hid their path down my face. It was the only place I cried. Since Clara's death I hadn't let so much as a single tear slip in front of another living soul. I needed to be strong for those around me, be the empress my mother, and Clara, and so many others believed I could be. Empresses didn't weep in public, didn't show emotion. Only in the safety of the water, with the sound to hide my weeping and the beating spray to wash the imaginary blood from my hands, could I cry.

Scrubbing at my skin never took all the blood off, no matter how hot I let the water get or how hard I rubbed. It wouldn't ever get rid of it, of all the lives and deaths that I now carried with me.

I dried off and dressed in a brand-new uniform. The local black fabric of Canafey was rougher than the ones from the palace, but I was thankful we'd found replacements for the cobbled-together garb we'd all been wearing since Red Cliff. The uniform gave us cohesion even when we were spinning away from each other like planets in a newly formed solar system.

Unwinding the wrapping from my hair, I undid my braid and ran my fingers through the curls to give my scalp some air. I walked out of the bathroom.

And straight into an argument between Emmory and Zin. They were toe to toe, shoulders tense and mouths set in hard lines.

"That's not the point I was trying to make and you know it."

"It is *exactly* the point, Emmory, I—" Zin snapped his mouth shut when he spotted me. "Majesty, there's food."

"Thank you. Good morning, Emmory." It seemed the safest thing to say.

"Majesty." He inclined his shaved head in my direction. Emmorlien Haris Tresk didn't show the slightest sign that he'd died on me only a few weeks ago. My primary BodyGuard's shoulders were back to their ramrod stiffness, and his impassive face didn't show the same worry for me that the others couldn't hide.

I knew it was there, though. We both did. Right this moment I wasn't entirely sure if the uneasy muscle twitch at his jaw was my fault or Zin's. So I nodded, not looking their way as I sat in a ridiculously ornate chair with carved lion heads for arms. I mechanically chewed and swallowed, knowing my BodyGuards were watching and calculating every gram of food that passed my lips.

It was so much like my parents watching me to make sure I didn't sneak my vegetables off onto Cire's plate that I couldn't stop the laugh. It quickly turned into a coughing fit when a piece of my toast went down the wrong way, but I waved everyone off.

"I'm fine." I coughed again, finally clearing the wayward

crumb, and pushed my plate away. Sipping at my chai, I watched Emmory over the rim of my cup. Zin turned his back on both of us and I raised an eyebrow that my *Ekam* ignored—mostly.

"Leave it alone, Majesty," he subvocalized over our *smatis*.

The array of chips in our heads provided us with short-range communication without the aid of additional equipment, data storage, and a host of other abilities depending on make and model of the processors.

"It's none of your concern."

"My BodyGuards, my concern," I replied, but didn't pursue the matter further. For one, Zin was still in the room; for the other, Emmory would talk when he was ready. Or when I ran out of patience and made him.

I took socks and my new boots from Stasia, putting them on and then sitting still as she wove my green curls up into several looping twists.

"Zin, is Hao hanging around outside?" I asked.

"I don't think so, Majesty. I believe he went to check on Gita."

"Go see, would you?"

"Yes, ma'am." Zin dropped his head forward in a bow and left me alone with my maid and *Ekam*.

"So was that just an elaborate ruse to get me out of the gym?" I asked half an hour later as Stasia finished my hair. "Or did you actually have something to talk to me about?"

"I've officially picked five Royal Marines to add to your BodyGuard detail," Emmory said. "We'll start rotating them into the schedule this evening."

"The same ones you've had on door duty?"

He nodded.

"Okay, files?" I held my hand out and Emmory brushed his palm over mine.

The door opened again, Zin and Hao entering.

Cheng Hao, my mentor from my gunrunning days, had saved us back on Red Cliff. I still hadn't found out if his presence at a hidden landing pad on the planet had been a coincidence or not. I wasn't given to the idea that the universe favored me in any fashion, so I was leaning toward not.

His uncle, Po-Sin, was the most feared Cheng gang lord in the galaxy—a position he'd earned through uncompromising brutality and shrewd business sense. I'd enjoyed working for—and with—them both, though of the two I felt like Hao was less likely to stab me in the back.

I'd thought Hao would remind me I owed him a favor and head back to his uncle, but he'd stuck around for far longer than I'd expected. Hao and our other impromptu allies—the smuggler king Bakara Rai and his companion, Johar—made for a merry band of criminals. I figured Rai was hanging around because I owed him money. With Johar it was harder to tell—I think she really just enjoyed being around so many women.

"Brought you a gun," he said, tossing a QLZ-77 in my direction. I caught it neatly, grinning at him when he set the weapon packs on the table out of my reach.

"How's Gita?"

"Better, Majesty. She's responding to questions and I got a smile out of her," Hao replied. The honorific still sounded strange coming out of his mouth, though he seemed quite at ease with it.

Whatever the level of my grief over Clara's murder was, it was nothing compared to my BodyGuard's.

Gita Desai was Clara's second child, and her gasp of pain when her mother died still echoed in my head at night. She'd been catatonic for the last week, straining my already minimal BodyGuard coverage even further.

"Do you think she's going to recover, or should we leave her here?"

"I think that depends on how long you are planning on staying in Canafey."

I shared a look with Emmory. Hao knew damn well I didn't have anything resembling a plan at the moment. Wilson, in collusion with Eha Phanin, my former prime minister, was presently in control of Pashati, Ashva, and half the worlds in the empire.

Meanwhile I had all the other planets, a fleet of ships—including forty-seven of our newest *Vajrayana* warships—and presumably the support of my people throughout the empire. Still, there were too many variables, too many unknowns, and I hadn't had a moment to catch my breath, let alone plan something.

"We have time," I said, knowing that wouldn't fool Hao in the slightest. "Any news about Wilson?"

Hao shook his head. "Not yet, I've got a call incoming in about ten minutes. I'll let you know after what they found."

"Do that." Because I could, I waved a hand at the door with a grin that Hao echoed.

"Majesty, if you'll excuse me also, I need to give Indula a hand with something." Zin followed Hao out of the room.

My *Ekam* watched the door, the frustration and pain surprisingly clear on his face, and I took another stab at proving my suspicions over what my *Ekam* and his husband were fighting about.

"How's Zin?" I asked.

Emmory blinked at me. "Majesty, please."

"Have you talked to him? He thinks he failed me, Emmory."

"Oh. That."

"Yes, that." I arched an eyebrow in his direction. "Was that what you two were talking about when I came in?"

He sighed and rubbed a hand over his face.

I wasn't sure it was any kind of relief to have my suspicions about the ongoing argument between the two of them confirmed. Crossing the room, I leaned on the windowsill. "We've all been through the wringer, Emmy. Are we going to be able to get our shit together before we leave here?"

Emmory's laugh was rusty and he joined me at the window. "To be honest, ma'am, have we had our shit together at all since we first met? I don't know about you, but I feel like we've been winging it."

"Good point." I leaned against him and laughed. "I had plans, you just kept messing them up. At least in the beginning."

"You mean that brilliant plan to steal a shuttle and try to run from a *Jarita*?"

I laughed. "Yeah, running from a battlecruiser in a shuttle was probably not my best plan, but I was pressed for time. How did you know I'd do that? I remember you saying Zin thought I would stay but that you knew me better."

"I do," Emmory said with a smile. "Portis said you wouldn't come home willingly. I had nearly three months to study you before we met on *Sophie*."

"And twenty years of Portis's reports on me." The pain was sharp, more so because I realized I hadn't thought of Portis for a while. My lover, my BodyGuard, Emmory's brother—Portis Tresk had been the best thing in my life since I'd left home, and his death had left a gaping hole I'd had no choice but to ignore in favor of more pressing issues.

Now the grief was fading without my ever having faced it, and I wasn't sure if I welcomed its absence or if the void left behind was something far worse.

"You were his opposite in almost every way." Warmth coated Emmory's voice and he rested his hand over mine. "It got to where I could tell he was frustrated with you based on how carefully he chose his words."

"He was less careful with his words in person. Ask Hao about it sometime," I replied, and Emmory chuckled.

"I'm sure. The more I read his reports, the more I realized you were making choices that I would make." He gave me a sideways glance. "If you'll forgive me the familiarity, we are a lot alike."

"There's nothing to forgive and you know it. You're also right about us. We make a pretty good team, the three of us."

"I'll tell Zin you said so." He laughed. "He'll be horrified. I'll speak to him again, Majesty, about what happened on Red Cliff. I was trying to explain my thoughts to him earlier, but they just got tangled."

"Tell him to forgive himself, and that's an order from me." I turned my hand over, linking my fingers with Emmory's, and squeezed. "And forgive yourself for missing the clues about Phanin. I did, too."

"It won't happen again."

I nodded. "Let's go home, *Ekam*. I want my throne back."

The door cracked open and Iza stuck her head in. "Majesty, Alba is here to see you."

The low rumbling of explosions rattled the chamber, and I moved from the window before Emmory could move me. He tipped his head to the side as the report came in, but relaxed and shook his head with a smile. "Other side of the building, Majesty, we're fine."

"Send her in, Iza. You go on," I said to Emmory. "I'm sure you've got more important things to do. If the shelling continues, I'll go to the shelter like a good little empress."

Emmory's expression didn't change. "Would your Majesty like a chance to meet the Marines before their duties officially start?"

"No." I grinned, waving Alba into the room. "I'll chat with them as they come into the rotation, Emmory. Thank you."

He nodded at me and at Alba and left the room.

My chamberlain watched Emmory go with an expression that said she desperately wanted to ask what was going on.

Thankfully, her training kept her mouth shut and she gave me a quick bow, her raven-black braid swinging down with the movement. "Good morning, Majesty."

"Have a seat, Alba. What have we got this morning?"

"Quite a bit, Majesty. I've got reports from governors on Baisl, Sumeria, and Taos about movement by Solarian forces. Admiral Hassan would like us to hold here at least a week to give her time to sort through personnel and to take care of what repairs we can manage in that time. Major Morri asked for some time this week to talk about Fasé. And there's a sizable email queue to go through."

"Pull up a chair, then," I said with a smile. "Let's get to work."

2

I sat on my balcony, my eyes closed, watching as Wilson killed Clara. There were no more tears for me, just a clinical detachment as I took the man apart, piece by piece.

"Yes, the bone in the meatball, so I've learned."

How did he know that phrase? I froze the recording and played it back. There was no hesitation from Wilson, not even something to indicate that his *smati* was translating my words, just the instant recognition that could only come from someone familiar with the Old Tongue.

It stood to reason he'd be fluent in Indranan if he'd been studying the empire and my family for as long as he claimed; however, *kabab mein haddi* wasn't nearly as popular as the Solarian saying about monkeys and wrenches. My father had used it frequently throughout my childhood—usually in reference to me—and he'd always said it in the Old Tongue.

"Your Majesty? Am I interrupting?"

I turned at the baritone, blinking away the vision of Clara's last moments, and smiled at my visitor. "Colonel Bristol. How are you this evening?" Hafiz was a distant cousin of mine. The Marine had the same dark brown eyes and wide jaw of my great-grandfather. He was much shorter than me and nearly as wide as he was tall.

"I'm well, ma'am. You?"

"Surviving." I liked the colonel. He was a solid man who was respectful, but not in total awe of me.

Hafiz laughed, a deep bell of a sound. "Right now that's a good thing, ma'am. A very good thing indeed."

"Have a seat, Colonel." I gestured at the little table set up on the balcony of my rooms. The balcony was invisible from the outside, hidden by a camouflaged shield that allowed the fresh air and the late-evening sunshine in but nothing else. "Have you eaten?"

"I did, ma'am, but don't wait on my account."

"I ate already also. Stasia is a bit of a stickler about that. Something to drink?"

"Yes, coffee, please." Hafiz sank back into his seat when I waved him off and poured him a cup of coffee. He took it with a nod of thanks. "We located the Solarian embassy staff. The Saxons had detained them and were forcing them to make regular reports as though nothing unusual were happening."

"That's going to go over well back in the Conglomerate, I'm sure."

Hafiz chuckled. "I think we've located any and all relations of yours, Majesty. I'm still waiting to hear from Director Ganej about the people on Pashati. Everyone else is accounted for."

"Leena and Taran are still with the director?"

"Yes, ma'am. We're trying to figure out the best way to transport them off-planet without risk. At the moment it seems safer to leave them where they are."

I was sure Wilson didn't care about the fact that Taran was technically no longer my nephew. We'd secured him and Leena during the initial coup, and they were currently safe with my loyal forces on Pashati. I'd feel much better if I could get them out of Wilson's reach.

"Everyone not on the homeworld has been moved to a crown-loyal military installation."

"Good." I wasn't taking any chances with Wilson's threat. All my surviving relatives, no matter how distant, were in danger. "Your family is included in that, I assume?"

He smiled. "They were already on base, ma'am, but yes, they're safe."

I nodded with a slight hum. I'd alerted anyone from my gunrunner days I'd even remotely considered a friend, though the idea that Wilson could get a drop on any of them was laughable.

I didn't want their blood on my hands.

"I'm glad to hear it," I said, standing. "Let me know if the situation changes."

"I will, Majesty."

"Anything else?"

"That is it, with your leave, ma'am?"

I nodded and Major Bristol put his cup down as he stood, then gave me a short bow.

"Don't hesitate to let me know if you need anything else."

I watched him go. As hard as it was for me to trust anyone new, I liked the man.

Settling back in my chair, I scrolled through a briefing on a Saxon attack from yesterday. Thankfully, none of our troops were seriously injured, but the Saxon forces were still out there and I was done messing around. I pinged Nakula on the com. He'd never admit it, but the spy had saved all our lives when he saved the governor of Canafey Minor—Jia Li Ashwari. Jia's possession of the lock codes for the *Vajrayana* ships had put those high-tech battleships in my possession. With them, we'd been able to take back Canafey and would hopefully be able to retake the home system as well.

"Nakula, what news do we have on the Saxon rebels?"

"Nothing yet, Majesty. I'm narrowing down their location, should have something in a day or two."

"See that you do, I don't want anyone else injured because of them."

"Yes, Majesty."

I disconnected the call and glanced over at the older Marine on guard at the door. Gunnery Sergeant Jasa Runji was a solid, short woman with buzzed gray hair. According to her file she was a widow with five children and eighteen grandchildren. She was an expert markswoman, and judging from the glowing recommendations in her file from Lieutenant Colonel Teesha Alexander, Emmory was lucky to have stolen her away from her post in the squadron.

"Is your family back on Pashati, Gunny?"

Jasa blinked at me as the question took a moment to sink in. "No, Your Majesty. They're scattered. My two oldest girls live on Ashva. The other girl and my boys live on Leucht and Mundi."

"Are they safe?"

She smiled. "Yes, ma'am. Safe and waiting for you to return."

I was saved from babbling an embarrassed reply by Emmory's arrival. Jasa braced to attention, her hand twitching its desire to salute. Emmory smiled and clapped a hand down on the woman's shoulder, tilting his head toward the door. Jasa nodded and left.

Alba came through the door. "Majesty, I have President Hudson on the com link for you."

"Thank you, Alba." I checked my shirt and smoothed my hair down, settling into the chair once again.

"Should I call Stasia?" Emmory asked.

"No." I laughed. "I think I look fine."

Alba gave me a smile and a nod to let me know I passed her inspection. "On the wall, ma'am?"

"Actually, send it straight to my *smati*. Keep yourself looped in so you can hear."

"Yes, ma'am."

The chime of the incoming com link rang in my ear. I held my hand up and pasted a smile on my face before answering. "President Hudson."

Chad Hudson of the Solarian Conglomerate was older than me, his silver hair meticulously styled and his wide eyes set deep in his pale face. "Empress, it is a relief to see you well. We have been watching the news about Indrana with a great deal of trepidation."

I'm sure you have, I thought, but kept those words in my throat in favor of something more diplomatic. "Thank you. It's a most distressing situation. I am pleased to inform you that your ambassador and the embassy staff are unharmed. Colonel Bristol informed me the Saxons had stormed the grounds and taken them hostage. I'm sure Ambassador Smith will give you a full report."

"I have already spoken with him, Your Majesty. He asked me to pass along his gratitude to you and your people."

"He's most welcome."

"Your Majesty, what are your plans now?"

I blinked at him. "My plans, President Hudson?"

"Yes, Majesty."

"They aren't any of your concern," I replied, a careful smile now on my face. "The issue with the Saxon Alliance is between us and them, and the issue within Indrana is not the Solarian Conglomerate's concern."

Hudson frowned. "Your Majesty, I realize this is all very

new to you and on top of that these are most upsetting circumstances. However, you must realize that by firing on the Saxon vessels you've violated no less than four provisions in the peace treaty signed by Indrana?"

Alba's hissing exhale was barely audible. I didn't move, letting the careful non-expression smooth over my face, wiping away my smile, and picked through my next words with care.

"I believe that treaty became null and void the moment King Trace blew a sizable hole in Red Cliff. Or, actually, strike that—it would have become useless when the Saxons attacked Canafey in the first place. Indrana has the right to defend her territory, President Hudson, treaty or no." I smiled, watched him swallow, and continued. "I realize you're used to dealing with my mother. I am not her. My education wasn't palace-sanctioned and diplomat approved, but I do know what I'm doing."

He jumped when I clapped my hand on the table.

"So, we will see to it that your people are packed and headed back to you within the week."

"You're kicking the embassy out?"

"Not at all, Mr. President!" I laughed, the sound ringing across the com link. "It's a war zone here. Far too dangerous. I wouldn't want anything to happen to citizens of the Conglomerate on my watch. When things are safe again we can talk about reopening the embassy."

"Your Majesty," he sputtered. "The Solarian Conglomerate would be more than willing to mediate discussions with the Saxons on Indrana's behalf. We can help you."

"I don't believe we need your help," I replied, a cool smile now on my face. "The discussion with the Saxons will be relatively short. You are welcome again for the rescue of your people. Have a nice evening." I disconnected the link and launched out of my chair. "Can you believe that man?"

"I wish I could say no, Majesty, but I'd be lying." Alba smiled and got to her feet.

"Lecturing me about treaties when those Shiva-damned bastards dropped a building on our heads. They held his people hostage! The man's brain is soft if he thinks I'm just going to sit politely at a table with the Saxons after all this." I stopped and pressed both hands to my eyes, dragging in a breath, exhaling it with a groan. "*Uff,* I sound like my mother."

"A bit, Majesty." Emmory somehow managed to say that without the slightest bit of sarcasm.

The door cracked open. "Your Majesty, are you all right?" Jasa poked her head into the room.

"I am supremely annoyed," I said, and then laughed. "I'm fine, Gunny. Alba, send Admiral Hassan a note and ask her to come down and see me as soon as it's convenient."

The room shook before Alba could open her mouth to reply. "Oh, bugger me."

Emmory rushed to me and pushed me away from the windows. "Majesty." He had us through the door before the second mortar shell impacted the building, his hand wrapped around my upper arm.

"I know, I know." I looked at Alba. "Also, find Hao and tell him I want to see him after this nuisance is over."

"Move, Majesty."

"I am moving."

Emmory hustled me out of the room. The mansion shook again when a third mortar hit, showering me with dust from the ceiling, and I muttered a curse. "I'm getting tired of these people."

"I know, ma'am. Nakula is working on it."

"So he said. He needs to hurry it up." My breath hitched when we reached the bunker deep within the mansion interior. Emmory was well used to my reaction and didn't press as I fought a silent battle with my claustrophobia before stepping into the windowless room.

The doors closed behind us and I squeezed my eyes shut. Focusing on a litany to Ganesh helped ease the panic in my chest. "I'm serious, Emmy," I said during a break in the litany. "Tell Nakula if he doesn't handle this soon—I will."

"Of course, Majesty."

I smacked him in the chest. "I heard that smile. Watch yourself."

Emmory chuckled aloud but fell into silence when the building shook again. The tattered forces of the Saxons were a bit more determined this time, it seemed.

I started pacing the length of the windowless room. I knew the dimensions by heart. Our first visit had lasted an hour and I'd counted every square centimeter of the place to try to keep the panic at bay. Governor Phillus's panic room was more spartan and a great deal smaller than the one back in my palace, with only a few chairs and a table at the far end of the sixteen-meter room and a desk at the other.

The Saxon attack on Canafey Major had been so swift the governor hadn't even had the chance to make it to his bunker. He'd issued the lockdown order on the *Vajrayana* ships in the yard from his office and then blown his *smati* out of his skull.

"Did you have a chance to talk to Zin?"

"Yes."

Emmory's response was grim and I made a face. "Not good?"

"No."

"Are you going to tell me?"

"I'm going to tell you again it's not your concern, Majesty."

"*Ekam*, I am the empress. You don't get to tell me what is and is not my concern."

"Fine." The word was clipped. "He is no longer feeling sorry for himself. Now he's angry at me because I said something stupid."

"What did you say?"

His shoulders sagged. "Majesty—"

"No, you'll listen. We're about to head out of here and go up against a man who's not only possibly smarter than both of us, but who's spent his entire life trying to destroy my empire. Distractions are not an option. I can't let either of you leave Canafey without having settled this."

"It's too late. I hurt him. I didn't mean for it to sound the way it did. I know you ordered him to stay. I wouldn't have blamed him even if you hadn't."

I crossed to him and put my hand on his shoulder. The depth of pain in Emmory's voice was a pale echo of what I'd felt when he died and it was the reason, as much as I disliked meddling in my BodyGuards' lives, that I kept pushing the issue. Emmory had died because of me; the least I could do was try to fix it.

"It's never too late. What did you say?"

"He thinks I was mad at him for staying with me. I wasn't, Hail, I swear. That's Zin's own insecurities about choosing me over you coming to life to snarl at him in the night.

"I have never blamed him for that. I can't change who I am. I swore an oath to you, to Indrana, and I'll follow through with it to the end. If something happens to me, that's fine. I'm okay with it. But I don't want to drag him down with me when I go." Emmory gritted the next words out from between clenched teeth as if each one were being pulled from him. "He almost died because of me. We've always known that was the reality, it just—"

"He was dying," I murmured, remembering Henna's words to me in the med bay and my own panicked desperation.

"It's not that I don't want this bond. It has been the most

precious thing in my whole life. He has been the most precious thing in my whole life."

"You tried to explain all that to him and mangled it, didn't you?"

Emmory closed his eyes. "Badly."

"Go apologize," I ordered. "Don't try to explain it. Just say you're sorry. He'll forgive you."

Emmory nodded and we lapsed into silence for a long moment. The image of him, still and dying on the floor of Hao's ship, rose up to lodge in my throat, choking the air from my lungs. "Emmy?" I was all too aware of the wobble in my voice. "What did it feel like when you died?"

I kept my eyes locked on the cold steel of the wall in front of me, not daring a glance back at my BodyGuard.

Emmory was silent for so long I thought he wasn't going to answer me. "It didn't feel like anything, Majesty. I was—" He paused, struggling for the words. "Gone. But not. The only thing I could feel was my bond with Zin as it stretched and frayed."

I squeezed my eyes shut and swallowed.

"Then everything snapped back into place." The sleeve of his shirt brushed mine as he came to stand next to me. "It was less than pleasant.

"Fasé thought the only reason she was able to bring me back was because of that connection between us."

Now I did look at my *Ekam*, surprised by the emotion in his voice. Emmory was staring at the wall. His face was impassive but his eyes were wet.

"She may have brought me back to life, but it was Zin who saved me."

"I owe him more than I realized," I whispered, putting my hand on his arm. "I am very glad you're not dead."

"As am I, Majesty."

23

3

Once the shelling was over, we returned to my rooms and I settled in to continue my study of Wilson, determined to pick him apart piece by piece. The file I was compiling was skeletal and filled so far with mostly useless information: Wilson was left-handed, his visual statistics useless in giving us any hint of the person he'd been. I was more certain than ever he'd had a body mod done, and it had to have been as deep as mine. I wondered if he could change it or if the same consequences—I was stuck this way permanently—were part of his modification.

Queuing up Hao's email detailing the call he'd had earlier, I reached for the whiskey at my elbow and took a sip. The attached video footage was from Shanghai Port and I couldn't stop my hand from shaking a bit as I spotted Portis and me, walking hand in hand along the concourse. Memz and Pip followed, waving good-bye to us and peeling off into the crowd.

The scene switched to a second feed and I gripped my glass with my other hand as Wilson's face appeared briefly from the shadows of a nearby stall. My treacherous navigator looked around, gave Pip a little shove toward a merchant, and vanished into the shadows.

I'd known my navigator had sold me out and we'd suspected that Shanghai had been the easiest port for Wilson to make contact, but my stomach still twisted painfully as the proof was revealed.

Hao's note in the email was short: *My contact found the wreckage of the mod shop you used on New Delhi. According to police records it burned down about six standard months before your Trackers brought you home.*

"The man has a habit of setting things on fire," I muttered.

"Majesty?"

I looked up to find Sergeant Fasé Terass, the Farian who'd saved Emmory's life on Red Cliff, standing in the doorway.

She was dressed all in gray—by my understanding it was meant to mimic Farian prison garb—and her hands were hidden inside the long sleeves of her shirt. Her red curls swung forward when she bowed.

"Fasé, how are you?" I set aside my cup and got to my feet, reaching for her hands and leaning down to press my forehead to hers.

"Alive," she replied in what was now our customary exchange since I'd stopped her from killing herself.

"Have a seat. Would you like something to drink?"

"No, thank you, Majesty." She did, however, take a chair, tucking her feet up underneath her like a child. "Major Morri told me she asked to speak with you."

"Yes, we haven't had a chance yet." I frowned when the Farian worried her fingers around the edge of her sleeve. "What is it, Fasé?"

"She will ask you for permission to take me home, Majesty. Please tell her no."

"Fasé, I am—this is a Farian matter. I wouldn't dream of interceding more than I already have."

"I don't deny that; however, the timing is wrong. Major Morri and I are both still members of the Indranan forces; we are both still under your command. You can deny her request, especially given the circumstances. It would be unwise to go into battle without Farians to help."

"Fasé, isn't it best if you go home? We can't provide the help you need." I reached a hand out. "You have given us so much already. I don't want to make things worse for you."

"I will go home, I promise, but not yet. I need to stay, and I can't do that if you give Major Morri permission to leave her post." Fasé uncurled from the chair and got to her feet as the door opened.

"Majesty, you wanted to see me?" Gita's face was still ashen and her eyes haunted, but her back was straight and her mouth was fixed in a line of grim determination.

I stood, but Fasé beat me to my BodyGuard.

"Gita." Fasé put her hand on the woman's arm and smiled. "There is comfort in small joys; don't deny yourself that." She looked back at me and dipped her head. "Majesty."

"We will speak later, Fasé. I am glad to see you up and about." Fasé nodded and left us alone.

I cupped the back of Gita's neck and leaned in to press my forehead against hers.

"Jaan hai to Jahan Hai," I whispered. I was so used to the sharp stab of pain in my chest that I barely flinched when it struck.

If there is life, then there is the world.

I didn't know if the proverb helped, but I would say it to her every day in the hope that it would somehow ease the ache. Someday both of us would believe the words that came out of my mouth.

I urged Gita into the empty seat across from me, taking both her hands in mine. "Emmory said you were up." I swallowed back the ridiculous question before it could slip out.

"I am, Majesty. I'm sorry for my absence. We are not in—"

"Don't you dare."

She blinked at my sharpness.

I squeezed her hands before I released her. "Don't you dare apologize to me, Gita Desai. If anything, I should be asking you for forgiveness."

"Majesty?"

"I'm sorry," I said. "Sorry that I couldn't save your mother." Shaking my head to silence her, I pressed on. "It is my responsibility. This whole mess has something to do with that man and my family. I'm sorry your mother was tangled up in it and I'm sorry for what it has cost your family."

"With respect, Majesty, Mother would have told you to shut up." A smile flickered over Gita's face before drowning in the sadness. "She'd have been more proper about it, of course, but you and I are soldiers. This wasn't your fault. I know you want to take the responsibility for it, but as far as I'm concerned the only one to blame is the man who pulled the trigger."

"I want him dead, Your Majesty." Gita gritted the words out. They were sharp and filled with a pain I knew all too well.

I nodded. "I swear to you we will see to it. You must promise me you will let me handle it."

She nodded, her dark eyes filled with resigned pain. "Yes, ma'am. It was your right long before it was mine. I just want to be there at the end."

"If I can make it happen, you will be. I give you my word." I bared my teeth at her in a vicious smile that my BodyGuard echoed. "Get cleaned up. If Emmory says it's okay, you're back on duty tomorrow morning."

Gita stood and bowed. "Yes, Majesty."

As she reached the door, it opened and I half rose from my seat, frowning in confusion.

Hao and Dailun came through the door, dragging a dirty and disheveled man with them. Bial Malik, my mother's *Ekam*.

Hao's former pilot, Dailun, was now my pilot—though how I'd ended up with one of Po-Sin's great-grandchildren pledging himself to me during our whirlwind flight across the galaxy was still something of a mystery. The pink-haired young Svatir-Cheng sported an impressive black eye and a look of annoyance on his pretty face.

Hao, by contrast, looked extremely pleased with himself and grinned at Gita on his way by.

Tu Winston and Raj Peche, Trackers who were among the best in the empire, followed in the gunrunner's wake, and Emmory came in the room behind them. He paused a moment to speak with Gita, nodding and gripping her shoulder briefly before closing the door behind her.

Sinking back into my seat seemed the best option. I crossed my legs and leaned back, raising an eyebrow at Hao. He bared his teeth at me in a wicked grin and shoved Bial to the floor.

"Your Imperial Majesty." Hao's bow was ridiculously extravagant.

"A gift, Hao? It's not even my birthday."

I was impressed Emmory hadn't moved from his spot by the door. I'd tried to kill Bial the last time we'd been this close to each other. Of course, that was when I'd been convinced he was part of the plot to kill my mother and my sisters.

Then he'd gone and saved my life during my cousin's attempted coup.

He'd disappeared from Pashati before I could thank him properly and turned up momentarily in the stronghold of

Bakara Rai before vanishing once more. I'd sent Dailun to meet up with the Trackers with instructions to hunt Bial down shortly before we'd taken Canafey. Saving my life didn't prove his innocence; it merely bought him enough time to explain himself while I decided if I would kill him myself or let someone else do it.

Emmory's relaxed posture was probably due to the fact that I wasn't armed. Though to be fair, right now I was more curious than anything.

"Bialriarn Plantage Malik. We saw you on Santa Pirata. You should have stuck around to talk."

Bial's golden hair had grown out some from the severe cut he'd worn when I'd arrived home. He had a handsome face, all angles and edges, and his skin was several shades darker than it had been the last time I'd seen him. I wondered just where he'd been in the sun long enough to get a tan.

He kept his blue eyes glued to the floor in front of him. "Your Imperial Majesty, I have—"

I cut him off with a laugh. "I'll bet that sticks in your throat like a cherry full of needles."

"It would hurt more if Your Majesty hadn't proven me right and lost her throne."

I held a hand up before Hao could kick Bial in the back, and he returned to his spot near the table. Leaning forward, I grabbed Bial's chin and tipped his head up, forcing him to meet my eyes. "I'll remind you that this shit-show we are currently in had nothing to do with my inability to rule an empire, but rather was because you didn't do your Shiva-damned job and let my dearly departed nephew poison my mother." I didn't raise my voice at all, but Bial flinched at my words.

"In fact, the only reason Indrana isn't in far greater danger is that *I've* managed to stay alive. With little thanks to you. After everything, you still think I can't do this. You still think I'm not fit to be empress."

"Prove me wrong," he said.

"I don't have to prove shit to you. You are a disgraced Body-Guard whose charge died in his care. You should be proving to me that you really care about this empire rather than expecting me to negotiate with you. If I want information from you, I'll have it." I snapped my fingers. "All I have to do is say the words."

My BodyGuards went to attention. Hao remained where he was, leaning against the table, but the smile on his face grew.

"The real issue here, Bial, is this: Are *you* going to prove me right: that you're nothing but an arrogant, self-righteous, failure? Or are you going to help me save Indrana?"

Bial blinked at me. "Majesty?"

"How much do you love Indrana, *Ekam-aiyeet*?" I shouldn't have even given him the honor of calling him BodyGuard, but the formal title for a previous *Ekam* found its way out of my mouth regardless.

I leaned even closer and stared him in the eye. "You went on and on about what a bad choice I was, how I'd ruin the empire. I'll grant you, I should never have been the first choice, but it turns out I'm the only one who can save the empire. Now you have two options: You can help me do that, or I'll have Hao take you out back and shoot you."

He stared back at me and the silence in the room ticked away.

"How much do you love Indrana?" I asked again.

"With all my heart and soul, Majesty." The reply was automatic, even through his confusion.

I released him and looked at Hao. "Get him out of here.

Clean him up and then toss him in a cell. I'll talk to him when I don't feel like putting my boot in his face."

Hao nodded and hauled Bial to his feet.

"Dailun," I called as the pink-haired pilot followed Hao and Bial out the door. "You have our thanks."

He bowed, actually lowering his head to the floor instead of keeping his eyes on me. "Without offense, you are family, *jiejie*. I would steal a star for you if you wished it."

"I don't need one right this second, but we'll keep it on the table. Get some rest, you've earned it." I held in the smile as I waved him out the door, letting it show only after Dailun's back was turned. Standing and holding out my hands to the Trackers still waiting near Emmory, I extended the smile to them.

"Tu, Raj, it's good to see you again. I'm assuming I also have you to thank for this?"

"Yes, ma'am. Though Dailun was a great asset; we could not have found Bial without him." Tu smiled at me as she bowed. "It's an honor to do our duty for the empire."

"Emmory will find you a place to stay. Come join me for lunch tomorrow, I'd like to hear about what our *Ekam-aiyeet* was up to."

"Yes, Majesty," they said in unison, and Emmory followed them from the room.

4

The sky morphed to gray in the predawn hours as the rain continued its steady patter on the windows and the roof. I was curled on the window bench in my room, staring out the windows at the rain.

"If you could do anything in the universe, what would it be?" Portis asked.

I rolled over to look at him. The suns of Calpis VII were high in the sky, baking us as we lay by the water.

"This."

"Lying on a beach?"

I laughed. "No. Well yes, but I meant traveling, doing business with Hao. Seeing the galaxy." I stuck my fingers into the pink sand, drawing spirals that looped in on themselves. "At some point I want my own ship."

"You just want to be in charge."

"Maybe, what's so wrong with that?" I flicked sand at him.

"Nothing." Portis laughed, holding his hands up in surrender. "You'd make a good leader, Cressen."

*   *   *

"I would give anything to have you by my side," I whispered, blinking away the memory and pressing a hand to my heart. I rubbed at the bruised spot a moment before I returned my attention to the summary Alba had prepared for me on the current status of the empire.

Reading things like this made me feel so unprepared for the task at hand, or rather the task facing me after I finished killing Wilson and everyone who had supported him. That task was something I was well suited for thanks to Hao's tutelage. But the unending deluge of statistics and dry-as-dust reports made my eyes cross the minute I started reading. I was beyond grateful for Alba's presence. My chamberlain understood the raw mess of data and was somehow able to put it into a format that didn't immediately send me into a coma.

I was going to be a horrible empress.

I groaned and dropped my head into my hands. My promise to Emmory when he dragged me home to be the empress was that I would do my duty. At the time I promised it, I had convinced myself that my only duty was finding the people who'd killed my sisters. Then I realized my mother was being poisoned and that I couldn't save her, and somewhere along the way I knew in my heart that I couldn't leave my empire out of the promise. I owed my people the same conviction as my family.

I was the last of the ruling line, maybe not the last Bristol, but the last female descendant of a line that stretched back to the beginning of Indrana.

And I was well and truly the last. There was no getting around that little secret, even if no one else but Emmory knew it at the moment. At least that would have meant I could have married Portis without any protests that a commoner would be introduced into the royal line.

I rubbed at my chest over my heart and then reached up to smear the stray tear away from my cheek.

The day would come when I had to decide what to do about the fact that I couldn't have children, but first I had to get my throne back.

"Morning, Majesty." Stasia came through the door, balancing a tray with one hand. "Breakfast?"

I smiled and waved a noncommittal hand without looking up from Alba's report. My maid was already well used to this routine and slid the tray onto the nearby table. She poured me a mug of chai and handed it over without comment, leaving me alone again to continue my reading.

Well over an hour had passed when Gita came into the room. "Morning, Majesty. Bial's ready to talk if you're ready to listen. Emmory's with him."

"Give me ten minutes," I said.

I closed out the report and abandoned my picked-at breakfast to throw on a clean uniform. I twisted my hair back, pinning it up at the base of my neck without calling Stasia, a move I was sure was going to get me a disapproving look from my maid. Lacing up my boots and drinking the last of my tea, I headed into the attached room, where my maid was talking quietly with Jasa.

As predicted, Stasia pointed at a chair. "Sit, Majesty." She undid my work and redid it in half the time, no doubt making it look better than my attempt. "Next time just call me, ma'am."

I held in my smile as I stood. Stasia probably had figured out what I was doing, but our daily struggle over my hair was still a good distraction for both of us.

Gita and Hao waited patiently on the other side of the door, chatting with Indula and Iza. The former policewoman had joined up with us during the attempted coup and stayed on ever since. Indula had been one of my mother's BodyGuards and was responsible for preventing Bial from taking us prisoner during the coup.

"Let's go." I waved Hao in front of me.

Hao smiled at Gita, giving her the briefest of nods before he fell into step with me. I watched his fingers brush over her hand as they passed.

The other BodyGuards formed up behind me. Straightening my spine as we hit the main staircase, I felt the weight of dozens of eyes on me. We headed down the stairs and across the wide foyer of the mansion.

I exchanged nods and the barest of smiles with the people we passed. Most of them were unfamiliar to me, though the longer we were here on Canafey Major the more repeat faces I saw.

Hao stopped at the doors. "The detention block is across the yard in the building to the west."

"We'll go first," Indula said, tapping Iza on the arm. They slipped through the door and several moments later Gita touched me on the shoulder.

"It's clear, Majesty," she said. "*Ekam* Tresk would like us to move quickly."

"Given the rain, I'd prefer to move quickly anyway," I replied.

We didn't quite sprint across the yard, and my Guards hustled me into the squat building, closing the door behind us. We all shook off the rain.

"Elizah, stay on the door. No one comes in," Indula said.

"Yes, sir."

Hao put a hand on my back. "Down the hall and to the left."

I took a breath, unsure where the sudden nerves came from. I didn't want or need Bial's approval, but the man was such a puzzle. Why hadn't he just disappeared? It was clear he had the talent for it. What was he doing in Santa Pirata, and why had he risked his life to save mine?

The questions cascaded through my brain, falling into a jumbled pile where they became an incoherent mess. Hao flexed his fingers against my back and gave me a knowing look. Giving me half a second to compose myself, he pulled open the door to the interrogation room.

Bial sat, cuffed to the table. His eyes locked on the wall to the left of Emmory's shoulder. They flicked in the direction of the door when we came in, but he didn't turn his head.

I shared a look with Emmory. He gave me a minuscule nod, so I crossed to the table and pulled the other chair out.

"Bial."

"Your Majesty." He dropped his chin, a surprising gesture of respect.

"Why the sudden obeisance?" Of all the questions I had to ask, that hadn't even been in the pile, and yet it slipped out all the same. I barely kept the look of surprise off my face.

Thankfully the question seemed to startle Bial just as much. "You are the Empress of Indrana, Majesty." The sincerity in his voice was reflected in his eyes. It was the same honest loyalty in Emmory's face when he'd knelt before me and sworn an oath to protect me with his life.

"It's as simple as that? Is that why you didn't let Nal shoot me?"

My former BodyGuard had thrown in her chips with my cousin and nephew in the plot to take the throne. It cost her her life. But had Bial not been there in the throne room to take the shot Nal leveled in my direction, it would have cost me mine.

"I swore an oath to protect the crown, Your Majesty. I failed where your mother was concerned. I wasn't going to fail with you.

"Whatever you think of me, Your Majesty, I am and will always be loyal to Indrana."

"He's telling the truth," Emmory said over our *smati* link. *"As strange as it may sound, he backed Ganda because he believes a matriarchy is the best thing for Indrana and thought she was the better choice given your history. When he realized there was something deeper than your cousin's push for the throne at work, he did the only thing he could do—try to protect the crown."*

I sat without moving, my arms crossed over my chest, and let the silence draw out until Bial shifted uncomfortably.

"Your Majesty, I have information for you on the men responsible for the deaths of your family members."

"The shit?" I shoved at the table, hitting him in the stomach with the edge. "Start with that next time, man."

"I was about to, Majesty, but then we got off track." *Befuddled* was probably the best word for the look on Bial's face and I resisted the urge to shove the table again.

"Get back *on* track," I said, resting my elbows on the table.

"I picked up Wilson's trail and followed it to Santa Pirata. There was a lot of money flowing out of various Saxon corporations owned by the king. Most of it is going into Bakara Rai's pockets. When the two things converged there I knew it had to mean something. It was just poor luck on my part that I was still there when you arrived, and even worse luck that you spotted me."

"What about the money?"

"Trace is hooked on Pirate Rock. It's buried well, but there's been a steady purchase of Pirate Rock over the last twenty years by a company I'm almost certain is linked to the Saxon king. Not enough for kingdomwide distribution, so it must just be for his personal use. It looks like Wilson was responsible for the initial delivery, but I don't have proof of that yet."

I'd suspected Trace was on something. The carefully worded reports coming out of the kingdom about one incident or another during his early teens indicated a kid desperately seeking some kind of relief from reality. He'd been on his best behavior during the visit to Indrana just before the war started, but I suspected that was due to my sharp-eyed BodyGuards.

His more recent behavior was wildly inconsistent with what I remembered of him and reminded me far too much of some of the drug-addicted underbelly I'd come in contact with over the years.

I just never thought he'd be dumb enough to go for something like Rock.

"That stupid fucking idiot," I muttered. The quick-cooling lava on the surface of Santa Pirata produced a rock very similar to Earth obsidian. Once compressed with the ash in the air, the resulting rock was powdered to create Pirate Rock. The highly addictive substance was packed into pipes and smoked, producing one of the most powerful highs known to humankind.

"Are you sure?"

Bial nodded. "He was careful to cover his tracks, but there's nothing else that much money could have been paid to Rai for, Majesty. I would ask Bakara Rai for the final piece of proof, should you need it."

"Idiot." I shoved away from the table to pace the room. "It's going to kill him." I muttered a curse. "Where's Rai?" I hadn't seen the man since we'd landed on Canafey. I attempted to contact him with my *smati*, but my call went unanswered.

"Majesty, what do you want to do with him?" Emmory asked, tipping his head toward Bial as I headed for the door.

"Do you have more?" I asked.

"I do."

"Then give Hao the rest of the information you have. We'll

talk after I have a chance to see it. Hao, take him to the mansion. We'll send a Marine your direction as soon as Emmory finds someone suitable to keep an eye on our *Ekam-aiyeet.* Don't restrain him, he's free to come and go as long as someone is with him. No weapon."

"Yes, Majesty." Hao executed a bow without the slightest bit of sarcasm and released Bial from his cuffs. "Get up." He prodded Bial with his foot.

I didn't look back as I headed out the door. "Iza, get Kisah, and you two track Rai down. I want to know why he didn't think it was necessary to let me know he'd been selling Shiva-damned Rock to the king of the Saxons."

"Yes, ma'am."

"Indula."

"Majesty?"

"Talk to me about Bial. What do you know about him?" Even as I asked the question I was kicking myself for not thinking of it sooner. Indula had served in my mother's Guard, and of all of us would have had the most contact with him.

"I gave Emmory a full report, ma'am. I thought he would have passed it on."

I slid my *Ekam* a sideways look. "Give me the highlights while we walk. I want to talk to Caspel."

Back in the privacy of my rooms, I paced a restless path from the couch to the door while I waited for Director Ganej to get back in touch with us. Emmory was in the hallway with Gita, and the shift change for the BodyGuards meant Caspian Yuri Kreskin, my *Dve,* Emmory's second-in-command, stood near the door and watched me with blue eyes that were now far too old for his baby face.

"You're going to wear a hole in the floor, ma'am."

I stuck my tongue out and he laughed. The chime for an incoming com sounded and I dropped into the chair, tapping the console.

"Majesty." Caspel Ganej, my director of Imperial intelligence, gave me a nod. The bustling activity of the loyalists' hideout flowed behind him. I spotted people setting up equipment as children ran through the chaos, and on the far side of the room a group of women sat cleaning and sorting weapons.

"How are you?" Caspel asked, drawing my attention away from the people behind him.

"Still alive. You?"

"Same," he replied, his mouth twitching with the urge to smile.

"Did you get in touch with Toropov?"

"Better, Majesty." He shifted his hand, revealing Jaden Toropov. The Saxon ambassador was a lanky older man with silver-blond hair and piercing blue eyes. His scarred hands spoke of a past I was only partially familiar with, and his lined face was very good at hiding secrets.

To say I was surprised that my intelligence director had let the man into his headquarters would have been an understatement, but the only reaction I allowed myself was to raise an eyebrow a fraction and glance at my *Dve*.

"Cas, tell Emmory to get in here."

"Your Majesty." Jaden Toropov inclined his head.

"I should tell Caspel to shoot you right now, Ambassador," I snarled.

"I realize your feelings toward the Saxon Kingdom are less than friendly at the moment, Your Majesty. However, you know as well as I do that things are not always as clear-cut as they might seem."

The edges of my laughter were sharp enough to make the

men on the other side of the transmission flinch. The door to my rooms opened and Emmory, along with Zin and Cas, slipped inside.

" 'Less than friendly' is accurate. You have fifteen seconds to convince me why Director Ganej shouldn't air out your skull."

"There are certain factions within the Saxon government who are supremely concerned about the direction King Trace's leadership is taking the kingdom."

"Caspel."

Grim-faced, my director pulled his gun out, and Toropov rushed on.

"Majesty, we do not want Trace in charge. He is dangerous. Out of control. He has brought us to the brink of war—"

"Oh, not the brink," I said with another sharp laugh. "We're *at war*, Ambassador. I'm going to let Admiral Hassan fly into Saxony and wipe the floor with your navy just like we did here at Canafey. There won't be anything left when she's done."

"Majesty, the man is unstable. Surely you saw that yourself on Red Cliff."

My wide-eyed look of astonishment had the ambassador paling. "You know, I believe I did witness that. He blew a huge hole in a Solarian neutral planet and killed a great many women and men. I was in the building when it dropped on my head. I was standing right there when he fucking shot Emmory. Not exactly the actions of a sane person."

"He's hooked on Pirate Rock."

I rolled my eyes. "I know that."

The shocked look on Toropov's face was priceless. "You know? How? You've been—"

"On the run?" I laughed. "Yes, but I'm also—as you should have figured out—not one to be underestimated, Ambassador. How I know isn't important, just trust that I know it, so I'm still not getting any information from you that's at all helpful to me." I didn't bother concealing the look I gave to Caspel.

Toropov's eyes slid sideways to Caspel and he swallowed. "Majesty, there are a number of us in the Saxon government who are prepared to back Trace's younger brother, Samuel Gerison, in a bid for the throne. However, we cannot fight the Indranan Empire and remove Trace from power at the same time. We are not strong enough for that."

"It is extremely challenging to fight two wars at once," I said with a snort. "How long has Trace been on the Rock?"

"Our best guess is it started right after his father's death, or possibly right before. Trace was always rebellious. It got worse after his father died." Toropov shook his head with a frown. "Either way, by the time anyone realized how badly he was hooked it was too late."

"Wilson's the one who gave it to him, Ambassador."

"We know that now." Jaden allowed what I suspected was a rare look of frustration to show on his face. "We were so close to avoiding a war with Indrana. Then something changed Trace's father's mind; I was sent to Indrana and could no longer influence him. After he died, all Trace wanted was revenge on Indrana."

"That's got Wilson's fingerprints all over it," I murmured.

"Trace is unfit to be king, Your Majesty," Toropov replied, neatly sidestepping the issue of money. "A sober Trace could have been a great king, but he is not and will not be anytime soon enough to save Saxony. My colleagues and I cannot stand by while he destroys thousands of years of hard work."

"Here's our problem, Ambassador. Or rather, your problem. See, I'm not particularly inclined to be helpful toward the Saxon Alliance right this second. Your king colluded with the man who killed my family. He shot my *Ekam*."

Toropov swallowed at the frozen shards in my voice, but I didn't stop.

"He killed several of my BodyGuards. He *tried* to kill me. The end result of this put a Farian in a desperate situation that has ramifications with our relations with the Farians beyond what any of us can see. Furthermore, *you* lied to me about Canafey. If you'd told me the truth we could have done something to stop it!

"So explain to me just what it is you can offer me that's going to give me greater satisfaction than wiping Saxony off the face of every star map in existence? And trust me when I say it will happen if you can't come up with something good."

"You are not quite in a position to make such threats, Majesty. With all due respect, how many ships do you have control of at the moment?"

I stared at Toropov for a long moment before I spoke in a voice that reminded me of my mother, but that hard edge Cressen had perfected was also present. "Don't test me, Jaden. I have enough of my own ships. Furthermore, I will call in every favor from every gunrunner I know if it is necessary. Trust me when I say the size and ferocity of the force I muster will be quite adequate for what I need."

An uneasy silence filled the space between us before Toropov bent his head in acknowledgment. "Your Majesty, if you will allow me to speak with my compatriots I will have an answer for you in a fortnight."

"You have a week. A standard week, Ambassador, and you'd better hope I like the answer you give me." I disconnected and made a face. "That was both unexpected and may have made our lives easier, Emmory."

"Without a doubt, Majesty."

"Can we trust him?"

"No."

My heart sank at his reply.

"However, it's worth waiting to see what he comes up with, ma'am. If Toropov is telling the truth and the Saxons are willing to deal with us in exchange for us not going to war with them?" Emmory smiled. "We both know what that would mean for Indrana."

"Not going to war with the Saxon Alliance is definitely preferable to the alternative," I agreed. "But I will put together the largest force of miscreants and criminals to wipe the Saxons out if I have to." I crossed my arms over my chest and stared out the window at the ruins of the Saxon assault on Canafey. Parts of the city still smoldered, and the violent scars cut through the rain-soaked orchard stretching out in front of me. "They may have started this war, but I'm going to finish it."

5

t would be easier if we could trust him," I said at last, getting
up from my chair to pace again. "But what about this has ever
been easy?"

"He's a politician, Majesty. It's a natural reaction," Emmory
replied.

"Which part?"

The dry question pulled a smile out of my *Ekam*. "Both. It
would be easier, but we all know that's not a wise choice."

"He hasn't exactly been forthcoming up to this point either,"
Zin added. "And it's damn suspicious that they only now want
to knock Trace off the throne. Why now? Why not do it before
he started an intergalactic incident? Why not do it when his
father died?"

"Because it gives them the perfect excuse to take him off
the throne." I spread my hands wide and laughed. "Killing
the head of the Indranan Empire and starting a war is a pretty
good way to prove someone is unstable. It'll sway the undecid-
eds who might follow the throne out of habit."

"Not to mention, the Saxons still come off as the winner in any altercation with Indrana. They can blame it on a

drug-addicted king but keep any territory they happen to acquire in the meantime."

"Like Canafey," I said, nodding at Cas in agreement.

"Precisely, ma'am. It would still be in Saxon hands if not for you."

"If not for Admiral Hassan," I corrected with a smile.

"Speaking of, ma'am," Emmory said. "She's here. I'll be right back."

"Fill her in on Toropov, will you?"

I waited until he was gone and then tipped my head at Cas and at the door. He took the hint, leaving me alone with Zin.

"He hasn't apologized yet, has he?"

A smile flared to life on Zin's face, disappearing too quickly. "Did you order him to?"

"You know I did. Just like you know he'll do it anyway, but we're kind of on a timetable."

"What did he tell you?"

"Initially? To mind my own business."

Zin chuckled. "He's right, Majesty. With all due respect, this is none of your concern."

"It is very much my concern, Starzin." My use of his full name was enough in itself, but my frozen tone helped to remove the rest of the amusement from my BodyGuard's face. "He is distracted. You are on edge. This split will spread through the rest of the Guards until our very foundation is shattered into pieces. You called me out when it was necessary and I'm doing the same for you now. Emmory will apologize, you will accept it. If you want to talk about what happened, fine, but actually listen to him."

"Is that an order, Your Majesty?"

"If you make me turn it into one, I will." I crossed to him and took his hands. "Zin, you almost lost him. Do you realize he almost lost you, too? You were dying right there with him and he's as terrified of that possibility as you are. This isn't about me, or your loyalty to me. It's beyond question—for both of you." I released him and pressed a hand to his heart. "This is about your love for each other. It has lasted and will continue to last. Do not second-guess this."

Zin sagged, his shoulders dropping, and his next words were in a whisper. "Thank you."

"You're welcome." I wrapped my arms around him, pressing my cheek to his. "Go talk to him. It will be okay, Zin. I promise you."

The door opened. "Majesty, Admiral Hassan—" Cas cleared his throat at the sight of me and Zin. "Admiral Hassan is here."

"Thank you." I let Zin go, walking with him to the door. Emmory gave me the Look as he came in the room and I answered it with a raised eyebrow.

"Admiral." I held a hand out to Inana.

"Majesty, you look well." The head of the Indranan Navy was a slender woman a dozen centimeters shorter than me with short black hair and brown eyes. Like Clara, her support upon my return had been valuable. The Hassan family had been at the side of the crown throughout history, but moreover her family and mine had always been close. Her younger brother had been one of my father's best friends up until his death in a shipboard accident just before the war.

"Doing better." I squeezed her hand and headed for the balcony. She joined me and we stood for a moment looking out over the remnants of the orchards to the east of the mansion.

"Governor Phillus was quite the horticulturist, from what I hear. He was responsible for the planting of most of those over the last eighty years."

Scorched earth and uprooted trees broke the rainbow rows

of flowers, more evidence of the Saxon strike on the planet that had cost the governor his life.

"It's a fitting memorial, I suppose. We'll have to make sure there's someone still alive to keep tending it." I turned from the view. "I talked with Caspel and with Ambassador Toropov a while ago." I filled her in on the afternoon.

"You know, that doesn't surprise me about Bial," she said when I'd finished.

"Really? Why?"

"The man is stiff, uncompromising even. He was a change from Ven, that's for sure, but your mother liked him and so did Ven."

"He would have had to at least trust him to do the job," I murmured. "Or Bial never would have been on that short list of replacements."

"Ven trusted him and more." Admiral Hassan leaned on the balcony railing and stared off into the distance. "Bial is fanatically devoted to the empire, Majesty. If you asked him, he'd say it's because those who don't learn from the past are doomed to repeat it.

"Bial is a student of Earth history and to hear him tell it, nearly everything that went wrong on Earth—or in the Solarian Conglomerate—was because men were in charge."

I didn't know why that surprised me; I'd heard similar sentiments from people in the palace when I was growing up. "I can't say I fully agree with him, but I can see where he might get the idea."

"So he may not have liked you, Majesty, and chose Ganda instead—though I'd hazard a guess that's because they kept him well in the dark about their plans—but when it comes to a choice between you or Phanin?"

"He'll side with the matriarchy." I nodded. "It would probably make him happier if Alice were empress."

"Why do you say that, Majesty?"

"She has Bristol blood," I said with a shrug. "Diluted and on the male side, but it's there. More than that, though, her temperament is better suited to the job than mine is."

Inana glanced my way, but I ignored the unasked question in her eyes and turned from the balcony to pace the length of the room.

"Admiral Mendez from Yandin is headed our way; she's pulling ships from pickets she thinks can take the vacancies as she heads toward us."

"Do you trust her?"

"I've known Kala for years, Majesty. She'll get what she can without compromising our security further."

I nodded. "How long until she gets here?"

Inana made a face as she did the calculations in her head. "She shouldn't be more than a week out. It'll give us time to finish up repairs on the fleet."

"That's fine, we've still got cleanup to do here on the ground. I'm not leaving until those Saxons are either dead or rounded up."

"We need to talk about what happens next, Majesty."

I didn't slow my stride, though Emmory likely caught the minute hitch in my step. "There's nothing more to talk about, Admiral. We're sticking with the original plan. You're going to Saxony and obliterating their navy unless Toropov can come up with a reason good enough to convince me otherwise. I'm going home to take back my throne. We'll meet back at Pashati, where hopefully we can win a battle without killing too many Indranans.

"At the end of it Eha Phanin and Wilson will be dead."

Inana opened her mouth, glanced Emmory's way, and closed it again with a sigh. Just before Clara's murder we'd had a plan to assault the Saxon Alliance on their own turf before we turned our attention back to the men who'd shattered my family and taken my throne.

Nothing significant had changed about that plan, except that in the week since Wilson had murdered Clara I'd come up with as many ways to kill a man slowly as I could think of, and now it was simply a matter of deciding which one to use.

No one else was going to be on board with this, probably because they knew that Wilson's actions and subsequent promise to wipe out everyone I cared about were nothing more than bait to get me to come back to Pashati.

I wasn't an idiot. I knew full well it was a trap. I just didn't care.

"Majesty." Emmory's smoke-coated voice floated through the tense silence.

"Don't you start." I spun on my heel and pointed a finger at him. "You know if you try to stop me I'll just take Hao and go on my own. You promised me, Emmory. Maybe you've forgotten, but I haven't. You promised me the men responsible for this, and damn you if you back out of that now that I know who they are."

"*We're* going home, Majesty."

"What?"

"You don't have to do this alone," Emmory said. "Your BodyGuards will follow wherever you choose to go, Majesty."

"*Ekam* Tresk—"

"With pardon, Admiral," he said, cutting her off. "But my place is at the empress's side. I have seen her fight. I have seen her put the needs of the empire before her own. I trust her to not act foolishly or rashly. And I know she can take care of herself. This is still the best plan, all things considered."

Inana's eyebrow hiked upward, but Emmory shook his head.

"Under normal circumstances I would agree with you that going to Pashati and letting the empress walk into what is most undoubtedly a trap is extremely rash. However, you and I both know that this is the last thing Wilson and the others would expect from us."

Admiral Hassan opened her mouth to reply, then closed it again with a sigh. She shook her head, her short black hair ruffled by the movement. "All right, I'm clearly outnumbered here. What are we going to do?"

"Your part in this hasn't changed, Admiral," I said, sinking into a chair.

All week I'd kept my emotions in check, kept everything bottled up. Emmory's unexpected support was like a sledgehammer through that wall, and I felt my anger seeping away, leaving my foundation in danger of collapsing. Folding my hands into my lap to hide the shaking, I inhaled. "You're still going after the Saxons. Hit them hard and then bring the fleet to Pashati in time to back us up.

"Meanwhile, we're taking a small force to Ashva. Intel says there aren't more than a few picket ships there and I'm fairly sure my former brother-in-law doesn't have complete control of the planet. Taking back that planet will give us a base of operations if we need it."

Major Albin Maxwell, formerly Bristol, had been installed as the new governor of Ashva, the other habitable planet in our home system. I was looking forward to having a chat with him, preferably with the business end of my gun.

"Once we take Ashva back, we'll touch base with Caspel and

the rest of the resistance and figure out how to get onto Pashati without being seen."

"And then?"

I bared my teeth at her in a smile that had terrified most of the gunrunning universe at one point or another and made my admiral shift uncomfortably. "I'm going to kill Wilson. I might let Emmory kill Phanin, I haven't decided yet."

The sun was setting, throwing streaks of gold and purple across Canafey's sky. Emmory stood by the windows, his hands clasped behind his back, and I was sprawled on the couch, a glass of whiskey in my hands.

I rolled the crystal back and forth, watching the amber liquid crawl up the sides and then slide back down.

"Thank you for backing me in there," I said.

Emmory didn't turn from the window. "You were surprised."

"I know everyone—you included—would be happier if I were locked safely in a box somewhere." My own imagery made me shudder, and I took a swallow of my drink. "I just can't, *uff*—" I broke off when the words failed to come. Draining the rest of my glass, I rolled off the couch and went to fill it again.

"I treated you like a spoiled princess when we first met, Majesty," Emmory said as I joined him at the window. "I was wrong."

"Emm—"

"Let me finish?"

"Sorry."

"I was wrong. You were a gunrunner when we picked you up, not some princess playing games. You spent twenty years surviving in a dangerous world. I have seen that world with my own eyes, and I have witnessed the damage it wreaks upon those who are not prepared to face it.

"You came home, Majesty. I know you didn't want to and I know you were planning on leaving as soon as you figured out who'd killed your family. But you didn't. You stayed. You figured out how to be a princess again and then how to be an empress."

Stunned tears filled my eyes and I blinked them away as Emmory turned toward me.

"Circumstances put us right back into that gunrunner world, and you kept us alive. We want to keep you safe because you are our empress, but none of us—not a single one of your people— wants to do that because we don't think you're capable of handling it on your own. And because of that, we'll follow you into this battle."

"I—"

The door opened and Stasia came in carrying a large tray. The moment was lost as Emmory moved to help her. I drank the rest of my whiskey, my head still spinning over the words from my *Ekam* and the crushing pressure of knowing that all my people were so willing to follow me.

What if I made mistakes? What if more people died because of me?

Emmory left without another word. I sat down to eat as Cas came into the room with Iza on his heels. Rai and Johar were behind her. The lanky mismatched pair of outlaws were like night and day: Rai with his dreadlocks and dark skin, Johar's black hair slicked away from her sharp face, her pale tattooed limbs currently covered in long sleeves and dark gray pants.

I set my silverware down. "Where in the fires of Naraka have you been?"

"Exploring," Rai said with a shrug, and folded his lanky frame into the chair across from me. Johar's eyes had lit up at the food on the table, but she miraculously restrained herself. At least until I tipped my head at it with a laugh.

Rai shoved his dreadlocks off his shoulder. "I regret to inform you, Your Majesty, that my attempt to collect the bounty on Eha Phanin was unsuccessful. Though I hear the collection team did manage to injure him, none of them were able to strike the final blow and all died in the attempt."

"You sent men to kill him?"

"Eh, it seemed a worthwhile investment for the potential payoff." Rai grinned. "I got the distinct impression that my men weren't the first ones to make the attempt. He will not be sleeping well for the rest of his life."

"Good," I said flatly. "That was my intention. I'm sorry for the loss of your people."

"They knew the risk." Rai made a face and waved a hand in dismissal. "Had they been better they would have survived."

"When were you going to tell me you were selling Rock to the Saxon king?"

"Ah." Rai got up again and retrieved a wineglass from the cabinet. He raised an eyebrow in question as he reached for the bottle on my table and poured himself a glass when I nodded.

Johar barely slowed her eating as she looked between the two of us. Rai sipped the merlot, rolling the stem between his fingers, and I let him mull over his answer.

"Client lists are confidential, Your Majesty," he said at last, his apologetic smile actually genuine. "Friendship is one thing. Business is business."

"You said back on Santa Pirata that we were doing business, if I recall. I'm paying you for that business and for the information."

"Too right." Rai saluted me with his glass. "To that end I will answer any questions I can, Your Majesty, so long as it doesn't interfere with the confidentiality of my clients."

"Did you sell to Wilson?"

"I may have, it's a common name, Majesty. I'd have to check my lists first."

It wasn't the answer I wanted, but I knew pushing Rai wouldn't get me anywhere. "Fine. Bial says the transactions started after the death of Trace's father."

"That would be close. I'd say four years after is more accurate."

"How much is he using?"

Rai studied me for so long I thought he wasn't going to answer, but then the man named a number that had me whistling.

"How is he not dead?"

"He's a medical miracle?" Rai shrugged. "As long as he keeps up with his payments I don't ask questions."

"Will you stop selling to him?"

Rai considered me for a moment before he shook his head. "There's nothing you can offer me that would justify it from a business standpoint, Your Majesty."

His raised eyebrow stopped my protest before I let it slip free of my mouth. Instead I tapped a finger on my lips and changed the subject. "What's it going to cost me to get unmarked transport to Pashati?"

"I can let you know after I get home and take a look at inventory."

"You're leaving?" I set my glass down, all pretense at casual flying out the window. "When?"

"In the morning," Rai replied. "This has been an enjoyable diversion, but I do have a business to run. Don't worry, Your Majesty. Johar has expressed her desire to hang around."

"I still want to see your empire," Johar said around a mouthful of food. She wiped her mouth with the back of her hand. "Besides, the fighting will be fun. Just like old times."

From behind Johar's back, Cas rolled his eyes toward the

ceiling and I accidentally inhaled my next swallow of wine. Coughing and laughing, I nodded. "That is true," I managed finally. "It has been a long while."

Rai finished off his wine and stood with a bow. "By your leave, Majesty, I have some things to take care of before I go."

Johar shoved a few more bites into her mouth and grabbed a roll as she stood to follow him.

"Rai, do a job for me when you get home?"

He arched an eyebrow.

"Find out who Wilson is. I want everything. I don't care what it costs. You tear his fake life down to the bones."

"Of course, Your Majesty."

6

"akula."

"Majesty." The spy bowed low in my direction and I swallowed down the laughter that threatened. Nakula Orleon was still grappling with the fact that the gunrunner he'd known was his empress. He did better in private, but whenever someone else was in the room with us, he defaulted to overly formal behavior.

The transition would be easier if Hao stopped making fun of him for it, but I didn't see that happening any time soon. I shot Hao a warning look and got a wholly unbelievable innocent smile in return.

"Colonel Bristol, please tell me you are keeping these two in line?"

Hafiz's mouth twitched as he tried to hide his smile. "Of course, Majesty."

I took a seat at the conference table. Admiral Hassan sat on my right; Alba was on the left. Jia sat across the table; the tiny governor was dressed in a light blue *salwar kameez* and it looked as though someone had fixed the messy haircut she'd given herself while on the run with Nakula. Her black hair now curved against the line of her rounded cheeks, and the circles under her brown eyes were gone. Nakula took a seat next to her, a gentle smile flaring to life on his face when Jia reached out and touched his hand. Colonel Bristol and his XO, Lieutenant Colonel Teesha Alexander, sat at the far end of the table with Hao.

"The numbers are iffy, but at last count we think there are somewhere around four hundred and fifty Saxon Shock Corps hiding out in the woods about thirty kilometers from the mansion." Colonel Bristol highlighted the areas on the projection map above the table. "They've got some road vehicles and a few light craft—which explains how they've been able to lob fire at us and then disappear. They're hitting us at random intervals, no distinct pattern that I can see."

"They're being led by this man." Nakula flipped the projection to an image. "Major Darius Travoy. According to what we dug up on him he's not particularly bright, nor one of the best soldiers the Corps has seen."

I studied the round-faced man in the out-of-focus image. He was paunchy for being a Shock Corps officer, and his hair looked like someone had stained a bristle brush orange and nailed it to his head.

"How's he managed to evade capture?" I asked.

"He's got fanatically devoted soldiers, and this man"—the image changed to an older man with cold eyes—"is smart. This is Sergeant Marcus Postoyev. Travoy may technically be in charge, but all the plans are coming from Postoyev." Nakula tapped the tabletop and the image disappeared. "We've got a meeting tomorrow night with some contacts of mine. They've been trying to pin down the camp, but if we can't do that we'll come up with a way to draw Travoy out into a fight he can't win."

I nodded. "I'm coming with you. I want to speak to your contacts."

Nakula made a face but didn't refuse me, and neither did Emmory.

Hao shot Emmory a glance and then raised an eyebrow, just a fraction, at me. "You are not," he said, his voice flat. "It's dangerous out there."

I smiled, a lazy baring of teeth that was good for scaring most people; however, Hao's expression didn't change in the slightest and we stared at each other for several minutes before I spoke again.

"It's dangerous everywhere, and don't you start. Worrying about my safety is his job." I jerked a thumb at Emmory. "You know I can handle myself."

Hao just returned my look with a roll of his eyes. "Things change, Majesty, like it or not. You're not a gunrunner any longer. There's no reason for you to go tonight. Nothing to justify the risk you'd be taking and you know it."

"He's right, Majesty," Emmory said.

"So much for trusting me to handle myself," I muttered, and got a look from all three of the men. "Is there anything else?" I asked, pushing out of my chair. No one said anything, so I nodded once and headed for the door.

"Majesty."

I skidded to a halt just outside the door of the conference room before I ran Fasé down. "How are you?" I reached for her hands and leaned down to press my forehead to hers.

"Alive," she replied, and let go of my hands, moving past me to Emmory. She reached up, pressing her palm to his chest. "It was the right choice; don't second-guess yourself just to remove the guilt." Emmory frowned at her, but Fasé just smiled. "I need to speak with Her Majesty alone, if that's all right?"

My *Ekam* nodded and headed down the hallway ahead of us. I watched Fasé with a raised eyebrow; the Farian smiled mysteriously and tucked her arm into mine.

Alba followed close behind while Lantle, Jasa, and Ikeki spread out in front of us.

"You are feeling better, I take it?" I said finally as we rounded the corner to my rooms. After the usual sweep, I ushered Fasé inside and closed the door. "What was that about?"

"Nothing, Majesty." Fasé settled into a chair, tossing a smile in Stasia's direction.

"Fasé, that makes no sense."

"I realize that." She dipped her head. "I will need you to trust me. It was something Emmory needed to hear. I will let you know when I can just how that came to pass."

"Okay."

"You will regret today, but it was necessary. Don't let it drag you into doubt."

"Do you realize how crazy that sounds?"

"I do, ma'am."

I stared at her. There wasn't a hint of expression on her face or in her golden eyes beyond a patient acceptance. I was struck all at once how alien she looked, something I'd never really seen before. The Farians adapted themselves to our worlds and their physical appearance gave the illusion they were human, but they weren't.

"She won't budge, ma'am," Stasia murmured in my ear as she set a cup down by my elbow. "She is ridiculously stubborn that way."

"So I'm learning." I looked back at Fasé, who was staring at the ceiling with a dreamy smile on her face. "Major Morri is going to be here in a few minutes. Would you like to stay, Fasé?"

"No, it's best if I go," Fasé said. She slipped out of her chair and crossed to my maid, giving her a quick kiss before heading for the door. "I'll talk to you again soon, Majesty."

"What is going on there?" Alba asked as soon as the door closed.

Stasia shook her head and sighed. "About this time yesterday, she started talking nonstop. Most of it doesn't make a lot of sense."

"I guess I will know what she's talking about tomorrow." Leaning back in my chair, I started the video of Clara yet again. What had started as an obsessive need to punish myself for failing her had turned into a study of Wilson that was probably also unhealthy, if I was going to be honest with myself.

Wilson gloated. He threatened. He grabbed her. Clara elbowed him. *"Hail! Your mother said no!"*

I'd watched this clip a thousand times, but this time her words rang out over the chaos and I leaned forward in my seat. I hadn't—

"Majesty, Major Morri is here."

I swallowed back my curse at the interruption and nodded. "Let her in."

The Farian major came into the room. Her red hair was white at the temples and cut to her chin, short where Fasé's was long. She was tall for a Farian, towering a good twenty centimeters above Fasé. The same tilted eyes and pointed ears as all Farians. Dio's eyes were a deep platinum.

"Your Majesty, thank you for finding the time to see me."

"Of course." I gestured at the seat across from me. "What can I do for you?"

"I'd like your permission to take Fasé home."

"Major, we are in the middle of a war."

"I know." She pressed her hands together and shook them in apology. "However, this is important. She is not well, and the sooner I get her home the faster we can figure out how to help her."

I found myself grateful for Fasé's warning. Had the major's request caught me off guard, I might have been more inclined to listen to her pleas.

"Major, I am sympathetic to Fasé's condition—you know I am. However, you're asking me to spare a ship when we have none to spare and to release not one, but two Farians from my service at a time when I need you most. Surely you can't expect me to weigh the good of the empire against one life? Even with all my love for Fasé—" I shook my head. "I cannot let you go."

Dio swallowed and shoved a hand into her short red curls. "The treaty rules—"

"I am well aware of the treaty. It still gives me the right to make the decision, especially in times of crisis."

"Majesty—"

"This is not a discussion, Major. You have asked and I gave you my answer. Have a good day."

"Yes, Majesty." Dio frowned as she got to her feet, but she bowed and left the room without further protest.

I wore my own frown and whispered a little prayer to the Dark Mother that I'd made the right decision and wasn't just keeping Fasé close to me because of the fact that she'd saved Emmory.

"All right, Alba, what's next?" I had little choice but to push my worry to the side and focus on the rest of my day.

"Admiral Hassan passed on some dispatches she thought you would want to see. The most worrisome are the ones from 8th fleet about the Solarian Navy."

I paged through the files on my *smati* before I found the one Alba was referring to—a notice from Admiral Bolio on the border between Indranan and Solarian space.

"The traffic patterns are showing a marked increase in battlecruisers and other, heavier vessels over the last week. He's requesting advice on how to proceed."

"It matches the reports from the governors the other day. Do we have Inana's reply? Never mind, I see it," I said before Alba could reply. Admiral Hassan recommended 8th Fleet keep at least four ships with weapons hot at all times and requested Admiral Bolio send her daily reports and contact her immediately if something changed.

"I don't think the Solarians will actually try anything." I was saying that more to reassure myself, but Alba nodded.

"It's most likely reactionary due to the tensions between us and the Saxons, coupled with you kicking out their embassy staff."

"We removed them from a war zone for their own safety, Alba." I gave her a stern look and she grinned at me.

"Yes, of course, Your Majesty." Alba consulted her list again. "I received an encrypted file from Director Ganej for you."

"Send it on to Zin, he'll know what to do with it."

"Yes, ma'am."

That afternoon I strolled through the interior gardens with Jia at my side. Gita, Kisah, and a young Marine named Henjai were set at intervals around the small space. Cas stood by the door, his arms crossed and his eyes constantly scanning the rooftops.

"I've finished contacting the other governors, Majesty," Jia said. "Thankfully Caspel's early intelligence that Phanin had control of more than half the planets of the empire was cautious exaggeration. There are fifteen confirmed, including Pashati and Ashva, that have governors and military control for Phanin. The others are solidly with the crown."

"That's a relief."

Jia laughed. "To be honest there is little the loyal governors can do besides remain loyal and take care of business at home."

"True." I nodded. "We will need them to be focused, especially if we need to bring the other fleets to Pashati."

"Do you think it will be necessary?"

"I hope not." It meant we had a bigger problem than any of us had planned for, and I didn't even want to think about what a protracted war with Phanin for control of the home system— let alone the rest of the empire—would look like.

"He does not have the faith of the people, Majesty. You do."

"The people hardly know me." I sat on a nearby bench and stared at the sun through the new leaves of the trees. "They liked my mother and we're counting on the love of my family to carry them through to support me. It's working so far, I guess."

"Treat your people as you would your own children and they will follow you into the deepest valley."

"Did you just quote Sun Tzu at me, Jia?"

She bowed, her laughter floating on the wind. "It is appropriate. Your people already love you more than you know, Your Majesty, and it is precisely because of the way you treat them."

"Majesty! Incoming!" Cas sprinted across the lawn as the other BodyGuards converged. I leapt to my feet, wrapping my arm around Jia and pushing her in front of me toward the door. Kisah grabbed her, dragging her into the mansion, and the rest of us followed close behind.

The explosion shook the building, rattling the door Kisah had slammed just in time.

"Move, Majesty." Cas locked his hand around my wrist and pulled me farther into the hallway. I didn't argue, my heart hammering against my chest as we raced for the shelter.

7

It was early evening the next day when Hao came into the room, exchanging a few words with Gita as he passed. My old mentor had slid easily into a spot that wasn't quite advisor but wasn't quite BodyGuard either. Whatever it was, he had an amazing amount of freedom to come and go as he pleased.

Emmory stood by the window, looking out over the quiet landscape. He seemed more relaxed and I hoped it was because he'd finally straightened things out with Zin.

"Emmory?"

"Yes, Majesty?" He didn't turn from his spot at the window as he answered me over our private com line.

"What's the deal with Hao? You've given him a lot of leeway considering who his uncle is."

Emmory didn't answer me right away and I resisted the urge to turn around in my chair and stare at him.

"Portis said we could trust him," Emmory finally said. *"According to him, Hao was quite fond of you while you worked together. Since he's joined us he has proven himself trustworthy. Though you don't have to worry—we are still watching him."*

"Do you really think I'm worried?" I laughed across the feed.

"Hao's saved my ass so many times, Emmory. Fires of Naraka, he saved all of us back on—" I broke off as two things slapped me in the face.

One was that Hao was watching me with a smirk. "You done talking about me?"

"No," I replied, and watched his copper eyebrow arch up in response.

The second was that I'd never gotten an answer as to why Hao had been on Red Cliff at the exact moment I needed him most, and I was just now realizing that my *Ekam* had been far more prepared for things to go sideways than I'd given him credit for.

"Emmory, why was Hao on Red Cliff? I swear if you don't give me an answer, I'll ask him."

"I wouldn't, Majesty."

"And why not, Ekam?*"*

"It would be awkward if he were to find out I offered him a job on Red Cliff at the same time as the negotiations."

"Shiva, Emmory," I groaned, trying hard not to let my expression show. *"And people accuse me of being impulsive. What's that going to look like when news gets out that my BodyGuard contracted a gunrunner to work for him?"*

"At the risk of being forward, Majesty, he's working for you right now. Besides, I do have contacts outside the normal channels. You don't think I contacted him directly, do you?"

"I'm not sure that's any better. What do you think he's going to do when he finds out he got suckered with a fake job offer?"

"It was a real offer, ma'am. If things had gone smoothly, Hao would have gone on his way with a lucrative job in his hold. Since they fell apart, he got his initial payment and a terminated contract with no hard feelings due to forces outside his control."

"He's going to kill you when he finds out."

"He's welcome to try."

This time my laugh was out loud and I rubbed a hand over my face before looking at Hao. "Okay, now we're done. What do you want?"

Hao studied me curiously for several moments before answering. "Nakula wanted me to ask if there was anything specific you wanted to know from his contacts before we head for the meeting tonight."

"You mean besides how soon can we put an end to the random shelling of my current home?"

"I suppose so," he said with a smile.

"Nothing comes to mind at the moment." I stretched. "Since you won't let me come with you, I guess you'll have to handle it on your own."

"Don't be petty."

"I'm still mad at you," I said to Hao.

"You can be as mad as you want, I'm still not going to let you go." He gave a little shrug. "You know I'm right. If it makes you feel any better, Colonel Bristol is going with us."

"It doesn't, but at least he's more honest than you two." I fiddled with my silverware for a second before I conceded the fight. "Fine, I'll get you a list of issues in an hour. Go away."

"Of course, Your Majesty." Hao dropped into a ridiculously dramatic bow that was a perfect copy of Nakula's.

"Get." I tossed a fork in his direction with a helpless laugh. "And stop making fun of Nakula."

Hao's answering laughter echoed for several seconds after he'd left the room.

"I can't believe you tricked Cheng Hao into being an emergency transport," I said to Emmory.

He turned from the window. "It was obviously necessary, Majesty. And I suspect Hao would make a big deal of it, but in the end he would have done it for free."

"Why do you say that?" I got out of my chair and joined him at the window, resting my forearms on the sill and looking out over the orchards. The setting sun bathed them in a golden sheen, the light slicing through the branches and into the buildings on the far side.

"He cares about you. Why else is he still here? You haven't paid him a single credit because he hasn't let you. I know gunrunners well enough to know that's not at all normal."

"Oh, you know gunrunners now, huh?"

Emmory shrugged a shoulder. "Portis said we could trust him if we needed him. He was right."

"We definitely needed him on Red Cliff." I laid a hand on Emmory's arm. "He saved us both."

"He did, ma'am."

The laugh took me by surprise and I struggled for breath, leaning against Emmory until I could get the words out. "Shiva, don't ever tell him about it. I'd never hear the end of it."

"I'll bear that in mind for when I need you to cooperate."

I ignored the threat. "You did talk to Zin, right?"

"Yes, Majesty."

"And?"

"It's still none of your business." He smiled. "But things are better, thank you."

I rubbed a hand over the back of my neck. "Major Morri asked for permission to take Fasé home. I told her no."

"Any particular reason why?" Emmory asked.

The chime of an incoming message cut off my reply and I moved away from Emmory to the console. "Caspel," I said with a nod.

"Majesty. I have a quick update for you. Ambassador Toropov wanted to let you know that he's still waiting on a proposal from his contacts back on Marklo. There's been no sign of the king since Red Cliff and things are in a bit of an uproar. He apologizes and promises to get you what you've asked for as soon as he can."

"He's the one who's on a deadline," I replied. "You can remind him of that. Admiral Hassan will be leaving Canafey as soon as the rest of the ships arrive. I suggest he tell his contacts to get their shit together."

"Yes, ma'am." Caspel gave me a sharp nod. "I will do that. I have some additional files on Phanin's movements here at home to get together for you. I'll send them once I'm sure the encryption is secure. Also, Alice is here. She wanted to give you an update on the other matriarchs and their daughters."

The image fuzzed as Caspel passed the com link along from his *smati* to Alice's. "Majesty."

"How are you?"

"Well enough." My heir smiled at me. "You, Majesty?"

"I'm all right, Alice."

"We have our first council meeting scheduled for tomorrow." Her exhalation was a little shaky, but she forced a smile and continued on. "Masami, Caterina, and Sabeen will com in with you from Canafey," she said, referring to the three matriarchs who'd been with me at Red Cliff and managed to escape. I hadn't spoken to any of them since before the battle for Canafey.

"Tej Naidu, Heela Maxwell, and Adi Desai are taking over their departed mothers' posts. The Surakesh family is in total disarray. Leena's aunt and mother are in Phanin's custody, along with the other inheriting daughters. Her sisters are safe, but too far away for us to coordinate effectively; the agreement seems to be to let Leena speak for the family at the moment."

"Are Phanin's captives still alive?"

"We think so, ma'am; there's no way to tell for sure." Alice didn't say what we were all thinking, that the fear of Wilson bringing them out for the cameras would mean their deaths.

"Good." I nodded. "We will talk again tomorrow then."

"Yes, Majesty. Have a good evening."

"Stay safe." I disconnected the com link and glanced up at Emmory.

"It's good." He nodded in approval. "Getting the council back up and running will convince the outlying planets of the crown's stability."

"I just hope it doesn't bring any unwanted attention to them."

"We both know it will, Majesty. Caspel is good at his job. He'll keep them safe."

"Like he kept Clara safe?" I covered my mouth with my hand as soon as the words were free. "Sorry. That was uncalled-for."

"It doesn't hurt my feelings, Majesty, and you're not entirely wrong." Emmory leaned against the console. "Caspel knows it and he'll make sure it doesn't happen again."

"What do you think Toropov's going to come up with as an offer?"

Emmory tipped his head to the side as I got up to grab a drink. "They'll have to start with returning the planets Indrana lost in the peace talks or there's little point in even having a discussion."

"I would laugh at him if he didn't put that on the table," I admitted.

Zin slipped in through the door. "Evening, Majesty. Emmory, Cas is outside," he said, and Emmory nodded.

They seemed better, more relaxed, and I smiled.

"All right, I need to get this list together for Hao and I'm sure you have something better to do than stand here and watch me."

"We'll see you in the morning, ma'am."

"Good night." I waved at them, grinning at the empty air when they disappeared into the smaller room on the other side of my quarters.

I settled onto the couch to compose my note to Hao, picking at the remains of my dinner while I wrote until Stasia appeared to clear it away. It took me almost an hour, but I finished it and sent it off to him.

Checking my queue from Alba, I pulled the first of the briefings she'd marked important and started reading.

"Majesty, I've got Caspel on the line for you," Emmory said over the com.

I blinked at the time in the corner of my vision; several hours had passed as I worked my way through Alba's urgent list.

"Thank you." I answered the call. "Caspel."

"Majesty." My intelligence director gave me a weary smile. "I have that information for you, transmitting encoded file now. Your BodyGuard will have the decryption protocols."

"Thank you."

"No trouble, ma'am." He glanced to the side. "I wanted to tell you earlier but I thought it best to do it out of Alice's hearing. You would be most proud of your heir, she has rallied the people in your name.

"They saved us yesterday. Colonel Regen decided to make a push against us; he called in an air strike." Caspel shook his head. "Women, children, men flooded the streets around the port. I have never seen the like."

"What happened?"

"Phanin wants the people to love him more than he wants me dead, apparently. He called the general off." A smile raced briefly across Caspel's severe face. "I think some people are still out there celebrating."

"Tell Alice I won't complain if this is all handled by the time I get home." I sent Caspel a coded message of my own and he nodded slightly when he received it.

"I will, Majesty."

"We'll speak again soon," I said, and cut the connection. "Zin, get out here."

"Majesty?" He emerged from the room, smoothing down his shirt.

I turned to the bar to hide my smile at his disheveled hair and cursed myself for not thinking before I'd called him. "Caspel sent me something. Take a look?" I passed the file over the *smati* link and then poured myself a drink.

"Troop movements on Pashati and the identification codes for the *Vajrayana* ships Phanin has, ma'am," Zin said after a moment. "Also the officer rosters and a message from Taran. I'll put that one through the decryption program first, ma'am, so you can listen to it."

"There's no rush, Zin. Have it for me in the morning with the rest of the reports. Tell Emmory I said good night." I saluted him with my drink as I disappeared into my own room.

I woke from a dead sleep, but not from a nightmare, and it took me several seconds before I realized that the shouting was what had dragged me awake.

Rolling from my bed, I jerked the door open a split second before Zin closed his hand on the knob.

"Majesty." Zin stepped in front of me, blocking my path across the main room.

"What's going on?"

The look on his face was grim, but I couldn't get a read on just what had put the expression there. Zin tilted his head, listening to instructions—presumably from Emmory. I socked him in the arm.

"What is it?" Adrenaline pumping through my veins cleared the last of the sleep away like a tidal wave. "Hao? Bugger me, Zin, what is it? What's happened?"

I didn't wait for an answer and miraculously evaded him, sprinting for the door. He caught up with me in the hall but didn't stop me. Gita and Kisah had been on the door and they'd started down the massive staircase ahead of me without instruction.

The bloody chaos in the foyer of the mansion didn't still with my arrival. I spotted Hao and Nakula and the breath I'd been holding rushed out on a sob. The sound was lost to the shouting, but my relief was cut down when I realized Colonel Bristol lay in an ever-growing pool of blood on the marble tile.

"No. Oh, Dark Mother, no." I rushed forward, slipping in the blood, knees banging to the floor with a force that would leave bruises by morning.

"He's gone, Majesty. I'm sorry." Lieutenant Hasai Moren, one of the Farians from Admiral Hassan's ship who'd joined us planetside, shook his head sadly at me. "There wasn't anything I could do." The Farian's arms were red up to the elbow.

I slapped a hand to my mouth, muffling the agonized moan. Only when I was sure my grief was contained did I remove it and reach the same shaking hand out to gently close Hafiz's eyes.

"Your Majesty, I'm so sorry."

"What happened, Nakula?" I held my arm up and Zin closed his fingers around my forearm, pulling me to my feet. My gray pants were soaked from the knees down, and the copper tang of Colonel Bristol's blood filled the air.

"We were ambushed. I don't know how, but someone who

knew about tonight's meeting talked." Nakula dropped to a knee when I turned around. "The Saxons hit us as soon as we got there. If it hadn't been for the colonel we wouldn't have gotten out of there alive."

I looked to Hao. The gunrunner didn't go to a knee, but met my gaze with an expression I'd seen several times over the years. Every single time it had boded ill for those who'd stirred his anger.

"He saved us." He gritted the words out, fury mixed with the knowledge that he owed his life to a dead man. It was a debt no one ever wanted, one that you couldn't pay back, not with all the money or favors in the universe.

I had more than my fair share of those.

"Find out who is responsible for this," I said. "I want them alive."

"We'll find them." Hao gave me a sharp nod and tapped Nakula on the shoulder. The spy got to his feet and, with one last look at Hafiz's body, followed Hao back out of the mansion. They crossed paths with Emmory as he came in, gun in hand, and whatever he said to them was too low for me to hear.

"Majesty, I will take care of Colonel Bristol's body. There is a burial plot being excavated—"

"He is a Bristol. I want him stored," I said to Lieutenant Moren. "We'll see that he goes home to his family when this is over."

The lieutenant opened his mouth to argue, thought better of it, and nodded. "Yes, ma'am. I will see that it's done."

Tears threatened, stealing my reply, and I clenched my teeth together to hold them in as Emmory approached.

"Stasia's on her way with a robe for you, Majesty." He pointed off to his left. "There's an office over there."

Bloody footprints trailed after me, rust-red stains on the

marble, as I followed Emmory out of the foyer and into the tiny office. I sank into a chair as Zin closed the door, shutting out the noise. The silence closed around me, heavy with grief, and I dropped my head into my hands.

"I forgot he went with them," I whispered. "I was so worried about Hao, I didn't even think."

"There wasn't anything you could have done."

"He was family."

"I know, Majesty. He was a good man."

"I am so fucking tired of hearing that." Standing up to pace seemed like a good idea until I remembered I was covered in Hafiz's blood, and I fell back into the chair with a bitter laugh. "How many more, Emmory?"

"You know I don't have that answer."

The door opened and Stasia slipped in, a tray balanced on one hand and a robe in the other. Emmory dipped his head in my direction and left the room.

"I'm so sorry, ma'am." Stasia set the tray down and draped the robe over the back of a chair. She wrung out a washcloth and stepped carefully around the blood trail, holding the steaming fabric out to me. "Face and hands," she said.

I cleaned them off, handed her back the cloth, and stepped out of my blood-soaked pants onto a clean patch of floor. Stasia passed the robe over and I slipped into it.

"Sit down." She pointed at a different chair as she rinsed out the cloth in the bowl of hot water, and I obeyed.

This time I didn't try to stop the tears as my maid wiped off my legs and feet. Stasia finished, tossed the cloth back on the tray, and wrapped her arms around me.

"Jaan hai to Jahan Hai," she whispered. "Don't lose hope, Majesty."

I buried my face in her shoulder and wept.

75

8

ajesty, I am so very sorry." Fasé smiled sadly at me from her spot on the window seat in her room as I came through the door later that day. She held out her hands to me, the gray sleeves of her plain top sliding away from her fingers.

I took her offered hands and leaned in to press my forehead against hers. "How are you?"

"Alive," Fasé replied. "I am sorry about Colonel Bristol. We spoke a few times, he seemed nice."

"Thank you." I glanced Stasia's way, but my maid shook her head and Fasé laughed softly at us. The sound grated on my ears, raking itself over my senses, and I resisted the urge to jerk from her grasp.

"She didn't tell me, Majesty. I felt him leave us." She released my hands and looked down at her own. "I can feel the heartbeats of everyone in the mansion—human and Farian alike. You all feel different, isn't that strange?" Her smile was distant.

"Our heartbeats?"

"Yes, ma'am. Yours is so steady, like the pulsing of a star. Even in the midst of tragedy, the pace of it never wavered."

"How?"

Fasé shrugged and made a sound in the back of her throat. "I do not know. Something is happening to me. But what it is, I cannot say. Maybe in time. Have you spoken to Major Morri?"

"Yes. I told her we couldn't spare the ship or the two of you at the moment."

"Good." Fasé smiled.

"Have you talked to her?"

"About this?" Fasé tapped her chest. "No, it is not her place to speak with me on what is happening. The news of my transgression was sent home. We are waiting to hear from the Pedalion."

"What is the Pedalion, Fasé?"

"Our wisest," she replied after a moment of consideration. "It is hard to put into Indranan. They are a governing body, of sorts, like your Matriarch Council, but more than that also."

"Will I be able to speak with them?"

Judging by the way the Farian blinked at me before she laughed, the question shocked her. "No one who is not Farian has stood before the Pedalion, Majesty. Even when we first made contact with humanity, all conversations were conducted through specially chosen emissaries."

"There's a first time—"

The knock at the door interrupted me and I glanced over my shoulder at Gita as she opened it. She pushed the door open and I got to my feet when Hao came into the room.

"Did you find them?"

"We did, Majesty, but—" Hao caught my arm as I tried to push past him. "Hail, it's not that simple."

I stared at him until he let me go with a sigh. Striding out of the room with Gita on my heels, I gathered Kisah and Iza in my wake. Hao pushed by them until he reached my side again. "Where's Nakula?" I asked, stopping at the head of the stairs.

"Downstairs," he said.

We went down the main staircase, my eyes straying to the now-pristine marble where just hours ago Hafiz died in a pool of his own blood. As if I were retracing my own bloody footprints, Hao led me into the same office just off the foyer.

I didn't wait for my BodyGuards to clear the room, snarling at Gita when she tried to step in front of me.

Nakula was inside and a young Marine with a tearstained face sat in the same chair I'd occupied when Stasia had cleaned the blood off my feet. She shot to attention, dark eyes wide in her round face. Her hands were cuffed in front of her.

"Your Majesty."

"Who is this?" I looked at Nakula.

"Your Majesty, this is Specialist Patka Modi, Colonel Bristol's—" Nakula cleared his throat. "Lover."

I arched a single eyebrow.

It wasn't totally uncommon, especially among the military. Marriages tended to be for specific alliances rather than love. Still it surprised me; Hafiz hadn't given any indication he'd felt anything but love and affection for his wife when he spoke of his family.

"The colonel was unfortunately less than discreet with her about our meeting last night," Nakula continued, his face shifting from uncomfortable to impassive with his words. "Specialist Modi was under the impression you were going to be with us."

"He didn't tell me he was going instead. I thought that the money they promised me would let us get away from all this. Hafiz was a good man. He didn't know what I'd done. I thought it would just put an end to the fighting." The woman started crying again and my temper frayed.

"Stop."

The command made her jump.

"Do we have a trail to follow?" I asked Nakula. A fury was

building in my chest, but Nakula's answer iced it over, filling me with the terrible realization of what I would have to do.

"Yes, ma'am. She gave us names and faces. We're running them down now."

"Good. I want Travoy's and Postoyev's heads at my feet before sunset." I took two steps forward and grabbed Specialist Modi by the collar of her shirt. Twisting my fist, I dragged her toward the door. Kisah and Iza both jerked in surprise when I kicked it open.

"Ma'am?" Iza asked, confusion in her eyes.

"Get out of my way," I snarled, hauling the stumbling, sobbing Marine across the foyer and out the front of the mansion.

The sun was peeking over the brightly colored awnings of the marketplace in downtown Tasht just outside the front gates of the governor's mansion. The Marines at the large doors looked from me to my prisoner to my Guards and back again, but they didn't move from their posts. The ones down farther by the front gates snapped to attention and I was sure there was a lot of rapid-fire activity on the coms.

"Hail, what are you doing?" Hao caught up to me, his voice pitched low even as the murmurs of the crowd outside the gates rose to drown him out. Nakula was at his side, his face wiped clean of expression, though his eyes betrayed his concern.

"Setting an example." I threw Patka to the ground. "Exacting justice." They were easy answers for a difficult question, one that I didn't have the time to explain to him. I knew, somehow I knew without a shadow of a doubt, that Wilson would be watching this and my response to Patka Modi's betrayal had to be swift and uncompromising.

I hated it. Hated that he'd backed me into this corner. Hated that this stupid, selfish young woman would die because she'd lost her faith in me—if she'd even had any to begin with.

"Justice, or vengeance?"

"Don't you dare moralize at me, Cheng Hao, after every-thing we've been through together. This woman just admitted to treason, to collusion with the enemy. She caused the death of my kinsman and put us all at risk because of her stupidity and selfishness. I could cite a dozen laws she's violated." I pulled my QLZ-77 free of the holster and raised my voice so the crowd outside the gates could hear me.

"Specialist Patka Modi has admitted to committing treason against the throne of Indrana. Her actions resulted in the death of Colonel Hafiz Bristol. We are at war. If you are not with me, you are my enemy."

"Hail, don't. Let your courts handle it." Hao put his hand on my arm.

"I swore I would take the responsibility myself. I've seen you kill for so much less than this." I shook his hand off. "Why are you trying to stop me?"

"Because there's still hope for you," he murmured, sadness in his gold eyes.

"No, there's not." I looked back at Specialist Modi.

"Please, Majesty." Tears rolled down her face. "I am sorry. I didn't—"

I pulled the trigger. There were gasps from the crowd, but then an awful silence descended. Emmory and Zin sprinted through the doors and down the stairs.

I didn't meet my *Ekam*'s eyes as I walked past him, slapping my gun into his chest before heading up the steps and back into the mansion.

I could hear Emmory's voice clearly from outside the door of my rooms, but I only half listened to the dressing-down he was giving to Gita as I watched and rewatched Clara's execution.

Hao leaned against the windowsill. Iza was by the door, and she jerked every time Emmory's voice rose.

"I don't care what your personal feelings are, Gita! Your job is to protect the empress. Sometimes that means even from herself! You don't stand there and let her kill a Royal Marine in front of hundreds of witnesses."

"The woman was a traitor by her own admission!"

"Then you let the Shiva-damned tribunal handle it!" The door shook from what I hoped was Emmory's fist slamming into it and not Gita's head. "If you can't separate your need to avenge your mother from your duty to the empress, I'm going to relieve you of your position. Now get out of my sight until I decide I'm not going to fire you just on sheer principle."

Gita's response was indistinct. I hit play on the video again. The door opened and closed behind me but I didn't look away from the gruesome image on the wall when Emmory sat at my side.

"You can't fire her, we're already shorthanded."

"I know."

"She couldn't have stopped me even if she'd wanted to, Emmy."

"I know," he repeated. "That's not the point, though. She didn't even try. It's our job to think of the things you won't. Nakula told me what happened. You should have let her command handle it."

I lifted a shoulder, watching as Clara fell to the ground once more. "It wouldn't have changed the outcome, and I told you after the executions at home that I'd rather pull the trigger myself than let someone else do my dirty work for me. I meant it. That woman caused the death of my cousin—she would have caused my death had Hao not bullied me into staying here. She deserved what she got and I'm not sorry to be the one to take responsibility for it. Besides, Wilson was watching to see what I'd do."

"You can't run an empire like a smuggler's ship, Majesty." Emmory reached out before I could start the video again. "Hail, enough."

"Clara said, 'Your mother said no,' just before Wilson shot her. It was hard to make out over the shouting. I don't know what she meant, though. Do you?"

I couldn't help but laugh at the confused frown on my *Ekam*'s face. "Did you think I was just watching it to torture myself?"

"I did," Hao said with a wave of his hand.

"Shut up."

This time, it was Emmory who hit the playback. Hao pushed away from the window and stood behind me to watch. As Clara fell, Emmory muttered a curse.

"Zin, get in here," he said aloud over the com and a moment later the door opened. "Clara was trying to tell us something and we missed it."

"Mother said no to a hell of a lot," I said as Zin watched the video, his jaw tightening. "I don't know how we can possibly narrow it down."

"She didn't want Wilson to know," Zin said, turning from us and pacing the length of the room. "That's the best reason I can think of for being so cryptic."

"Get to work on it," Emmory replied.

Zin responded with a nod and left the room.

"Back to the original issue, Majesty."

I crossed my arms and stared Emmory down. "I'm not sorry for it."

"I know, and that's what worries me. There's already video circulating. With no context it looks like you just dragged a

Marine out into the yard and killed her. The Solarian news outlets are going nuts."

That was what I'd done, I couldn't deny it. "It's what Wilson wanted. I knew he'd be watching, or have someone there to record it. He wanted to see how ruthless I'd be, Emmory, and I'm tired of pretending to be civilized. The Solarians can fly themselves into their sun for all I care; this isn't their business."

"You used a young woman's life to prove a point?"

"No, *he* used her!" I flung a hand toward the window. "And she wasn't an innocent. She knew damn well what she was doing, or did you forget the bit about her thinking I would be out there with Nakula instead of Hafiz?"

That shut him up.

"I didn't enjoy it, I didn't want to do it, but it had to be done."

"Release the footage of her confession," Hao said. "It's more than enough of an explanation."

"It also announces that Hafiz was having an affair to the whole galaxy," I said with a shake of my head. "I won't do that to his family. Not without some kind of warning first. Have Alba get with Admiral Hassan's staff to draft a release detailing Modi's crimes and leave it at that. Don't argue with me, Emmory. I'll take the hit for this; it's my responsibility. The rest of the civilized galaxy has been whispering about me for long enough. Now they can all see the rumors are true."

Getting up from my seat, I gave Hao a look and jerked my head at the door. He arched a metallic eyebrow in reply, but followed my unspoken order and ushered Iza out the door in front of him.

"I've got a meeting with the Matriarch Council—what's left of it—this afternoon. You can bet your ass this is going to come up. I need a united front here. Not just for them but for Wilson. If it looks like we're fighting among ourselves he'll only keep throwing more lives into the fire."

"Forgive me, Majesty, it's your life I'm concerned about. No one else's."

"I can manage my own life, *Ekam*, thank you very much."

Emmory's mouth twitched. "You could have fooled me."

I laughed in response and we both pretended it wasn't hollowed out with pain.

9

I could not have been more nervous as I sat in the chair at the head of the conference table and waited for Alice to link into our coms. The matriarchs who'd been with me on Red Cliff—Masami Tobin, Caterina Saito, and Sabeen Vandi—sat on one side of the table. Admirals Hassan, Fon, and Dewan were on the other.

"Before we start, does anyone have anything to say about this morning?" I glanced around the table. "As I said in my statement that Alba released to the news lines, Specialist Patka Modi was found guilty of treason by her own admission and the crown's justice was administered accordingly. This was the result of outside influences attempting to meddle in the affairs of the Indranan Empire. The crown's response to such actions will always be swift and uncompromising."

Caterina Saito surprised me with a firm nod. "Nothing to say, Your Majesty. You did the right thing."

"Ruling is messy," the elderly Masami said with a shrug. "Even more so in times of war, Majesty. You have to trust your own judgment on this; even if we would have done differently, we support your decision."

I glanced at Sabeen Vandi; the youngest member of the matriarchs was the newest member of the council because of the unexpected deaths of her mother and older sister. She'd never expected to take her sister's position and I suspected had suffered from the same sheltered upbringing many of the younger noble daughters experienced. She'd handled herself well during our flight from Red Cliff, but now Sabeen was staring at the tabletop and worrying her bottom lip between her teeth. I let the silence drag on a moment more and then cleared my throat.

She jerked her head up. "Majesty?"

"What's on your mind, Sabeen?"

"Nothing, ma'am. It's fine. You did—"

"Sabeen, don't lie to me. What's on your mind?"

Still she hesitated, the war between the respect for her empress and the words she wanted to say playing out so clearly on her face.

"It was cruel," she blurted. "You didn't even blink, ma'am. If it hadn't been for Hao you wouldn't have hesitated at all. Specialist Modi was stupid and in love. That wasn't justice; you murdered her in full view of the empire. How could you be so callous?"

"You watch your mouth." Masami came up out of her seat at Sabeen's words. "That is your empress you're speaking to, Matriarch Vandi."

The rest of Masami's words faded into the background as I was twelve years old again, railing at my mother for denying a petition of clemency for a young man who'd been sentenced to death.

"He made a mistake, Mother. How can you be so cruel?"

"A mistake?" Mother laughed and swept a glass off the table. It

shattered when it hit the floor. "That's a mistake, Hailimi. This young man's decisions resulted in someone's death. The law says the consequences are he forfeits his own life. The judges saw fit to give the sentence. I can't just overturn their rulings, disregard their wisdom, because his sister happens to be a friend of yours."

"He was stupid and in love and you're going to murder him for it and Kaileen will never speak to me again!" I shoved my chair back so hard it fell to the floor just like the glass. "I hate you. You're horrible and heartless."

"Haili!" My father's voice cut through the chaos, so full of shocked disappointment I couldn't look him in the face. Dodging his outstretched hand, I ran from the room, Tefiz following after.

"Masami, that's enough," I said, and the matriarch sat back in her seat. Sabeen was in tears, her face buried in her hands. I waved the others to the opposite side of the room and crouched down next to her chair.

"Sabeen."

"I—I'm s-sorry."

"There is nothing for you to apologize for. Dry your face. We don't have a lot of time for this. Yes, she was in love, and yes, she did something incredibly stupid. We are not children, Sabeen, and our stupidity has consequences. For Specialist Modi it was the death of the man she loved and the loss of her own life. I know it seemed cruel. I know I seemed cruel.

"I executed a Royal Marine and I did it because it was the only possible response to the men who are trying to destroy our empire." I tipped her face up to meet mine.

"I have to think about more than myself, Sabeen, and that means being cruel at times. There are billions of lives at stake. Had Specialist Modi considered that before she made her choice, she might still be alive. And so might Colonel Bristol."

"Yes, Majesty."

I smiled sadly and squeezed her chin. "Never be afraid to speak out when you think I've gone too far. I am not so arrogant as to believe that I will always be so clearheaded. Some of us are not made for death and war, there's no shame in it. I need people like you around to remind me, okay?"

"Yes, ma'am."

The incoming signal buzzed and I nodded in Gita's direction as I moved back to my seat. She put it on the screen on the far wall.

"Alice."

"Your Majesty." Alice dipped her head and the camera panned back to reveal the others in the room with her. Matriarch Saba Hassan smiled at the sight of her daughter sitting on my left, while Ellin Prajapati gave me a quick nod in greeting.

The new matriarchs were my cousin Tej Naidu, Heela Maxwell, and Adi Desai, who barely remembered to acknowledge me before she found her sister and offered a sympathetic smile that Gita answered with one of her own.

"Leena," I said to my former sister-in-law. "It's good to see you. How is Taran?"

"He's as well as can be expected, Majesty," she replied with a soft smile. Leena was not a matriarch, but her aunt and mother were in Wilson's custody and her family scattered. I wanted as many voices speaking our unified message for Indrana as I could get, and right now she was the only Surakesh of note.

"Majesty, we should not stay on for long. Caspel is reasonably sure we can conceal the signal, but with all of us in one spot it is dangerous enough without advertising where we are."

"Understood. Proceed, Alice."

"The first issue is the safety of members of the royal family and members of the matriarchy. For posterity, the list of the dead is as follows..." Alice read off the names of those who had been killed, starting with my mother and sisters and working her way down the list to finish with Colonel Bristol. "A moment of silence for all those who have gone to temple, and our apologies for being unable to give you all the rights and rituals due to you at the time of your deaths."

I pressed my hands to lips, heart, and head.

"Our sisters are still in the custody of the traitor Eha Phanin," Alice continued. "The first issue is to discuss if we should mount a rescue operation."

I shook my head. "We will not."

"Majesty," Leena protested. "My mother is in that madman's clutches. My aunt, possibly my sisters, you cannot—"

"I am aware of that," I said. "And for the moment, they are unharmed. The others are unharmed. Wilson will be waiting for a rescue attempt and you are all on precarious ground as it is. Moving before we are ready will only result in repercussions I don't think any of you are prepared for. Keep watching the palace, get any information you can, but don't make a move until I am home."

The older matriarchs nodded in agreement, while the younger ones watched me with worried frowns much like Sabeen had worn. Alice, by contrast, gave no hint of her preference and merely nodded.

"Understood, Majesty. We will wait until you have returned." Alice checked the item off her list with a tap of her finger. "The next issue concerns the news reports flooding in about Her Majesty's execution of a Royal Marine. At present we've answered any questions with a fairly standard line that we were not present and cannot comment on a situation where we are missing essential details."

"Good. Keep it that way."

"Majesty, can we know the details?" Tej Naidu thankfully looked more like her mother, with dark hair and eyes, than like her dead sister Ganda. "This secondary story coming through the news lines is not very flattering to the empire."

"Specialist Modi betrayed the empire," I replied, meeting her gaze with a steady look. "She sold classified information that led to the death of Colonel Bristol and interrupted a vital mission here on Canafey. She did so with the idea that I would be present at the meeting that was ambushed and admitted without coercion that I was the original target."

Tej nodded. "Understood, Majesty. She deserved her fate."

"Agreed," Alice said. "Does anyone have questions or objections on this?"

No one else spoke up, so Alice tapped on her list again. "Majesty, you issued a statement on Santa Pirata about Phanin's actions. The council would like permission to draft our own for release to the Indranan people. The general tone would be in line with your statement, condemning his actions and his association with an outsider who obviously holds ill will toward the empire as well as making known our support for you."

"Granted. Send a copy to Alba when you release it."

"Yes, ma'am."

"I'm going to record another message before we leave Canafey. One for the people of Pashati and Ashva asking them to hold the line against these men trying to destroy our empire."

Alice nodded. "That's all I have, Majesty. Does anyone else have questions? We've got about five more minutes before we need to sign off."

Leena raised her hand. "Majesty, what are your plans?"

The words to tell her about the plan to go to Saxony were on the tip of my tongue when my common sense kicked in. *Don't give your plans away before you put them into action.* Po-Sin's voice was sharp in my memory.

I swallowed down the words I'd been about to say and instead I said, "I'm coming home."

She laughed. "We know that. I meant what are your plans for taking back the system?"

"I understood the question, Leena," I replied. "Our plans are need-to-know."

"Majesty, we're the council," she protested. "How is that wise to keep information from us?"

"You are not a member of the council, Leena. You are there as a temporary." I tried to keep the snap of annoyance out of my voice, but judging by the way her shoulders jerked, I failed. "And you don't need to know because there's nothing you can do about the plans we're developing. Furthermore, there's plenty that could go wrong should Wilson's men get hold of someone who knows the plans. So my answer remains: I'm coming home."

"Enough, Leena, we are out of time." Alice cut her off before she could open her mouth again. "Thank you, Majesty. We'll talk to you again soon."

"Stay safe, all of you."

A smile ghosted across Alice's face as she nodded at me and cut the connection. Silence descended in the room and I glanced around the table, taking stock of the women's expressions.

Inana frowned, her eyes locked on some spot outside the window.

"Admiral Hassan, thoughts?"

"Sorry, Majesty, I was just—" She shook her head. "Any particular reason you didn't tell the matriarchs we are headed for Saxony?"

"They don't need to know," I repeated. "I don't want to take any chances of Phanin or Wilson finding out until it's too late."

Inana nodded, but she was still frowning, and I raised an eyebrow at her.

"What is it?"

"I don't know," she said after a moment. "I'm just uneasy, Majesty." She rubbed a hand over her face. "I probably just need to get some sleep."

"Good advice for us all," I agreed, getting to my feet. The others followed, talking quietly among themselves as they left the room. "Inana?" I called out before she could leave the room with the other admirals.

"Yes, ma'am?"

"Let me know if you can pin down what's making your gut twitchy."

She nodded. "I will, ma'am."

Emmory came back into the room, exchanged a nod with Gita, and tipped his head toward the door in a silent order. She left, Fasé slipping by her with a worried expression.

"Majesty, we must speak." Her eyes darted around, looking in two directions at once and making the hair on the back of my neck stand up. I'd known Farians could do that, but I'd never actually seen it happen. They were usually so careful because of how unnerving it was.

"Fasé, what is it?"

"Please tell me you didn't tell Leena what our plans are?"

I blinked at her. "Excuse me? How did you—"

"Did you tell her?"

"No. No, I didn't tell her." I shook my head, glancing over at Emmory. His grim look made my stomach twist. "What is going on?"

Fasé sagged against the table, relief washing over her face. "I was afraid I was too slow. I didn't want to message you on the *smati*, I thought it might—I don't know. *Mata, íosi bin*," she muttered to herself in Farian. "It's so hard to keep everything straight. The days are blurring and there's too much—"

"*Dhatt*, Fasé." I took her by the shoulders and pushed her into a chair before she slid to the floor. "Take a deep breath. You're as white as a sheet."

"I'm always as white as a sheet, Majesty. I'm a Farian." Her laugh was shrill enough that I contemplated slapping her to bring her back to reality.

Emmory put his hand on her shoulder. "Fasé, you're not making much more sense than when you found me."

His touch seemed to ground her. Fasé put her hand up over Emmory's and took a breath. I grabbed for the chair behind me, pulling it close to hers and dropping into it.

"I saw Leena with Wilson," she whispered. "It was fragmented, so much more jumbled than anything else I've seen. I saw you telling her about our plans for the attack on Pashati. I saw the palace in flames."

"What do you mean, you saw her?"

Fasé tapped her temple. "Here, I saw them, Majesty."

"We don't even have those plans yet, Fasé."

"I know, it doesn't matter. Everything is out of order in my head. All I know is what I've seen, Majesty. You can't trust Leena. I'm sorry. I know it's a lot to ask of you to trust me, but—"

"Emmory, get on the com with Caspel. I don't know where they were for that conversation we just had, but tell him to get the matriarchs out of there. Tell him I said to do it and we'll tell him why as soon as they're safe."

Emmory nodded, releasing Fasé and turning around to send

the message. My stomach continued to roll. I couldn't ignore the timing, or the way that Fasé's words matched up with my own sudden hesitation over Leena's questions.

Why would she betray us?

"Majesty, Caspel said they're still at the secondary site. Leena is gone already, claiming she needed to get back to Taran. The other matriarchs are with Alice. He got them out the door the minute I said he needed to move."

I pressed my hand to my mouth. "Shiva, Emmory. She's got Taran, if she's—"

"Caspel's on it already, ma'am. If she's flipped on us we'll make sure Taran is safe."

"I can't believe she would do this to us."

"We don't know anything for sure yet, Majesty. It's better to not take any chances. Caspel said Leena doesn't know the location of the main headquarters but that she's been to several outlying sites. He requested a com link in about an hour."

Fasé put a hand on my arm. "I'm truly sorry, Majesty."

"We'd all be a lot sorrier if Alice and the others ended up dead." I sent a message to Tazerion, telling him to com me immediately. "I don't know what you saw, Fasé, and I hope to Shiva you are wrong. But we won't take the chance."

I blew out a breath as my com chimed and answered Taz's call. "We have a problem," I said.

"So I heard." My childhood friend, Tazerion Benton Shivan, was the new leader of the *Upjas*. The rebellious group campaigning for male equality in Indrana had found a certain amount of legitimacy during the coup and my ascension to the throne.

My older sister, Cire, had been in love with the group's former leader. Her death had weakened Abraham's will enough that the *Upjas* split into factions. The more violent offshoot had been dealt with just before I left Indrana and—at least for now—it seemed the bulk of the *Upjas* were solidly on the side of the throne.

I suspected Taz's relationship with my heir played a large part in the acceptance of the *Upjas*.

"I've got a handful of people at the base where Taran is staying, Majesty. They'll get him out of there and keep him safe."

Taz and I had been best friends. My mother had been in talks with his about our marriage before I left home. Now he was just a reminder of the life I'd left behind, and we fumbled with a mix of the familiar and the new every time we talked.

"Thank you."

Taz smiled and lifted a shoulder. "Have you—" He stopped, glanced around, and then continued. "You look like shit, Hail. Get some rest."

"I've been a little busy."

"I know, and it's not going to stop any time soon. You're safe there; take advantage of that while you can."

"I will." I laughed at the look I got in reply. "I will, I promise."

"We'll see you soon."

"Stay safe."

It was his turn to laugh. "I don't have much choice; apparently I rate BodyGuard status now. There's two mean-looking people following me around all the time." He shifted his hand and showed me the pair of Guards by the door. "Alice doesn't seem to care that I've been taking care of myself for longer than these two have been alive."

"Welcome to my life," I said with a grin, and waved at him before I cut the connection.

10

"he site we used for the meeting was hit by an air strike not
half an hour after we'd gotten Alice and the others to safety."
Caspel and Alice both wore looks of grim determination. "I'm
sorry, Majesty, it just never occurred to me that she would be
involved like that."

I waved off Caspel's apology. "What is the status of the
Surakesh family?"

"I've detained three of the matriarch's children, Majesty. As
for Leena's aunt and mother, we have no way of knowing if
they're actually prisoners as Leena claimed, or if they're working with Wilson the same as she is."

"Keep them in custody," I replied with a nod. "Either way it's
safer for you and for them." I leveled him with a look. "Question them, Caspel. Find out what they know. I am tired of being
surprised."

"Yes, Majesty."

"The *Upjas* were able to retrieve Taran and move him to
safety, Majesty. We're not sure if Leena was planning on trying
to grab him." Alice smiled. "But he's safe."

"Pass my thanks on to Taz," I said, giving her a smile in return. "Caspel, Toropov?"

"Nothing yet, Majesty. He's still trying to get an answer."

"Tell him I'm running out of patience, Caspel, and he's running out of time."

"I will, ma'am." He nodded once at me and then disconnected.

I shared a look with Gita and got up to pace the room. "Majesty?"

"Leena's defection is a shock, but more worrisome is the fact that Fasé knew about it before anyone else," I said, leaning on the windowsill and staring out at the darkening sky. "If I was to believe her, she can now apparently see the future, and I have no idea how to wrangle that into submission in my head."

"It's not unheard-of, Majesty, though you'd have to ask Major Morri or Fasé about it for any detail. I know a little about Farian culture from my ambassador security days and I can try to answer any questions you have."

"The future, Gita. You're asking me to believe that everything is already set in stone."

Gita shook her head. "That's not the way it works. Again, my knowledge is limited, but it's more like they see the possibilities." She looked up at the ceiling for a moment, visibly trying to collect her thoughts. "It's much like our Tracker program, ma'am. Certain Farians are picked at a very young age to see if their talent bears out. Those who pass certain tests are meant to become future-seers; the others go back to their regular lives."

"It's insanity."

"Possibly, ma'am." Gita smiled and shook her head. "In this case it bore out, unless you think Fasé is somehow working with Wilson and it was to his benefit to give Leena up?"

"No," I replied. "I'm trying not to be quite that paranoid." My *smati* pinged with an incoming call and I answered it.

"Your Majesty, I'm surprised your handlers let you answer this call all on your own."

"They do occasionally remember that I'm in charge. How were you able to get through to me?" I waved a hand at Gita, pointing at the door, and she frowned at me.

"Oh, I have my ways."

"What can I do for you, Wilson?" The moment I said his name she snapped into motion.

"Just called to congratulate you, or is it commiserate? Both would work, I guess. I was so sad to hear about your cousin's death. But congratulations on that public execution—it was gripping stuff. I thought your mother was ruthless. You are on a whole other level."

"My mother was a diplomat," I replied. "I'm something entirely different."

"Yes, the gunrunner empress." Wilson waved his hands in the air. *"The news lines are loving that moniker. Personally, I think it's a bit childish, like something one of your BodyGuards thought up."*

I didn't even have to feign the yawn. "Did you call for a reason?"

The muscles on the side of his jaw tightened and this time his smile seemed forced. *"Like I said, just called to congratulate you, kiddo."*

"We should meet soon so you can do that in person."

Wilson raised his eyebrows at me. *"I'm looking forward to it."*

I disconnected the call and forced myself to stand still instead of raging only because the room was now filled with people.

"Majesty, how did he call you directly?"

"I have no idea, though he's in the palace and my *smati* is on record."

Zin muttered a curse that was vicious enough to be out of

character for him. "We need to scramble signals on everyone before we leave here."

I held a hand out to Emmory and passed the recording along to him. "Show the others."

As Emmory passed it around, I went to the window, letting the murmurs swirl through the air as they watched it.

"You did well, Majesty. He was trying to get a reaction out of you and he failed."

"He was showing off. He—" I exhaled in frustration as something attempted to claw through my anger but vanished under the seething surface before it could draw breath.

"What is it?"

"I don't know." I turned to him and made a face. "That's unhelpful, I know. I'm sorry."

"I trust your gut, Hail," Emmory replied in a voice too low for the others to hear. "Let me know when you've figured it out."

"I will." I mustered a smile that my *Ekam* didn't echo; instead he lifted a hand and glanced back at the door.

"Hao and Nakula are back," he said. "Colonel Alexander is reporting that the Saxons have been routed. All are accounted for, either surrendered or killed." Emmory put a hand on my back. "Hao is requesting you downstairs."

"We should go then. He always got grumpy when I kept him waiting." I crossed the room and exited, heading down the hallway toward the stairs. I spotted Hao and Nakula, both men dirty and disheveled with a bag on the floor between them. My spy wore a concerned frown, while my mentor had that same canary-eating grin that happened when he was immensely pleased with himself.

I was surprised to see Bial there, with Johar at his side. I hadn't laid eyes on mother's *Ekam* since our conversation several days before. They, too, were dirty, as though they'd participated in the battle against the Saxons.

Walking down the stairs to the first landing, I leaned on the railing. "What is that?" I asked Hao, gesturing at the bag by his feet.

Hao just continued to grin. Nakula cleared his throat. "As Her Majesty requested—the heads of Travoy and Postoyev."

"Nicely done," I replied, a smile spreading across my face. "Pack them up and ship them to the palace. I want Phanin to see the fruits of his association with the Saxons."

"Yes, Majesty." Nakula looked a bit shell-shocked, but he didn't argue.

"Johar, did you enjoy yourself?"

"Immensely." She grinned. "Your people are well trained and excellent fighters."

I gave Bial a nod and he returned it with a surprisingly deferential bow.

"Good work, everyone," I said loud enough for the others in the foyer to hear me, and tapped my hand on the railing before I turned and headed back up the stairs.

Three mornings later the leaders of my ragtag army gathered around the conference table. I leaned against the wall as Hao and Nakula talked quietly in the corner with Johar and Alba. Gita stood like a statue by the window, her hair lit by the sunlight. Iza, Kisah, and Indula were all by the door. Major Morri and Senior Tech Ragini Triskan occupied chairs at the far end of the table, while Admiral Hassan and her staff were clustered in small groups around the sun-streaked room.

Emmory and Zin came into the room with my other three BodyGuards trailing behind.

I caught Inana's eye and nodded. She crossed to the table and banged a fist down. "All right, people, let's get rolling."

Everyone moved to the table. I settled on a chair away from the windows after Emmory glared at me, punching Hao in the leg for his snickering when he took the seat on my right.

Admiral Hassan cleared her throat once everyone was seated. "I'd like to extend my welcome to Admiral Mendez."

The newest admiral to join the fleet with a host of eighteen ships gathered from various pickets around the empire was a muscular older woman who'd escaped from Yandin before the governor there could replace her with a commander loyal to Phanin.

"In a week the Indranan fleet will be headed for Marklo, except for the ships we're leaving here at Canafey to protect the system. Using a split approach, we'll come at the Saxon homeworld from both sides. The *Vajrayana* ships will be divided into three groups..."

"Are we taking my ships to Ashva?" Hao asked over our com link.

I didn't look away from the diagram Inana had brought up from the center of the table. *"Most likely. If they don't want to stay I'll call in those ships from Po-Sin."*

"Unnecessary, sha zhu, they will fight."

"Don't think I don't know what you're doing." I nudged his foot with mine under the table. *"I keep owing you favors at this rate, I'm going to have to do something drastic like give you part of the palace when this is all over."*

"I'm hurt you would even suggest such a thing." Hao didn't blink, but there was amusement sparkling in his eyes. *"Maybe just a nice house in the country and a pension to retire on."*

"You're too young to retire. Besides, you'd die of boredom."

"Uncle always says he was a fool not to quit while he was ahead. I like to think I'm smarter than him."

I swallowed back my laughter and gave Admiral Hassan an innocent smile when she looked my way.

"With any luck, we'll be able to hit them hard enough to cripple them permanently. Then we'll head for home," she said, and gestured in my direction. "Majesty, if you'd like to share the second part of this plan."

Using my *smati*, I switched out the image hovering over the table to the Ashvin system. "We're taking a small strike team home aboard the *Pentacost* and coming up on Ashva from the night side with the mercenary force. Sources say Shul set up only three destroyers there. We'll give the picket force a chance to surrender. If they don't, we'll wipe them out. Once we have control of the planet, we'll wait for Admiral Hassan's ships to arrive." I looked to Inana, who picked up the flow easily.

"When we arrive, we can either draw Admiral Shul and his ships away from Pashati or fly in to meet them in battle."

I zoomed the image in to the very edge of the southern continent. "Either way, it'll provide enough distraction for us to put the *Pentacost* down here on Pashati and then make our way across to rendezvous with Caspel and the loyalist forces. From there we'll determine what the best course of action is."

"Your Majesty, what happens if we get hung up at Marklo?" Admiral Fon asked. "With all due respect, you won't have a lot of time once you make a move on Ashva, and ten mercenary ships don't stand a chance against Admiral Shul when he comes to meet you. Even if he only takes half his fleet to Ashva, he's got three *Vajrayana* ships under his control."

I nodded. "I'm taking one *Vajrayana* ship with us as well as Senior Tech Triskan, possibly more technicians also; we'll need to talk about that and make a final decision on the numbers needed. The senior tech here has something up her sleeve to deal with Phanin's *Vajrayana*."

"Yes, ma'am." Admiral Fon nodded at me.

"Additionally, we've got 5th Fleet on standby. I suspect Phanin isn't going to let Shul attack Ashva directly, no matter how much I goad him. Which means he doesn't have a whole lot to do if there's no ships in the space above for him to fight. If we're already on the ground at Ashva and he does come after us, we'll have a better chance of surviving." I shook my head. "I can't believe they'd bombard the planet."

"But it's a chance," Emmory said.

"True," I agreed. "If necessary, Admiral Dewan with 5th Fleet believes she can get home in under fourteen hours. I don't want her to move unless it is absolutely required. I'd rather Shul think that the other fleets aren't going to involve themselves in the fight until it's too late for him. But if we need her, she can be there to help."

Shul was dead the second my boots hit the dirt on Ashva anyway, or sooner if I needed it. But I wasn't about to tell a roomful of naval officers that I'd authorized the assassination of one of their own—even if he was a traitor.

"Is anyone else going to bring up the sheer ridiculousness of allowing the empress to walk right into what is undoubtedly a trap? How extremely dangerous it is to let her even leave here? This man wants to kill her. Why are we making it easier for him?" Colonel Teesha Alexander tapped a slender hand on the table in a staccato rhythm.

Colonel Bristol's replacement was a stern-faced older woman whose demeanor reminded me painfully of Clara.

Opening my eyes wide in mock surprise, I said, "Shiva's bones! You know, none of us thought of that."

"Manners, *sha zhu*." Hao smacked me in the back of the

head, eliciting several shocked looks from the people around the table and a suspicious cough from Admiral Hassan that sounded a lot like covered-up laughter. "It's a valid question."

"Admiral Hassan and I have had this conversation. My *Ekam* and I have had this conversation. Hell, even the matriarchs and I have had a discussion about it. I'm not sure what part of *I am the damned empress* is unclear here."

"The problem is that it's all too clear, ma'am. That's exactly why I'm asking the question. You're our empress; if you die they win. It's as simple as that." Colonel Alexander shook her head. "It's not about if you can, Majesty. It's about if you should. This Wilson knows how to push you, that's clear enough to all of us. He shot Matriarch Desai for precisely that reason. He had Colonel Bristol killed. You dragged a member of my company out into the yard and shot her in the head. It's all over the news outlets now and they are not being favorable in their commentary."

"Teesha, you'll want to watch your words," Inana said.

"I'm not saying she didn't deserve it, ma'am." Colonel Alexander held her hands up. "Naraka, I would have shot her in the head for what she did if I'd gotten to her first. I'm asking if Her Majesty is thinking things through or if she's just letting Wilson push her into reacting." She pressed her hands together in front of her forehead and shook them in my direction. "Majesty, forgive me, but you won't even defend your actions to the media because you know you'll have to hurt Hafiz's family to do it. I get it, he was a good man, a great commander, but he was human and he made mistakes. You're letting your affection for your cousin impair your judgment. Your family is the soft spot, it's your weak point. Wilson is playing you and it's clear he knows just how to get you to go down."

There was silence for a heartbeat, and then the noise level in the room soared as some spoke up in my defense while others raised their voices to agree with Colonel Alexander.

I pressed fingers to my mouth as I tuned out the fighting. Colonel Alexander's words rang in my head along with Emmory's from before. I couldn't blame any of them for thinking I was trying to beat Wilson at his own game instead of just reacting to him. No one here really knew me well enough for that leap to be obvious—except for maybe Hao.

"That's enough," I said, and even though I'd kept my voice low, everyone stopped talking.

"You're not wrong, Colonel." My laugh was short and sharp. "Not entirely anyway. This is Wilson's game, so I'm forced at least in some way with the option of nothing but reacting to whatever he throws at me. Which isn't to say I'm not fully aware of it and doing everything I can to make sure I think things through. However—"

"Your Majesty, if I may?"

I blinked at Hao's formal tone as much as the interruption and gave him a curious look but gestured at the table for him to proceed.

He got to his feet and surveyed everyone around the table with that little half smile he wore when he was deciding just how he was going to play a room.

"I realize none of you know me and most of you have no reason to trust me given my occupation." He grinned at the nervous laughter that answered him. "However, I have known this woman for longer than any of you. I have fought with her, bled with her, and I trust her with my life. So, let me tell you a story.

"Nearly twenty years ago in a fit of insanity I took an interesting young woman and her ridiculously protective companion on board my ship. They both had skills that made me decide to keep them around, but it wasn't until about three years later I realized what a good decision I'd made." Hao shoved his hands into his pockets and looked out the window. His eyes went soft, unfocused, as he remembered.

"We were meeting with a man who was a high-ranking member of my uncle's organization. A man who, for reasons I won't get into here, I couldn't stand."

Everyone's eyes were glued on Hao, but he was oblivious as he recounted an event I'd forgotten all about. We'd had to do a job for Fen Ah, and though Hao didn't say it out loud there'd been something about the set of his jaw when he talked about the man that made me uneasy.

I'd dug, even though I knew I probably shouldn't pry into my boss's personal affairs. Though the only information I could find linking them on previous jobs was mention of a File 44, a heavily censored Solarian Conglomerate report that alluded to the deaths of several agents of the SC government, one of them a woman named Mei. Other than that there'd just been the ghosts in Hao's eyes and an uneasy feeling that I couldn't shake.

When we'd met Fen Ah for the first time the man's sly smile and overly familiar behavior with Hao was like nothing I'd seen my boss put up with. It had made my skin crawl.

"She didn't act rashly. She knew I didn't care for the man and despite my orders to leave it be she kept poking at it. But when she met him she didn't walk up and punch him," Hao said, shaking me out of my reverie. "I would have had to kill her if she'd violated our laws so blatantly. Instead, she somehow goaded Fen Ah into assaulting her in full view of my uncle. Because she was my crew, I got to exact justice for her." Hao's smile was so cold several people shifted uncomfortably in their seats.

"Your empress and I have fought back to back. I have saved her life. She has saved mine. Over all the years, nothing has ever meant as much to me as that moment. Without even knowing why, she walked a man who'd evaded justice for decades straight into a trap that cost him everything in just a matter of minutes." He pointed down at me. "This woman doesn't act impulsively—ever—and it would be in your best interest to remember that."

Everyone in the room stared at Hao. He lifted a shoulder and sat back down.

"Close your mouth, Majesty." Emmory's voice was in my head, and I swore it was filled with laughter.

"Well." Inana cleared her throat and smiled at Hao. "Thank you, Captain, for your input. Colonel, I'm assuming that addresses your concerns."

"And then some, ma'am." Colonel Alexander was grinning at Hao. "I like you, Captain."

Hao winked at her.

"There goes the empire," I muttered, and those closest to me snickered. "All right, we've got that settled. Let's hammer out who's staying and who's going. My BodyGuards, Hao, Dailun, Johar, and whatever Marines Emmory and Colonel Alexander decide on will be headed for Pashati with the mercenary ships and one *Vajrayana*. Admiral Hassan, I'm assuming you have a crew picked out for it?"

"Yes, ma'am."

Nodding, I tapped a hand on the table. "Obviously the matriarchs will stay here where it's safest. I'm leaving Governor Ashwari in charge of the whole system with their support and council. Nakula will stay as head of security. Any and all decisions will go through him. Trackers Winston and Peche are taking over temporary bodyguard duty for the governor. Alba, you'll be assisting Jia."

"Majesty, no." Alba bit her lip as soon as the protest slipped out. Grief etched itself over her face.

"Alba." I reached for her hand. "You have performed your duty far above and beyond what I hired you for and I am so grateful for everything you have done. But I won't take you into this danger. You're not trained for it. You can do more good for the empire here right now. Jia needs your help, and Fasé and Stasia will welcome your company."

And I don't want your blood on my hands, too. I didn't say that out loud, but I was pretty sure my chamberlain saw the words in my eyes. She forced a smile and nodded twice.

"Yes, ma'am. I'll do my best."

"I'll see you after." I squeezed her hand and let her go.

"Your Majesty." Major Morri stood, her hands folded in front of her. "I will be accompanying you. It would be foolish to undertake this mission without a Farian, and I have combat experience."

I glanced over my shoulder at Emmory and he nodded. "All right, Major. You're on board."

"Thank you, ma'am."

"We'll be leaving the day after Hassan takes the fleet out. I want a complete supply list seventy hours from now. Hao, coordinate with your new friend there." I jerked my head at Colonel Alexander.

"With pleasure, Majesty."

I rolled my eyes as I got to my feet. "Everyone else, you know your jobs. Go do them."

11

The week sped by, every day packed with preparations for our departure and for the upcoming battles. I spent the bulk of my time with Jia—going over a priority list for Canafey—or with Emmory, discussing our plan for getting onto Pashati without being detected.

Jia had the run of Canafey well in hand, and I was sure Alba would be able to help her with anything she couldn't manage to juggle.

My chamberlain was still unhappy with my decision, but she didn't pout or fuss. Instead she threw herself into her new role as Jia's assistant with the same dedication I'd received.

Nakula couldn't seem to figure out if he was supposed to be angry with me for leaving him behind or relieved that he got to stay with Jia. I tried to hide my amusement from him, but judging from his sidelong glares I wasn't entirely successful.

"Majesty." Stasia passed me a cup of chai.

"Thank you." I looked away from where Jia and Alba were in deep discussion with Commander Pescadari about the best placement of the ships Admiral Fon was leaving to picket the system.

"I've packed our gear, Majesty. Zin said he'll get it over to the *Pentacost* this evening."

"Just my things, Stasia," I said with a smile. "You're staying here with Fasé."

"Majesty, my place is with you."

I shook my head as she continued the argument we'd been having for well over an hour. "I am not going to need a maid the next few weeks and we both know it. Fasé, however, does need you."

The incident with Leena had pushed Fasé back into silence, and she'd remained hidden in her room for the entire week refusing to speak with anyone.

"Majesty, I shouldn't leave you alone—"

"Hush. I won't be alone." Putting my cup down, I stood and wrapped my maid in a hug. "I am so grateful for all you've done. Let me do this for you."

"You've already done so much, ma'am. She's alive because of you." Stasia choked on a sob. "I wouldn't have—I can't imagine my life without her."

"And that's why you're staying." I released her, cupping her face and kissing her forehead. "I know I can't keep all of you safe, but I'll do whatever I can. I promise I can dress myself in the meantime."

She choked on a laugh and I winked at her. "Stay with your love, help her heal, and I hope when I see you again some of the grief is gone from your eyes."

Stasia murmured, "Yes, ma'am," and dropped a little curtsy before she left the room. I watched her go, wiping the tears from my eyes with the heel of my hand.

"Softy."

I elbowed Hao in the chest. "You'd have done the same."

"I have a time or two." He shrugged. "Mel and the others

are resupplied and ready to go. Your technician is on board V7 along with the contingent of Marines Teesha insisted we bring along."

"Teesha, is it?" I teased him, and Hao grinned.

"*Colonel Alexander* seemed to think we needed a full squadron. Even though I'm pretty sure you're not taking them all down to the surface."

"Shiva, I'm not taking any of them if I can help it. I want to get on the ground unnoticed." Emmory and I had already discussed it, and the best scenario was to send the Marines down as a distraction, which would allow them to meet up with the loyalist forces and give our group some cover.

I didn't want to attempt this with people I didn't know at my back, but Emmory hadn't budged on my five new Marine Body-Guards, and for the last week they'd spent all their spare time training with the other BodyGuards in preparation for the trip.

"All joking aside, *sha zhu*, he's got to know you're coming," Hao said quietly. "He did everything but lay out a welcome mat, and that call he put in to you the other day was decidedly creepy."

"I know." I made a face. "Colonel Alexander had a point, Hao. How do we keep from walking right into a trap?"

"We set our own." He rolled a shoulder. "Before you ask, I don't have anything yet, but I'll let you know if I come up with something."

"Think fast. We don't have a lot of time." I tapped him on the shoulder. "I've got a call with Alice."

"Is that the polite way of telling me to get out?"

Laughing, I shoved him at the door. "I'll talk to you later."

Hao gave an exaggerated bow and left the room. I sat back down and answered the chime, keeping the com on my internal viewer rather than throwing it up on the wall.

Alice and Caspel sat next to each other; they both looked exhausted. "Majesty."

"What's your status?"

Alice shook her head. "Not good, ma'am. We've lost two major bases within the capital thanks to Leena's betrayal. Even with Caspel keeping things as compartmentalized as he tends to do, she got her hands on an awful lot of information before she took off."

"Are you safe?"

"We are, Majesty. Don't worry. Taran is with us now. Taz's people brought him in a few days ago once the fighting had died down. I'd love to try to get him out of the city but I don't think we can risk it," Caspel replied.

"What about Toropov?"

"I haven't heard from him, Majesty. I don't know what's going on, I'm sorry."

"Send him a message and tell him he's got forty-eight hours to give me an answer. After that he's out of luck."

"I will." Caspel's mouth tightened a fraction. "Majesty, whatever you have planned, you need to get back here as fast as you can."

"Understood. Keep fighting, we'll see you soon."

They both gave me sharp nods and the com went blank. There was no one to hear me mutter a curse as I got up, rubbing both hands over my eyes and sliding them up to link my fingers behind my head.

The slender thread of hope we had was stretched to the breaking point and I didn't know how much more we could take. If something, anything, went wrong we could lose everything.

I headed for the door, pulling it open and nodding to Gita when she came to attention. "I'm going to go say good-bye to Fasé."

Gita and Zin followed me down the hallway and across the mansion. I stopped outside Fasé's room and tipped my head at Zin, jerking it to the side. He nodded and continued down the hallway, leaning against the banister that looked out over the massive chandelier hanging in the wide-open space between the floors.

Gita swallowed, her eyes darting from Zin to me and back again. She folded her hands together and I saw her fingers shaking before she bowed. "Majesty, please don't leave me here. I promise I am completely aware of my duty. My mother's death won't—"

"Bugger me, hold up." I put a hand on her head to stop her desperate babble. "Stand up. I'm not leaving you here, Gita. I wanted to apologize."

"Apologize?" She blinked, confusion running across her face.

"I put you in a bad position the other day. I got you in trouble with Emmory; moreover, I made it difficult for you to do your job. That's something I swore not to do. I know I can be a difficult charge—"

Zin coughed and I shot him a glare.

"At times. I don't regret what I did, but I should have waited for Emmory rather than letting you take the blame for it."

"Majesty, there was no blame." Gita shook her head. Her earlier fear over being left behind had melted away and a steely resolve filled her eyes. "I would stand by your side and watch your back as you did it again. She broke the law and earned her death. I trust you. You know Wilson better than the rest of us."

A laugh escaped. "I don't know him at all. I just recognize his type. Spoiled, angry, thinking the universe owes him something just because he exists."

"As do I, Majesty. You had to stand up to him, knowing full

well it could cost you not only the support of your own people but support across the galaxy." Gita pressed her palms together again and touched them to her forehead, lips, and heart. "I do not need an apology. I just need to know I can be with you through the end of this."

"And beyond, I hope," I held out my hand. She grabbed me by the forearm and we shared a grim smile.

Releasing her, I turned and knocked on Fasé's door, turning the knob at the sound of her voice and slipping into the room alone.

"I wondered how long you were going to stand out there," Fasé said by way of greeting, and I laughed.

"I needed to reassure Gita she was still coming with us. Fasé, I want you to stay here where it's safe. Stasia is staying with you."

A ghost of a smile passed Fasé's pale lips. She'd changed clothes, the gray drab outfit replaced by black pants and a short-sleeved shirt. The dark color made her red hair and gold eyes even more brilliant in contrast, and the shadows under her eyes gave her face an unnatural gauntness. "Major Morri has already been by to tell me she's going with you—" She paused and glanced out the window. "Which is fine, but Stasia and I will be going with you also, Majesty."

"Fasé, you can't. You're not well." I sat on the edge of her bed and laid a hand over hers. "I appreciate everything you've done."

"Of course, Majesty." There was that same ghost of a smile. "I would do it again in a heartbeat."

"The lives of my BodyGuards are something I will never be able to repay. However, I swear to you that I will do whatever is necessary to help you." I squeezed her fingers. "I mean it, so don't try to claim I can't or that you don't need my help. When we're done here, you will all come home and we will fix this."

"No, ma'am." Fasé shook her head and tapped her chest with

two fingers. "I don't need you to fix this. I need to go with you. We started this together and we should finish it together."

"I don't want to put either of you in danger."

"It's not your job to protect us."

"That is precisely my job."

Fasé stopped me when I started to rise and slid her other hand out from under mine so she could press it to my heart. "Trust this, ma'am. It is steady as a rock. It has never led you astray. Don't second-guess it now when you need it most. You know we need to go with you and it's simply fear trying to tell you what to do."

Words stuck in my throat, so I nodded in response.

Fasé smiled, the first genuine one I'd seen since Emmory died. "May my gods watch over us, Your Majesty."

The quiet hum of Hao's ship vibrated underneath my boots as I walked down the corridor. We were a day out from Canafey, almost a week away from our long approach to the dark side of Ashva, and our lack of a decent plan on how to defeat Wilson was eating at me.

Spotting Cas in the common area, I clattered down the stairs and hopped over the doorway. In order to accommodate the addition to our ranks, Hao had sent the bulk of his crew to Mel's ship, which meant my *Ekam* was slightly less anxious about me roaming around unattended.

"Majesty." Cas offered up a smile but surprisingly didn't get up from his seat or look away from whatever it was he was working on.

I sat next to my *Dve* on the heavy leather couch. It was an odd luxury on a spaceship, but so very much in keeping with Hao's personality that I hadn't been surprised to see it.

He'd probably have given me the same line about life being good to him had I asked why it was there.

115

"What are you doing?" I asked.

"Scanning Pashati news reports to see what we can use for intel. Emmory thinks we can pull together a decent idea of Phanin's forces if we combine this with what Director Ganej has. If you give me another ten minutes I'll be done with this batch, ma'am."

"Take your time," I said. "I'm not in any rush." Moreover, I didn't have anything specific to talk to him about. Leaning back against the leather, I watched Cas work and smiled.

He'd been so uncertain in the beginning, my baby-faced Guard. Watching the others like a hawk, taking all his cues from Emmory and Zin, and Jet.

Now Cas had a much harder face, born from the breakneck speed of the last few months and the loss of too many women and men he'd called friends. I knew Willimet's death had hit him with the same force Kisah had felt, but he'd hidden it better, buried it beneath his duty to me as we ran for our lives.

His blue eyes flicked back and forth as he skimmed the news reports for any scrap of information that would prove useful to us.

I sat with my pain while he worked. The thought of Jet made me hope his family was safe. I wouldn't put it past Wilson to go after Reva and her daughter just to hurt me.

Ten minutes on the dot later, Cas rubbed his eyes and gave me a tired smile.

"Anything useful?"

"A few things that have potential. I passed them on to Iza; she's got a knack for spotting truths in the lies. What did you need, ma'am?"

"Nothing really." I smiled. "I just saw you in here and thought I would join you. We're still trying to come up with a plan for infiltrating the palace, but I'm coming up blank so far." I huffed out an aggravated sigh. "Bugger me. I think most of it's because I can't get a handle on Wilson. What do you think?"

"Of Wilson, ma'am?"

Nodding, I got up to pace the room. A long table and benches were bolted down by the far wall, and a midsized galley with a low countertop bar took up the opposite side of the room.

"He's angry," Cas said. "Not just mad, but furious. Did you notice every time we've seen him it's like he's trying to keep from screaming?"

"What do you think he's mad at?"

Cas made a face. "Hard to say, beyond the obvious that it has something to do with you. It could be anything."

"I tend to have that effect on people who are trying to kill me."

He grinned at my comment and then sobered. "He was so familiar with you in that last call, ma'am. He called you 'kiddo,' which seems ridiculous, as he doesn't look much older than you. You don't recognize him at all?"

Pausing in midstride, I rolled Cas's words over in my head. That had been the thing trying to rise from the depths of my anger. It was too easy to dismiss Wilson treating me like a child as part of his arrogance.

"If he's someone from my past, he's had a body mod done."

"It's not unreasonable. An enemy you made while you were running guns?"

I shook my head. "It's nothing we can rule out entirely, but I doubt it. Anyone I pissed off in the last twenty years would want me to *know* who they are. Wilson's like—"

"A ghost," Zin supplied as he came into the room, Bial and Johar trailing behind. I'd found it curious that Emmory had insisted on bringing Bial with us instead of leaving him back at Canafey. Whatever my feelings for the man, he'd made himself useful by giving Hao all the information he'd dug up on

Wilson since the time he'd fled Pashati. And it appeared Johar had appointed herself his unofficial shadow, so at least I didn't have to worry about keeping an eye on him.

"He's not anyone you've been associated with, Majesty. I know that much. Bial backtracked him to about 2983, but before that it's like he didn't exist."

"People don't just pop out of nowhere, Zin."

"You did, Majesty," Bial said.

I shot the former BodyGuard a look as he lowered himself into a chair. He met the look with a smile that was genuine if still a bit uneasy.

"Cressen Stone didn't exist until 2991 when you walked out of that illegal mod shop on New Delhi. Your mod guy was good and backdated all the information into the system so that it wouldn't be as obvious. Cressen got a birthday and a home planet and all the things that we take for granted when we actually live them. It's one of the reasons your disguise held up so well over the years. The information was there, you just had to sell it. There wasn't anything strange to make people like him want to go digging for more information."

I turned to look where Bial was pointing and saw Hao and Emmory in the doorway.

"He's right. We did a thorough check on you and Portis. You came back squeaky clean, a few minor brushes with the law one would expect from an orphan. Portis came back exactly who he said he was with a dishonorable discharge that a follow-up told us was genuine. Nothing raised a flag, and believe me, Po-Sin would have never approved my request if there'd been something in your history to make us suspect you weren't who you said you were."

I pressed a hand to my stomach at the abrupt spike of loss the thought of Portis brought forth. No one in the room seemed to notice, so I took a deep breath and kept going.

"Wilson obviously doesn't care about that," Bial said. "In fact it's almost like he's flaunting that he appeared out of nowhere."

"I've run down every treaty, every agreement, every proposal your mother said no to over the last twenty-odd years." Zin shook his head. "Nothing. I can't find a single connection to Wilson."

"That's the year before the war started."

"Majesty?" Zin frowned at me.

I waved a hand in the air and continued to pace the room. "You said Wilson appeared in 2983?"

"That's the first record I could find, Majesty," Bial said. "He booked a passage on a freighter on the fifteenth of Shravana at a space port near Basalt III."

"That was the year before the war started. And—" Something was dancing outside my reach and I hissed in frustration. "Cas pointed out he called me 'kiddo.' What if he's someone from my childhood?"

The men looked at each other, and I could see Emmory and Bial both trying to sort through a list of possible suspects in their heads.

"Why?" Hao asked. "I'm sure you were a difficult child, *sha zhu*, but enough for someone to want to kill you?"

I punched him in the arm, unable to stop the laughter, which I'm sure was what he'd intended. "Not just about me, remember? This is about my whole family and from the sounds of it my mother was the starting point, not me."

"Fair enough." Hao pointed at Zin. "I'd say go back further than twenty years. Look at everyone who was around Hail and her mother from the time she was born."

"That is a wide fucking net," I murmured. Hao was right, though, and I nodded in agreement. "Look back further, Zin. We're missing something. I don't like the timing of Wilson's appearance, and his familiarity makes me uneasy."

"Yes, ma'am."

That worry in my head was still there, but I pushed it aside and headed back to the couch. Hao beat me to my spot with a grin, so I kicked him in the boot before I went to lean against the wall next to Emmory.

"Next problem, how are we getting into the palace? I'm pretty sure neither Wilson nor Phanin will slither out to meet me if I shout their names from the street."

"More likely he'd have a sniper drop you, Majesty," Emmory replied. "It's what I'd do."

"Me, too." I crossed my arms over my chest and made a face. "We storm the palace and a lot of good people get killed in the process."

"Drop a nuke on him from orbit," Hao said. "No hassle, no mess." He waved a hand. "Beyond the obvious nuclear fallout."

"And the enormous hole in my capital, you ass. Never mind the civilian casualties." Lucky for Hao there wasn't anything within throwing distance.

"I'm just tossing ideas out, don't get snarly."

"Something in the halfway decent range would be great," I said.

"We could do something like that bank job on Marakesh?"

"The one where she almost lost her arm?" Zin asked, and Hao tipped his head to the side. "Probably not a good idea."

"Good point. What about that other job in New York?"

I laughed. "That one was such a comedy of errors from start to finish. Do you remember when Portis—" My voice caught and Hao raised an eyebrow but I ignored him. "When he got so mad at us that he walked into that bank alone and in less than five minutes had charmed the guards into letting him into the vault?"

Hao's laugh was tinged with sadness. "He let us in the back door and we carried a hell of a lot of money out of there."

"I'm not sure how that plan—what little of it there is—would work with Wilson," I said.

"I walk in there and charm the pants off him." Hao shrugged. "Let you in the back door."

"Are you trying to get shot in the head? Because that's exactly what would happen. Wilson knows you. You'd be dead before you got three words out."

"Wilson's going to be prepared for anything you can throw at him, ma'am," Cas said. "Perhaps it would be best to let us come up with something?"

I wanted to argue, but he was right. Wilson had obviously spent a lot of time studying me and my family. It was entirely likely any plan I came up with was doomed to failure before we even had a chance to put it in motion.

"Fine, you all hash out a plan. I've got a call to make." I gestured at Hao. He got up from his seat and followed me from the room, and together we made our way up to the bridge. Johar followed after a brief word with Bial.

"Cressen, may I ask a question?"

Her use of my old name mixed with the proper phrasing was odd, and I stopped by the stairs leading up to the bridge. "Sure, what?"

"Your parents, how did they meet?"

"Excuse me?"

"Was it arranged? Or did they fall in love?" Johar looked to

Hao for help, but the gunrunner shrugged. "I know in a great many places of the galaxy, men get to pick their wives. Do you really do the opposite in Indrana?"

I laughed as I realized what she was trying to ask. "Yes, Mother picked my father from a group of suitors. There were other young nobles in the running."

"Those who lost were upset, yes?" She frowned. "That is a loss of an opportunity to be very powerful."

"I'd imagine some of them were, but nothing that created a scene. One of them was a good friend of my father's, as a matter of fact; he used to joke about it with me."

"How strange."

"It's the way things are done in Indrana." I smiled. "Men are used to it. There was no reason to fuss."

"Sweets, men always fuss," Johar said. "That sort of shit happens all over the galaxy, surely you would have seen it." Johar waved a hand in the air. "You have no idea how many men I've killed because they couldn't take no for an answer."

12

Jiejie." Dailun didn't look up from the controls as we came onto the bridge. "We are making good time to Ashva. Captain Mel and I have come up with an entrance to the system I think will keep us off the scanners."

"How long?"

"One hundred and thirty hours, give or take." He wiggled his hand at me. "We could do it in half that if we used the bubble, but that would draw a lot of attention on our arrival."

"I'd rather spend the time," I agreed with a nod, sliding into the chair next to him. "Are we going to be safe to contact home?"

"I'd send a burst transmission to see how the situation plays out on Pashati first. That way they can contact you back if it's safe to do so," Hao replied, leaning against the console.

I shot the message off to Caspel. A three-second burst that simply said, *Any news?*

"So all we can do now is wait for them to answer?" I asked Hao. "Got a deck of cards?"

"How about we talk about your plan for dealing with Wilson?" Hao asked. "Because I know you're thinking of one. You might be content to let your *Ekam* plan an assault on your palace, but I know you, Hail. You're going to be the one to kill him whatever the cost."

"I was actually considering challenging him to a fight to the death and then shooting him when he agreed," I replied with a grin that Hao didn't answer. I sighed. "I don't know yet and honestly I suspect that, as much as I hate it, we might have to wing this one."

"We've had worse odds."

"I'd feel better if I could manipulate him like Fen Ah." Hao's wince didn't escape my notice and I reached out a hand. "He's long dead, honored brother," I said in Cheng, using an endearment I hadn't directed at Hao for years. "He can't hurt you."

Hao glanced at Dailun, who was studiously not listening to our conversation. "Scars remain painful for a long time, even after those who dealt them are turned to ghosts." He forced a smiled and threaded his fingers through mine, squeezing them quickly before he released me.

I knew Hao wouldn't answer, but the question was still on the tip of my tongue when the com link buzzed.

"*Jiejie*, I have Caspel on the line."

I turned in my chair, crossing my legs as the GIS director's face appeared on the screen on the console. "Still alive, Caspel?"

"Yes, Majesty." The hawk-faced man gave me a sharp nod. "Better even. I have Ambassador Toropov with me."

"You cut that close, Jaden," I said.

The Saxon ambassador smiled mirthlessly. "My apologies for the delay, Your Majesty; even when urgency is required my comrades can take a ridiculously long time to decide on matters."

"I'm going to hold off on accepting that apology until I hear what you have to say," I replied.

"Your Majesty. The provisional Saxon government under the

leadership of King Samuel Gerison is prepared to offer you the following in exchange for your assistance and your promise to not bring Indrana's military forces to bear on Saxony until all measures and peace talks have proved fruitless. As follows: All the planets the Saxon Alliance has taken from Indrana, including the ones conceded to us during the peace talks of 3001 and the more recent incident at Canafey. We are also prepared to accept responsibility for the War of '84 and to discuss reparations once we are financially able to do so."

"You are shitting me."

"I am very serious, Majesty."

"You don't have that kind of power."

"I will, if you help me." He smiled. "King Samuel is prepared to reward me quite handsomely for my assistance.

"In addition to that, I can also provide you with a way to get onto Pashati and into the palace without Phanin's forces knowing about it." Toropov gave me a shrewd look. "I'm assuming that is something you need, yes?"

I looked at Caspel, who nodded minutely. "I'm going to chat with everyone here about this new development and get back to you," I said, and Dailun cut the transmission when I waved my hand. "Tell the others to get up here. We need to talk."

"Yes, ma'am." Emmory nodded.

I tucked my hands behind my head and threw a foot up on the console, ignoring Hao's raised eyebrow. Toropov's offer could change everything. I had to make a decision—one that had the potential for either victory or our complete destruction.

I tossed through ideas as the others filtered in. I could do the most obvious thing and throw Toropov's offer back in his face, raze Saxony to its foundations like I'd promised. That left me at home without the benefit of Hassan's full fleet and only one *Vajrayana* ship plus a band of mercenaries to take Ashva and then hope nothing went sideways before we could get in position to take Pashati. There wasn't time to list all the things that could go wrong with that plan.

Or I could take his offer. Recall Inana and all her ships and tell her to make a beeline for home. I didn't have to send my people to die in a pointless war with the Saxons and I could focus all my attention and resources on defeating Phanin and Wilson.

I'd get back the planets we'd lost. Saxony would admit it was their greed that started the war over Canafey in the first place. That was more important than the money anyway. I'd let the Saxons clean up their own damn mess and their new government would *owe* me. It was hard to see a downside to the offer.

As long as there weren't any hidden strings. Which was, truth be told, something I was extremely wary of where Toropov was concerned.

Soon the bridge was crammed with BodyGuards and Marines; I could hear Emmory filling them all in, the words filtering through my racing brain. Hao kicked my leg, so I dropped it to the floor and stared at my hands for a moment before I looked up at the expectant faces of my people.

"I've just received a very interesting offer from the Saxon ambassador. As Emmory just told you, he claims there's a faction supporting Samuel Gerison, who doesn't want Trace on the throne any more than we do. He's offering us all the territory Indrana lost in the war and also a way onto Pashati unseen in exchange for letting them take care of matters internally. Saxony will admit their responsibility for the War of '84 and I have a somewhat vague promise of future reparations. Thoughts?"

I glanced Fasé's direction, hoping the Farian would have something to say about our future, but she was staring at the floor.

"It's too good to be true, ma'am," Lantle said, the older Body-Guard shaking his head with a frown. "What's the catch?"

"I don't know," I replied. "Honestly I thought the same thing myself, but I can't think of anything that Toropov could do to us that wouldn't make it a decent trade-off."

"He could betray you, Majesty. This unseen way onto the planet or into the palace could be a trap." Indula shook his head. "I don't like it."

"Worst case—besides the empress getting killed—is that we'd have to go after the Saxons after we clean up at home, right?" Kisah looked around the room and several people nodded in agreement with her. "We'd lose the element of surprise we've got now, but we'd have a lot more ships at our disposal to go after the Saxon Navy."

"Majesty, I've had some contact with the ambassador," Gita said. "I was on his security detail during a visit to the islands. He's very good at his job, ma'am. He's dedicated to his kingdom, but he's honest. I don't think he would have made the offer if he was intending to double-cross us."

"Caspel trusts him." Zin smiled at my raised eyebrow. "You glanced at him, ma'am, and he gave you a nod. We don't have any reason to think he'd steer us wrong. This offer gives us a chance not only to end this coup but to end any future war with the Saxons before it even starts."

Looking Emmory's way, I waited while my *Ekam* finished mulling things over in his head. "I don't like it," he said, and my heart sank.

The breath I'd been holding while I waited to see if Emmory would agree with me slid out as a silent gust of air.

"However, we have few choices. Even knowing it could be a trap, it's still our best option to take his offer. Call Admiral Hassan. Shul can't defend against 5th Fleet and all Hassan's ships. Those odds are too great for the number of ships he's got. If we don't have to deal with the Saxons until later—or at all—it only works to our benefit."

"Sir, what about the danger to the empress?" Cas spoke up.

I got the feeling my *Dve* was bringing up that point for the record rather than forgetting all the previous times I'd been in danger, and judging from Emmory's look he knew it, too.

"We've been in a war zone since Red Cliff. Is there anyone in this room who thinks the empress can't handle herself?"

No one said a word. Several grins were shared among my people, and I shook my head with a smile.

"I'll put together a message to Admiral Hassan," I said. "Hao, contact the rest of the ships and let them know we've had a slight change of plans, but don't go into much detail. Let's find a place to stop so I can talk with Ragini and the others face-to-face so we can come up with a better plan for assaulting Ashva.

"We'll want to give Inana a chance to catch up with us anyway. Emmory, send Caspel a message and we'll visit with him again when we stop. The rest of you get some sleep—we're all going to need it."

The chorus of "Yes, ma'am" bounced around the bridge and then everyone was moving.

"Fasé?"

She paused at the doorway. "Yes, Majesty?"

"Why didn't you say anything?"

"Better to trust the experts." She smiled at me over her shoulder. "Experience is always more reliable than the babblings of a half-mad prophet." Waving her hand, she left me alone with Dailun on the bridge.

I leaned back in my seat, staring out the window of the bridge at the star-scattered blackness. So many lives in my hands; had I made the right decision?

"Sometimes it's the only choice, honored sister," Dailun said in a voice that barely carried over the noise. He didn't look away from the console. "Good or bad is irrelevant. We walk the path laid out for us. Going back is never an option."

"Someone should have told Emmory that when he decided to drag me home," I muttered under my breath.

Dailun laughed. "I do not think your *Ekam* would have cared, *jiejie*."

"You're probably right." I went back to looking at the stars.

13

Majesty, are you sure?" Admiral Hassan's frown carried across the light-years.

"I'm not—that's why I want your opinion." I shook my head. "The consensus is that Toropov shouldn't be trusted on general principle. But Caspel seems to trust him, and I trust Caspel. Emmory agrees that while, in all likelihood, it's a trap, we can't pass up this opportunity."

"It is an awful risk," she said, shaking her head. "If you're wrong and we take the whole fleet into a trap, you could lose everything."

"I'll likely be dead, so I doubt I'll care."

Hassan sighed but didn't chastise me for my flippancy. "If you think it's best, ma'am."

"I have zero experience with this, Inana; can we all quit pretending otherwise? Your opinion matters and if you really think we should pass on the offer, then that's what we'll do."

"No." Hassan sighed again. "It's making the back of my neck twitch, but maybe that's just because we've finally caught a break. You're right, Majesty, and so is Emmory. We'll turn the fleet around and head for home."

"We're already several days ahead of you, but we're going to find a place to hide for a bit and refine the plans for the assault. I'll send you what we come up with and meet you outside Ashva. We'll stay in stealth just outside the system and proceed from there."

"We'll do a short float to cut the distance," she replied. "There's no way a fleet this size is going to be stealthy anyway, so there's little point in sacrificing the time by going the long way around. I'll split them up, though, and keep two-thirds of the fleet back out of the system when we hit Ashva. We'll see if we can't lull him into some complacency."

"True." I gave her a vicious grin. "I don't mind him seeing you coming. If we're lucky he'll assume I'm with you. But I'd also love it if Shul totally underestimates what he's about to be dealing with."

I didn't remind Hassan I was still planning to have Shul killed at the first possible moment. Though I doubted she'd forgotten my plans on that particular subject, it was no doubt easier for her to pretend otherwise.

She answered my grin. "I'll remind you our luck has not been the best, ma'am."

"We're still alive at the moment. We'll bounce all communication through V7. Hopefully, if they spot her they'll think she's a scout and not realize the rest of us are sneaking around out here."

"Yes, ma'am."

"Oh and Inana? Call Admiral Dewan and tell her it's time to join the fight. I want her to head for Ashva immediately and we'll rendezvous just outside the system. If we really don't have to worry about the Saxons, I want as many ships as I can get my hands on without compromising our borders. If we can get an impressive enough show of force, maybe their ships will stand down and we can do this without killing any more of our people—on either side."

Inana nodded. "We'll do it, ma'am. See you at home."

I returned her nod and shut down the coms. Turning around to face Emmory, who was leaning against the back wall of the bridge, I raised an eyebrow. "There goes nothing."

"It's our best chance," he replied.

We stared at each other for a long moment. Emmory's face was carefully neutral, not giving away a hint of how my *Ekam* might be feeling about the whole thing.

"Say it," I said, heading past him off the bridge. I threw Dailun a salute as we passed and he returned to his chair.

"Say what, Majesty?"

I laughed.

"Say I'm being reckless or thoughtless or any one of a hundred other things. I'll agree with you."

Emmory followed behind me as we headed down the corridor toward our quarters. Despite the lack of Hao's crew, we'd stayed put in the same bunks as when we first came on board. I paced across the room and dropped onto my bed.

"If anything, ma'am, you should be saying that to me." Emmory leaned on the doorframe of our quarters and looked around the empty room. "I know what I said in front of everyone else, but I am taking an extraordinary risk with your life. If we are wrong—" He rubbed a hand over his mouth, unable to finish the sentence.

"We will deal with it," I said. "I'm not trying to brush off your concerns, *Ekam*," I continued when he gave me the Look. "I'm being realistic. You said it yourself, we don't have many options and this is risky. However, maybe that's a good thing."

"How could it possibly be a good thing?"

"I like to look at all my options, but once I make a decision, that's it and it's time to move." I smiled. "We take any pre-cautions against a double-cross that we can, but we take this chance because it's against everything that everyone would be expecting of me." I spread my arms wide and gave him a sad smile. "In the end, we'll do it, because there's no other option, and I don't know about you, but I really don't like to lose."

Emmory chuckled, smoothing over the tension. "I know, Majesty."

"You know, the irony of me fighting so hard to get back a throne I never wanted has not escaped me."

Emmory glanced behind him into the hallway and then closed the door. "Having second thoughts?"

Suddenly restless, I shoved out of my bed and paced the length of the room. My hands were clammy and I rubbed them against my pants as I walked. "Second and third ones? Prob-ably more. Emmory, you know I've had them since that first moment you called me 'Highness.'"

"I'm not having doubts about going after Phanin and Wil-son. It's the same as with Ganda and Laabh. Neither of them have the best interests of the people of Indrana on their minds. We all know that. I'll see this through to the end, whatever it may be." I leaned a shoulder on the wall next to him. "What about after? I don't doubt I am the best option for this whole crisis, but am I really good for the empire in the long term? A barely civilized, barren, ex-gunrunner empress doesn't have all that good a ring to it."

Emmory turned to face me but didn't immediately wave off my concerns or insist I was wrong. Instead, he smiled and the rare sight eased the knots in my stomach.

"Hail." My name was an exhalation. "Have you spent your whole life trying to plan ten steps ahead?"

"At minimum." My attempt at a smile died before it started.

Emmory reached up and cupped my face with a hand. "Why don't we try to get through this alive first? Then worry about what we're doing after. I won't try to convince you one way or the other, ma'am, but I will support whatever you decide to do."

I blinked at him, stunned speechless by the unwavering support in his eyes, and threw my arms around his neck in a hug. "I would have been so honored to call you my *jeth*," I whispered.

"It would have been an honor to have you call me brother." He squeezed me once and let me go. "It is equally an honor to be your *Ekam*, Majesty."

"I'm going to remember you said that," I teased before the tears in my eyes got the better of me.

There was a knock at the door. Emmory reached over and opened it and Zin poked his head in. "Emmory? Do you have a minute?"

"What's up?" Emmory nodded at me as he turned and headed out of the room. I didn't follow.

Stretching, I toed off my boots and headed for my bunk. Most of my email was still being filtered through Alba, but she was flagging things she felt I should read, and the first one to catch my eye was a video message from Bakara Rai.

"Hail, your gatekeeper refuses to tell me where you've gone and for some reason Johar agrees with her. I can verify a sale of Rock to Wilson Pembroke in the Indranan year 2996. I'm attaching his credentials for you now and a photo that seems to match your adversary."

"You bet it does," I murmured, pulling up the photo and then dismissing it in favor of the file.

Waterloo Corporation was founded in the Indranan year 2967 by Wilson Pembroke. It was a Solarian Conglomerate company and its founder and CEO was a citizen of the SC. But there was nothing on the founder, no publicity shots, no news, nothing until 2984, when he started funneling what money he legally could into the Saxon war effort.

I was sure there was a lot of illegal funneling also and sent Rai a reply. "Thanks," I said. "Can you look into what he was up to for the sixteen years between the company's appearance and the start of the war?"

I dumped all the data into the file Zin had started along with a note for him to look at it when it was convenient and settled deeper into my bunk to mull over the new information.

The klaxon jarred me awake and I rolled from my bunk, snagging my boots as I bolted from the room. I hit the stairs for the bridge and took them two at a time. Emmory was already there, as were Hao and Dailun.

"What is going on?"

"Unwelcome visitors," Hao said. "They dropped out of warp almost on top of Mel."

"Do we have an ID on them?" I jerked my boots on and my fingers flew as I laced first one and then the other.

"I don't even know how many there are yet, Hail. Incoming, grab onto something," he said.

I stopped lacing my boots and grabbed for the railing, hanging on for dear life as Dailun sent the *Pentacost* lurching to the side.

"V7 is reporting at least two dozen craft, possibly more, all small ships. They're not reading anything bigger than a cruiser."

"Is it a damned swarm? I thought this sector was cleared." Hao scanned the console in front of him. "And where's the carrier?"

"A swarm?"

I glanced away from Hao at Emmory. "Unaffiliated pirates sometimes band together. Better chance at taking down a big score, even though it means they have to split it with the other survivors."

"They don't turn on each other?" Emmory was so clearly surprised I couldn't stop my laughter, even though the *Pentacost* shuddered again and Hao swore.

"They're pretty strict about it. If you were going to violate the agreement, you'd better make sure the score will set you for life, because no one would work with you ever again and for these independent smugglers that's a death sentence."

"There's also the matter of the actual death sentence," Hao said. "You'd never live to spend the payday."

"Majesty, I've got a com from Captain Saito on the V7. She wants to know if they should open fire."

"Tell her to hold off. These little ships are going to be harder for her to hit and there has to be a carrier out there somewhere. We're in the middle of nowhere. They couldn't have traveled this far on their own."

"That's what really bothers me about this," Hao said. "Oh mother—" He bit the curse off with a glance in my direction. "The *Fairchild* just opened fire on the *Bronx*."

"That answers that question," I muttered. "What kind of weapons do you have on this bucket?"

"Two guns at mid and one aft. But my gunners are on the *Bronx*."

"I'm a better shot anyway. Emmory, tell Indula to get on that tail gun."

"You're going to owe me a new ship, Hail!" Hao shouted at me as we left the bridge.

I flipped him off and slid down the stairs, Emmory on my heels. "A little warning would have been helpful," I said as we passed by Fasé, who was headed for the crew quarters with Stasia.

"That's not how this works, Majesty," she singsonged back at me.

Gita met us in the hallway. "What is going on?"

"Swarm," I said, grabbing her by the arm. "Someone on the *Fairchild* sold us out. Come with me. Emmory—"

"Got it, Majesty." He ducked into the turret.

"We haven't seen the carrier ship yet. At the moment it's just smaller fighters," I said, and strapped into the gunner's seat. The targeting computer came up as my *smati* linked in to the guns.

Captain Mel's dreadnought was fighting desperately against at least ten smaller ships. The *Bronx* had good enough shielding to withstand the attacks, but eventually something would get through.

"Hail, are you up?" Hao's voice was in my head as the *Pentacost* juked to the side. Gita swore and braced herself against the opening of the turret. *"I've got two on my tail, let's scrape them off."*

"Make that one now," Indula said, his voice gleeful. *"Second one is coming up on your side, Your Majesty."*

"I see him."

I exhaled, eyes tracking the ship as it flew into my sights, and fired. The ship disintegrated and I heard the cheers echo up from below us.

"Dailun, take us in near the Bronx*! Let's pick some of those fleas off her."*

Four of the other ships were pouring fire into the *Fairchild* until its shields failed and it came apart in a violent blue-green explosion.

The *Pentacost* swooped in—Emmory, Indula, and I firing at the smaller craft attacking the *Bronx*.

"Winged him. Indula, can you finish him off? He's headed your way."

"Got him, Majesty."

"Three left," I muttered. *"Come on, you bastards, what's the matter? You don't want to play anymore?"*

"Incoming! I've got a warp signal and—Dark Mother preserve us." Ragini's voice was breathy with shock over the coms.

The *thing* that dropped out of warp like a stone was the biggest ship I'd ever seen. *"Bugger me, what is that?"*

It fired, and the shot vaporized two of our remaining ships. Gita swore viciously.

"Ekam, we have to get out of here. Now."

I whipped around to stare at her.

"We can't leave them—"

"Hey, Hao?" Captain Mel's voice echoed a bit over the coms. *"I don't know what the shit this new ship is, but our warp is down and I think my drive containment is failing. Recommend you get the hell out of here. We'll see if we can't hurt it enough so it won't come after you."*

"I hear you, Mel. Thanks."

She laughed. *"Means shit to a dead woman. Just promise me you'll punch the fucker responsible for all this."*

"Consider it promised."

I watched the *Bronx* turn toward the massive ship, but the space around us shimmered as we floated into warp and in the blink of an eye we were thousands of light-years away. "Gita, what in the fires of Naraka was that?"

My BodyGuard squeezed her eyes shut for a moment before removing her hand from her mouth. "A nightmare, Majesty," she replied as Emmory appeared at the doorway to the turret. "A Saxon experimental vessel I'd hoped they hadn't made a reality."

"Why is this the first I'm hearing about it?"

Gita shook her head. "I have no idea, Majesty, other than to say that with everything else it probably wasn't important enough to brief you on." She exhaled a shaky breath. "Who else followed us to the rendezvous point? We'll need to be ready to jump again. There's no telling if the *Fairchild* gave away our emergency plans in addition to our route."

"Only V7 followed us into warp. We're not going to the original spot," Emmory replied. "Captain Saito, Hao, and I had a separate plan."

"You knew about that thing?" I asked.

"No, Majesty." Emmory shook his head. "I just knew something would probably go wrong. I need all the specs you have on that, Gita."

"Yes, sir." She passed them along with a touch of her hand to his.

The ship shuddered again, this time more seriously, and the three of us shared a worried look before we sprinted for the bridge. Hao and Dailun were speaking back and forth in rapid Cheng.

"There's something wrong with the ship," I murmured.

"I'm getting that." Emmory grabbed for me, pinning me to the railing as the *Pentacost* listed dangerously to one side and Dailun fought to straighten her out.

"*Nali! Nali,*" Hao said, jabbing his finger at the console map. Dailun glanced down at his own display, gave a sharp nod, and sent the ship to the right until the massive blue star filled the bridge window.

"Emmory, get her into a suit." Hao didn't look back as he spoke, but the tone of his voice made my blood run cold.

"How many do you have?" Emmory asked.

"There's fifteen in the cargo bay."

"What? No."

There were twenty-four people on board the *Pentacost* between my people and what was left of Hao's crew.

Emmory's grip on my arm tightened and I had to follow him off the bridge or face being dragged down the stairs.

"Captain Saito, do you copy? Pentacost *is being forced to land on G4T83, unclear as to issue but Captain Hao is recommending evac as soon as we touch down. Advise you land V7 as close as possible while still maintaining safe distance. Keep your shields up."*

"Roger that, Ekam *Tresk."*

"Be advised we only have suits for fifteen of the twenty-four on board, Captain."

"We'll prep a team with extra suits and put them in a shuttle, Ekam.*"*

"Thank you, will pass that along to Captain Hao." Emmory propelled me down into the cargo bay, where Zin and the other BodyGuards were already putting on their suits.

Stasia, who was not wearing a suit, handed one over to me with a smile. "We'll be fine, Majesty," she lied. "I'm sure it's nothing."

Heart breaking, I shimmied into the suit, using all my strength to keep my breathing and heart rate even. Zin and all the other BodyGuards were already dressed, ready to go out into the airless terrain.

Zin handed me the helmet and I froze. "Majesty?" His voice was muffled through his own helmet.

"I'm fine, give me a second." My voice was hoarse and I tried to ignore my shaking hands as I took the helmet.

The *Pentacost* shook again, this time with the familiar jolt of landing.

"Deep breath," Emmory said, putting a hand on my arm. "Put it on."

I gave him a jerky nod, took a breath, and slammed the helmet on. The lights came on, the air washed over my face, and I shoved everything else aside. *"Let's go."*

We filed into the airlock.

"Gravity is one and a half times Indranan standard," Cas recited over the coms. *"We're going three across with the empress in the middle. Zin, Gita, Kisah are in front. Emmory and I on the sides. Iza, Indula, Major Morri in the back. The rest of you follow behind. You'll feel like you're trudging through mud, but keep the pace up. We need to get as far away from the* Pentacost *as we can."*

I am leaving good people behind to die. I squeezed my eyes shut. I hadn't seen Johar, Fasé, or Bial in the cargo bay, or the five Marines of my detail from Canafey.

There was a chorus of assent from everyone and at Emmory's nod, Zin reached out and hit the door panel.

"Om Klim Kalika-Yei Namaha." The words echoed against the inside of my helmet. I latched onto the mantra to the Dark Mother as the door to the outside opened. Emmory's hand on my back and the increased gravity further grounded me to the rocky terrain as we stepped outside and broke into a run.

The surface of the desolate world was covered in jagged rock laid bare without the smoothing influence of wind and rain. V7's white hull shone in the distance as they came in for a landing as close as they dared.

I spotted the shuttle taking off before the *Vajrayana* landed. It blew past us back toward the *Pentacost.* *"Hao, get your shit and get out of there,"* I snapped over the coms. *"Johar, you drag them out if you have to."*

"Sure thing, Hail," she replied. *"They put Stasia and Fasé into the spare suits and they're ready to go. Just waiting for the shuttle. Bial and I are seeing what we can do to keep things in engineering under control."*

I fingered the tether at my waist. It was connected to Emmory, wrapped around my waist, and then connected to Cas, who was outfitted with an EVA pack in the event of an emergency.

Or rather, a bigger emergency than the one we were currently facing.

"Down! Down! Down!" Emmory shouted abruptly as he and Cas grabbed me around the waist and slammed me to the ground. A millisecond later I felt the ground shake from what I could only guess was the *Pentacost* exploding.

The increased gravity contained the blast radius to a third of its normal size, but with no atmosphere to slow it down the shrapnel raced away from the ship at a lethal speed.

"I'm hit!" Iza's voice rang over the com.

"Get pressure on it now before you lose your air." Emmory barked the order.

"Already on it," Indula replied. *"It's her leg, sir. We're going to need transport."*

"Ekam, my radiation warning is off the charts." Gita's voice was cool in the chaos.

"I know, so is mine," he replied. *"V7, do you copy? We need immediate extraction. One wounded and suit compromised. All in party have been exposed to a lethal dose of radiation. Need treatment in next eight minutes."*

"Clock is started," Zin said, and flashing red numbers began the countdown in my vision.

I squeezed my eyes shut, holding back the useless tears as my BodyGuards hauled me to my feet and propelled me forward. *"Hao?"* My voice cracked and I bit my lip until the pain cleared away the panic. Static answered me.

"Speak to me, you asshole. Tell me everyone made it off." I opened my eyes again, but my vision was blurred by unshed tears.

"Focus, Majesty. We need to get you inside." Emmory kept a hand on my back as we slogged toward the V7.

I choked down my fear, trying to focus on each torturous step away from the wreckage. The reality, the cold, awful knowledge that I might have lost even more people I cared about, wove a thread of splintered glass through my throat.

"Hao, damn you." My voice cracked. *"Answer me."*

"I really, really liked that ship, sha zhu.*"*

This time I couldn't hold in the hot tears or the sob I knew was audible to everyone on the channel. *"I'll buy you a new one,"* I managed.

14

The next several minutes were a blur of barely contained chaos. The shuttle that had collected Hao and the others with only seconds to spare had enough time to throw up their shields, protecting the occupants from both the blast and the radiation of the *Pentacost's* failed containment.

We were not so lucky, and what followed was a mad rush to get us to V7 and the medical bay before the clock ran out.

"I'm sorry, Majesty," Major Morri said, shaking her head. Her Farian biology had protected her from the radiation. "I wish there were more I could do."

"Stop apologizing. I'm not expecting miracles from you, Major." I leaned my head back against the pillow when the nausea threatened.

Emmory and Cas had practically carried me in a desperate sprint the last forty-five meters to the V7 with everyone but Iza and Indula on our heels. A second shuttle had screamed out of the bay to get to us. However, Emmory had snapped orders for Cas to keep running and for the others to board the shuttle.

The shuttle with Hao stopped to grab Indula and Iza and carted them back to the *Vajrayana* ship.

I'd made it to the med bay with plenty of time left on the clock flashing in the corner of my vision, and the efficient staff had me in treatment before the others boarded the ship.

Iza and Indula, however, were outside the safety window and now both were in containment while their bodies fought off the brutal effects of the exposure.

"Majesty?" Zin came into the room with a smile. "You have some visitors."

I spotted Hao, Dailun, and Johar in the doorway behind him. Stumbling off the bed and across the room, I threw myself into Hao's arms, not caring about the sobs hitting the open air. "Don't. Ever. Do. That. Again."

Hao caught me and hugged me tight. "I'm all right, little sister," he murmured against my hair. "Remember who you are."

"I don't care right this second."

Hao released me with a smile, giving my hand a squeeze before he let it go.

I grabbed Dailun with one arm and Johar with the other, hugging them both close with only slightly more restraint than I'd shown with Hao.

"Everyone else is all right?" I asked as I let them go.

Johar nodded, a smile on her severe face. "Your Marines and Bial were most helpful; thank you for leaving them. They kept the containment up far longer than my damage estimates. Without them we would all be dead. Fasé said to tell you that she will speak with you soon and that your maid is well."

Dailun had wiggled out from under my arm and gave me a small smile. "If you will take no offense, *jiejie*, Hao and I would like to go find Dr. Brek and mourn for our friends."

"Mel didn't make it?" It had seemed unlikely, but I was holding out hope.

"I can't raise her," Hao said with a shake of his head. "I know

145

her well enough to know she'd have gone down fighting. And if the containment went on that ship, it would have made a hell of a boom."

"Let's hope it did some damage to that Saxon ship on its way out then."

Hao nodded. "Captain Saito has found quarters for us; we will be there if you need us."

"I'll come find you when they let me out of here and share a drink for the lost." I watched them leave, waiting until I was alone with Major Morri again before I carefully went back to bed. She didn't hover, and instead settled into a nearby chair. We sat in companionable silence until Emmory and Captain Saito came through the door.

"Your Majesty." Captain Isabelle Saito was an imposing figure with broad shoulders, a square jaw, and a utilitarian buzz cut. The only thing she had in common with her matriarch cousin was the distinctive look of their Japanese ancestors.

"Thanks for coming to our rescue."

She smiled. "Anytime, ma'am. Your *Ekam* thought we should sit down and talk about how to proceed, if you are feeling up to it?"

"I'm fine." I waved a hand. "Just a little shaky still. Have we been in contact with Admiral Hassan?"

"No, ma'am. We were waiting to see what you wanted to do first."

"I don't know. I'd like to let things settle and see what happens," I said, and arched an eyebrow when the pair shared a look. "What?"

"Please tell me you're not thinking of taking on that Saxon ship?"

"I could. I'd be lying."

"Majesty, we have one ship," Emmory said. "We can't take on that monstrosity, *Vajrayana* or not. It makes more sense to head for Ashva and meet with the fleets as we planned."

"One *Vajrayana* ship that is better than a handful of normal ones, and I'm willing to bet that that Saxon bastard is still out there looking for us. I don't want to get caught just hanging around waiting for Admiral Hassan, or worse, have that ship waiting for them when they get to Ashva."

Captain Saito smiled. "This is a very good ship, but still no match for that Saxon monstrosity or for the picket we think they have at Ashva. Not all by ourselves, Majesty."

Her words sparked an idea to life in my brain. "The picket at Ashva is just a few ships, yes?"

"Three destroyers according to our reports." Zin nodded. "We have to assume otherwise. We can't go into this thinking we're safe."

"Dhatt." I held a hand up. "You're right about that. I get it. But there's no reason to not continue on. We were never planning to assault Pashati or Shul's fleet on our own anyway, and I may have a plan for taking out the picket at Ashva without having to fire a shot. All this really means is we've got a lot less cover on our way home. However, we can probably get to Ashva faster now, and that will cut down on any concern there. I suspect the V7 hasn't really tested the full speed of her engines during this trip?"

"We have not, ma'am." Now Captain Saito grinned, the expression lighting up her face. "I'm sure engineering will love to see what she can do."

"Within reason, Captain," Emmory said. "Let's not run ourselves into even more trouble."

"Of course, *Ekam*. The safety of the empress is paramount." Captain Saito nodded.

I held a hand out and she took it. "Thank you, Captain. You saved our lives today. It won't be forgotten."

"I was just doing my job, ma'am," she replied, but her cheeks reddened in pleased embarrassment. She bowed low when I let go of her hand.

"I'm lucky to have citizens like you. We'll speak again soon."

"With your leave, ma'am. I'll go pass along your instructions."

I watched with carefully concealed amusement as she turned on her heel and left the room. "So damn young."

"Most of the ship is, Majesty. Admiral Hassan had to get creative with postings for the *Vajrayana* ships."

"To be fair, she wasn't expecting us to end up with nothing but this ship to transport us to Ashva."

"What is the plan, Majesty?"

"I'm working on it. We'll talk about it when I have something solid."

"Fasé asked to see you if you feel up to it," Emmory said.

I swung my legs off the edge of the bed, ignoring Major Morri's disapproving look. It was a toss-up if she was frowning over me or Fasé.

"How is she?" Emmory asked Major Morri as he reached for my arm.

"Her Majesty is fine, *Ekam*. You, on the other hand, could use some rest."

I got the Look when I snickered.

"I'll be fine, Major. Thank you." Emmory took my arm and led me from my room and toward the door. Zin was quiet on my other side.

"Is Emmory okay?" I subvocalized the question, keeping my eyes straight ahead. We headed down the corridor. It was empty, almost unnervingly so.

"He waited until both you and Cas were treated, ma'am. It put

148

him right at the time limit. Dr. Adelle wanted to keep him for another round of treatment but he refused."

"Do I need to shout at him?"

Zin's chuckle was strained in my head. *"I already did, and while you're welcome to try, I'm not sure you'd have any better luck. To be fair, he is out of danger, ma'am, just pushing himself harder than any of us agree with."*

"Keep on him, Zin. After this I want him to get some rest, even if you have to have Dr. Adelle or Major Morri knock him out."

"Yes, ma'am."

We reached her quarters. I knocked once and heard the muffled "Come in, Majesty" before opening the door.

"Emmory, Zin," Fasé said, holding her hands out to my *Ekam* and his husband. They crossed the room to her and took them. Silence filled the room as something passed between the three of them and I felt suddenly like a schoolgirl watching a party through a window—uninvited and unwelcome.

Then Fasé smiled and released my BodyGuards, holding out her hands to me. When I closed my fingers around her slender ones, the feeling vanished and I leaned down to press my forehead to hers.

"You wanted to see me?"

"Yes, sit. All of you." She waved to the seats around the little table, folding her hands in her lap as we sat down. "Things are shifting," she said. "I felt it when Hao's ship exploded."

I tipped my head to the side, studying the Farian when she didn't continue. Fasé kept her eyes focused on her hands, fingers entwined and still. I counted heartbeats as we waited, for what I wasn't sure, but an army couldn't have moved me to speak in those moments.

"At the start of it," Fasé said at last, breaking the stillness that had settled over the room, "there was light glinting off a shattered mirror. Seven pieces of reality split apart to make the world. Seven gods born into existence to show us the way the world should be made.

"You humans always have the need to organize and name things. When we first met the only way our emissaries could get you to understand the concept was by naming the unnamable— putting our gods into boxes." She glanced at me through her lashes with an almost mischievous grin. "They're not really named after the days of your Earth week."

"I seem to recall my lessons having a footnote to that effect," I murmured. "Something about humans not being worthy to hear the names?"

"Names have power, Majesty. To give the names of the gods to unbelievers is to lessen them." Fasé lifted a slender shoulder. "You are young, foolish. Humanity still fights and rages and desecrates the stars as you once did your own planet." She raised her head, looking right at me with her golden eyes. "We considered wiping you out when we first saw you. The elders were horrified by the hatred that spread like a plague wherever you went."

"*That* was not in my lessons."

"You are the first humans to hear it. I would advise against telling Major Morri or anyone else that I have told you."

"Fasé, why are you telling us this?" Emmory asked.

"The stars are changing. I am changing. I made a choice that set this all in motion. Her Majesty made a choice when she wouldn't let me end it. Things continue to cascade.

"I am not a future-seer, but I am getting better and I can feel the change here." Fasé thumped her own chest. "There are things you will need to know in the days to come. It's why I asked the empress to let me stay with her."

"What things?" Zin asked.

"That I don't know yet, and I may not. Like I said, I cannot tell apart the futures with any degree of certainty. This might creep up on us like a jaguar and devour us all before we can stop it; there is no way to know for sure except to go home—and we can't do that yet."

"Home?" I echoed. "You mean your home?"

Fasé nodded, her strange ghost of a smile back. "It was the future-seers who stopped the elders. Humanity was needed, they said, though they would not elaborate then, and they continue to hold their secrets close after all this time."

I didn't know what made me ask the question, but it slid out onto the air before I could stop it. "Fasé, how long?"

"Long before you all started dreaming of traveling to the distant stars."

Hao answered the door of their quarters with a drink in his hand. He passed it over to Emmory without comment, and my *Ekam* surprised me by drinking from it before he handed it to Zin.

Zin took a drink and passed it along to me.

I saluted Hao with it and knocked back the rest of the glass. The sharp taste of Canafey's local vodka burned in the back of my throat and I only just managed not to cough.

"To the dead," Hao said, taking the glass back from me and filling it again.

"Henna." I reached out and touched Dr. Brek on the shoulder as I passed. I was filled with relief that she had been on the *Pentacost* with us.

I settled into the corner of the couch, listening as Dailun told a story about the gunner twins and Big Bob. Henna occasionally corrected him, her head resting on Johar's lap and her feet propped up on the opposite arm of the couch.

There had been new faces on the *Pentacost*, but I felt the loss of the crew I'd recognized. It was far worse for Hao and the others, and the silence between stories grew longer as the night wore on. Hao stared morosely into his glass, swirling the vodka around but not drinking it. Dailun had his eyes closed and rested his head on his knees.

"I have to break in a whole new crew," Henna murmured, twisting her face up in disappointment. "Answering so many stupid questions about my eye and repeating the rules about touching and making noise." She rolled over and looked at me. "It was bad enough when you left us, Cressen. This is a million times worse. I thought maybe you'd come back after you got hurt on Candless. Was a surprise you didn't."

Bugger me.

My hope that Henna's drunken ramblings would slip by and disappear into the silence were fruitless as Johar perked up.

"I've been to Candless, bunch of savages. What happened?"

"Bolthouse gang double-crossed us over a deal for some neoprene explosive," I replied with a shrug. "Navigator took one in the temple. I took one in the stomach."

"She took a fragmentation bullet in the stomach. It shredded her." Hao's voice was frozen over with an unidentifiable emotion.

"Killed her twice before we got there," Henna agreed cheerfully. "Don't know how Portis and that man barely qualified to be a veterinarian kept her alive. Cressen's just stubborn, I guess."

"You're the one?" Johar's eyes were wide. "You're the one who wiped out the Bolthouse gang?"

"Portis and the rest of the crew helped," I replied, determined not to glance in my Bodyguards' direction.

"That was fucking epic retribution. Why didn't you put your name on it?"

"I was doing a public service." Forcing a smile I didn't feel,

I leaned forward and stole the glass from Hao's hand, tossing back the rest of the vodka as I stood. "Good night, everyone."

Hao followed me to the door but didn't say anything until Emmory and Zin were out of the room. "You were terribly injured, *sha zhu*," he said in a low voice. "I saw the scans, I talked to the doctor. You were—"

I leaned in and pressed my cheek to his. "Whatever you're going to say out loud, if you love me, don't say it," I whispered against his ear. "Good night, honored brother."

Hao frowned, his metallic eyebrows furrowed as the door closed between us.

15

how me how it's done, Ragini. You don't need to explain. I just want to see it." I leaned over the senior tech's shoulder and pointed at the schematic on the screen.

Ragini Triskan had saved our asses several times during the battle for Canafey, and her knowledge of the *Vajrayana* ships was the reason I'd wanted her with us rather than leaving her behind with Admiral Hassan's fleet and the bulk of the *Vajrayana* ships.

Ragini tapped her console and let the simulation play out.

"So we'll be able to control them?"

"It looks good, ma'am. I can't promise anything, though. They're bound to have people on those three ships. We can get in through some code vulnerability that really should have been spotted in early testing and get control of the ships. I just don't know how long it will take them to lock us back out."

"Shul isn't going to have anyone on board that knows the ships as well as you do," I said, and she ducked her head at the praise.

"Probably not, ma'am."

"That's all I need then. We're not building the whole assault around this. At a bare minimum I want the option to knock those three *Vajrayana* out of the fight. If we can get them to fire on Shul's ships, that's a bonus; if it looks like they're starting to beat you at your own game, I want you to lock them down."

"I'll get with the others, ma'am, see if we can come up with some better firewalls."

"Good." I tilted my head to the side and pursed my lips in thought. "Have we fixed that vulnerability issue on our end, Ragini?"

"Yes, ma'am. I wrote a patch for it while we were still on Canafey and distributed it to the rest of the fleet."

"Good woman." I clapped my hand down on her shoulder. "When you have a workable plan, pass it on to Zin. He's the one putting everything together."

Ragini nodded, but her brain was already occupied with the problem, so I left her alone and headed back into the hallway with Cas at my side.

"How are you doing?" I asked, slipping my arm through his as we walked down the corridor.

Cas smiled. "No longer nauseous, ma'am, which I will admit is a huge relief."

"You're right about that."

Captain Saito and Emmory had agreed that we needed a few days of rest and it wouldn't affect our arrival at Ashva. We'd still get there long before Admiral Hassan, and this gave me more time to work up the plan I'd told Emmory I had.

Three days after the attack by the mammoth Saxon ship, we remained camped out on planet. We made a lot of preparations for the fight back home, but otherwise we'd all appreciated the opportunity for some downtime.

"I remember a time when you would have frozen up at my familiarity," I said with a laugh.

"Only a few months ago, Majesty," he replied with a laugh of his own. "The last few months have not been what I expected when I accepted Emmory's offer of a BodyGuard position."

"That is the understatement of the century, Caspian." I gave his arm a gentle squeeze. "I haven't said it lately, but I'm proud of you."

"I'm just doing my job, ma'am."

"*Hai Ram!* Everyone keeps saying that to me. You're all going above and beyond the job." I flipped my hand out, smacking him in the stomach. "So just say thank you."

"Thank you, Your Majesty." Laughter danced in his blue eyes.

I sniffed and lifted my chin as we continued on our way.

"I spoke with my grandmother," Cas said. "She made it to a crown-loyal base shortly after the fighting started."

I released his arm and had to swallow my emotions down before I could speak. "I'm relieved to hear that."

"So was I. She said not to worry about her." He laughed. "From the sounds of it she was ready to take her sewing circle and lead the charge on the palace herself."

"That would be a sight to see."

"For certain—"

The ship shifted out from underneath us and klaxons blared over the coms. I grabbed for Cas, just missing him, and the sickening sound of his head hitting the floor came a heartbeat before my own impact into the corridor wall.

My lungs refused to cooperate for several panicky seconds before I managed to drag a breath in. "Cas," I wheezed, rolling over and reaching for him. He was still, unresponsive, and I grabbed for his wrist, sending an order to my *smati* to check for a pulse.

Alarms rang both inside my head and out. Ignoring the

screaming pain, I pulled myself upright, hovering over my unconscious BodyGuard. "Caspian, wake up."

I slid my hand under his head, and my stomach sank when I encountered the sticky sensation of blood.

"Majesty, where are you?" Emmory's voice was calm over my *smati.*

"Corridor J, third deck. Cas is hurt. Concussed, most likely, bleeding from a head injury and unresponsive. What's going on?" I waved to the two crewwomen I spotted at the end of the hall and they rushed in my direction.

"He hit his head, and he's bleeding. Get him to medical."

"Yes, Majesty. Are you hurt?"

"I'm fine." I got to my feet, bracing myself on the wall when the *Vajrayana* shook again. *"Emmory, what in the fires of Naraka is going on?"*

"Stay where you are, Majesty. I'm headed your way."

"That's not a damn answer, Ekam, *and don't waste your time. I'm going to the bridge."*

I took off down the corridor, vaulting up the stairs to the second deck and narrowly avoiding a collision with Gita as she skidded around a corner.

"Ma'am, are you hurt? You're bleeding."

"Crashed into a wall. Cas took the brunt of it. This is his blood." I wiped my hands off on my pants. "I left him with some crew and they're taking him to medical. What's going on?"

"It's that Saxon behemoth."

"Because of course it is," I muttered as we made it to the bridge and stumbled through the door. "Plans to get us off the ground, Captain Saito? Or are we just going to sit here and let them keep taking potshots at us?"

"We just got the engines online, ma'am," she replied, and

slapped her hand down on the console next to her chair. "All hands, hang on to something—we're getting out of here."

Gita looped an arm around the railing at the same time I did, and we both braced ourselves as the V7 surged off the planet surface. "I've got her, sir," she said aloud. "We're on the bridge."

The chatter on the bridge bounced across the air.

"Shield strength at eighty-seven percent. Whatever they are hitting us with is sucking the life out of our shields."

"Weapons, what are they firing at us?" Captain Saito demanded.

"The sensors are saying they're laser missiles, ma'am, but I've never seen any that strong before."

"Can we evade?"

"Negative, ma'am. Another salvo incoming, deploying countermeasures."

"Helm, put us on a course of zero-three-three," Isabelle said, and I tightened my grip on the railing as the V7 dodged. The ship shook again.

"Shields down to seventy-nine percent."

"Engineering, how soon until we can go into warp?"

"We need about five more minutes, Captain."

"How did they find us?" My question wasn't directed at anyone specific, but Ragini answered me.

"I don't know, Majesty." She frowned at the data on her console. "They shouldn't have been able to follow—"

"Captain, I have an incoming message from the Saxon vessel."

Isabelle looked in my direction and when I nodded, she turned back to her communications officer. "Put it on-screen."

Trace's face filled the air in front of the bridge window. His eyes were bloodshot and filled with glee when they settled on me. "Hail, there you are."

I raised an eyebrow. "Did you need something?"

"We need to talk."

"I don't think you have anything to say that I'm interested in hearing."

"You'll listen anyway!" Trace slammed his fist into something near him; the crunch echoed over the com link. "I'm hearing some disturbing rumors that my brother did a deal with you. They'll stab you in the back the first chance they get. You have to listen, Hail. You owe me."

"Captain Saito, when we are ready to float into warp, you let me know." I subvocalized the command while keeping my eyes on Trace.

"Yes, ma'am."

"When I say go, get us out of here."

"Trace, I owe you a punch to the mouth and that's about it. You got yourself into this mess and you'll pay the price for it." I wasn't going to waste my breath telling him I didn't trust Toropov and the other Saxons. I knew what his kingdom was capable of, and the same men advising his brother had doubtlessly advised Trace during the war.

"You can't run from me, Hail. I'll find you. I'll find you and I'll keep shooting pieces out of your ship until you listen to what I have to say about Wilson."

"You haven't shot any pieces out of my ship."

"I will. Your shields won't hold out forever and there's nowhere you can run that I won't find you."

"And why is that?"

Trace was either in the first stages of withdrawal or dangerously close to overdosing on whatever supply of Rock he had left. It was obvious he wasn't thinking clearly, and I was hoping my question would rattle him enough to make him slip.

He laughed and waggled a finger at me. "I don't think so, Hail."

"We're ready, ma'am."

"Go," I said to Captain Saito, and gave Trace a little wave before the connection was cut and we warped away.

Emmory, Zin, and Hao skidded through the door of the bridge a few seconds later.

"So, we found Trace," I said. "Captain, where are we headed?"

"We warped to a system about half a light-year from here," she replied. "We could have warped straight to the Ashvin system, but I was fairly certain you didn't want to show up with a massive Saxon ship in tow."

"That was definitely not in the plans," I said, and crossed to the navigation officer. Leaning over the young woman's shoulder, I poked at the charts until I found a spot that suited me. "When we come out of warp, toss us right back in headed for these coordinates."

"Majesty?" The lieutenant glanced at Captain Saito for confirmation.

"You want to rabbit, Hail?" Hao asked, and I nodded.

"I'll explain it later, Captain. These engines should be able to take the abuse. We need some breathing room." I looked over at Ragini. "I need to know how he found us."

"Yes, ma'am."

"Can we stand up to that ship in a fight?" I glanced at Gita, and she shook her head.

"I don't know, ma'am. Not if it's armed like the specs that I saw. The *Vajrayana* are powerful, but the shields on that thing are amazing."

"And their weapons are obviously going to be a problem." I frowned and pointed at the weapons officer. "I'm declassifying that information as of now. Gita, get with Commander Gui there and transfer your files about that ship to him. Captain, where's the best place to talk about this?"

"My briefing room." She jerked her head to the left of the bridge.

"Call whoever you think needs to be involved." I squeezed Ragini's shoulder on my way by her chair. "Let me know the second you have something; there's no way he just guessed where we'd be."

"Yes, ma'am."

"Cas is in the med bay with a concussion and a laceration on the back of his head," Emmory said. "Dr. Adelle says he'll be fine."

I exhaled and mustered up a smile. "Good. Trace said he knew something about Wilson, Emmory."

"You can't trust anything he says."

"I know." I rubbed at my face. "I just—*dhatt*. Why would he go to all this trouble?"

"I don't know, Majesty. We'll worry about it later. Right now, what's the plan?"

"Honestly, I don't know yet, but I've got an idea. I'm hoping that rabbiting will buy us enough time to come up with something."

I stood by the door of Isabelle's packed briefing room, Emmory on one side of me and Hao on the other.

"Ladies and gentlemen," Gita said, and the crowd fell into silence. "Meet the *Likho*; it is a new class of ships for the Saxons that up until a few days ago Indranan military intel was convinced was merely an experimental design. Let us all hope this is the only one in existence.

"She has a warp engine capable of performing more than a thousand floats of normal duration without having to refuel. She can act as either troop or fighter carrier, but she's also no slouch in a fight." Gita brought the schematics up on the display. "The limited data I have suggests that the shields are a new matrix generated by plasma repeaters set at several points within the ship rather than one central location. The size of the *Likho* doesn't allow for anything else. I don't have specs on this, so there's no way of knowing how they're going to respond to the *Vajrayana*'s weaponry."

"Well, that's good news," I said.

"The other good news is that the locations of the repeaters are known." Gita highlighted them on the ship. "I'd highly suggest aiming in that direction when we decide to take a shot. If we're lucky, taking one or two of those out might give us enough of a break in the shields to do some actual damage."

"What about the weapons?" Captain Saito asked.

"I've given Commander Gui the information I have. They didn't do a lot in terms of upgrading the weapons. When you get right down to it, their technology is still a good dozen years behind Indrana's. What they've done is crammed as much of their heavy artillery into the ship and focused on these."

A new schematic took the place of the ship. The missile didn't look all that different from your standard military grade, but the whistles from several of the officers as the specs popped into the air next to the image confirmed it was something new.

"Captain, permission to get to work with BodyGuard Desai and the rest of the weapons crew to figure out some counter-measures," Commander Gui asked.

Emmory nodded at Captain Saito's questioning look.

"Granted, Commander, get to work."

The room emptied out enough to give me breathing space. Clearing my throat and looking at the remaining faces, I pushed away from the wall and leaned on the table.

"Until we can figure out the *Likho*'s weaknesses, our best bet is to keep running. Gunrunners like to use a technique we call rabbiting—using quick warp jumps to stay ahead of the pursuers."

"Your Majesty?" The chief of engineering raised her hand, my *smati* identifying her as Ani Werez. "With all due respect, we don't know enough about the *Bristol*'s engines to know how she'll handle it."

I rubbed a hand over my face. "This is a bit like trying to use an unfamiliar vehicle as a getaway car."

Hao laughed. "Would now be a bad time to point out my ship would have been fine for this plan?"

I made a face and smacked him. "Hao, tell Johar to take Bial and get down to engineering. I want her studying up on the ship's systems. Chief Werez, between you, Hao, and Dailun I'm pretty sure you'll be able to handle anything that comes up."

"Yes, ma'am."

"Why the quick jumps?" Captain Saito asked.

"For one thing it'll burn less fuel—we're not running on full. For another I have no idea if that beast of a ship can catch up to us in warp and I really don't want to find out. Regardless of how they are tracking us, if we're bouncing around enough, it's going to take them a little time to figure out where we are. I'll take any advantage I can get."

"So this is our plan? Just run from the madman?" Coming from anyone but Hao, that question would have been too insulting to consider. As it was, Captain Saito shot him a look that could have melted the hull of her ship.

"That's the first part, yes. I'm still working on the second part, but we have to burn some time up because I do not want to go toe-to-toe with Trace unless I know for sure Admiral Hassan is right around the corner."

"Fair enough." Hao waved a hand at Chief Werez. "Let's go take a look up your girl's skirt."

"Hao." I pressed a hand between my eyes and sighed.

The diminutive chief didn't smile. She crossed the room, stopping well within Hao's personal space. "Captain Hao, this is an imperial vessel, not some gunrunning junker. You will treat the *Bristol* with the respect she is due or we can find you suitable quarters outside the ship."

Hao looked down at the young officer without a hint of a smile on his face. "Duly noted, Chief. I apologize for the insult. You are correct. I'd forgotten where I was." He gestured at the door. "After you."

They left the room and I sighed. "Captain—"

"I'll speak to her, ma'am. I'm fairly sure Chief Werez wouldn't actually space someone without checking with me first."

"It's not that." I waved a hand. "Hao can take care of himself, and it's a good idea to not let him get too comfortable or we'll find this ship actually being used for gunrunning." I raised an eyebrow at Isabelle. "Why did Chief Werez call the V7 the *Bristol*?"

"Oh, that." Captain Saito bit her lip and looked at the floor. "The crew may have unofficially named the ship, ma'am. It's a little nerve-racking to fly around in a vessel with just a number."

I nodded, waiting for her to finish with a raised eyebrow.

Captain Saito swallowed, then glanced at Emmory and back at me before she straightened her shoulders. "Welcome aboard the *Hailimi Bristol*, Your Majesty."

Emmory chuckled. I closed my eyes and sighed.

16

Expecting an attack from an opponent who has the advantage doesn't do a whole lot to improve one's chances in the fight. That didn't stop the crew of the *Hailimi Bristol*—for Shiva's sake—from preparing as best as they could for the upcoming battle.

We floated out of warp near an abandoned mining system, the hulking wrecks of equipment still hanging in the blackness of space. I stood with Emmory near the back of the bridge, my hands locked onto the railing. There was no way of knowing how soon Trace would arrive, and despite my hope otherwise I knew he would show up.

"The clock is started, Majesty," Captain Saito said, and I nodded in acknowledgment.

Johar and Hao needed a half hour to make some modifications to the *Bristol* that would allow us to burn less fuel with our jumps and hopefully would help the engineering crew stay ahead of any potential problems repeated jumps might cause.

We just didn't know if we'd have the time.

The clock ticked away the minutes, each one seeming to last

longer than the one before it. At the twenty-one-minute mark I commed Hao.

"How are you doing?"

"Almost finished," he replied. *"This is going faster than expected, so slightly less than ten minutes left."*

The alarm of an incoming warp signal made my stomach drop. "Good, because we're going to need every second. They're here. Tell Chief Werez we're going to need power to the thrusters."

"Will do."

"Majesty, that was twenty-one minutes and forty-four seconds from us floating into the system to their arrival," Ragini said. "Whatever signal he's following has to be traveling at FTL speeds, but I checked the coms already."

"Check them again."

"His warp drive is better than ours," Captain Saito said with a frown.

"I hate to say it, but I think his everything is better than ours," I murmured back at her.

"They're targeting us."

"Evasive maneuvers, Ensign Kohli," Isabelle ordered. "Commander Gui?"

"Yes, ma'am?"

"You are cleared for any countermeasures you deem necessary, but fire back on my command only. Understood?"

"Yes, ma'am," he replied.

Despite the target lock, no missiles streaked across space from the *Likho*. Instead the Saxon ship just hung there in the vacuum, waiting.

"What are they doing?"

"Waiting," I replied. "He wants to talk. Send a com request."

When the image came up, Trace was lounging in the captain's chair on his bridge. He grinned. "We could do this all day, Hail;

at the end of it I'll still have plenty of fuel left. Eventually you're going to have to stop and listen to what I say. You've got to want to know about Wilson. Why are you making this so difficult?"

I leaned my forearms on the railing. "I'm not going to believe anything you have to say about Wilson. You've been working with him all this time, or did you forget?

"Rock does that, you know, melts your brain down. When they crack your skull open they're just going to find a puddle in the bottom."

"You don't know anything." He threw a hand in the air and I spotted the tremor before he dropped it back in his lap. "That's why you're losing this. Why you need me."

"I don't need anything from you. I'm going to take back everything Saxony has stolen from us and then some. You started this mess, Trace, when you made a deal with the monster who murdered my family."

"I didn't know who he was." Trace's easy dismissal had me hissing air between my teeth in barely controlled rage. "Look, you're outclassed here, Hail. Just surrender, we'll have a conversation about Wilson, and then I'll help you get your throne back and all you have to do is let me keep Canafey and a few other pieces of territory. It's a win-win situation."

"Canafey is mine."

Trace was too far gone to recognize the deadly tone of my voice, but Emmory shifted next to me and the others on my bridge went very still.

"God, the arrogance, Hail; you think you own everything, but you don't even have control of Pashati! You're pathetic."

"Coms, cut the line. Chief Werez, warp us out."

Emmory put a hand over mine on the railing as the screen went black and the *Bristol's* drive kicked on. *"Take a breath,"* he subvocalized over our private channel.

"I almost let him get to me there," I admitted. *"Sorry."*

"It's fine, Majesty, you just can't expect him to make any sense, or to care at all about the people he's hurt."

"The nerve of that man. I'm the one who's acting like I own everything? He's—" I broke off.

"Majesty, what is it?"

I snapped my fingers as a plan started to take shape. "An idea," I said aloud. "Possibly a plan. If we do this right we sucker Trace into a fight against the whole 5th Fleet and I don't care what kind of firepower he's got, it won't be enough."

"Admiral Dewan is still three hours from Ashva."

"I know, we're going to have to keep rabbiting and buy some time until she's close enough." I looked at Captain Saito, who was watching us intently. "Let me think on this for a bit. Keep us on the warp schedule that engineering set up, Captain, and I'll get back to you when I have things figured out."

"Yes, Majesty."

I pushed away from the railing and headed for the door. The pattern of warping into a system and then right back out again would hopefully buy us a bigger window every time we did it, even with the *Likho's* better warp drive.

Emmory caught me by the arm when I staggered into the wall. I muttered a curse. The adrenaline was leaching out of my system and I realized I was going to crash soon.

"Make sure everyone gets some rest, Emmy," I murmured, stumbling again through the door of my quarters.

"I will, Majesty."

I didn't resist when he pushed me gently toward the bed, and I was out as soon as my head hit the pillow.

The klaxon woke me from a dead sleep. I scrambled out of bed, still fully dressed, and sprinted out into the corridor. Emmory and Zin caught up with me at the stairs. I grabbed for the railing as the familiar queasiness of floating into warp washed over all of us.

Once I had my bearings I started up the stairs, taking them two at a time and double-timing it to the bridge.

"Sorry, ma'am. We cut that one a little too close," Captain Saito said as a greeting. "I was hoping we'd stretched our lead to forty-five minutes, but no dice. The engines are starting to protest a little, but Chief Werez says the modifications your people made are making a significant difference."

"Isabelle, you look like shit, have you slept?"

"Yes."

"In her chair," her XO said under her breath, and I grinned in her direction.

"Ragini?"

The senior tech had her head bent against Dailun's as they pored over schematics of the *Vajrayana*. "Ma'am?"

"Any luck?"

"Not yet, ma'am, but we've eliminated a lot of possibilities. There's definitely something tied into the com system, but it's just transmitting, it's not the source. If I shut it down it just comes back in a different spot in the system."

The *Bristol* made an awful noise and we dropped out of warp with a jarring thud. I managed to keep from falling completely on top of Ragini at the last moment and the top edge of her seat drove into my midsection, relieving me of air.

"Bugger me, that's going to bruise," I muttered. "What happened?"

"I don't know, Majesty. Engineering is saying the drive stalled. They're trying to get it back up." Isabelle shoved out of her chair and leaned over the navigation console. I joined her.

We'd dropped out of warp near a cluster of planets and

asteroids. "Get us over there," Captain Saito said, pointing at a spot on the far side of the screen. "I want cover. That bastard is going to come out of warp on top of us otherwise. We can at least outmaneuver him in there."

As if she'd summoned him, the *Likho* appeared on our scanners. Isabelle swore and the klaxon sounded again throughout the ship.

"Weapons fire," she said.

Gita nodded from her spot next to Commander Gui and the *Vajrayana*'s plasma beam cut a swath diagonally across Trace's ship.

"Got him, ma'am," Gita's voice echoed over the cheers in on the bridge. "That should slow him down a little."

"Helm, get us out of here." Isabelle settled back in her chair.

"How long until we can warp again?" I asked Hao over the com link.

"I need ten minutes," Hao replied.

"How am I supposed to do that?"

"Talk to him. Keep getting him angry—he's not thinking clearly as it is. You're not going to like it, but we're going to need to scrap the rest of the planned warps and go straight to the Ashvin system."

"I don't, but we'll manage. It's better than being stranded a really long way from home without a warp drive." I made a face.

"Helm, take us to seven-zero-zero-five," Captain Saito ordered. "Half power."

"Aye-aye, ma'am. Half power. Heading seven-zero-zero-five."

I made it back to the railing just before the *Bristol* moved and watched the clock in the upper corner of my vision slowly tick off the seconds.

"Incoming fire on header niner-four."

"Deploying countermeasures."

The *Bristol* shook but continued on her path for the questionable safety of the asteroid field.

"Shields at ninety-nine percent."

The next salvo from the *Likho* missed us but slammed into the asteroid nearby, and I felt the shudder of the ship as several massive chunks of rock, moving slowly enough to slip past our shields, slammed into the hull.

Alarms rang out over the chatter on the bridge. The ensign at the helm never blinked once as she continued to navigate the *Bristol* deeper into the asteroid belt. Trace kept throwing shots in our direction, alternating between aiming right at us and at the surrounding rocks.

"He's narrowing down our evasive pattern," I murmured to Emmory. "Captain, open up a com link to the Saxon ship."

"Ma'am?"

"I'm going to distract him." I leaned against the railing, crossing my legs at the ankles.

Captain Saito nodded reluctantly and moments later Trace's face appeared on the screen.

"Trace." I smiled at him. "You're shooting a little wild there."

"My aim is spot on and we both know it. Stop now, Hail, or the next shot is going to do a hell of a lot more damage."

"I thought you wanted to talk."

"You shot my ship. Do you know how much damage you caused?"

"Oops," I said.

"I could say something very uncharitable about you right now, Hail."

I grinned. "Go ahead, it won't hurt my feelings. Better men than you have called me some pretty spectacular things."

"Why are you being so difficult?"

The man was deranged and I wasn't sure I could keep my temper for the ten minutes Hao needed. "Why am *I* being difficult? We could have come to a resolution on Red Cliff that would have saved millions of our people from going to war. You decided to drop a building on my head instead, remember?" I kept the smile on my face even though my words were sharp. "Turn around and go home, Trace. Leave Wilson to me. I don't need your help, whatever it is. You keep pushing this and you're going to end up dead."

"You can't tell me what to do!" His face turned a dangerous shade of purple and flecks of spittle shot from his mouth.

"I'm not telling you what to do," I replied as the clock in my vision hit zero. "I'm just buying us enough time to get out of here."

He frowned in confusion. "Hail—"

"Sorry, have to run." I winked at him and the screen vanished.

Moments later we floated into warp. As soon as the dizziness had passed, everyone went to work again.

"Majesty, we found it." Ragini called me over to her station. "There's a tracker code embedded in the life-support system, and it piggybacks in the coms to send a signal on an uneven pattern. I can't turn it off without shutting everything down."

"Don't worry about it. Now I want Trace to follow us." I dropped into a crouch next to her chair. "The thing we were talking about with the *Vajrayana* ships at Pashati—do you think you can do that with other ships?"

Ragini frowned in thought. "Which ships, ma'am?"

"The *Sarama*-class ships that are going to be at Ashva," I replied. "We'll need those destroyers for the fight against Trace's ship, but can we shut them down right after we win?"

"It'll be tricky, Majesty. But let me see what I can do."

"You've got nine hours. Dailun can help." I patted her on the

172

shoulder as I stood, and pointed at Captain Saito as I passed her. "You and Commander Gui with me, Captain."

"Yes, ma'am."

Emmory preceded me out the door and we headed back to my quarters with Zin and Gita trailing behind. "This is about to get messy," I muttered. "Have I mentioned how much I dislike planning things on the fly?"

"Only a dozen times, Majesty."

I punched Emmory in the shoulder. "Hush."

Fasé and Stasia were in my quarters, heads bent together in quiet conversation, when I came through the door.

"Sit, sit." I waved my hands before either of them could rise. "Hao and the others will be here in a few minutes." I took a spot on the couch next to Fasé. "How are we doing?"

She shook her head. "Everything has been quiet for some time, Majesty. I can't just call it up at will yet. The images will come or not on their own."

It wasn't the answer I wanted, but I knew better than to press. Fasé looked wan and there were dark circles under her eyes. Stasia shook her head at my questioning look, the shadows of worry creeping through her expression.

"We've got this last warp in the engines, hopefully, and we can't afford to wait for Admiral Hassan and her ships. Gita tells me we're not going to survive long in a straight-up fight against that ship. However, Admiral Dewan should almost be at the rendezvous point, so we won't be alone for long.

"I have a plan for how to take Ashva and get rid of Trace. If we can pull it off, we'll have the orbital defenses, and even better, a base in system in case—Shiva forbid—we get drawn into some long fight with Shul for Pashati."

The door opened and shut again as Gita let Hao and the others into the room.

There was quiet as people shuffled around. I stayed where I was, hands folded at my waist, until everyone had settled.

"We know that Ashva currently has a picket of only a few *Sarama*-class vessels, which in theory this ship could handle with relative ease. But given the circumstances, we don't want to alert the fleet at Pashati and risk them sending several battlecruisers—or worse, a *Nadi*—to stomp us into pieces.

"If they do, we'll only have six and a half hours before they show, so we'll need to coordinate with Admiral Hassan and make sure she hits Ashva as close to that window as possible."

"Majesty, what are you planning?"

I grinned at Emmory. "We're going to fly in like we own the place. Which, technically, I do."

Laughter echoed around the room. Emmory gave me the Look before telling everyone to shut up. I grinned and tossed the rough plan up onto the far wall. "In nine hours we're going to warp into the Ashvin system near Ashva. We'll come screaming into the destroyers' scanner range blaring a warning of an attack..."

Half an hour later I wrapped up the briefing and people started filtering back out of the main room of my quarters into the corridor. I gave Captain Saito a stern look on her way out of the door.

"You get some sleep, Isabelle. In a bed. That's an order."

"Yes, Majesty."

"Same goes for you, Fasé. Stasia, see that she does."

The women bowed their heads. "Yes, ma'am."

Hao waited until we were alone in the room. I raised an eyebrow when Emmory ushered the other BodyGuards away from the door and it slid closed. Hao hitched a hip up on the briefing room table but didn't speak, so I leaned against the wall near him and crossed my arms over my chest.

He broke first. "Hail, what are you doing?"

"Getting my throne back, and trying to keep Trace from killing us all in the meantime."

"The other night—"

I couldn't stop my inhale, or my hand from reaching for the nonexistent gun on my hip. "I told you to leave it."

"I'm doing this in private for a reason, little sister." Hao didn't move, didn't blink. "Do they know you can't have children?"

"Emmory knows. I don't know if he's told Zin." The sick feeling of betrayal slid through me. "What's it going to cost me to get you to keep your mouth shut?"

Hao's eyes snapped wide and the string of curses that followed could have blistered the paint off a ship's hull. "You think I want to blackmail you?"

"Judging by the incredulity in your voice I'm guessing that's not what you are getting at."

"I would never betray you like that." Hao fisted a hand. "If I didn't think your BodyGuards would interrupt us I would kick your ass, *sha zhu*. How could you?"

"I—" Words failed me and I pressed a shaking hand to my mouth as I sagged against the wall.

Hao crossed to me, grabbed me by the shoulders, and shook me once. My head rapped back against the wall and the pain grounded me. "You are family," he said, and let me go.

"I'm sorry." I dragged in a breath, then another, and reached for his hand.

"I wanted to know what you were going to do about it, Hail," Hao said, his fingers curling around mine. "If the secret gets out, how are your people going to react?"

"I named Alice as my heir because of this," I said.

"You named a widowed matriarch with no children as your heir," Hao said gently. "I'm not saying she was the wrong choice, but you need to think further ahead."

I wasn't even going to ask how he knew all this. My former mentor was smarter than most people gave him credit for and had no doubt been poking around in Indranan politics and history since he discovered who I was.

"I've been a little busy."

Hao waved his free hand in the air. "The answer's already there in front of you, Hail. You just need to start thinking like an empress."

"Now you're going to be vague?"

Hao grinned, then leaned in to kiss my cheek. "It's more fun this way."

I pulled him into a hug. "You're a horrible pain in my ass, but I'm glad you're here."

"I'm headed back to engineering," Hao said as I released him. "Take your own advice, Majesty. Get some rest. Don't stay up worrying about what can go wrong." He grinned at me when I opened my mouth to protest. "I know you, *sha zhu*, never forget that."

I shoved him out the door, waved a hand at my BodyGuards, and retreated to my quarters. Once alone, I paced the length of the now-empty room. The meeting had wrapped with nodding heads and confident smiles, but now the heavy weight of uncertainty pressed against my chest.

This was one of the riskiest things I'd ever planned, and the whole of our campaign rested on its success. There were far too many opportunities for things to go sideways, and I hated trying to run an operation with that kind of margin for error.

For a moment I considered waiting for Admiral Hassan or

trying to figure out a way to squeeze one more float out of the engines.

However, the entirety of 5th Fleet would be more than enough to handle one Saxon vessel, even one as terrifying as the *Likho* pursuing us. There was a greater risk of Ashva's picket force opening fire with Admiral Dewan there, not to mention the orbital defenses around the planet. I was counting on the chaos of Trace's arrival to keep the destroyers from asking too many questions.

If I could pull this off, we'd do it without firing a single shot in the air at our own people and the loss of life on the ground would likely be minimal.

17

enna, Tefiz." There was a rush of relief at the sight of my former Guard and the previous intelligence director on the screen in front of me. They had moved to Ashva shortly after I took the throne.

"Your Majesty." Tefiz smiled. She looked so much better than the last time I'd seen her, broken and defeated from the death of her wife and my disappearance. Now a sense of purpose lit up her eyes and she was almost vibrating with excitement. "Admiral Dewan and 5th Fleet are just outside the system and will be at Ashva inside of an hour after you arrive. We are ready to move on your signal."

"We're going to be coming in hot. What about the orbital defenses?" I'd sent them the specs on the *Likho* to study in case they could give us any suggestions.

"Most of the civilians working there are loyal to you, Majesty. They're not trained in hand-to-hand fighting, but they know their base and their systems. We've got enough military on our side to take care of the others. We'll assault the governor's mansion at the same time."

"Do we know if Governor Joshi is alive?"

Governor Turi Joshi hadn't been seen or heard from since the coup and I worried the elderly woman was beyond our help.

"My sources say she's still alive, ma'am. I will let you know as soon as we find her."

"You take Albin alive, Fenna. You hear me?"

"Yes, Majesty."

Albin Maxwell. My sister's husband. Traitor. He'd thrown his lot in with Phanin and Wilson. He was as responsible as Laabh, and possibly Leena, for Cire's and Atmikha's deaths, and I was going to make him pay.

"Good."

"Majesty, be careful," Fenna said with a worried frown.

I faked a grin. "We're just fighting a massive Saxon ship with nothing but us and three enemy ships; what could possibly go wrong?"

Tefiz snorted and slapped Fenna on the back. "She'll be fine—don't worry. We'll see you on the ground, ma'am."

I cut the connection and leaned back in my chair. "How's Cas doing, Emmory?"

"Better," he replied. "And Iza is awake."

"We should go see her while it's quiet."

The corridors were empty, most of the crewwomen occupied with preparations for our upcoming battle. Or, in Hao's case, still fighting to keep the *Bristol* in warp and in one piece.

Dr. Petra Adelle met us at the door of the containment room. "Morning, Majesty."

"Lieutenant." I nodded in response to her bow. "How is she?"

"A little disoriented, but her vitals are good. Better than I expected, honestly. She's recovering quite a bit faster than Indula is."

I followed her over to the field and put my hand up when Iza struggled into a sitting position. The doctor slipped through the field to help her.

"Majesty," Iza said.

"Glad to see you awake. How's your leg?"

"No pain there, ma'am. Major Morri was able to repair the shrapnel wound without any trouble." Iza glanced over at the sleeping Indula. "He saved my life, ma'am. He didn't have to stay with me."

"Of course he did," I replied. "You would have done the same and we both know it."

Iza grinned. "You've got me there, ma'am. I'm sorry we're not going to be well enough to help you take back your throne."

"It's fine. Rest up, Iza. We'll handle it from here." I tapped my hand against the field, sending ripples bouncing across the blue light. Iza nodded and lay back down.

"Keep me updated, Lieutenant," I told Petra when she came back into the room. "Where's Cas?"

"Over there, ma'am."

"Majesty."

"Do not get up," I snapped at my BodyGuard when he started to sit up. Cas flushed and I patted his hand. "Don't get up, Cas. How's your head?"

"Hurts, ma'am, but Dr. Adelle says I'll be all right in a day or so." He nodded to Emmory over my shoulder. "Sir."

Emmory returned the nod.

"What's going on?" Cas asked. "I've gotten some spotty updates but nothing thorough."

I leaned against his bed and filled him in on the events since we'd crashed and burned in the corridor. "You'll stay put until we're on the ground again, understood?"

"Yes, ma'am." Cas didn't attempt to hide his disappointment and I laughed.

"Still plenty of fight left for you to be involved in, Caspian. We're all going to be standing around for this bit anyway. I'll see you later."

Emmory reached past me and squeezed Cas by the shoulder. With a final nod, we headed out of the med bay.

"What now, Majesty?" he asked.

"Now we need to find someone to pretend to be the captain of this ship."

I once walked into a Zheng-owned warehouse and back out again with four boxes of their brand-new QLZ-57 handguns. After Hao and Portis had finished shouting at me for being "stupid, reckless, and death-obsessed," my boss had wanted to know how I'd managed to pull off the feat. Unable to give him a decent explanation, I'd merely shrugged and replied, "I just walked in like I was supposed to be there, and nobody questioned me."

After the second round of shouting died down, Cressen's Rule 17 was born. People are funny creatures and more often than not, if you act like you're supposed to be somewhere—especially if it's someplace you're not supposed to be—no one will question you.

In all my years, I had never attempted to do this with a ship, let alone with a crazed monarch on my tail. So as the *Bristol* made her approach to Ashva's orbit, I was nervously pacing the hallway outside the bridge.

We'd spent the last several hours preparing, swapping out bridge crew positions to make it look more like the bridge of one of the *Vajrayana* ships under Shul's control and doing some cosmetic adjustments to make us look like we were hurt a lot worse than we really were.

Captain Saito had stepped aside for Jasa. My older Marine had performed perfectly under the pressure of both Hao and me shouting questions at her for the better part of an hour.

Ragini was still on the bridge, but buried in the back at a console so she could work her magic while the ships in orbit were distracted.

On the ground, the resistance movement was starting its assault on the orbital defenses and the governor's mansion. We were hoping to use that added distraction to keep the ships in orbit from asking too many questions.

However, with the arrival of Trace's ship, I was sure they'd welcome us with open arms rather than suspicion. If they didn't see through our ruse before that happened.

If.

I stopped when Hao stepped into my path, and growled at him when he shifted so I couldn't go around. "What?"

"Calm down."

"You calm down."

Hao choked on a laugh. "Hail, you're behaving the exact opposite of how this rule works."

"I'm not in there." I jabbed a finger at the door. "I can be as antsy as I please."

"A leader leads by example, not by force," he murmured, and the words stopped me cold. Hao met my glare with a blinding smile and a wink.

"When did you start reading Sun Tzu? Last thing I remember was you saying that dead guys had very little to teach us."

"I changed my mind," Hao replied. "You were right."

"I'm sorry, what—"

"We're being hailed by the Ashva ships," Emmory said

182

before I could gloat. He tossed the image from the bridge onto the hallway wall so we could all see.

"Unidentified Indranan vessel, this is Captain Tauji with the destroyer *Hanuman's Mountain*. Please slow to one-half impulse and provide your identification or you will be fired upon."

It was a hell of a challenge, especially since we all knew this older-model *Sarama* wouldn't stand a chance against the *Vajrayana* ship.

"Helm, bring us down to one-half impulse, and coms, open me up a channel." Jasa looked calm and relaxed in the captain's chair. "Captain Tauji, this is Captain Hibi Daido aboard the *Eha Phanin*. Our identification code is—"

I rolled my eyes at the ceiling. It shouldn't have surprised me that Phanin had named one of the *Vajrayana* ships after himself, but it had and I'd snorted out loud when we saw the names listed in Caspel's message. The arrogance of the man was astounding.

We'd picked the *Phanin* because the captain was not only relatively unknown but a woman, and Jasa's build matched the photos we had.

I wasn't going to deny that I liked the slap in the face of using Phanin's name to fool his own ships into standing down.

"Captain Daido, your identification checks out. What brings you all the way out here? Last I heard they were keeping the *Vajrayana* ships behind Shaibya."

"You heard right, but we were sent out here to reinforce the picket. Admiral Shul has received intelligence that the rebel forces may attempt to take over Ashva before they head for Pashati. We got jumped en route by a Saxon ship we've never seen before."

"A Saxon ship?" Captain Tauji's eyebrow arched toward the

ceiling. "I'm not seeing anything on the scanners," he said with a frown. "Is your ship in immediate distress?"

"No, sir. We are pretty banged up, but we'll be okay. You're going to need our help when this beast shows up."

I tuned out whatever Jasa was saying to the captain as I contacted our troops on the ground. *"Tefiz, are you ready to move?"*

"Yes, ma'am."

"Go then. May the Dark Mother watch over you."

"And you, Majesty."

I returned my attention to Jasa just in time to hear Captain Tauji let out a very unprofessional curse.

"Look at the fucking size of that thing!" His eyes were wild when they settled back on Jasa. "We can't fight that, Captain."

"You can and you will," Jasa replied. "Or you'll explain to Emperor Phanin why you abandoned your post. I'm sending you the information we managed to gather from our encounter. It includes specific firing targets we think will hurt them."

The *Likho* was screaming toward us, and I knew that the seconds until Trace opened a com link and started shouting my name were ticking rapidly away. I held my breath until Captain Tauji gave a sharp nod and disconnected.

Emmory slapped the panel, opening the door, and the real bridge crew flooded back in. They swapped out seats with effortless efficiency.

Captain Saito and her crew had come up with a battle plan for dealing with Trace. Using the information from Gita about the ship itself, and the *Vajrayana*'s superior maneuverability, they were counting on the destroyers to provide a distraction and little else.

I braced myself against the railing and watched the battle unfold.

The destroyers were small enough and fast enough to get in

close to the Saxon ship. They spun around the behemoth like a pack of wolves around a cow, darting in to take a shot at the head of the ship, then scrambling out of the way before Trace could get a lock on them.

Which was a good plan since a direct missile hit from the Saxons would likely cut straight through their shields and vaporize the *Saramas*.

I'd no sooner had the thought than a lucky shot from the *Likho* clipped the edge of the destroyer called the *Ruby Knight* and sent it spinning off away from the planet. The other two ships redoubled their efforts and their weapons cut past the Saxon's weakened defenses, opening gaping wounds to the blackness of space.

"Commander Gui, fire," Isabelle ordered.

"Aye-aye, ma'am."

We fired our plasma beam into the same spot where we'd hit them before, and a gushing plume of fire spat from the ship's side.

"Shiva," someone murmured.

"Captain, open a direct link to the Saxon ship. Make sure those destroyers can't hear me."

"Yes, ma'am."

The image of the bridge appeared, and smoke filled the air. "Trace?"

A young man appeared in the frame, blood flowing from a wound in his head. He blinked at me in confusion. "Ma'am? Uh, Your Majesty?"

"Where's your king?"

"Gone, ma'am. They went to the escape pods. That last hit—" The bridge shuddered underneath him and he grabbed onto the nearest console. "That last hit clipped the reactor."

"Isabelle, get on the coms and tell those destroyers to get

185

away from that ship." I hissed the order, but she was already moving.

"Navigation, back us up. I want all power to the front shields."

"Where's your captain?" I asked.

"He went with the king."

My gut rolled. "What's your name?"

"Ensign Pavel Zima, ma'am."

"Ensign, get your ass to an escape pod. You have my word we'll rescue you and your crewmates and you'll be fairly treated."

He mustered a smile. "Too late for that, ma'am. Not enough pods on this ship. I drew the short—"

Before he finished, the screen went black and seconds later the Saxon ship exploded into a brilliant sphere of white and orange that vanished almost as quickly as it appeared. It faded quickly from sight and I was surprised by the tug of sympathy in my gut.

"Take us up, Helm!" Captain Saito ordered. "All shields to rear and port side."

"Dark Mother have mercy on your soul." I murmured the prayer as we turned tail and ran.

18

We didn't get far before the shock wave hit us and the *Bristol* rocked with the impact on her shields. The shrill chorus of alarms filled the air as the debris from the Saxon ship blew past us. One by one the alarms died out as the crew brought the ship back under control.

"Damage report, Captain?"

"We're all right, ma'am," Isabelle replied. "Banged up and probably in need of some major repairs, but we're not in any immediate danger."

"Did the destroyers get out of range?"

"Seems so, ma'am." Ragini answered my question. "Do you want me to start?"

"Do it." As soon as the shaking stopped I let go of the railing and headed for Captain Saito's chair. "Can I steal your seat for a moment, Captain?"

She got up out of the captain's chair and I sat down, crossing one leg over the other. "Let's bring all three ships up on the com link when I say. How's that third ship, Ragini?"

"The *Ruby Knight* is down for the count, ma'am. Life support is still up, but their weapons and navigation are both toasted. We won't have to worry about them."

"Good."

"*Hanuman's Mountain* is hailing us, ma'am." The communications officer looked over her shoulder at me.

"Ragini?"

"We've got weapons control and shields, ma'am," Ragini said.

"Acknowledged," I replied. I exhaled, counted to fifteen, and then nodded. "Do it."

"Done, ma'am. Clock is running at three minutes." This was the estimated time it would take any one of the destroyers' technicians to get control of their computers again.

"Captain Daido, what in Shiva's name—" The question died in Captain Tauji's throat when he realized who was staring at him.

"Gotcha." I winked.

"Your Majesty, I have coms up for all three ships," the com officer said.

"Captains, this is your empress speaking. You will surrender your ships and prepare to be boarded, or in two minutes and thirteen seconds I will blow all three of you to pieces. Since you are all traitors to the crown, I won't lose any sleep over it," I lied.

"Your Majesty, the *Indranan Star* is hailing us."

"Put them on the screen also," I said.

Captain Tauji was still gaping at me as the screen split and a disheveled young man with a lieutenant's insignia on his collar appeared. He bowed ridiculously low, almost disappearing from the screen with the motion.

"Your Majesty, this is the *Indranan Star*. We surrender. Please do not fire. Captain Gorai is in custody and my companions and I have control of the bridge."

"Thank you, Lieutenant…"

"Bosconi, Your Majesty. Long live the shining star of Indrana."

"Good job, Lieutenant Bosconi." I nodded once, and the young man relaxed.

"There's one ship I don't have to write off. Captain Tauji, you are running out of time and I promise you even if you had forty-five minutes instead of seconds it wouldn't help."

"You're not the empress."

"Turn the life support off." I gave a smile I hoped would leave him with nightmares in the years to come and watched Captain Tauji swallow. "No point in wasting a perfectly good ship."

"No, wait!" The man's shoulders sagged. "We surrender."

"We surrender?" I raised an eyebrow.

"Your Majesty."

"Wise choice. You'll wait for further instructions, and I should take this opportunity to note that the orbital defenses for the planet are also now in my control and I believe my people are knocking on the governor's door as we speak. So I would advise a healthy dose of common sense." I glanced over my shoulder at Ragini, who nodded in confirmation.

"*Ruby Knight*, I expect full cooperation with my Marines when they dock with your ship. Any resistance will be swiftly dealt with, and I'll warn you now I'm not in the mood for mercy." I gestured at Ragini to turn the coms off. "Did the shuttles launch?"

"Yes, ma'am," Jasa answered. "Colonel Hagen and the other two teams are on approach."

The three shuttles from the *Bristol* were crammed to the hold with Royal Marines who would take charge of the ships until we could bring up some more personnel from the ground—or until Admiral Hassan got here, whichever came first.

I only hoped we didn't need to fight anyone else between now and then.

"Majesty, I've got an incoming call from Fenna," Emmory said quietly.

I reached a hand out for his arm as I joined in the *smati* conversation. Fenna was spattered with blood and soot, but she smiled when she saw my face.

"Orbital defenses are secure, Majesty. I see from the displays they bought your ruse."

"They did." I grinned. "We're going to need to land all these ships and swap out crew as soon as possible."

"I'll get with Commander Bosche, she's our naval contact. We'll have crews for you by the time you land."

"Have you heard from Tefiz?"

"Not yet, ma'am. I'll see if I can get in touch with her."

"We'll do it, Fenna. You focus on the job there. We'll be on the ground first, and the destroyers will follow as soon as my Marines have control. I want crews ready."

"Are we expecting trouble?"

I laughed, the sound drawing attention from everyone on the bridge. "Always. We'll talk again when I'm on the ground."

"Yes, ma'am."

Emmory disconnected. "I'm trying Tefiz now."

"Captain, I'm assuming you want your chair back?"

"If you don't mind, Majesty."

I got up out of Captain Saito's chair, exchanging a smile with her as I paced toward the main window. The hum of the bridge filled in the silence as she took over the conn and the *Bristol*'s crew continued with their duties.

"I'm picking up ships on the radar. It's 5th Fleet."

I blew out a breath that Captain Saito echoed, and we grinned at each other. "How many escape pods launched from the Saxons?"

Isabelle frowned as she looked at the scans. "Looks like at least two dozen? I don't know how many people each one holds but they're decently sized."

"Admiral Dewan is on the com, Captain."

A slender woman with dark hair cut short around her face bowed to me. "Your Majesty, Captain Saito, it's good to see you in one piece."

I smiled. "We couldn't hold the party for you, sorry about that. There are some escape pods for you to pick up. One of which likely has a very grumpy king in it. I'd be careful—"

"Majesty." Emmory interrupted me, and I glanced over my shoulder at him. He was leaning on the console, shaking his head. "Those aren't normal escape pods. I think they've got reentry capability. One of them was trying to hide in the debris from the explosion."

"You think it's Trace?" I crossed to him and followed his finger as he traced the pod's route.

"Possibly. None of the others are making an attempt to get to Ashva."

"He's going to want transportation that can get him out of the system. Bugger me, we can't let him get away. Admiral?"

"Yes, ma'am?"

"Sorry to leave you with the cleanup; we're going to have to go after him. Keep an eye out for movement from Pashati. Captain Saito, follow that escape pod's path and get us on the surface. How soon can we be on the ground?"

"We're ready to land, Majesty. Mostly we were hanging around to give the shuttles backup if they need it."

"Send a message with a reminder that the orbital defenses

are trained on them with orders to blow them to pieces, and then turn it over to Admiral Dewan's people. If even one of my Marines gets so much as a scratch during boarding I will execute everyone on board."

It was a bluff I could afford to make. I just hoped Captain Tauji didn't try to call me on it.

"Yes, ma'am."

"Keep trying Tefiz," I told Emmory, and leaned against a console as the *Bristol* began its descent into the atmosphere.

"I suppose trying to get you to go back to your room while we land is out of the question."

"Pretty much, this is the fun bit."

Ashva gleamed in the main window, a little pearl of a planet. The massive glaciers of the north glowed greenish-white in Dasra's dim light, vanishing into the pure blue waters of the Mishan Ocean.

The shields flared when we hit the atmosphere, the red fire obscuring the rambling brown-green fields that surrounded Ashva's largest city.

"She's right here," Emmory said into his com, and then turned to me. "It's Tefiz."

I pulled up the com on my *smati*. *"What took you so long?"*

"Sorry for the delayed response, Majesty. We were a bit busy." My former BodyGuard winked and rubbed the back of her hand over her cheek, smearing blood across her face. *"I'm fine, before you ask. The mansion is secure, ma'am."* She jerked my brother-in-law into the frame, and the terrified look on his face was one of the most deeply satisfying things I'd ever seen in my life.

"Thank you, Tefiz. We'll be there shortly, I just have to make a quick stop first. You have our leave to start without us as long as you make sure he's still alive when we get there."

Albin whimpered. Tefiz grinned and cut the connection.

I tapped Hao on the shoulder on my way by. "Come on. Tell Johar and Bial to meet us in the cargo bay."

"Majesty, what are you planning?"

I gave Emmory a sidelong look. "Are you really going to waste your energy trying to talk me out of this? I'm not letting Trace get away."

We clattered down the stairs, meeting Gita and Zin at the bottom. Zin handed me a Hessian 45 and a new holster. I put it on as I stepped over the doorway into the cargo bay. *"Captain Saito,"* I said over the com link. *"Do you have a target for us?"*

"Yes, ma'am, patching it through to your smati *now."*

I blinked twice as the sheer map overlaid my vision. "Unknown number of targets," I said to those assembled as the ramp to the ship lowered, revealing a pristine field behind me. "At least one is King Trace. Try not to kill him; I know he's a pain in the ass, but I think Toropov would prefer we keep him alive."

"Gita, you stay on the empress."

"Yes, sir."

I grinned and we raced down the ramp. The adrenaline was coursing through my system, and my heart thudded against my rib cage. Captain Saito had put the *Bristol* down on the edge of a lentil field, and as we cleared the ship I spotted the smoking trail Trace's escape pod had left in the earth behind us.

I may have started this hunt, but Emmory was the undisputed leader as everyone looked to him for direction. He tapped Hao and Johar on the shoulders, pointing to the right.

"Circle around," he said. "They're probably making for that town in the distance. We can cut them off over there. Zin and Bial, go left."

Zin nodded, tangling his fingers briefly with Emmory's

before he took off with Bial for the cover of the tree line. Hao tossed me a grin and a wink, and then he followed Johar into the field, the pair disappearing easily into the green.

"We following this?" I gestured at the trench cut into the ground.

"We could." Emmory shaded his eyes with a hand and pointed again at the cluster of buildings in the distance. "Trace may not be cognizant enough to plan ahead, but I suspect his guard will be. They'll aim for that abandoned mill as a spot to regroup and figure out their next steps."

"Have I mentioned lately that I'm really glad you're on my side?"

His grin was quick. "Let's get this done, Majesty."

The three of us took off at a run, skirting around the edge of the field and heading for the same tree line Zin and Bial had used for cover. We cut back into the field, using the scattered earth from the escape pod as cover until we reached the low, crumbling wall that arced around the remains of the building.

Whatever the structure had been in its life, time and weather had worn the three stories down. The only hint of the third floor was a jagged edge of wall on the eastern side still clinging to the floor below. The entire south wall was gone, leaving a semiclear view into the interior. I still couldn't see our targets, but I could hear Trace's voice and shared an incredulous look with Gita as the volume rose. Ivan's rumbling bass echoed back, and a third voice I didn't recognize joined in.

"Are you getting this?" Zin asked over the *smati* link.

"I think they can hear him in town," Hao replied. *"Emmory, Johar and I have vantage points in the field. Don't want to get any closer, I'm afraid they'll see us."*

"Not if they keep going on like they are," I muttered.

Hao chuckled. *"We don't have a clear shot. Let me know what you want us to do."*

"Stay where you are. If you have the chance, move in. Otherwise you can keep them from bolting that direction."

"There's a stairwell on that far wall that looks intact." I grabbed Gita by the arm. "Come on, I've got an idea."

"Majesty?" Emmory stuck his hand in my way.

"You wait for Zin. When I give the signal, you three come in through the door." I pointed at the wall closest to us. "Or the gigantic hole next to it, I don't care. I promise they will be too distracted by us to notice."

Emmory pulled me in, pressing his forehead to mine. "Don't get killed," he said, and released me.

My reply stuck in my throat, so instead I nodded and took off with Gita at my heels. Hitting the wall at a run, I boosted myself up and over, and rolled out of the way for Gita. We lay flat to the weathered stone for a long moment, but Trace's ranting hadn't slowed in rhythm or volume. My *smati* translated the Saxon's words into Indranan.

"This is an unmitigated disaster, Ivan! We need to get out of here."

"I am working on it, Your Majesty. If you will please keep your voice down."

"Don't tell me what to do! And you, *Captain*, you worthless sack of shit. You said that ship was indestructible!"

I peeked over the edge of the stairs in time to see Trace take a swing at the cringing man in the corner. The captain covered his head with his arms, so Trace kicked him in the side.

"Majesty, enough, we need him to fly the ship."

"Thoughts, Gita?" I subvocalized over our *smati*.

"The captain isn't a threat; neither is Trace really, though he's

unpredictable and that's never a good thing. Ivan's the real threat. He's packing and his charge is on an enemy planet. He won't surrender, he'll die first."

"My thoughts as well." I carefully freed my weapon from its holster and trained it on Ivan. *"Emmory, you're about to hear a weapon go off. Get moving."*

A memory filtered into my head as I lined up my shot, of Ivan laughing—or trying not to laugh—as he helped a winded nine-year-old Trace back onto his feet. My finger froze on the trigger. "Bugger me," I muttered, squeezing my eyes shut and trying to shove away the feelings rising up in my throat.

The sound of the laser blast was loud in the silence.

19

van dropped, dead before he'd even realized the shot was fired. Trace dove for the ground and the Saxon captain curled himself up into an even tighter ball.

I looked to my right, where Gita lay with her own weapon out. The weapon she'd just fired.

She gave me a slight smile. "Just doing my job, Majesty."

Emmory and Zin burst into the ruins, guns trained on Trace and the captain. "Drop it." Bial was right behind them, and I spotted Johar and Hao outside the window at Trace's back.

Trace had rolled to his feet, his own gun out. "I've shot you once—don't think I won't do it again."

"Drop your gun." Zin's voice was so calm it threw a chill down my spine. "Or I will kill you."

"Do it then," Trace sneered. "I don't think you will. I'm worth more to you alive, BodyGuard, and we both know it."

"Men." Gita rolled her eyes, took aim, and shot Trace in the hand. The laser drilled through his hand and his gun. He dropped the now-useless weapon with a cry.

I covered my mouth with both hands in a failed attempt to hold in my laughter.

Trace clutched his hand to his chest, wailing at the top of his lungs. "Damn you, Hail. Come down and fight me!"

"I already beat you," I said, coming up on a knee at the edge of the landing. "You've got two choices—let Zin take you into custody, or resist. I'd recommend not resisting, but I'm pretty sure you're not going to listen."

Zin handed Emmory his gun and peeled off his uniform jacket. "Turn around and put your hands on your head."

In a move that surprised no one, Trace rushed at Zin, who shifted out of the way, bringing his left hand down hard on Trace's ear and sending him crashing to the ground.

I'd been the recipient of that move a few times and found myself grateful that my BodyGuard had been gentle with me, even when I'd been trying to take his head off.

"I could just shoot him in the knees, ma'am," Gita said.

"I know," I murmured in reply. "But Zin deserves this."

Zin stepped back, his hands folded in front of him as Trace scrambled to his feet again. Blood flowed from a cut on the Saxon king's cheek and he swiped impatiently at it.

"Turn around and put your hands on your head."

"What is wrong with you?" Trace spat. "Kowtowing to a bunch of women? It's unnatural."

Zin just smiled and made a "come here" gesture at Trace. This time he didn't move when Trace tried to punch him; instead he grabbed Trace's fist and pulled him downward, hitting him in the chest with his forearm. The impact was hard enough to lift the king of the Saxons into the air.

Trace went down hard, wheezing in the silence as he rolled onto his back.

"Maybe you should shoot him. This is embarrassing," I said to Gita. "Come on, Trace, I thought you were good in a fight."

He glared at me as he slowly got to his feet.

"Turn around and put your hands on your head," Zin repeated.

Trace lifted his arms, wincing as he turned. Zin glanced my way and I shook my head as a warning that the Saxon wouldn't give up so easily. I was right and as Zin approached him, Trace whirled around, trying to catch Zin in the head with his elbow. However, Zin leaned back out of the way of the strike, his right hand coming up and locking onto Trace's jaw as he drove his knee into Trace's.

I was fairly certain that bouncing Trace's head off the floor wasn't a necessary part of that move, but I wasn't about to chastise Zin for it. Trace went limp and Zin let him go.

I jumped down from my spot on the stairs. "Downside is now you have to carry him." I crossed to the Saxon captain still cowering in the corner. "Get up. Are you armed?"

"N-no."

"What's your name?"

"Captain Petrov, ma'am. Alexander Petrov. I would very much like to surrender."

"I accept your surrender. Bial?"

"Yes, Majesty?"

"If you'll take Captain Petrov into custody for me and see that he's transferred to wherever the remains of his crew are being held."

Bial nodded and pulled a pair of cuffs from a pocket. As the others took care of the prisoners, I crouched by Ivan's body and closed his eyes.

"You had to shoot him, Majesty," Emmory said.

"I didn't," I replied, getting to my feet and turning in time to see the surprise on Emmory's face. "I mean, we did need to shoot him, but I couldn't. I froze, there was a—I remembered his laughter and I froze. Gita shot him." I mustered up a smile and patted him on the chest. "That pep talk about protecting me sank in, I guess."

"Majesty—"

"I know we can't take his body back with us, but we should contact someone in the town and have them come get him. It doesn't seem right to just leave him for the animals." I walked away from Ivan's body and out of the ruins without looking back.

An hour later, I kept my attention on the window as the *Bristol* swooped low for a landing at the private port near the governor's mansion. It was less for the view and more to avoid my *Ekam*'s scrutiny.

"That is a lot of people," Zin said from behind me with a low whistle.

"I guess they weren't happy about Phanin's takeover."

"They could be on his side, ma'am," he replied.

"No. They'd be shooting at us." I grinned over my shoulder.

"It's still a problem," Emmory said, bracing himself against the jolt as the *Vajrayana* ship touched down. "I have less than a dozen BodyGuards without armor and it's forty-five meters from here to the mansion."

"Even at a sprint that's a long time for someone to line up a shot." Zin studied the crowd, a frown creasing his face.

"Or a rocket launcher," I murmured.

Emmory closed his eyes and sighed.

"Well, we're going to have to give that crowd something or they're going to rush the tarmac."

We all turned to look at Hao, who was standing back by the door with his arms crossed.

"*Ekam*, do you trust me?"

"As far as I can throw you."

Hao grinned. "I suspect that's a decent distance. I'll take it as a compliment." He gestured at me. "Come on, Your Majesty. Let your Guards coordinate your transportation with someone in the governor's mansion. We'll go talk to your people."

I exchanged a quick look with Emmory, who surprised me by nodding. "Cas will meet you in the cargo bay, Majesty."

With Cas on one side and Hao on the other, I walked down the *Bristol*'s ramp and out into the midday sunshine of Ashva. The roar of the crowd nearly flattened me.

Johar and my Marines had disembarked before us and set up a stack of cargo crates behind a makeshift shield generator Johar had somehow cobbled together in less than ten minutes. Cas boosted himself up and then offered me a hand.

The silence that rolled through the air was almost as stunning as the cheers. I looked around, unable to see any of the far-off faces, but I knew there had to be cameras around and so I smiled.

"Citizens of Indrana. It is good to be home." I folded my hands and pressed them to my heart, lips, and forehead. "I grieve with you over the murders of our beloved matriarchs and promise you that justice for those responsible will be swift and uncompromising. For now, go home to your families. You have done great works here today in liberating your planet from the traitors to our empire. Go home and celebrate your freedom, grieve for the dead, and prepare for tomorrow. We still have a lot of work to do."

"Jaya ma!" the crowd shouted back at me, several thousand voices raised to the sky. Then the chanting started, "Long live the gunrunner empress," and I had to bite my cheek to keep my laughter from dancing out into the air.

"Majesty, we've got transport incoming," Emmory said in my ear. *"Zin and I are headed to the cargo bay. We'll see you in a moment."*

"Acknowledged." I climbed off the crates, Cas following me.

The transports arrived at the same time that Emmory and the rest of my BodyGuards walked down the *Bristol's* ramp and we piled into them.

"Eyes up, everyone," Emmory said. "Tefiz may have secured the mansion, but something could go sideways."

"For us?" The mock surprise in my voice had the others in the vehicle laughing. I grinned at my *Ekam* and leaned forward in my seat to adjust my holster. Checking over my equipment gave me a certain amount of comfort, and after I finished with my new Hessian 45 I settled back with a quiet sigh.

"Captain Saito passed on a message from Admiral Dewan; she's been in contact with Admiral Hassan and they're expecting to arrive in about eight hours."

"I wonder how long it's going to take Shul to realize he's lost Ashva. Do we have a check-in schedule for the picket here?"

"Colonel Hagen was working on it, ma'am," Zin answered for Emmory. "We think we can fake a few of them and buy us some time. Probably just enough for Admiral Hassan's fleet to get here, but even if they can't the 5th Fleet has decent firepower and Admiral Dewan thinks she can hold off any assault until they do arrive."

"Good. I won't worry about it then," I said, just to hear Zin chuckle.

The transport came to a stop and I was sandwiched between Emmory and Zin, someone's hand on my head pushing it down between them as we hustled through the open doors and into the governor's mansion.

"Your Majesty, Shiva's blessings on you." The Marine captain saluted as she greeted me.

"Thank you, Captain...?"

"Coulet, ma'am. Anjali Coulet." Her left arm was in a sling, but her smile was bright. "*Dve-aiyeet* Ovasi and Governor Joshi are with the prisoner. She asked if I would get you settled and then take you to her."

"We can skip the getting settled part, Anjali," I replied with a smile of my own. "My people can take care of that when they get here. First let's have Major Morri take a look at your arm."

"It's nothing, just a—" Captain Coulet broke off at my look. "Yes, Majesty."

The Farian moved past me and laid a hand on Anjali's arm. One eyebrow arched up. "Broken in three places is not nothing, Captain."

I reached a hand out to steady the Marine as Dio healed her.

"May you feel better," Dio said, and she helped the captain take off the sling.

"Thank you very much." Anjali folded her hands together and shook them slightly. "Now, Majesty, if you'll come with me."

We followed her through the narrow corridor and into the mansion itself. Ashva's agricultural history meant the governor's mansion was more functional than fancy, and we passed through hallways void of decoration beyond the occasional landscape painting.

I'd only known Albin Maxwell briefly before I'd left Pashati and had studied up on him while still at home. My former brother-in-law was a mediocre naval officer who'd achieved his position within the Indranan Navy thanks to his mother's name rather than any particular skill of his own. Why my sister chose him for a husband I didn't understand.

"*Tefiz, we're almost there,*" I subvocalized over the com link. "*Has he talked yet?*"

"*No, ma'am. But he's close to cracking. Not much spine on this one.*"

"*Am I going to help or interrupt if I join you?*"

"Might be enough to shake him," she said after a moment's pause. *"I'm assuming you have a plan?"*

"I do." I held a hand in Johar's direction. "Can I borrow a knife?"

"What's your preference?"

"Something sharp and scary looking."

Anyone else would have laughed. Johar tipped her head to the side and studied me as we walked down the hallway. Then she nodded and planted her foot onto a nearby chair. She reached into her boot, pulled out a slender knife, and started moving again before Kisah could skid to a halt behind her.

"That was a present from my father," she said, handing over the eighteen-centimeter-long weapon. "The handle is Jupiter spider bone and the blade is Damascus steel. He had a man on Earth make it for him the year I was born."

The blade was narrow, barely a few centimeters at its widest point, but the distinctive rainbow of the rare steel was still visible. The handle was stark against my skin, and surprisingly heavy.

"It's lovely," I said, turning it over my fingers. There wasn't any point in asking her for something less sentimental. Johar wouldn't have offered it up if she didn't want me to use it.

Captain Coulet hesitated at the door, but I reached past her and touched the panel. "She's expecting us." The door slid open and I stepped out of the way so Emmory and Cas could go through first.

I rolled my shoulders back and followed them with Hao and Johar on my heels.

The sun streamed in through the massive window on the left side of the room, its cheery warmth a strange counterpoint to the weeping man sitting in a chair. I smiled slightly when Tefiz stepped away, burying the expression before Albin raised his head to stare at me in terror.

"Your Majesty." Tefiz executed a bow that was only a little rusty.

When she came up I leaned in and pressed my cheek to hers, not caring about the blood that smeared over my face as I pulled away with a murmured blessing. Tefiz snorted and rolled her eyes at me but didn't say anything out loud.

"Governor Joshi." I held a hand out to the elderly woman as she came up out of her bow.

"Your Majesty, it is with great joy in my heart that I greet you." The elderly woman's dark eyes sparkled with relief and she squeezed my hand in hers.

"Are you all right? Do you need medical assistance? We have a Farian."

She waved her free hand. "Tefiz already made sure I was taken care of. Thank you, Majesty. If you will excuse me, I would like to see who of my staff survived our little occupation."

"Captain Coulet."

"Yes, ma'am?"

"Go with the governor and keep her safe."

She saluted and followed after Turi. I waited for the door to close before I turned to my former brother-in-law.

"Ha—Your Majesty—" Albin's panicked stammer broke off into a whimper when Tefiz reached out and cuffed him on the ear.

I tapped the blade of the knife against my lips as I circled Albin's chair, watching him shift and fidget as he tried to keep an eye on me without actually moving.

Grabbing a chair from the nearby table, I spun it in front of him and dropped into it. "Albin, it is such a pleasure to see you again."

20

That's a lie," I continued, flipping the knife between my fingers. "We never did have the chance to get to know each other, and now that I know you're responsible for my sister's death I'm not in the mood to do much more than slide this into your ear as slowly as possible and call it even."

Haunted brown eyes snapped up to meet mine and Albin's handsome face twisted into an expression filled with a surprising amount of regret. "I—"

I stopped him with my boot between his legs and he whimpered in pain. "Here's how this is going to work, Albin. I'm going to ask you some very pointed questions. Your answers determine how much unpleasantness there is. If we're able to verify the truth of it and I'm satisfied with what we learn, you might get to live out the rest of your life in a prison cell. If I'm not"—I smiled and watched him swallow hard—"Johar here once took thirty-eight days to kill someone and if I ask nicely she might help me try to beat that record."

"That was a long time ago, Majesty, I've learned some new things since then," Johar said. "We could probably get ten more days, maybe even more."

Albin made a noise like a dying cow and slumped over in his chair.

"Oh, for Shiva's sake. Did he really just faint?"

"It would appear so, Majesty." Emmory pulled Albin back upright and I leaned in, slapping him across the face several times in rapid succession until his eyes fluttered open.

"Who is Wilson?" I hit him again, harder, until the confusion gave way to fear.

"I don't know. I swear. He just appeared one day while I was on leave at Bahmai Port. He told me that Atmikha wasn't my daughter; that Cire had been seeing that *Upjas* rebel even before we were married."

"You killed them all because you were jealous?" I tightened my grip on the knife and Albin's eyes slid from mine down to the blade in my hand. "You're not going to die quick, you spineless coward. I am going to cut you into pieces."

"No!" He shook his head so violently he almost unseated himself. "It all got out of hand so quickly. I didn't want—I loved her. I just wanted her to love me back. Wilson said he could make Abraham disappear. All I had to do was recommend Admiral Shul to Cire when the command of 2nd Fleet came available."

Tefiz's curse lit up the air. I ignored her and fixed Albin with a look that had him crumbling into sobs. "I swear that's all he had me do. I did it, but Abraham didn't vanish and Cire continued to ignore me in favor of the empire. I told Wilson he couldn't be trusted to hold up his end of the bargain and that we were through. I got a posting with Admiral Shul because he was grateful for my support. I'd just gotten home the day before they died." His mouth wobbled. "I was supposed to go out with them but I wasn't feeling well that morning."

"You had to have known something was wrong when they

died!" It took all my control not to bury Johar's knife in his throat. "You didn't say a word. You ran like the gods-damned coward I've always known you to be."

"There wasn't anything I could do. They would have killed me if I'd said anything!"

"They killed your mother, you worthless sack of shit!" I grabbed him by the shirtfront and hauled him into the air. "Shot her in the head! She didn't die a coward, sniveling and whining. She was loyal to the very end." I threw him back into the chair and only Emmory's presence kept it from tipping over backward. Albin sobbed as I loomed over him and I rolled my eyes in disgust. "Get him out of my sight before I decide he's not worth keeping alive."

Cas and Jasa moved at my words and grabbed the weeping Albin by the arms. I dragged in one breath after the other, trying to get my anger under control as they hauled my brother-in-law from the room.

"Admiral Verrier was in charge of 2nd Fleet, Majesty," Tefiz said the moment the door closed behind them. "He died of what the doctors said was an aneurysm in 2997. He was older; there was no reason to suspect foul play." She rubbed a hand over her face and swore again. "Cire talked your mother and Admiral Saini, who was in charge of Home Fleet at the time, into appointing Admiral Shul as his replacement."

The awful pieces of this puzzle were starting to fall into place. I turned to the window with a hand pressed to my mouth. Wilson had set this whole thing in motion with exquisite care. I dropped my hand, taking the knife and flipping it between my fingers. The blade flashed in the sunlight.

"He's been playing this deadly game of Chaturanga for my whole life," I murmured.

"He did say it had been years of work," Emmory said from my side.

"I am so far behind I'm not sure this is a game I can win." I blew out a breath. "We still don't know anything, Emmy."

"We know some of it," Hao said. "Maybe it's time to put that all together in one place."

An hour later I was sitting on the floor of an office in the mansion, scrolling through the limited information we'd managed to gather on Wilson and tossing important pieces up onto the blank wall in front of me.

Gita leaned against the wall behind me, talking quietly with Tefiz and Kisah. The others had gone to finish locking down the mansion, Emmory surprisingly content to leave two Marines on the door once I promised to stay in the room.

I glanced to my left where Bial was sitting. Johar was staring out the window humming a little tune to herself.

"How did you know to go to Santa Pirata?"

"Majesty?" He blinked at me, confused by the abrupt question.

"You were at Santa Pirata because of the drug, yes?" I waved a hand at one of the dates on the timeline I was constructing. "Your report said Wilson was there in 2996, and Rai confirmed he sold Rock to the man at the same time."

"Yes, ma'am."

"How did you know?"

A surprising blush appeared on Bial's sharp cheekbones. "I used your reports, Majesty. They were extremely helpful."

It was my turn to blink. "When did you get your hands on those?"

"I had access from the moment I became *Ekam*, but I didn't

really look at them until after we realized your empress-mother was being poisoned. For not having any training you followed Wilson's trail extremely well."

"I lost him."

Bial lifted a shoulder. "Because he went to Santa Pirata, and no one in their right mind would have sent a nineteen-year-old-girl to Bakara Rai, Majesty."

Johar tipped her head to the side. "He's right," she said. "Bakara would have eaten you alive. You're lucky you didn't run into someone who valued money more than being able to sleep at night."

I suspected I had Portis to thank for that. No doubt my new BodyGuard had run interference with anyone I'd come into contact with. The anger flared only briefly. I'd been so close to Wilson and I'd lost him because of deliberate interference.

"Portis was protecting you, Majesty." Tefiz's voice broke through the silence as if she'd read my mind.

"I know," I said. "It's over and done. There's little point in being angry with a ghost anyway. It's just—*dhatt*." I blew air out between my teeth. "We could have stopped this before any of it started if he'd let me go."

"We had Trackers follow the trail from there."

"Trackers who disappeared," I countered, and Tefiz gave me a nod in acknowledgment.

"Wilson was at Santa Pirata for the Pirate Rock, which we can be reasonably sure he took to Saxony and either gave or sold to Trace." I looked back at the scattered data we'd collected. "He shows up and disappears. Over and over like a ghost. In '67 he's alive on paper, then nothing for sixteen years? Then he's there when my father is murdered in 2990 and he skulks about in the shadows whispering to my brother-in-law, recruiting Admiral Shul. Addicting the king of the Saxons to Rock.

"Then, nothing, *Hai Ram*," I muttered, slamming a fist into my knee. "He vanishes again. There's a nearly ten-year gap between that and when he reappeared on Pashati to kill my sisters. So what the hell was he up to that whole time?"

There was a beat of silence before Kisah spoke up. "He was waiting, Majesty."

"Waiting?" I turned my head to look at her, and Kisah pushed away from her spot near the door.

She enlarged one of the images on the wall. A headline about the war between Indrana and the Saxons. Another battle lost, more territory conceded by Indranan forces. "I had a cousin whose air scooter got stolen when we were kids. She tracked down the girl who snatched it and sat outside her house every day for a week until she drove it out of her family's garage. Gayla let her get down the block and out of sight of any cameras before she tackled the girl and stole her scooter back.

"We already know Wilson is patient, ma'am. We may not know why, but we know he's spent years planning to destroy your family and Indrana." She tapped a finger against the image. "He was waiting to see if Saxony would win the war."

"It makes sense," I said, resting a hand on her shoulder. "If he wanted to destroy my family, then destroying Indrana would be the best way to go about it." I squeezed once and then let her go. "However, we didn't lose."

"No we did not." The blond Guard grinned at me. "The war hurt us, but the Solarians' intervention kept the Saxons from running over the top of us completely."

"And when the peace treaty was signed he had to move to plan B."

We turned to look at Zin as he came into the room, followed by Emmory and Admiral Dewan.

"Yes, the plan to wipe out my whole family." My flippancy

had a sharp edge to it that made everyone wince. "Admiral Dewan, welcome to Ashva."

"Your Majesty," she said, her voice carrying that same curious sigh of relief everyone's seemed to these days, as if she couldn't quite believe I was alive until she saw me standing before her.

"I think wiping out your family was always part of the plan, Majesty," Zin said. "It's just a question of how he was going to go about it. When the Saxons didn't completely destroy Indrana, Wilson had to shift things around.

"I've been searching video feeds for any recognition of Wilson since before the coup, Majesty," Zin continued as he crossed to the wall. "Obviously we had other things to focus on, but I finally got a hit." He tossed an image up on the wall. "After the treaty was signed in 3001, a survey drone pulled this photo off a street in Tibat, the capital city of the southern continent on Kerala."

The image was blurry but I could make out Wilson's face.

"We got a lock on Eha Phanin's face from a camera a few blocks down so we know this man is the same person."

"They passed each other on the street," Johar said with a shrug. "Not even Rai would kill someone with that flimsy of a connection."

Zin grinned at her and brought up another file, this one a video. He zoomed in on the men's hands and as they passed each other Wilson handed something over to Phanin. "Shortly after, Phanin's career went from quiet backwater politician to the rising star of Kerala, and by 3003 he'd been elected to the General Assembly and moved to Pashati. The biggest contributor to his campaign? Waterloo Corporation."

I frowned. "I guess now we know what he was doing while he

waited for the Saxons to wipe us out." I nodded, then glanced in Johar's direction. "Call Rai, see if he's found anything else."

We made it two hours before someone on Pashati started questioning the brief check-ins from Captain Tauji and actually looked at the scanner data.

I leaned back in the chair in the office I'd taken over and watched the screens showing me the orbital defense station, Admiral Dewan's bridge, and Caspel on Pashati.

"Admiral Hassan is still five hours out, Majesty," Emmory said as a fourth screen flashed an incoming message notice. "This is going to be close."

"We'll be all right," I replied, accepting the call. I let my best gunrunner smile spread over my lips as Admiral Shul's face appeared on the screen.

Wilson's admiral had a narrow face with sharp cheekbones. He opened and closed his mouth several times before clamping his lips shut, and I watched his jaw muscles flex as he struggled with the surprise. I let him wrestle with that for several minutes before I spoke.

"I am granting you one opportunity to surrender, Temar Shul. You'll be tried and convicted by a military court for treason and then executed. It's more of a mercy than you deserve, but I'm offering it. Order your fleet to stand down, lock all your ships down, and give me the codes."

Shul's laughter was supposed to be sharp with disdain, but the waver of his next words ruined his effort. "Fuck your mercy, you bitch. What have you got? Twenty ships? I'm going to erase you from the pages of history."

"I was hoping you'd say no," I said. "Think of me when you're choking on your own blood."

The flicker of fear in his eyes just before I cut the connection was more than satisfactory.

"Admiral Dewan, you're in charge of Ashva's defense until Inana gets here. I'll leave you to it."

"Yes, Majesty." She nodded and closed out the call. The captain at the station did the same, and I looked to Caspel.

"I want him dead, Caspel. Make it happen and tell your operative to get the hell off the ship as soon as it's done."

"Yes, ma'am."

"Any news on Leena?"

"Nothing yet, Majesty."

I was surprised that Wilson hadn't tried to contact me to gloat about her betrayal, but so far it had been silence from the palace.

"I have a few files for you," Caspel said, and my *smati* beeped with the incoming message. "Should be helpful."

"Good." I nodded. "We'll see you soon. Stay alive."

"You also, Majesty."

I got up out of my chair after Caspel had ended the call and I leaned against the windowsill, tapping my fingers in a restless rhythm as I stared at the pale lavender clouds. The light of the setting sun washed it all in waves of gold.

The sounds of the door opening and closing filtered through my thoughts, but I didn't turn around. We were almost home. Just a few more battles to win and it would be over. I didn't let myself consider the possibility that we could lose.

Did I really think I could rule an empire once the shooting was done?

"Majesty, Emmory said you have a message from Caspel for me to decrypt?" Zin asked.

"Yes." I passed it over to him with a smile.

"Hail, they're not going to let me eat until you come over here and start."

I turned around, grinning at Johar. She stood at the table, glaring at Stasia, who glared back without the slightest hint of fear even though Johar could have killed her easily. "Did you get hold of Rai?"

"He hasn't messaged me back." Johar shrugged. "You know how he is."

"If *I* have to message him and remind him we're on a timeline I'm going to get annoyed."

"I like it when you're annoyed with him. It's fun; he doesn't know how to react." Johar grinned at me.

"Majesty, are you ready to eat?" Stasia asked.

"We'd better. Johar gets grumpy when she's hungry." I headed to the liquor cabinet with a laugh and poured myself a drink.

Zin touched my hand. "Here, Majesty," he said, passing back the file from Caspel with Toropov's message on it. I took a seat at the little table and put the screen up on the wall.

Toropov's face appeared. "The ship will be at Juno Port, Your Majesty. It's a Saxon-registered courier ship by the name of *Avangr* with diplomatic immunity, so you shouldn't have any problems getting through Pashati's planetary defense grid. Phanin seems under the impression I am being held prisoner by Director Caspel." He flashed a brief smile.

"I have made contact with my people at home. According to them Trace is still nowhere to be found, which gives Samuel a lot more leeway, though I have cautioned them to proceed carefully and to wait for things here to go into motion before they make their move. I will warn you as well, if Trace is not back on Marklo it means he's up to something. I don't have access to our ship movements, but about half the fleet is still loyal. If he makes a move on Pashati it is not something that has been approved by anyone in the government." Toropov paused and rubbed at his nose. "I look forward to a reply from you. God-speed, Majesty, may we see each other soon."

The screen went blank, the recording over.

"I wonder what Ambassador Toropov is going to say when I tell him that his king is in my basement?"

Stasia slid a tray of food in front of me and I dug into it with a smile. The others got their own food and joined me around the table. We ate in silence, the only background noise the sounds of utensils on plates and cups being set down.

Half an hour later, I poked at the remains of my dinner lying on the table in front of me as I mulled over the contents of the video.

"It's an easy way in," I said finally.

"Almost too easy," Emmory answered, and I lifted my head.

"True. I'd feel a whole lot better about this if Toropov had been on my side from the beginning."

"To be fair, ma'am, he's the Saxon ambassador. His first duty is to his people." Zin tapped at the edge of his cup in thought. "He's demonstrated that loyalty. I would be more concerned if he'd been willing to involve himself in Indranan politics from the outset."

"We trust him to give us a ship that's going to fly us right through a defense grid capable of blowing us out of space. That's if the damn thing doesn't just go up the second we close the doors, or if a platoon of Phanin's men aren't waiting for us at the port—either here or after we land on Pashati. The life-support systems could be compromised and we'd all be unconscious before we could do anything about it. I don't fancy waking up in Wilson's hands, and you lot wouldn't wake up at all. I don't—"

"Hail." Johar's quiet word interrupted my rant. Her lips twitched at the look I threw her, but she didn't quite smile. Emmory did, so I kicked him under the table.

216

I grabbed for my chai and took a drink, unable to explain the sharp-toothed monster suddenly snarling away in my chest. We had a long way to go before the end of this.

"I'm sorry; I don't know what's got me so on edge."

"You don't have to apologize, Majesty," Emmory said. "Toropov hasn't given us a reason to trust him, though I'd say this offer of his is an attempt. It's just a hell of a risk to take."

"Caspel didn't tell him about the Saxon ship. I wonder why?"

"He's probably waiting for the go-ahead from you," Emmory replied.

"We can make it work," Zin agreed. "Ragini and I can go over the ship and make sure there is nothing strange with it."

"Hao and I can help also," Johar said. "We'll be able to spot any less-than-legal modifications."

Emmory nodded. "Actually, let's get on that now. We can get the specifications for that courier ship and we can take a look at it."

Zin pushed away from the table with a nod in my direction. Johar followed suit with a nod of her own.

Stasia began clearing the table, waving off my attempts to get up and help. When she finished and Emmory and I were alone in the room, I pulled a leg up onto my chair and rested my chin on my knee.

"What is it?" Emmory asked.

"Something is scratching at the back of my brain about this, Emmory. I just can't get a handle on what it is. Who in the hell is Wilson? He recognized an Indranan saying without blinking an eye. He acts like he knows me, when he forgets to pretend otherwise.

"What possibly happened to him—what could my mother have done—to give rise to this desire to burn a whole empire to the ground?"

"Why do you assume your empress-mother did anything?"

"I—" I broke off and blinked at him in shock. "What Clara said, and he's obviously angry. I'm not blaming her. I just need to know. Wilson's unpredictable and I can't plan with that kind of chaos stirring things up."

"I'm not suggesting that you're blaming her, Majesty. You're looking for logic from a man who clearly has none. Maybe your mother didn't actually do anything. Have you considered that? Maybe Wilson just thinks she did. Maybe she said no to a favor, something so ridiculously inconsequential that there's no record of it at all."

"It wasn't inconsequential to him. He killed my whole family because of it," I whispered.

"I know, Hail." Emmory smiled gently, but his eyes echoed the grief of my words. "And I'll say it again, you're looking for logic from a man who clearly has none. He wants vengeance. Don't misunderstand me, he's got a plan and he's following it. Whatever happened, he's spent his whole life working up to this moment. You haven't." Emmory got up out of his seat and came to kneel next to mine. I turned my head to look at him, pressing my cheek into my knee. My *Ekam* reached out, resting his hand gently on my face.

"I need you to promise me you'll remember that. Don't let him push you into seeking vengeance of your own. You can't beat him at his own game. He's had too many years to prepare, and your rage over your family is no match for the fury he's carrying."

There was something in Emmory's eyes, a glitter of concern I hadn't ever seen, chasing itself over the silver lines within his eyes.

"I promise." The words came easily and I meant them.

21

Emmory answered the quiet knock at the door, letting Hao and Gita into the room. They were both disheveled and dirty and I wondered if they'd been up to more than just crawling around the innards of the Saxon ship for the last two hours.

"Ship's clean," Hao announced, dropping into a chair. "I still don't trust Toropov, but as long as we're going in with eyes open we're good to go whenever you're ready."

"I thought Johar was going with you?"

"She's talking with Rai," he replied with a wave of his hand. "Gita offered to help."

Resisting the urge to grin at my BodyGuard was difficult, so I turned back to the window. "There's no movement from Pashati," I said. "I don't know if Caspel's operative was successful or not, though I suspect I'll hear about it either way when it happens. I do find it interesting Shul's not hauling ass in our direction."

"He's not in charge, ma'am," Gita said quietly. "Wilson, or Phanin, is probably trying to figure out if you've set a trap."

I nodded absently, watching a plume of smoke rising off in the distance. The fighting on Ashva had mostly been contained to the mansion grounds, but there were two military bases in the capital where crown forces had gone up against Phanin's men, and the smoldering rubble was still throwing curls of black into the air.

"The big question is, do we wait for Admiral Hassan before we head for Pashati or go now while things are still fresh?" I murmured the question.

"Tefiz asked me to let you know that King Trace is demanding to speak with you," Gita said.

"I'm sure he is," I replied, not turning from the window. I was also sure he was about to start going through some serious withdrawals. "Make sure Tefiz knows to keep a doctor nearby. There's a very good chance he'll die before he sobers up."

"Yes, ma'am." Gita nodded and left the room.

I stood in the silence for several minutes before I looked at Emmory. "What now?"

"We'll wait for Admiral Hassan, Majesty," he said, moving to the door again and opening it. "Get some rest. I've got everyone else on a rotation. We've been going at it for a while and we'll all feel better coming at this with clear heads."

I woke with Fasé's face centimeters from mine. "That's a good way to get shot," I said.

She smiled. "And waste all your hard work? I don't think you would, Majesty."

"What's going on?"

"Johar's coming with news for you." Fasé moved back from me and settled cross-legged on the end of the bed. "You need me to be here."

I sat up and rubbed both hands over my face. "Do I need to tell you that's more than a little strange?"

"Emmory already did." She lifted a slender shoulder and smiled. "I am getting used to it."

I looked around the barren room and then got to my feet with a sigh as the door opened. "Did you get some rest?" I asked Emmory.

"I did, Majesty. Admiral Hassan floated out of warp an hour ago. She said to tell you she'd be on the surface as soon as possible."

"Good. Any movement from Pashati?"

"Not as of yet." He shook his head.

Fasé followed me through the door like a pale shadow and perched on the arm of the couch when I sat down. The main door opened, and Zin and Gita came in with Hao and Johar on their heels.

"Rai sends his apologies for the delay, Hail," Johar said. "He needed to verify the information, and given the age of it, that proved to be a tad difficult."

I nodded, crossing one leg over the other and leaning back against the couch. "What did he find?"

"Ironically it was something he had all along." She raised a black eyebrow and shook her head with a laugh. "Around 2983 Indrana's calendar, a black-market mod shop on Basalt III owned by Flip Bavenkov burned to the ground. There were no clues, and obviously the cops didn't spend a whole lot of energy looking for the perpetrator. One less illegal mod shop was less work for them.

"Flip owed Rai money, but he'd been pushing us off for a while. Rai suspected he was lying about how many clients he was bringing in, so he put a pair of eyes on the shop door—a young street girl no one looked at twice."

Johar tossed the gritty image onto the concrete wall; Wilson's face was visible beneath the streetlight as he left the building. "The place went up in flames not ten minutes after she saw him leave."

"We already suspected he modded his appearance," I said with a frown, and pushed to my feet to examine the image of Wilson more closely. "This doesn't help a whole lot."

Johar's grin was fierce. "Rai was annoyed, Hail. You know how he gets. He saved every image the girl recorded, even after he decided it wasn't worth going after whoever killed Flip. These are the three men who went in before Wilson came out. The cops found three bodies in the ruins of the building. One of them was Flip. The other two they couldn't identify." The three images went up on the wall one after another.

"Obviously the last one seems a likely candidate given his features, but we're running facial recognition on all three of them now, Majesty," Zin said. "It might take a while but we—"

His voice was drowned out by the sudden buzzing in my head as my eyes landed on the last image—a handsome Indranan man. His was a face I had seen almost as much as my father's for the first ten years of my life. The air left my lungs in a rush and my knees gave out. The sound that ripped from my throat terrified everyone in the room, but the looks on their faces were quickly lost to the tears that blurred my vision.

Fasé was the only one who didn't react. The Farian stayed where she was as I fell to the ground, her voice rising above my grief and the chaos it caused. "Emmory, don't."

My *Ekam* was on a knee by my side, his hand on my shoulder. "She's—"

"Experiencing a painful truth. It has to happen. Let her be."

Emmory removed his hand but didn't move away. I buried my face in my hands, images colliding in my head.

That same handsome man spinning me in a circle in the garden on a warm summer night.

Laughing with my father.

Hugging my mother.

A photo in a frame on my father's desk. My father's arms slung over the shoulders of Janesh and Hemel, his best friends, all of them grinning at the camera.

"*Sha zhu.*" Hao had, of course, ignored Fasé and crouched in front of me. He wrapped a hand gently around my wrist and pulled my hand from my face. "Who is he?"

"A ghost." My voice felt raw in my throat as if I'd been screaming. I dropped my hands and stared past him at the image. "Janesh Raja Hassan was one of my father's best friends. He died on board the *Shiva's Creation* in an explosion along with Hemel Anbami on the thirteenth of Shravana 2983."

I remembered the look of stunned grief on my father's face, and Cire's tears and mine when he'd told us the news. Our joy at his unexpected return crashed into sorrow so fast it had left me breathless. Pace had only been three and while she hadn't understood the reason for it, our sadness had set her wailing.

"He was the older brother we'd never had and then he was gone." I pressed the back of my fingers to my mouth, swallowing down the nausea that threatened. "I thought he loved us. He said he loved us. But he lied. He killed them all, my whole family!" The tears streaked down my cheeks as the awful truth sank its teeth into my heart.

The door opened. "Majesty, Admiral Hassan is here. Should I—" Kisah broke off when she spotted me on the floor, and she looked to Emmory for guidance.

I slipped out of Hao's grasp, got to my feet, and was through the door before Kisah could say anything else, or anyone could

223

stop me. Scattering naval officers and BodyGuards as I plowed through them, I grabbed Admiral Hassan by the throat and slammed her into the opposite wall.

"Did you know about all this?" I pressed my gun to her temple.

Emmory skidded to a stop behind me but didn't grab me, probably for fear of the gun going off. My finger was on the trigger and I was a heartbeat away from pulling the damn thing.

My BodyGuards brought their weapons up and aimed them at the stunned naval officers in the hallway. Emmory's command was steady, uncompromising, and slid into my bones, giving them some of their strength back. "I'm going to say this exactly once: Anyone who is not the Empress of Indrana or one of her BodyGuards will keep their hands well away from their weapons."

"Hail, let her go." Emmory issued the request to me over our *smati*.

I backed up a step and Zin holstered his own gun, reaching past me to relieve Admiral Hassan of her sidearm. He gave my arm a reassuring squeeze on the way by.

"Admiral, inside." Emmory gestured at the door. "The rest of you wait here. Zin?"

"I got it," he said, handing the admiral's gun over to Jasa and moving to disarm the other officers in the hallway.

I followed Inana back into the room. Fasé hadn't moved from her spot on the couch arm and she gave me a sad smile when I met her golden gaze.

"Majesty, I don't know what's going on." Admiral Hassan's eyes were wide, confused fear grappling across their surface. Her voice, however, was calm, with only the slightest tremor in my title echoing the look in her eyes.

"Your little brother"—I snarled the words, the guttural fury in them making her flinch—"murdered my *entire* family!"

Old pain surfaced in her eyes and I watched her swallow as she chose her next words carefully. "Majesty, my little brother has been dead for twenty-eight years." Inana's gaze slid toward Emmory, a plea for intervention or information. "I don't know what you're asking of me."

Emmory pointed at the image of Janesh on the wall.

"No," Inana said. "This isn't possible. Where was this taken?"

Johar retold the story. Inana pressed a hand to her mouth, the other arm wrapping around her waist. Her grief and horror were real and I felt the first stinging sharpness of guilt worming its way past my own pain.

"Your Imperial Majesty." Inana dropped to her knees at my feet. "On behalf of my family I beg your forgiveness for this awful deed. I didn't know he was still alive. I didn't know what he was planning. We haven't spoken since the day the *Shiva's Creation* left port." She bowed her head. "I understand if you can't believe me and will offer my resignation and submit myself into your custody."

I stared down at her bent head, emotions warring behind my façade of cool consideration. I wanted to trust her, wanted to forgive her for something she wasn't involved in. Inana had been one of my closest advisors this whole time, one of the few people I felt I could trust. I couldn't have been so wrong, couldn't possibly have read her deception as loyalty simply because I wanted it so much.

The part of me that had kept me alive for so many years— through gunrunners and assassins—whispered that this was part of Wilson's plan. Get me to trust and then rip it all away.

Or worse, Inana really didn't know about all this and Wilson was hoping that I'd kill her anyway. My gun was still in my hand and I fought to keep it pointed at the ground.

He thought he erased his tracks, baby.

Out of nowhere, Portis's gentle voice smoothed over shattered nerves and grief. He was right. Wilson had been meticulous in covering his tracks from the moment he disappeared. Every move he'd made was one of careful precision designed to wipe Janesh from the fabric of the universe so that there wasn't any way to trace who he was now to who he had been. He wouldn't have been so stupid as to confide his plan to his older sister and leave her alive. Leave her as a witness to his deeds.

He'd screwed up. Hadn't known about Rai's determination to get his money from a mod shop. He wouldn't have expected to be spotted by a girl and that Rai would save his image for all these years just waiting for his chance at payback.

I exhaled and holstered my gun. Putting my hand on Inana's head, my fingers sank into the twists gathered at the base of her neck. "I believe you and there's nothing to forgive. I'm sorry for doubting you, sorry for—"

Admiral Hassan's shoulders shook as the tears came. I moved away, letting Emmory drop to a knee at her side to comfort her, and swallowed down my own tears.

Fasé slipped her hand into mine. "She hasn't betrayed you, ma'am, but you know that already. Don't feel guilty over a perfectly natural reaction. At least this time you didn't kill her."

"This time?"

Fasé smiled. "It's still hard for me to figure out which future I'm seeing is ours and which belongs to some other choice. I'm not very good at this yet."

"You'll get better?"

"Possibly, it's hard to tell." She dropped one eyelid in a slow wink.

"Are we going to win this?"

She laughed, the sound like a bell that chased the grief from the air. "Don't ask me silly questions, Majesty. It doesn't work like a database you can just pull information from when convenient."

"Does Major Morri know yet?"

Fasé gave me a look, her sweet face surprisingly cold for a moment. "She does not. It's none of her concern."

"I don't have to be able to see the future to know that's going to cause a problem at some point," I said. "I don't want you to ruin your life for me, Fasé. That's not how this works."

"This from the woman who was prepared to die with me," Fasé countered dryly. "We're past protesting the choices we made. You and I both know we'll do whatever is necessary." She reached up and pressed her free hand over my heart. "We are linked, all of us. You've always lived your life that way. The rest of us got dragged into your orbit, but we're happy to be here."

Warmth wrapped around my heart, spreading outward and chasing the last of the pain away. The words stuck in my throat, so I pulled Fasé into a tight hug, pressing my cheek into her red curls. "Thank you," I murmured.

As we separated I saw Emmory help Inana to her feet. The admiral wiped the tears from her face and gave my *Ekam* a small smile. She straightened her shoulders and looked in my direction.

"Majesty, your fleet is here and we are ready to escort you home."

I gave her a nod. "I'm ready to go home, Admiral. Let's move this affair somewhere with a bit more room."

As we moved into the hallway, Zin and the others were already handing weapons back. I took Inana's sidearm from Jasa and handed it over.

"The information learned just now does not go any further. I will kill anyone who breathes a word of it. Is that understood?"

There were murmurs of assent from the assembled officers.

"Admiral Fon and I have worked up a plan, Majesty. I sent it ahead to Admiral Dewan so she'd have time to look at it before we got here. We think it will work. I've got the bulk of the fleet out of the system so Shul can't get a good count of our forces."

"I gave Caspel the order," I said over our *smati*. *"With any luck Shul will be dead before we even get to Pashati."*

Inana nodded once.

We passed through a patch of sunlight cast through the wide windows from the rising sun. I frowned at the red mark on Inana's uniform, my brain taking entirely too long to recognize it for what it was as time slowed to a crawl.

The shot obliterated the window, spraying us with glass, and tore through Admiral Hassan's chest. Everything snapped back into speed. Emmory grabbed me, jerking me out of the sunlight and away from Inana as she fell to the floor.

22

hooter! On the roof, next building over." Zin was already on the com shouting orders.

Johar leapt to her feet and exited gracefully through the ruined window, disappearing from sight. Hao rolled his eyes and followed Zin's more sane path down the hallway and to the stairs for the next level. I desperately wanted to follow but I knew there was no way Emmory was letting go of me.

Admiral Fon scrambled forward on her hands and knees, pressing both hands to the bloody mess of Inana's chest. "Captain Poole, call medical. Get someone here on the double! Inana, damn you, don't die on me."

I reached for Inana's outstretched hand. "Hang on," I whispered. "Emmory, where is Major Morri?"

"I don't know. I've already called her, Majesty. Keep your head down." His fingers were in my hair, pressing against my scalp, holding me down and away from the line of fire.

Inana convulsed, her fingers tightening around mine, and Admiral Fon swore.

"No, don't you dare," I snapped. "That's an order, Admiral. You stay alive."

"Let her go, Majesty." Fasé crawled past me, staying below the level of the windowsill, and untangled my fingers from Inana's. She was a bubble of calm in the chaos, her pixie face serene as she pushed Admiral Fon away and pressed her own hands into Inana's blood-soaked chest.

I couldn't understand a single word Fasé recited in the sing-song Farian language. Calm washed over me, my panic easing at the sound.

"Fasé!" Major Morri sprinted down the hallway, dropping to her knees at Emmory's hissed warning. "You must not."

Fasé spat something in Farian that made the already fair-skinned Dio pale even more. Inana arched her back, dragging in a huge breath, and Fasé slumped onto her heels.

"You can do the rest," she said, wiping a bloodstained hand against her temple.

"You should not have—"

"Don't argue with me, Dio. She's still in dangerous territory and we need her alive."

Major Morri gaped but then nodded and put her hands where Fasé's had been. She murmured the traditional benediction under her breath and moments later Inana's eyes opened.

I scooted closer, reaching out with a smile. "Welcome back."

"I was—" Her eyes flew to Fasé, who winked.

"You were," she said.

I leaned a hip against the table as Gita finished picking slivers of glass out of my face. She handed me a cloth and I scrubbed away the remnants of the blood on my face and hands.

Fasé brushed a hand over my face as she passed me, and the little rush of healing rolled through me. Major Morri followed her, a frown permanently etched into her face, but she didn't say a word.

At least, not until the door closed, and then she started railing at Fasé in Farian while the rest of us watched and Gita murmured a broken translation from my right side.

"You are making things worse for yourself, Fasé. Defying the gods themselves will lead to—sorry, Majesty, I don't know that phrase." Gita frowned and tilted her head to the side as she listened.

"I suspect it's something along the lines of *epic shitstorm*," I whispered, and Gita choked down a laugh.

"The major said: We must go to the Pedalion now before it's too late." Gita listened as Fasé responded. "I'm not beholden to them. There are bigger things at work here. I can see now. We'll go after, but I will follow this through and you cannot stop me." Gita frowned as Fasé continued. "I don't know what she's saying, ma'am."

The pair of Farians stared at each other. I arched an eyebrow upward when Major Morri sighed and nodded her head. There'd been a definite power shift between them and I now had the impression that the major was no longer the ranking Farian in the room.

"Are you going to share with us?" I asked Fasé.

She smiled at me. "Gita got the bits you'd understand. I did not realize your Farian was so good, but we should practice. It will come in handy later." Gita nodded and Fasé rubbed her hands together. "I believe Major Morri understands the importance of the situation."

"I'm still not sure I do."

Fasé laughed at me. "It's all right, Majesty. You will." She patted my shoulder. "I need to go lie down." She left the room.

Major Morri stared at the door, her frown now more worried than upset.

"Is there something I need to know that she's not telling me?"

"She's apparently told you more than me." Dio shook herself and met my gaze. "My apologies; it is complicated, Majesty. I confess I don't understand a lot of it myself. I should send a message home, but—" She broke off, looking back at the door, and sighed. "Fasé has always gone her own way. I guess I shouldn't be surprised."

"But you are."

"I am." She nodded. "I won't lie, Majesty. This, whatever it is, carries potentially massive consequences. Consequences not only for Fasé and myself, but for you, for Indrana; possibly even for the whole of Faria. I have not seen someone with this power for an age; she barely tired herself out with Admiral Hassan."

Dio gestured at Emmory. "She brought your *Ekam* back from the dead and is still as sane as the day I met her. And now she can *see*. That doesn't happen to someone as old as she is.

"My personal feelings for Fasé make me worry for her, but she's right and I can't interfere with what may be the will of the gods."

I couldn't stop my eyebrows from shooting upward, and Dio laughed.

"I know your feelings on the subject of gods, Majesty. But trust me, the Farian gods are not quite so intangible an idea as yours may be."

I was saved from coming up with an inoffensive reply by the arrival of Zin, Hao, and Johar. All three shook their heads and I muttered a curse.

"They're good," Johar said, dropping into a chair and swinging a leg up over the arm of it. "Found the perch but barely any track to follow."

"Admiral Hassan?"

"They took her to the hospital to check her out," I replied.

"She's not dead?" Hao's incredulity was echoed by Johar. Zin seemed unsurprised, most likely because Emmory had already told him.

"Fasé," I said.

Johar chuckled and shook her head. "That Farian is handy to have around."

"If I die, let me stay dead." Hao disagreed, poking me with a finger. "No offense, *Ekam*."

"None taken," Emmory replied. "Zin, get a team together. I want that shooter found."

"We'll go with you," Hao said, and Johar nodded.

I touched a hand to Major Morri's arm. "Are you going to be all right?"

"I'll survive, Majesty. Thank you." Her wan smile didn't match her reassuring words, but I let her go without protest and turned back to Emmory.

"I know you're not going to let me outside right now, but as soon as it's safe I want to go to the hospital."

"Let's go look at that information about Wilson again, Majesty. He knows more about us than we know about him. I want to change that. Johar, before you all take off, go get Bial and meet us at the empress's quarters."

"Sure." She hopped up.

I nodded in agreement and followed him from the room. We took a different route back to my rooms, one that avoided any windows. Lantle and Ikeki were at the door, bleary-eyed and out of uniform.

"Go back to sleep, you two," Emmory said, and they nodded.

"I'm going to change." I headed for the bedroom, closing the door behind me.

Alone in the room, I dropped onto the bed and pressed my shaking hands to my face. My tears were silent, leaking from between my fingers and dripping onto the floor.

I'd almost killed Inana. Then she'd died right there in front of me. And Janesh.

"No. His name is Wilson; Janesh died a long time ago." I took a deep breath and got to my feet.

Forward was the only way to go; every other path was a dead end.

I splashed water on my face and changed into fresh clothes. By the time I emerged into the main room, the others were gathered around a rapidly growing timeline projected on the wall.

"You look like you need a drink," Johar said.

"I'm not going to argue with you." I crossed to Zin's side and studied the information.

"Now that we know who Wilson is, it should be a lot easier to narrow down what request she refused that would have driven him to this," Zin said.

"You don't need to." I took the glass from Johar with a smile and sipped at it. "I know why."

No one said a word. I reached my free hand out and tapped on the beginning of the timeline. "Janesh died in 2983, but Wilson appeared as the head of a company in '67. Do you know what else happened in '67?"

No one spoke.

"My mother picked my father to be her husband." A tear slipped free and I brushed it away. "From a very short list of candidates: my father, Janesh, and three others. They used to joke about it." I forced myself to relax my grip on my glass before it shattered. "Janesh would tease my father whenever Dad complained about court. Say he was glad to have dodged that life." I drained my glass and set it carefully on the table. "She said no." I pressed my fingers to my mouth and squeezed my eyes shut, felt the tears leak out even though I tried to stop them.

When I opened them, everyone was watching me. This time I didn't wipe away the tears. "People we loved have died because of this man's hubris. Thousands of lives have been lost. A war fought.

"All because he couldn't take no for an answer. I am done with compromises and diplomacy. Wilson is going to die. I am going to be the one to kill him. If you have a problem with that, there's the door."

No one moved.

"Majesty." Bial went down on a knee. "I, Bialriarn Plantage Malik, give myself willingly to you, Hailimi Mercedes Jaya Bristol, Empress of Indrana. You are the shining star in the blackness of space. The hope of the lost and forsaken. The spark that must not be extinguished. I pledge my life and loyalty to you until you release me or death takes me."

The oath shocked me almost as much as the fact that his eyes were clear of hesitation over his decision.

"We are with you, Your Majesty, to the end of this and after," Emmory said, also going to a knee. The others followed, except for Johar and Hao. Johar just grinned at me.

Hao lifted his glass in salute. "I was with you long before this and will remain so."

My mind was already sorting through our options as we drove to the hospital that afternoon. Inana was alive, but would she be well enough to lead the fleet into battle? If not, Admiral Fon was Inana's second-in-command. The diminutive admiral had gone with her to the hospital before anyone could stop her. Thankfully our sniper didn't try to take a second shot on the heels of her first, and everyone made it there safely.

"Your Majesty." The girl at the desk bobbed an uncertain

curtsy and tossed nervous looks at the grim-faced BodyGuards around me. Gita and Cas were at my back, Kisah and Elizah on either side.

"We're here to see Admiral Hassan." Emmory spared the girl a brief smile and a raised eyebrow.

"Yes, of course. I'll call Dr. Hemdine."

Moments later a young man rushed through the doors, trying to smooth down black hair that refused to cooperate. He skidded to a stop, nearly colliding with Emmory, and his dark eyes went saucer-sized on his face. "My apologies, *Ekam*." He cleared his throat, then looked past Emmory to me. "Your Imperial Majesty." He started to extend a hand, thought better of it, and gave a little wave that was even more inappropriate.

I don't know how I managed to keep my face blank as I nodded. "Dr. Hemdine."

"How did you—" He glanced back at the receptionist. "Oh, right. Gatik Hemdine, Your Majesty. Chief heart surgeon."

"Is Inana going to need surgery?"

"No." He shook his head. "I was called in to consult when they brought Admiral Hassan in this morning. It was...odd."

The kid was so clearly nervous, but I was fast losing patience and I knew Emmory didn't want to be standing in one spot for much longer. "Farians were involved, Doctor, and mine seems to be odder than the norm. May I see my admiral?"

Gatik jumped as if he'd been stung. "Yes, sorry, Your Majesty. Farians explains it...sort of, I'm not sure. I'd like to show you the results of her scans first, if I may. I haven't shared them with Admiral Hassan."

"You may, though I suggest we move, Doctor. Before my *Ekam* gets restless."

"Yes, ma'am. Right this way." He waved us past the desk and

down the hallway. Emmory sent Lantle and Cas on ahead and the pair turned into the office on Dr. Hemdine's direction.

"Clear," Cas said. "No windows."

"You have five minutes, Doctor. Make them count."

Gatik swallowed and tapped a few spots on his desk, bringing a three-dimensional model of what I assumed was Inana's heart into the air. "Your Majesty, this is the scan we did of the admiral's heart when she was brought in."

"It looks good," I said. There was no name for the feeling rolling around in me. We'd come so close to losing her.

"It does. Too good. She was shot, Your Majesty."

"Yes." My voice was flat. "I was there."

Gatik bobbed his head in apology. "What I mean, ma'am, is there is a distinct difference between this tissue"—he reached out and traced a path around Inana's heart that covered the right atrium and the right pulmonary artery—"and the rest of her heart. All of this is new."

"New?"

Emmory was faster than the rest of us. "The shooter hit her right where he was aiming. He took a chunk out of her heart."

"Fasé said she wasn't dead." My voice echoed a little in the shocked silence.

"Technically she probably wasn't, Your Majesty," Gatik replied. "Brain death takes a few minutes. But Admiral Hassan was missing a sizable portion of her heart and Farians, to the best of my knowledge, cannot grow organs. They can't even repair damage of that magnitude in the time frame I'm hearing about."

"Is Inana going to be fine?"

"She *is* fine, Your Majesty. Better than, if the truth is known. That part of her heart is brand-new compared to the rest of it."

Gatik shook his head. "I'd like to speak with your Farian if it's possible."

"I doubt it will be."

"Majesty, the advancements we could make if she'd be willing to—"

"I'll mention it to her, but you know the Farians aren't willing to tell us how they heal humans, Doctor. This is even more unusual than that and I'm not going to—I can't force her to do anything she doesn't want to do." I softened the denial with a pat on his shoulder. "Even were she to agree to speak with you, I doubt you'd be able to understand her answers. You're going to have to chalk this up as a miracle and move on."

"I'd like to talk with Admiral Hassan now."

"Yes, ma'am." He gestured at the door. "She's three doors down and on the left."

"Emmory," I said, and followed my *Ekam* from the room.

Admiral Hassan was sitting on the edge of the hospital bed arguing with Admiral Fon when we reached her room. I leaned against the doorframe, arms crossed over my chest, and watched with interest.

"You need to rest, Inana."

Hassan sighed loudly. "I'm fine, Gerté, better than fine. I feel—" She groped for a word. "Alive."

"You shouldn't be," Admiral Fon countered, a frown carved deep into her forehead. "I saw that wound, Inana."

"I'm not going to argue with Fasé for saving me, if that's what you're getting at."

"I'm just saying, everything has a cost, a price. What will this—" Gerté broke off when she saw me and bowed. "Your Majesty."

"Admirals." I came into the room, reaching a hand out to

Inana and leaning in to press my cheek to hers. "I am glad to see you upright," I said, my voice thick with unshared feelings.

"It is preferable to a slab in the morgue."

Gerté huffed and crossed her arms.

"I am obviously interrupting something." I looked between them.

"She's worried for my immortal soul," Inana replied with a roll of her eyes. "It's an old argument, Majesty. One I won't bore you with. Dr. Hemdine has pronounced me fit to return to duty, haven't you, Doc?"

"There is nothing wrong with you now," Gatik replied. "I can't see a reason to keep you here."

"You'll ride back with us. Dr. Hemdine, I was told my Body-Guards were also brought to this hospital."

There was a pause as the doctor consulted his *smati*. Then he nodded. "Yes, Your Majesty. They're on the second floor."

"Can we spare a moment?" I asked Emmory over the com link, and he gave me a nod.

"Cas, take Elizah and Lantle up the stairs. Give me a sitrep on the rooms."

Cas nodded and left the room with the other two Body-Guards trailing behind him. Several minutes later Emmory got a report that pleased him, judging by the look on his face, and we headed up.

"Majesty."

"Do not get up." I stopped Iza with a hand before she could get out of bed. "Both of you."

Indula grinned at me. "Majesty."

"How are you?"

"Much better, ma'am. Thank you." He nodded, smothering a cough and shooting me a second grin.

"Is he behaving?" I asked Iza.

"Mostly, ma'am. He fusses about the treatments, but one of the nurses can get him to shut up."

"They have a nice voice," Indula muttered, sticking his tongue out at Iza. "And they read, unlike this savage. Majesty, please save me, I am trapped in here with no one intelligent to talk to."

Iza rolled her eyes, and the other BodyGuards chuckled. The banter between the pair had increased since their confinement together, and I shook my head as I smiled. I was going to miss them.

"Majesty, we should get moving," Emmory said.

"We'll see you again shortly." I leaned in and pressed my forehead to Iza's and then to Indula's.

"Good luck, Majesty."

"Stay safe."

Emmory and I headed for the door as the others said their hurried good-byes, and then we all went back downstairs and out the side exit to where Lantle waited with the car.

I'd just stepped out of the door when the shot came. Elizah crumpled, dead even before she slammed into me, knocking us away from the vehicle. Emmory swore, trying to cover me even as we fell.

I crashed shoulder first into the ground and rolled sideways before my *Ekam* could crush me. "Bugger me, I am tired of this," I muttered, looking up in the direction I thought the shot had come from.

The flash of something reflecting the setting sun caught my eye and I pulled my gun free as I scrambled to my feet and took off down the nearby alley.

I could hear Emmory shouting and switched off my com link before the yelling could start in over my *smati*. I was going to get in trouble for it, but I didn't let the thought slow my feet as I ran up the alley wall, catching the lip of it and hauling myself up the rest of the way.

I spotted the sniper, now running across the rooftops, and leapt from my perch to the next building over. I landed in a crouch and lined up a shot as the figure crossed the roof ahead of me. The sunlight was in my eyes and my shot snapped at the heels of the sniper. They swerved to the right behind a vent.

Pushing to my feet, I raced across the roof, keeping my eyes locked on my target as they sprinted from their hiding place a moment later. I followed, not slowing as the sniper leapt off the side of the building. The roof next door was lower, barely visible on the far side. I took the jump without hesitation, rolling to my feet and leveling my gun for another shot.

Before I could take it, Johar launched herself from behind a rooftop entrance and slammed into the sniper, sending them both rolling across the surface in a tangle of limbs.

I skidded to a halt, weapon at the ready as the pair grappled. The man grunted when Johar landed two sharp punches to his back, but he somehow managed to slide free of her choke hold before she could lock it down.

His uppercut connected with a crunch that made me wince, and Johar spit curses into the air along with her blood.

"Oh, you've done it now," I murmured as the sniper tried to scramble away. I fired a shot into the rooftop and he recoiled back into Johar's fury. "Don't kill him, Jo. I want to talk to him."

I heard the crunch of feet hitting the roof behind me but didn't look around.

"Majesty," Emmory said as he came up on my side.

"I know." I watched Johar grab the man's head and slam her forehead into his nose. "I'd apologize but we both know I'm not sorry. Elizah's dead, isn't she?"

"Yes."

I hadn't had the time to get to know the young woman now staring sightlessly up at Ashva's steadily darkening sky, and that made it somehow even worse. I couldn't hide my relief that the sniper hadn't instead targeted Cas, who'd been standing right next to Elizah.

Zin and Hao emerged from the same rooftop entrance.

Hao, spotting Johar still beating on the now-unconscious sniper, shot me a look. "Really?" He moved to separate them.

"Johar, I do need to be able to question him."

Hao dragged the sniper to his feet and over to me. He slid to the rooftop with a dull thud when Hao released him. His head lolled back to reveal a face with sharp cheekbones and a short beard. Johar wiped the blood from her face with her sleeve and started frisking him, tossing the weaponry into a pile several feet away.

"We went to a lot of trouble to keep Emmory alive, Majesty," Zin said as he holstered his weapon. "It seems a waste for you to give him a heart attack by running over rooftops after a killer."

"He wouldn't have killed me."

"No, but gravity might have," Hao muttered, glancing over the edge and shuddering.

I studied the unconscious man at my feet. "Both times he could have taken me out, but he shot the person near me instead. Wilson wants me alive so he can kill me himself."

Emmory's inhale was audible, as was his deliberate exhale. "Lantle's here with the vehicle. I'll get Her Majesty to the transport if you'll clean up here?"

Zin nodded. "We'll be right behind you."

"Wait," I said, putting a hand on Emmory's arm. I knew I

was pushing my luck, but I was relatively sure the danger was past. "I want to question him."

"We're going to do that, back at the safety of the mansion."

"I have a plan." My look to Hao for support was pleading, and wasted as it turned out.

"Don't look at me for backup," he said. "I came up the stairs, like a sane person."

"Shut up."

Emmory started to protest, sighed, and gave me the Look. "What do you need us to do, Majesty?"

"Just stand there and look menacing." I looked at Johar. "Is he clean?"

"Yup."

"Did you ever run the skull game?"

Johar's eyes lit up in delight. "It's been a while, but I love that one." She looked around. "We don't have anything to fake the drop with, though."

"I know. I'll work around it."

Johar grinned. "I'll just follow your lead, then."

I gestured at our sniper. "Get him up."

She hauled him upright, shaking him until he groaned. I crossed to the edge of the building, the three men silent shadows in my wake.

Johar locked her fist in the sniper's shirt and lifted him over the edge so his feet were dangling in the air. "I would not squirm too much," she said as he regained consciousness and clutched at her arm. "And pray you paid enough for this shirt."

"Who are you?" I asked.

One of his eyes was swollen shut, but the other flicked to me and then to the men behind me. "Kin Simon."

"What's Wilson paying you to kill the people around me?"

He didn't answer and I sighed.

"Look, I'm not in a good mood. You killed one of my Body-Guards. A very sweet girl whose little sister I'm going to have to face when I get home. And you shot my admiral."

"I killed your admiral."

I let the grin spread over my face. "Admiral Hassan is a bit sore and rather pissed off, but very much alive."

"That's impossible."

"I'm very good at impossible," I said, pleased with the confused terror on his face. "Now, did Wilson give you a list of targets or were you just randomly picking and shooting?"

Kin swallowed, glancing past my shoulder at Emmory again. "I was given a list, but he said it didn't matter who I killed as long as I made sure they were standing next to you when I did it and as long as I killed these two last." He pointed at Emmory and Zin.

Fury was a living thing in my gut, but I wrestled it under control and stared the sniper down.

"I hope he paid you up front. You had to have known this wasn't going to end well for you."

"He did. I put it in a savings account for my family."

I swore internally but kept my face expressionless.

Johar was not so immovable and her face twisted with rage. "I'm going to hunt your family down and light them on fire one by one."

Kin wasn't moved by her threat. "She won't let you. I've heard the stories, but I don't believe them."

"You probably should have," I said. "Drop him. We'll recover whatever we can from his *smati* after we pick it out of the mess on the street."

"Wait!" Kin scrabbled at Johar's arm. "I can get you into the palace."

Putting my hand on Johar's shoulder, I looked Kin in the eye. "I take my hand off her and you go for real. Why would I need your help to get into *my* palace? I know the place inside and out. Those usurpers inside couldn't hope to find even half the passages in the time they've been in there."

"They won't have to. They'll ping your *smatis* the second you get within range."

Johar glanced back at me with a look that very clearly said: *Can I drop him now?*

I shook my head and mulled over the information. If he was telling the truth it was going to be all but impossible to get into the palace without being seen. We could try to modify Rai's cloaking device to get us past whatever sensors the palace was sure to have. However, if this guy had a better way in, it was worth it to at least see what it was.

"How do you know this? I'm pretty sure Wilson didn't share his genius plan with a hired assassin."

"I'm a professional, Majesty. I did my research when I took the job and made sure I had something to cover my ass when things went south." Kin's laugh was ragged. "I know people who know things."

"What a bloody load of rot," Johar said. "Can I just drop him? My arm's getting tired."

"Hush," I replied. "I'm going to need a name, Kin, before I'm at all inclined to keep you alive."

"Shanja Kaif. She works in the maintenance department. She was working on a repair in the south wing when Eha Phanin came into the room next door. He was having a conversation with Admiral Shul about you and told the admiral not to worry about trying to keep track of you. He said they had that covered and your *smatis* would be targeted the second you got close to the palace. They're counting on you to try to break in."

"That plan to nuke the palace from orbit is sounding better all the time," Hao muttered.

"It really is," I agreed, and spotted the way Kin's jaw tightened. "Something to say?"

"You wouldn't bomb your own people, Majesty."

"Everyone seems to think they know me," I replied. "We're done here."

"Majesty, please."

"Now it's *please*? You shot my people, Kin. You should have done a bit more research into what I do to people who kill the ones I care about." I took my hand off Johar's shoulder and walked away.

23

The mood back at the mansion was somber. I waved Stasia off when she offered me chai, ignoring her concerned frown and continuing to clean out the dirt from under my nails with Johar's knife. I had tried to return it to her but she'd refused and told me to keep it. The sheath she'd unstrapped now had a home around my leg.

She, Hao, and Zin had stayed behind to collect Kin's *smati* while the rest of us returned to the relative safety of the mansion. The admirals had already returned and were deep in a heated discussion on the other side of the room.

Dailun dropped into a chair next to me. "Hao had me go over the ship again to see if he and Gita missed anything. Everything is clean, *jiejie*. It will get us to your home without them being the wiser about the cargo."

"Good."

"I am sorry about Elizah. She was nice." He reached out and put a hand on my arm. "You did her justice. It was the right thing to do."

I didn't look at him. "I find myself caring less about right these days and more about just ending this."

"With all due respect to my cousin, blowing up your palace is a rather dramatic gesture."

"It is." I sighed. "It would put a pretty definitive end to this, though."

"At what cost?" Dailun shook his head. "It is unlike you to be so rash. Do not let his rage infect your heart and make you act without thought."

"His rage infected my whole family, killed the man I loved, and ruined my life. It's a little late for keeping it out of my heart."

Dailun smiled. "It's only a danger if you let it rule you."

"Majesty, will you come take a look at this?" Admiral Hassan called from the far side of the room, and Dailun followed me, peeking over my shoulder at the image floating over the table.

"Given that Admiral Shul knows we're here, there's only a few options open for bringing the fleet to Pashati," she said. "We can drive all the ships straight at them, sending the *Vajrayana* out in front to catch them off guard. Or we can split the fleet and send half around the system to come at Pashati from the night side."

"They both have problems, Majesty," Admiral Fon said. "The first gives Shul plenty of time to get sensor data on our fleet and prepare accordingly. We can't forget he has *Vajrayana* ships also."

"They're good ships, Admiral, but they're not magic. Besides, he's only got three. We've got a lot more."

Gerté frowned at my remark but continued. "If we split the fleet the problem is obviously that we're splitting it. We don't know if he has ships hiding out in the system somewhere, or if something goes wrong with one group or the other. There's a lot of variables."

Dailun tapped a point on the hologram just outside Pashati. "Why not just warp in here?"

The surprised exclamations and cursing from the assembled naval officers allowed me to cover my laughter with a cough.

"Young man, you do not warp one ship let alone a whole fleet into that close a proximity to a planet," Gerté said. "The unmitigated disaster that would happen if someone calculated wrong! You could fly the ship right into the planet."

Dailun seemed offended. "Only if you're a terrible pilot." Then he remembered his manners and bowed, keeping his eyes on her. "With respect, Admiral. It is more than possible to do when the proper precautions are taken. I can show your navigators and your pilots the way to fly."

"You know, he may be onto something."

"Inana," Gerté protested. "Be serious."

"I am. Not the whole fleet, but what if we kept a third of it behind? They'll stay hidden out of the system so Shul won't have accurate data. Then they warp in after we've already engaged his ships in battle. We'll grind them to dust between us."

"We can't risk a third of the fleet."

"It is not difficult. I promise," Dailun said. "Watch." He grabbed some glasses off the bar. "*Jiejie*, will you stand on the opposite side of the table?"

I moved. Dailun took up position by the image of Pashati that was floating above the table. "You warp in here, above or below the planet." He held the glass up away from Pashati and then put it on the table below. It was a decent distance away from the planet, but still unnervingly close for the naval officers. "You have your navigation fixed away from the planet so that moment you come out of warp, you do this."

He slid the glass across the table at me in an arc. I caught it and set it to the side.

Dailun repeated the gesture. "You do this with each ship on a five-minute delay. It gives everyone enough time to get out of the way."

"You'll need to draw Shul's ships away from the planet so we don't risk a collision there," I said as I caught the last glass he slid to me.

Inana nodded. "We can handle that. He's not going to sit right next to Pashati and fight us. The man's a traitor, but he's not an idiot."

"What about the orbital defenses?" Gerté asked. She still sounded skeptical, but her look was thoughtful. "The ships that are coming in are going to be well inside the OD's range, and they won't be able to defend against that kind of firepower."

"We're going to need to go in first," I replied without hesitation. "Give us eighteen hours. We'll have control of the orbital defenses just like Fenna did here by the time you guys are ready to warp in."

Inana stared at me. "It's a waste of my breath to try to argue with you, isn't it, Majesty?"

I smiled. "We all knew I was going to the planet surface the moment he killed Clara. Now that I know who he is, it's only more certain. I'm going to end him. I'm sorry. I know he's your brother, but—"

"My brother died a long time ago, Majesty," Inana replied. "This monster was born in his place and I will rejoice with you when it is dead."

I nodded at her. "As long as we're all on the same page. We're headed for Pashati tomorrow."

"How is he?"

Tefiz shook her head. "Not good, Majesty. The doctor has asked for permission to move him to the hospital."

I nodded as we headed down the stairs to the holding cells in the mansion. "Approved. I want him in a locked wing and guards on the main doors as well as the door to his room."

Tefiz held the door for me. "We'll be just outside, ma'am."

I walked down the corridor alone. The wing was empty except for the cell at the end where Trace was being held. I could hear the sounds of violent retching, and the sour smell of bile stained the air.

Trace was on his knees, his head resting on the edge of the toilet, and a surprising surge of pity blossomed in my chest.

"Did you come to say 'I told you so'?" he asked.

I leaned against the plasti-glass front of his cell. "I'm not sure gloating is helpful."

"It wouldn't make me feel any worse," he said, flopping onto his back and looking up at me. "I'm pretty sure I'm dying, Haili."

"You might be." I slid down to the floor and wrapped my arms around my legs. "What were you thinking, Trace? Rock? Of all the shit you could have picked."

"You sound like my mother." He covered his face with his arm. "We had the biggest fight before I left for Red Cliff. She found out. She was furious." He rubbed at his chin and turned his head to look at me. "I can't blame her. I fucked up. Ruined my life, the lives of my people, because all I could think about was the next hit. Though let's be honest, I was a terrible king and not just because of the drugs."

"Wilson picked you, Trace. He used you."

"I know that now. To be honest I'm not sure it would have made any difference if I'd known that then. I spent a lot of time even before my father died enjoying the perks of being a prince. He knew exactly what my weakness was." He offered up a wry smile. "And at the time I was so angry about my father's death, Haili. All I wanted was to see Indrana pay for it."

"It's what Wilson wanted, too." I leaned my head back against the wall. "You said you knew something about him, before on the ship. What was it?"

"I was—" He rubbed at his face and shook his head. "I'm sorry, Hail. I don't know. This drug, it makes you—everything gets out of order," he whispered. "I'm sorry. I know it means shit, but I am."

"I know," I replied, but couldn't find it in my heart to forgive him.

"Come in." I wiped the tears from my face with the heel of my hand as the door opened and Emmory slipped inside. "Did you know Elizah was a dancer before she joined the Guard?" I asked, closing out the file I'd been reading. "I wonder why she stopped."

"She applied for the Guard several years before you came home. When I interviewed her she just said it was a more stable source of income than the dancing had been. We didn't talk about it beyond that."

"We shouldn't have gone to the hospital."

"Majesty—"

"I'm serious, Emmy. I should have thought that through better. Should have realized that he'd be out there waiting. I knew that wasn't some random taking a shot at us." I thumped my fist into my chest and looked up at the ceiling. "I fucked up and that girl's dead because of me."

"It was her job, Majesty. It's my job and Cas's job. Every BodyGuard you have knows the risks. We swore an oath to keep you safe."

"Where in that oath does it say you should die from random gunshots?" I snapped.

"You just said yourself it wasn't random." Emmory shook his

head. "Wilson wants to hurt you and he'll do it the best way—by going through us." He crouched by my chair. "And we're fine with that, as long as you're still standing to finish this and you're still standing at the end. We're fine with it."

"You'd better hope one of you is alive with me at the end, or I'm going to have Fasé bring Wilson back and I'll spend the rest of my life killing him."

Emmory chuckled, the deep rumbling traveling through the air. "I don't doubt it, Majesty. Let's hope for all our sakes that doesn't happen."

I forced a smile, keeping my fears buried deep and hoping that Emmory wouldn't spot them lurking behind my eyes. If I was the last woman standing at the end of this, I wouldn't be the winner and we all knew it.

"So, what do you want?" I asked, getting up out of my chair to pace the confines of the room.

"I put a call in to Caspel. I thought it would be a good idea to talk to him before we leave."

"I've got some questions for Toropov," I said. "Mostly revolving around how we're not going to get blown out of the sky before we can land. Plus we should probably tell him we have Trace in custody, huh?"

The chime of an incoming message rang out from the nearby console. I dropped back into my seat and Emmory hit the receive button after a nod from me.

"Caspel."

"*Ekam*. Majesty." Caspel gave me a nod. "Sorry for the delayed welcome back to the system."

I laughed. "We've all been a bit busy. How are you holding up?"

"Well enough, ma'am. Looking forward to your return."

"Can I talk to Ambassador Toropov?"

"I'm afraid not, Majesty." Caspel shook his head. "He escaped to the palace a week ago. Or at least that's what he told Phanin." His grin was wicked. "Jaden is going to convince them that Saxony is still a viable ally, especially with Trace taken out of the equation."

"Speaking of that…" I grinned at him. "I may have captured Trace."

"What?" Caspel blinked at me in obvious shock, and I didn't stop my grin from spreading wider. I'd surprised my taciturn intelligence director, and that was an impressive feat. "Sorry, Majesty. Where is he?"

"Currently he's in a holding cell in the medical center going through withdrawal."

Caspel's laugh was incredulous. "I'm terrified to even ask what happened, Majesty, or how you accomplished that."

"It's a long story, I'll tell you when we get on the ground. Can we trust Toropov?" I asked. "It seems like he's playing all the angles he can get here."

Caspel dipped his head. "I won't argue that, Majesty. He's looking out for his country. I admire the loyalty in what is a difficult situation. But he's genuine and he likes you." He grinned and lifted a shoulder when I raised an eyebrow. "The plan to go to Phanin was to give the Saxon courier ship an excuse to show up on the scanners. Once you're in the atmosphere you can divert to these coordinates and we'll meet up."

Emmory nodded when he received the file and I gave Caspel a brief smile. "We'll see you soon then."

"Shiva willing. Stay safe, Majesty."

"You, too." I disconnected, staring off at the wall as I drummed my fingers against the console top.

"What is it, Majesty?"

"Nothing. Nerves, I guess." I shook myself. "I'm assuming you have the list of who's going with us locked down?"

"I do. Stasia isn't happy about being left behind again."

"I don't blame her."

"Fasé handled it. Major Morri will be coming along so we'll have a Farian for each team. Johar wants to bring Bial. I told her that I'd talk with you about it."

"He did swear his loyalty to me. I can't think of a reason not to bring him. Did she say why?"

"Honestly?" Emmory laughed. "I was afraid to ask, it's almost like he's her new pet."

"It's Johar." I choked on my own laugh. "I wouldn't put it past her. Can we think of a reason not to take him? He's a good shot, will be helpful in the palace, and I'm reasonably sure he's not going to flip sides and betray us."

"I agree," he said.

"Do you know where Zin is? I want to go over everything we have on Wilson, see if we can't figure out his weaknesses."

"I'll go get him." Emmory left me alone and I leaned back in the chair, stretching my arms over my head. Emmory came back with not only Zin but Hao and Gita as well.

"Let's lay him all out here," I said. "I want to know this bastard inside and out before we head for home."

24

It was past midnight when we boarded the Saxon vessel—
Avangr. I went straight to sleep, but my dreams were crowded
with my parents' faces and I woke up ill-tempered and edgy in
the tiny crew quarters. The dim blue lighting ghosted around
the ceiling, hiding the pale washed-out features of the diplomatic ship. Saxon ships were always a strange off-white inside
and though I couldn't explain why, the color made me uneasy.

Fasé was there, perched on the bunk across from me. "What
is it about being trapped that scares you?"

"What?"

"The few times I've felt your heart skip it's usually when
you're closed in." She tipped her head to the side, her red curls
slipping down to curtain half her face. With the lighting, she
looked even more alien. "What happened?

"You don't know?"

Fasé gave me a look. "It was in the past, Majesty."

"I got trapped under the palace as a girl. It was dark and I
couldn't move. It was terrifying. I thought I was going to die.
Why are you asking me this?"

"You will need to master it."

My eyebrows went up and I laughed. It was loud in the silence. "Fasé, I'm almost forty, it's a little late for that, don't you think?"

"I would if it didn't mean the difference between your end and your beginning." Her voice was sharp as a knife, and the cut of it had me wincing. "Shul is dead."

"How do you—" I cut the question off at her smile and rubbed my hands over my face. "Bugger me, I was hoping that would happen a little closer to our arrival."

"They saw the opening and had to take it." She lifted a shoulder and stared dreamily at a spot on the ceiling. "They may still survive. I hope so. It would be helpful."

Sliding from the bunk, I wiggled into my pants and tucked in the black tank before I tugged the sweater over my head. "What time is it?"

"05:00, we're an hour away from Pashati. They've had us on the scanners for a while now, but it seems like Toropov's ruse is holding up."

"Is he going to be in danger when we don't land where we're supposed to?"

"Possibly." Fasé hopped down and crossed to the door. "However, he's an old man and exceedingly tricky. I suspect he'll be fine." She tapped the panel and the door slid open just as Gita was about to knock. "Next."

"Majesty?"

Fasé slipped by Gita, her laughter dancing on the air behind her as she headed down the corridor.

"Don't mind her. Come in." I waved Gita in and sat on the edge of the bunk to put my boots on.

"With respect, ma'am. She's getting weirder by the day."

"Be thankful she's not sitting around watching you sleep," I replied. "What did you need?"

"I was thinking about Wilson, ma'am, and how Cas pointed out that he seems uncontrolled whenever he's speaking with you."

I stood up. "Keep going, we're headed for the bridge."

"Use that against him. If you push him enough he'll crack. I don't think it will take much."

"I wouldn't call someone who's spent the last thirty-odd years trying to bring down my empire uncontrolled."

Gita smiled. "You are ruining his plans. His carefully laid, exquisitely detailed plans. Wilson *is* controlled, but not around you because you remind him of everything he should have had and didn't get when your mother said no."

The courier ship was cramped, better suited for a crew of eight to ten people than our nineteen women and men; I could hear the Marines in the small open area by the exit hatch as Gita and I hit the open stairway.

I took the stairs two at a time up toward the second level of the ship.

"He's had all the time in the world to put this together, and now it's unraveling under his feet. You're more intelligent and more focused. You're not carrying around that same fury."

"He murdered my family, Gita. I think it's safe to say I'm pretty angry."

"You're angry, ma'am, and rightfully so. However, most of it is new and fresh and hasn't eaten you alive. You're too self-possessed for that. Maybe if you spent the same amount of time Wilson has consumed by jealousy and revenge you'd lose it the same way. But your advantage is that pain. It's giving you an edge that hasn't been lost to madness yet."

Gita stopped me with a hand on my arm before I could open the door to the bridge. "We all know this is going to end with a showdown between the two of you. As your BodyGuards we should interfere, but we won't. Not even Emmory will take this away from you. Just remember that you have the advantage. You already have what he wants."

"I will." I opened the door and came face-to-face with a nervous Ikeki.

"Majesty." My BodyGuard bowed her head.

"Breathe before you pass out," I said with a smile, tipping the blonde's face back up to meet my eyes. "You're going to do fine." I resisted the urge to tease her that we'd all die if she couldn't convince the orbital defense that she was Saxon. She was tense enough as it was.

"Majesty," Emmory said with a nod. "We're almost ready here."

I joined Hao where he was leaning on the far side of the bridge out of the range of the console cameras.

Dailun got up from the console so Lantle could take over flying the *Avangr* and crouched out of sight.

Ikeki fidgeted in the Saxon uniform until Emmory cleared his throat. She straightened her shoulders and nodded. "I'm ready."

"Good," Lantle said, "because they're hailing us."

Emmory patted her shoulder and slipped through the doorway. Everyone held their breath as the face of an officer with Pashati Orbital Defense came on the screen.

"Please identify yourself," the young woman said.

"Courier vessel *Avangr*. Lieutenant Helga Osweilen. We are here at the request of Ambassador Toropov."

"You are expected, Lieutenant," the officer said after a moment. "Please proceed to coordinates 28.617227 by 77.208116. I am sending them to you now. Do not deviate from this course. You will be met by an escort once you have cleared the atmosphere."

"Thank you," Ikeki said, trying to make her Indranan as

accented as possible. The woman simply gave her a sharp nod and disconnected.

"My turn." Dailun slid into his seat again. "Coming up on Pashati's atmosphere," Dailun said. "Preparing for reentry."

I spotted the glimmer of Shul's fleet—or whoever they'd picked to replace him—as Dailun turned the ship and we started down through Pashati's atmosphere; so many ships, so many lives that were soon going to be over.

"Do we have a plan here?" Hao asked. "They're going to expect us to land at the palace, and for obvious reasons that's a bad idea."

"Hush." I elbowed him. "Of course we have a plan. Caspel's working on it."

"Incoming message, *jiejie*."

"Put them on audio only," I said.

"Saxon vessel, you will proceed to the landing docks at the palace. Deviate from that path and we will blow you out of the sky."

"Acknowledged," Ikeki replied.

"I'm talking to Caspel now," Emmory said. "He's got it covered. Once you're at the coordinates we talked about, Dailun, drop low and hit the throttle. They'll take care of the rest on the ground."

"Okay," he said. "Everyone brace for reentry."

The *Avangr* sliced through Pashati's atmosphere. Snow blanketed the terrain beneath us, broken at the edges by golden strips of sand banked against the hard blue of the frozen ocean waves.

Dailun banked us hard to the left and hit the engines to full power as soon as we leveled out. I could imagine the angry swearing that was happening in the cockpits behind us as the two fighters gave chase.

"Emmory, I don't mean to be pushy, but they're lining up

shots on us." Hao's voice was calm as the ship shook. "Back shields at eighty-seven percent." We shook again. "Sixty-four."

"We're almost there. Dailun, can you see the landing area?"

"Your faith in me is astounding, *Ekam*."

I choked on my terrified laughter as the tiny landing spot came up in the window. Emmory really was banking on the skills of a pilot he'd only known a short time. The *Avangr* shook a third time and then a fourth.

"Shields at twenty-two percent."

"Now, Caspel." Emmory gave the command out loud. "Set us down, Dailun."

"Everyone brace yourselves." I locked my fingers into the back of Dailun's chair and seconds later the floor dropped out from underneath us. Gravity kicked in when Dailun cut the thrusters and we plummeted away from the Indranan fighters toward the ground.

"Someone on the ground is firing on the fighters," Hao reported, his voice ridiculously calm.

"*Yatta,*" Dailun hissed, slamming his hand back down on the thrusters, and we jerked to a stop. He brought the ship down the last few hundred meters. "Landing gear out." We settled to the ground for good, and a collective exhale filled the bridge.

"Great job," Hao said, reaching out and slapping Dailun on the back.

I ruffled his hair as I got to my feet. "Second that. Thanks for keeping us all alive."

"Majesty, let's go," Emmory said.

"Those fighters are smoking ruins."

He shook his head at Hao. "They are, but this ship is too visible. Caspel is waiting with transportation. We need to move."

"He's right, come on." I followed Emmory off the bridge and

down the stairs. The ramp was already open and the Marines were unloading gear under Johar's direction.

Bial gave me a nod as I passed. "Welcome home, Your Majesty."

I smiled and headed down the ramp. Emmory and Cas, along with the rest of my BodyGuards, formed up around me and we sprinted across the clearing into the nearby tree line. Hidden among the boughs of evergreen trees, Caspel and the people with him went to a knee in unison.

"Your Imperial Majesty. We celebrate your return to Pashati and look forward to seeing you once more in your rightful place on the throne."

"Thank you." I had to swallow back the lump that was suddenly in my throat as I crossed to Caspel. Grabbing him by the shoulders, I helped him up and pressed my forehead to his. "Thank you for holding faith and holding the line."

"Given a thousand chances we would back you a thousand times, Majesty." He smiled up at me and the others around him murmured their assent. "We have vehicles waiting and it's best if we get you safe as soon as possible." Caspel cleared his throat and I turned away from the clearing.

"I'll follow your lead."

I exchanged greetings with the others as we headed for the ground vehicles. There were so many young faces, both women and men. They were dirty and tired, but the lights in their eyes and the warmth of their voices were genuine.

I was home and my people truly were happy to see me. Gita was right—I had everything Wilson wanted.

25

The chorus of "Your Majesty" echoed in the room when I walked in, but Alice's voice was the loudest and rather than going to a knee, she rushed across the room to me. I caught her in a hug, and tears filled my eyes.

"I am so glad you are safe," I whispered, pressing my cheek to her hair.

"You as well," she replied. "Welcome home."

I let her go. "Up, everyone up." I reached a hand out for Taz, allowing myself to squeeze his fingers but nothing more.

"Taran is safe with a family I know in the country. Only Alice and I know where," he said over our *smati* link.

"Thank you." I let him go and looked around the room. "We still have a long way to go. The fight is not over. But we are home once more, and those who thought to destroy Indrana will soon learn she is far stronger than they believed. We are the shining star in the blackness of space and we will not be easily extinguished."

Cheers echoed through the air. I nodded to the crowd once and then turned, slipping an arm around Alice's waist and waving to Taz to keep up as we headed out of the room.

"Over there." Alice gestured at a doorway down the hall. "We've been using this for meetings."

"What is this place?" I glanced over my shoulder at Caspel.

"Training facility for deep-cover operatives," he replied. "It's why Phanin's people don't know about it. Only the operatives and I were aware of its existence."

"Have you heard from your operative on Shul's ship?"

Caspel shook his head. "Not yet, ma'am. But I also haven't seen anything on the news about an execution and you can bet if they'd caught my operative we'd be hearing about it. They're keeping the news of Shul's death as quiet as possible, but the rumors are swirling."

I settled into a chair at the head of the long table, well aware that Alice and Taz were both staring at me, as were the majority of my BodyGuards.

"You really had Admiral Shul killed?" Alice squeezed her eyes shut. "I'm sorry, Majesty. It's just—I didn't actually think you'd do it."

I grinned. "It's all right, Alice. I gave Shul the option of surrendering. He declined and there are certain individuals involved in this who will not get the benefit of a trial."

"We'll want to get the news out on our own lines, Majesty," Caspel said.

"We'll film something as soon as we're done here. There's a lot to catch up on. I'll go first."

Once the shock of Wilson's identity and the news of Trace's capture had died down, Alice and Caspel set about filling us in on the movement on the ground.

"Most of the fighting has been concentrated in the bigger cities. There have been scattered reports of troops out in the smaller towns and around the countryside, but they don't seem to live very long." Alice smiled. "We owe our people big-time,

Majesty. The civilians in the capital have been instrumental in sabotaging supply lines and overwhelming Phanin's troops."

"He misread their mood," I replied.

"More like he once again failed at killing you," Taz said with a shake of his head. "This would have gone very differently if the people thought you'd died. Don't get me wrong, Alice is popular and a great choice as your heir, but you are their empress."

Alice looked at the tabletop and my mouth twitched as I held in a smile.

"We're focusing on the capital," Caspel said, pulling up a schematic on the table surface. "The red areas are the spots Phanin has control of currently. The green is all ours."

I could see the concentration of red around the palace and spreading out toward the southern docks. A wedge of green speared into the northern edge of Phanin's controlled territory and extended back into a semicircle sliding down toward the bayside of the capital.

"Who's in charge of our troops?"

"We are, Majesty."

I turned from the table and was out of my seat at the sound of General Saito's voice. The commander of the Trackers released Emmory's hand and bowed low to me. I snorted a laugh, grabbing the woman by the neck and pressing my forehead to hers.

"Kaed, we are pleased to see you alive."

"Likewise, Majesty."

I released her, greeting Commander-General Suvish of the BodyGuards and Lieutenant General Triskan in the same way. I didn't let my new Army commander go right away. Instead, I pulled back and grinned at him. "I have a surprise for you, Aganey."

"Majesty?" He frowned at me.

Ragini gave a cry when I stepped aside and launched herself

across the room at her father. General Triskan blinked, barely able to register what he was seeing before she hit him in the chest, wrapping her legs around his waist.

"I don't care what the news lines are saying about you," Taz murmured. "You're a softy."

"He was very worried about his girls," I murmured back as Ragini assured her father that her sister was safe with Admiral Hassan.

"General Vandi sends her regards, Majesty," Kaed said, wiping tears from her dark eyes. "She's occupied at the front and couldn't get away."

"That's all right, I'm sure I'll see her soon enough." I looked across the room where Esha Suvish was greeting the other BodyGuards. "Have I told you thank you lately for your Trackers, General?"

Kaed laughed. "You have not, Majesty, and you're most welcome. As sad as I was to lose them I know it was in the best interest of the empire."

"We'd better get back to it." I moved to the table and leaned against it, studying the palace and the layout of Phanin's troops.

"With your permission, Majesty, I'd like to take Hao and a few others to scout this area." Gita reached past me and touched a spot where there was a several-block gap between our forces and Phanin's.

"Do it," I said after a moment. "There's a way out of the palace in that area. I have an idea for how we might turn it into a way in."

"Yes, ma'am." Gita nodded and moved back across the room to speak with Hao. I watched them talk for a few moments before Hao waved a hand to Johar. She acknowledged him and waited for Bial to finish speaking with the BodyGuard commander before she tapped him on the shoulder and jerked her head to the door.

"Majesty?" Caspel touched me on the elbow. "Are you ready to film?"

"Yes."

"The light's going to be better over here," Alice said. I followed her, fixing my shirt. Alice fussed with my hair for a minute while I grinned at her. "That's the best it's going to get, I'm afraid."

"I'm announcing I had someone killed, Alice. Not trying to win a fashion contest. I think we'll be fine."

She stuck her tongue out at me and my surprised laughter echoed through the room, silencing everyone.

Caspel took advantage of the sudden quiet. "We're filming in five, people. Keep those mouths shut. You are on camera, Majesty, going live in four, three—"

I straightened my shoulders, lifted my chin, and looked at Caspel as he waved two fingers and then one at me. "Citizens of Indrana, I am home and soon this dark chapter in our history will be over.

"I wish to inform you of the execution of Admiral Temar Shul. He was offered a chance to surrender and refused. The images that I'm about to show you are graphic, so please prepare yourselves."

After a moment, I nodded to Caspel, who inserted the proof his operative had provided of Shul's death. Several people in the room with us turned away, hands over mouths. Alice swallowed and stayed where she was off to my right, her eyes never wavering from the image in the air. I spotted her fingers tangling briefly with Taz's and smiled. Then I looked back at Caspel and at his nod, I continued.

"I'll offer that same chance to my enemies now. Surrender.

Face the justice of the people of Indrana for your betrayal of
this empire. I will not promise leniency and many of you will
face execution for your part in this attempted overthrow of my
throne. However, I know many of you have been dragged along
in this treason. Now is your chance to lay down your weapons,
walk away from the traitor Eha Phanin, and prove your love for
Indrana." I drew in a breath and exhaled slowly. "This is your
only chance at any kind of mercy. Choose your side wisely."

"Camera off, Majesty."

"Right. That's done." I checked the countdown going in
the corner of my *smati*. "We've got about ten hours before
Admiral Hassan gets here, Caspel. Let's talk about how we're
going to take the orbital defenses out without completely ruining them."

"Majesty?"

I looked up from the schematic of the palace interior and
smiled at Alice. My heir was dressed in the same dark green
pants and long-sleeved shirt as before. She'd discarded the
heavy leather vest she'd been wearing earlier and her hair was
twisted back away from her face. "Have you gotten any sleep?"

"Have you?" She closed her eyes and didn't quite curse under
her breath. "I'm sorry, Majesty."

"Taz is rubbing off on you," I replied with a grin. "I slept on
the way home but your point is noted. What did you need?"

She took the seat I gestured to. "Caspel received word from
Admiral Hassan. The fleet is four hours out from Pashati."

"Good." I kept myself from correcting her that it was only
part of the fleet. We'd decided back on Ashva it was safer to keep
the plan to warp a third of the ships into the space near Pashati
a secret.

"He also said that it appears at least one battlecruiser and possibly three destroyers bolted from Phanin's fleet shortly after your announcement."

"Do we know where they are headed?"

"Toward Admiral Hassan." Alice shook her head. "We have no way of knowing if they're acting on orders from whoever is in command of the ships here or if they are coming over to your side. Caspel already sent Admiral Hassan a message to be on the lookout for them."

"Let's hope they're on our side."

"General Saito is leading a squadron of Marines in an assault on the Pashati Orbital Defense headquarters. From there we'll have control of the unmanned stations."

"And the manned ones?" There were three in orbit around Pashati. Two of them would be out of range of my stealth fleet, but the third could still inflict quite a bit of damage if we couldn't get them to stand down.

"Nothing yet, ma'am. General Triskan's daughter is working with a few others to see if she can hack into the system. Her talents are being wasted as a senior tech."

"Tell me about it," I replied. "Though I am not going to complain, she was right where I needed her to be." I reached across the table and put my hand on Alice's. "Just like you. I'm proud of you. You've done an amazing job here."

"My empire needed me, I was happy to—"

"Oh stop." I rolled my eyes at her. "Don't give me formulaic cowshit, Alice. This hasn't been easy on any of us, but you and I both know I took off and left you here and then everything went to shit. You've had to run an empire without me and deal with Phanin's treachery.

"You've done that all. Moreover, you've behaved like an empress the whole time. I'm paying you a compliment. Say thank you."

"Thank you, Your Majesty."

I squeezed her hand once and let her go. "You're welcome. Go get some sleep. Things are about to get really crazy around here."

"Yes, ma'am."

I watched Alice go, then got up and stretched and wandered out in the adjoining room. A group of fighters were huddled around the potbellied stove, passing around bent and chipped cups with steam rising into the air in little curls.

"Don't get up," I said when they saw me and started to rise.

A young woman with deep brown eyes smiled at me and handed me her cup. "It's hot, Majesty."

I took the metal cup with a grateful smile, all at once missing Stasia but still so grateful she was out of danger.

Hao slipped in through the door and gestured at me. I followed him back into the room and he dropped into Alice's vacated chair with a sigh.

"Well, our sniper was telling the truth about Phanin having the *smatis* tagged. We got within forty meters of the palace and then it was as if Gita hit a tripwire. The bastards dropped on us out of nowhere."

"Is everyone okay?"

"Cuts and bruises." He shrugged. "Close quarters in those alleys. Most of the fighting ended up being hand-to-hand. It presents a hell of a problem, though," he said with a shake of his head. "You and *all* of your BodyGuards aren't going to be able to get into the palace without setting off some bloody great alarm inside."

I set the cup down on the edge of the desk and muttered a curse. "What if we deactivate our *smatis*?"

Hao was shaking his head before I even finished the question. "I wouldn't do it. You'd be going in there blind. It's suicide." He pushed to his feet. "Johar and I are going to do some exploring. As far as I can tell, they're not locked into our hardware, just the official ones. Give us a few hours to see if we can figure out just how they're tracking and if we can do anything about it."

"Admiral Hassan will be here in four. Be careful."

"I always am." He grinned at me.

"On Pluto, you asshole," I shot back. "You jumped off a Shiva-damned building."

"Given the choice between that or getting shot, it seemed like the more reasonable option." He winked. "I'll see you in a few hours. Get some sleep."

"You're not my boss anymore."

Hao's laughter lingered long after he'd closed the door. I went back to work trying to find us a way into the palace, even though it now seemed like the only way I could end this would be to draw Phanin and Wilson out into the streets.

"Majesty, Tazerion would like a word." Zin stuck his head through the doorway.

"Send him in, and is there anything to eat?"

"I'll see what we can find."

"Thank you." I rubbed at my eyes as I settled back in my chair.

"Majesty." Taz came in and bowed. His gray shirt was pushed up to his elbows and there were grease stains on his pants.

"What have you been crawling around in?"

"That courier ship." He rubbed a hand over his forehead, smearing the black mark that decorated his left temple even further across his face. "We can't use it for more than parts. It's too big and obvious to use for transport and with no weapons it's useless in a fight."

"So you're tearing it apart?" I laughed. "I'm not sure that's what Toropov was intending when he loaned it to me."

Taz grinned. "Given you've got his king in hock I think you can get away with it."

"True." I tipped my head to the side and studied him; Hao's earlier words about thinking like an empress were ringing in my head. "So, doesn't look like Alice hates you."

"Oh, for Shiva's sake, Hail." He groaned.

"What?" I grinned, ruining the innocent look on my face. "I'm just saying."

"You are a brat," Taz replied, and then he sighed and gave me a sheepish smile. "She's amazing."

"I know."

"Smart and funny, though honestly I think besides her family no one's ever seen that side of her. She lost her husband seven years ago."

"I know. He was with Imperial Tactical Squad. They were doing relief work on Ugho after a hurricane. They were clearing a building and the foundation shifted." I'd been surprised that Alice's family hadn't pushed her to remarry right away since she hadn't had any children, and Hao's words about my choice of heir floated back into my brain.

"She's done a great job, Hail. The people were scared. This could have so easily gone the other way, but Alice rallied them to the throne's side."

"Caspel said the same thing." I smiled. The solution to my problem had been in front of my eyes, just like Hao said. "You're going to end up being Prince Consort after all."

"I don't think—" My words sank into his skull and he blinked at me. "Hail, what in the fires of Naraka is that supposed to mean?"

I lifted a shoulder, though from the expression on Taz's face my nonchalant attitude wasn't fooling him. "Alice is the heir."

"You're the empress." Taz leaned forward, both hands on the

table. "Don't tell me you're going to all this trouble to get your throne back only to give it away."

"Alice is obviously a far better choice than Phanin. In all honesty, she may even be a better choice than me. I didn't earn any of this, Taz. It just fell into my lap because Wilson murdered my sisters."

"Hail—"

"No, listen to me. I *earned* my spot in the world that Emmory and Zin dragged me away from. Ask anyone, even Hao, though he'd make some joke about it to hide his pride in how well his damn prodigy did. You ask anyone out there in the galaxy and they'll tell you Cressen Stone was one of the best there was."

"You had twenty years to do that job, Hail. You've only been empress for a few months, a few chaotic months at that. Comparing the two is going to give you the answer that you were better at being a gunrunner than an empress. If you walk away from this, you won't know if that answer will be the same twenty years from now."

"With so many lives at stake, can I afford to run that kind of long-term experiment?"

"With so many lives at stake, can you afford to walk away?" Taz countered. "None of your people are going to question your choice, so I will. Their loyalty is to you, not to Indrana, whatever they try to tell themselves.

"I'm not saying Alice isn't competent, Hail, because we both know she is."

"Are you just trying to get out of being Prince Consort?"

Taz smiled and shook his head. "I'll do my duty, for Indrana. I'm just asking you to think about why you're doubting yourself. If you're running away from this because you're scared, it's the worst choice you could make."

26

I leaned against a console in the back of the unofficial War Room of Caspel's base, hidden by shadow and Gita's frame as people filtered in through the door. Admiral Hassan's fleet was inbound on the massive display in the center of the room, a replica of Pashati glowing in the dimness and the bright red of Phanin's ships speeding away from the planet.

They would tangle with Inana's ships several hundred thousand kilometers from us and all we could do was watch.

"At least they waited to move out," Gita said, not looking away from the display. "That's a relief."

One of our major concerns was how long Phanin's ships would wait before engaging Inana's. The faster they rushed out to meet our fleet, the longer it would take for the ships that were warping in to rejoin Inana's fleet.

Even though the majority of them were *Vajrayana*, if the battle was too far from Pashati it would mean the difference between victory and defeat.

Thankfully, whoever they'd picked to replace Admiral Shul didn't seem to be nearly as experienced, and they'd issued the orders to engage with Inana's ships only an hour away from Pashati.

The running commentary from General Saito's com link rose in pitch on the far side of the room.

"General Saito and her forces are in control of the Orbital Defense headquarters," Caspel announced.

I stomped my left foot on the ground and the sound was quickly echoed by others until the noise level in the room was deafening. It died out, replaced by the low hum of voices as we waited to hear from Admiral Hassan.

"It is hard not to feel useless just standing around waiting," Gita said.

We'd discussed—very briefly—the idea of mounting an assault on the palace at the same time as the battle in the space above Pashati was raging, but had discounted it almost immediately. Wilson would be prepared for something like that and we still didn't have a good way into the palace or a way to mask our *smatis* from whatever scanning devices he had set up.

"It is," I agreed. "I'd be just as useless up there on a ship, though. Inana is in her element and at least this way she doesn't have to worry about me."

Gita laughed. "She's still worrying, Majesty. Trust me."

"I survived just fine on my own before I got tangled up with you lot," I reminded her. "And before you say it—I was usually the one pulling Hao out of trouble, not the other way around."

"Slander and lies," he said, emerging from the shadows on my other side.

I reached out and smacked him. "One of these days you're going to time that poorly and I'm going to shoot you."

Hao grinned. "We found a way into the palace."

"Is this a 'good-news, bad-news' situation?"

"I guess." He lifted his hands. "If you count us not having a way to keep your *smatis* off the radar yet bad news, but technically we already knew it."

"How are we getting in?" I kept one eye on the countdown to engagement as I waited for Hao's answer.

"Remember what the sniper said about the maintenance tech overhearing Phanin and Shul? We had an image of her from his *smati*. Johar and I found her."

"She's in the palace," Gita said with a raised eyebrow. "That still doesn't solve our problems."

"We found her apartment, which is not in the palace."

I choked down a laugh at the look Hao shot her before he continued. "Johar's keeping an eye on it to get an idea of her schedule. Once this is over, can I steal Ragini? I have an idea for figuring out what they're using to ping *smatis* in that radius." He waved a hand at the center display and beyond where Ragini was hacking her way into the three *Vajrayana* ships Phanin controlled.

"Sure," I said. "Wait, you're not sticking around?"

Hao shook his head. "Space battles are boring if you're stuck on the ground. I'm going to get some sleep."

"I hate him a little right now," Gita murmured after Hao walked off.

"You and me both." I stifled a yawn with my hand.

"Majesty, Admiral Hassan is on the com."

I pushed away from the wall and crossed to Caspel. "Admiral." I greeted the image on the screen.

"Majesty." Inana nodded her head. "We are T-minus forty-three minutes from engaging with the enemy forces. Currently outnumbered two to one, but we have the advantage in capital ships. Four ships from the enemy have surrendered; I don't know that we can trust them not to turn on us in battle. Acting captain Hideo Marion with the battlecruiser *Kali's Revenge* said to tell you: trebuchet, Caspel."

A wide smile spread across my director's face. *"Auho*, Admiral. That is very good to hear. You can trust the ships, they are loyal to the crown."

Inana looked at me and I lifted my hands with a helpless laugh. "Caspel's the spy." I suspected it had something to do with his missing operative, but I wasn't about to say that out loud in front of all these people. "Use the ships—we need all the help we can get."

"Yes, Majesty." She gave me another nod. "We'll speak after."

"For Indrana," I replied, and the words echoed around me.

After that there was nothing left for me to do but watch as the two forces collided. It was obvious from the outset that Admiral Hassan had the experience, even if her opponent had the numbers.

"All ships, you have your assigned targets. Fire when in range."

"Shields at eighty-two percent."

"Firing solution delta-niner-alpha."

"Twelve missiles incoming, firing decoys now."

"Brace yourselves."

"Impact! Decks fourteen through twenty-three."

"Damage report, Lieutenant."

"This is Dr. Smith in the med bay. We have wounded filtering in now."

The chaotic chatter of the battle was hard to filter through, even with my *smati* doing the bulk of the work. Inana's voice was a cool presence through the whole affair, keeping her people in line and taking each new development without any reaction.

Only I recognized the minuscule tremor in her voice when

another of our ships went down. Phanin's new admiral wasn't as experienced, but he wasn't going down without a fight.

The frantic gasping of the woman seated in front of Caspel overrode all the noise.

"Incoming! I have a warp signature at—that's not possible."

Caspel leaned over her shoulder, whipped his head around to stare at me, and then muttered an unflattering curse.

"That's unkind," I said with a laugh.

"That's dangerous," he replied, shoving a finger in the direction of the screen. "Why didn't you tell me?"

Hurt laced his words. I swallowed down my amusement to a soft smile. "It was better this way. Not for lack of trust in you, Caspel, believe me when I say that."

"Majesty, I cannot—"

"*Cire's Light* just took a direct hit!"

I turned back to the display just in time to see Admiral Fon's ship on the display flicker and vanish. "No." I closed my eyes and pressed my palms together, bringing them to heart, lips, and forehead.

"What happened?"

"They got back control of one of the *Vajrayana*—V34. They were able to fire their plasma cannon," Ragini said. Her eyes were wet with tears as she looked up from her station. "I can't get back in, ma'am. Hasa was in charge of that one. She was on the—" Ragini broke off and I crossed to her, clamping a hand down on her shoulder.

"Breathe, Senior Tech." I kept my voice firm as I issued the order. "There are other lives out there depending on you." I looked back at Caspel. "Contact the first two *Vajrayana* ships that came out of warp. Tell them to zero in on V34 and turn it into slag if they have to."

The other ships continued to pour out of warp like clockwork and arced away from Pashati on a course to intercept the two battling fleets. I let Ragini go and she bent her head back to her work.

The arrival of the *Vajrayana* ships changed the tide of the battle from shocked misery to determination. Phanin's forces were caught in the grip of a vise that crushed them until one by one the ships either surrendered or were put out of commission by Hassan's people.

It wasn't over, but I let myself relax just a fraction as the mop-up began. The difficult task of driving Phanin and the others out of the palace would be infinitely easier with control of the space around Pashati.

Caspel was smiling when he joined me. "That went far better than I expected, Majesty." His smile faded somewhat. "Which makes me a bit nervous, if I'm being honest."

"You're not alone in that, Caspel. However, I'll take the easy win, for all that it wasn't." Images of Gerté's face surfaced in my head. I was going to miss the outspoken admiral, and Indrana would miss her expertise.

Emmory came through the door and crossed to us. "Majesty. Caspel." He nodded at both of us.

"*Ekam*, is the transportation ready?"

"Transportation?" I looked between them.

"I thought you'd want to com the palace, Majesty," Caspel said. "And see if they are ready to surrender. Obviously, we don't want to do it from here, so Emmory suggested an alternate location."

An hour later we pulled up outside a nondescript building just on the edge of the capital. I kept a tight hold on the scarf wrapped around my hair as we piled out of the vehicle and rushed for the door.

The air inside was musty and cold. The lights clicked on as we headed down the corridor behind Caspel. He led us through the maze of hallways until we reached a tiny windowless room.

"The building is shielded. It should make it very difficult for them to track where the signal is coming from," Caspel said as I sat in the metal chair. "Just let me know when you're ready."

Crossing my legs and draping an arm over the back of the chair, I nodded at Caspel.

A harried-looking Phanin answered our com, a white bandage decorating the left side of his head. His eyes flew open and the shocked gasp was enough to get me to lose control of my grin. It spread across my face before I could stop it.

"Your fleet is defeated and what few ground forces you have will soon follow suit. Let's discuss the terms of your surrender, Eha Phanin."

"You sent me severed heads!"

"Oh good, you got my present."

"You sent people to kill me!"

Of all the things I'd expected him to say, that wasn't on the list, nor was the wholly incredulous tone in which he delivered it.

"You know, now that you mention it I remember saying something to some friends about how happy it would make me if you were dead." I raised an eyebrow and smiled.

"I lost an ear!"

"How terrible for you." I slid a look in Emmory's direction and my *Ekam* lifted a shoulder.

I focused on Phanin once more. The man was sweating, clearly nervous. Not at all how I would have expected a man who masterminded the attack on Red Cliff to behave. Unless it had all been Wilson's plan from the start.

"However, I feel like I should remind you of the number of times you've tried to kill me. Missing ears notwithstanding, we're not even close to being even."

Phanin swallowed. "I won't surrender without a promise of clemency."

My laughter cut through the air like a blade as I got to my feet. "I don't know why you think you have any room to bargain with me. You are already dead, Eha. You just don't know it yet." I cut the connection and turned away from the console.

"What is it, Majesty?"

I shook my head at Gita's question. "I was not expecting him to want to surrender."

"Phanin's a lot of things, but not a coward," Emmory said. "Cowards don't execute a plot to overthrow an empire, not even with someone like Wilson behind them. Something about it didn't feel right."

Pointing in Emmory's direction, I nodded in agreement and paced the room. "You think he was trying to draw us into a trap?"

"It's possible. What are we going to do now, Majesty?"

"You want me to say we're going to wait for the ground troops to roll in and take control, then sort through the prisoners," I said with a laugh. "In a perfect world that's what we'd do."

"It's not a perfect world, Majesty."

"It's not, *Ekam*." I leaned against the console. "So instead we're going to figure out a way into the palace, and while the ground troops are distracting Wilson and the others we'll sneak in and rescue the matriarchs."

That earned me the Look.

27

Steam rose from the mug in my hand, curling lazily into the still morning air. The cold concrete of the rooftop seeped into my pants and settled into my skin, but for once I didn't mind the chill.

Emmory leaned against the concrete edging running around the top of our headquarters, his only concession to the cold a dark gray hat pulled low over his ears. It matched the one that covered my hair, the remainder of my braid tucked securely into my jacket.

Fasé was on my other side, perched on the lip of the rooftop like an eagle about to take flight. Her golden eyes were soft, unfocused, as she stared at the rising sun.

"Everything I tell you can change simply from the telling. I don't have the skills to sort through the mess when it overwhelms me. The future-seers are picked at young ages and put through rigorous training. According to Dio there hasn't been a case where a Farian my age suddenly developed the talent to see the future with any clarity. Yet here I am." She lifted a slender shoulder that was clad in a heavy jacket scrounged up by Taz. "If this was a result of my bringing Emmory back or just the way things were supposed to be I have no way of telling."

"So if you say we're going to win, the act of simply saying it will possibly change the outcome?"

"Yes and no." Fasé nodded. "The future isn't set, Majesty. It's a rushing river. If I reach in and pull a rock from the river or throw a rock in, it changes the course of the river's flow. Some of it doesn't change the flow much. You throw a small pebble in—"

"Nothing will really change," I finished, and nodded. "If we throw a boulder in it will change a lot of things."

"Or a whole lot of pebbles," Emmory said.

"Precisely." Fasé smiled at the rising sun, the glow illuminating her face. "The future-seers are trained to figure out which is best and what could possibly justify throwing—or removing—a boulder."

"I survived for thirty-eight years without someone whispering the future in my ear, Fasé. I'm pretty sure I can keep doing okay."

"I know, Majesty, but it doesn't stop me from wanting to avoid the futures I see where you are dead, or he is, or all of us are." She reached out and swirled a finger through the steam coming off my cup, looking at me for the first time in our conversation. The moisture collected on her skin and Fasé flicked it out into the air beyond the rooftop. "Untrained as I am, it doesn't stop me from feeling the pull that something extremely important hangs in the balance here."

We fell back into silence and I let it drag out as the sun inched higher into the sky. Finally, I leaned into Emmory, bumping his shoulder with mine. "Thoughts?"

"I am with you, Majesty, to the end of this," he said, his voice wafting through the air with the same graceful laziness as the steam. "We all are. I also know that laying too much trust in something like this can bring disaster. Our instincts were honed into weapons by our experiences. We shouldn't ignore them."

The tension in Fasé's body vanished with Emmory's words. I sipped at my chai to hide my smile. I'd suspected that the whole purpose for this early-morning meeting in the cold had been because Fasé was concerned we'd rely too heavily on her newfound talents, but Emmory and I were both seasoned veterans and we knew the value of practical experience.

"Thank you," Fasé said, slipping from the ledge onto the rooftop. She folded both hands and bowed low, then rose and made her way across to where Gita stood guard by the door.

I watched her go, turning back to the sunrise as Fasé slipped back into the building.

"The silence from the palace is worrisome," I said.

Emmory nodded. It had only been a day since our conversation with Phanin. His ground troops hadn't surrendered, but they weren't advancing from the territory they currently held either.

My generals were downstairs in the middle of planning the next wave of our attack. It was a meeting I'd opted out of, feeling certain that I would have very little to contribute. So instead Alice was down there and I was starting to think more and more that it was the right choice.

Indrana would be better off with someone like Alice at the helm. Especially with Taz at her side. A fresh start to the empire, a new dawn of leadership ready to take the people to a more equal future.

"Majesty?"

I blinked and looked at Emmory; he was frowning at me and it deepened when I forced a smile. "Yes?"

"You've got that look on your face."

"What look?"

"The 'I'm not qualified for this' look," he replied, twitching an eyebrow skyward.

"Technically it's more of a 'there are a ton of other people who are more qualified' look." My joke fell flat. Sighing, I leaned into Emmory and put my head on his shoulder. "I just want what's best for Indrana, Emmy, and I can't say with any certainty that I am that person."

"You could listen to the rest of us when we say it."

"You're biased and we all know it," I replied.

Emmory wrapped his arm around me and squeezed me against his side. "It's been an experience I would gladly repeat all over, Majesty."

"Even the bit where I kicked you in the face?"

His laughter rumbled out into the air and I joined in. The sound floated across the air, slowly fading out into silence. We sat together, watching the sunrise, until Hao cleared his throat behind us.

"We've got our way in," he said.

Johar closed the door behind the last of my BodyGuards and folded her hands at her waist, waiting for me. I leaned against the desk, crossed my legs at the ankles, and gave her a nod.

"There are two problems facing us: One is getting near the palace and two is getting into the palace. Our enemy set up a field around the compound specifically coded to the signal coming from *smatis* with the royal code identifier." Johar looked around the group. "It sets off an alarm if any of you cross the line and makes it impossible for any of us to reach the palace undetected.

"Hao and Ragini have been at work on a device modified off Bakara's cloaking program. We think it will open a window in the field for long enough to allow us to slip inside."

"So that fixes problem one," I said. "What about actually getting into the palace?"

"Don't be pushy," Hao replied. "We've got that covered. While Ragini and I were working, Johar made contact with Shanja Kaif. She agreed to open the door to the tunnel in your rooms and leave it open."

"I take it you didn't tell her you threw Kin Simon off the roof?"

Johar shrugged a shoulder. "It didn't come up. Besides, he brought it on himself."

I couldn't argue with her reasoning. It wouldn't have done a whole lot of good anyway. Johar's moral compass skewed to the opposite of most people's. I'm not sure what it said that I agreed with the way she'd handled it—or with the fact that Kin Simon really had brought it on himself.

"Emmory, take Kisah and Hao and go test the device."

"Yes, Majesty."

Hao raised his hand.

"What?" I asked.

"We already did that."

"Excuse me?"

"Sorry." He dropped into a ridiculously dramatic bow. "We already did that, Your Majesty."

I pulled my Hessian free, but Hao just laughed, so I put it away.

"Cas, Gita, and I went and tested out the device already, Majesty. It works."

My *Dve* tipped his head in my direction, too slow to hide his smile, and I kicked his boot.

"Hao's a bad influence on you."

"Yes, Majesty."

"Let's get moving, then," I said.

Emmory cleared his throat.

"What?"

"Perhaps we should wait for your generals to finish, Majesty? Consulting with them wouldn't be a bad idea."

"It wouldn't be, but it's also exactly what Wilson will expect. It's common knowledge by now that I hate doing things without a plan, Emmory, so maybe we should do them without a plan." I looked around the room at the others, pleased with the number of people nodding in agreement. "They expect us to try to use the chaos of a ground attack to hide our presence? We'll go in before the attack even starts."

"For what it's worth, Majesty, I think it's a good idea," Cas said.

"We did just determine your judgment is corrupted, so that's not much of an endorsement," Zin murmured with a grin. He cleared his throat and gave me a short bow. "However, Your Majesty, I am also in agreement. Moving now gives us an element of surprise we wouldn't otherwise have."

Emmory didn't react to his partner's words, and the room fell into silence as he continued to stare at the wall past my ear. I leaned my hands back on the tabletop and waited. Finally, my *Ekam* sighed and looked at me.

"BodyGuards and you two," he said, pointing at Johar and Hao. "The Marines will stay here. Go gear up, we leave in five minutes."

Everyone filed out of the room. Emmory grabbed me by the upper arm before I could follow Hao. "Majesty, you will stay by my side at all times. You'll do as I say, when I say it, or I will knock you out now and leave you here with Zin to stand guard. Am I understood?"

At least a dozen snarky responses rose up in my throat, but they all died on my tongue when I looked into my *Ekam*'s eyes. I could see everything my *Ekam* normally kept hidden behind an impassive mask: all his concern and devotion, the fear and resignation.

I nodded once. "Perfectly," I said. "You are in charge, *Ekam*."

28

Heart pounding in my throat, I followed Emmory into the darkness surrounding the headquarters and took off at a run toward the capital. If Fasé hadn't seen what we were up to, I suspected she'd notice the sudden change in my heartbeat.

I was practically plastered to Emmory's side. The weeks of our ordeal had meshed us in ways that only battle could. Zin was on my other side, moving at the same pace.

Hao and Cas led the way. Johar was behind them and the rest of my BodyGuards came behind us in a standard formation.

The streets of the capital were quiet and it made me uneasy.

"Where is everyone?" I asked Emmory over the com link.

"Caspel said the majority of civilians close to the palace fled in the early days of the coup. There was fighting in the streets. It's safer on the outer edges of the capital."

"Explains why we're headed in the opposite direction."

"This was your idea, sha zhu,*"* Hao replied.

"I know." I scanned the darkness ahead of us, now seeing the rubble and battle damage I had missed before. There was debris piled in a nearby alleyway, as though someone had made a last-ditch effort to clean up before fleeing.

Johar froze and flung her hand up. She flashed a series of numbers, then pointed to the left.

I poked Hao in the back and jerked my head toward the alley we'd just passed. He nodded and we all slipped behind the pile of debris.

"Lantle, you and Gita check farther back, see if we have an exit," Emmory ordered.

Johar skidded around the corner, tapped a finger to her lips, and held up her fingers in a series that totaled eighteen.

There was a pause, and then three pairs of footsteps headed down the street toward us. I could hear the voices of Phanin's troops floating on the night air and slid my Glock from its holster as silently as I could.

"All I'm saying is maybe we should take the opportunity when it's presented and get the hell out of here."

"Yanna, I swear if you don't shut up—"

"You saw those photos, same as I did. His throat was slit from ear to ear. Now, if you want to hang around and wait for the gunrunner empress to give you the same attention, that's on your head."

"It's not like she cut Shul's throat herself, you big coward." A third voice joined the fray.

"That's the problem, Vam! She was light-years away and Shul still wasn't safe," Yanna replied. "You two chuckleheads think Phanin's going to protect us from that?"

"Phanin? No," Vam said, contempt dripping from his voice. "But Wilson? Sure. He's got a plan and by all accounts he's got Bristol doing just what he wants her to do."

"I don't like him. Don't you think there's something off about that guy?" There was the sound of a brief scuffle and Yanna cried out in pain.

"You'd better watch your mouth, or you will end up with a

vented throat," the first speaker warned. "Wilson's men don't tolerate anyone talking about their boss like that."

"All the more reason to get out of here, and speaking of, it's cold. Let's get back to the palace."

Their voices trailed off as they moved away from us. Once Johar was certain the street was silent once more, she grinned at me.

"I really wanted you to lean your head out there and say boo," she whispered. "I think Yanna would have pissed himself."

Muffled snickering met her announcement and Emmory sighed. "Gita says there's a doorway at the back of the alley and it leads through to the shops on the other side. If we cut through we'll be almost to the spot where the tunnel comes out of the palace."

I wanted to object, but the alleyway wasn't the place for it, so I nodded and holstered my gun, following Emmory into the darkness.

Once we were inside, I grabbed my *Ekam* by the arm. "I think we should go back."

Emmory frowned at me. Everyone else just stared.

"Majesty, we won't get another chance like this," Cas protested. "They've just lost their navy. The ground forces won't be able to hold out for long. They don't know we're coming."

"Am I the only one who heard those men say Wilson had a plan and I was following it like a lamb to the slaughter?" I scanned the group looking for support. Hao had an eyebrow raised but was otherwise silent.

"Everyone out," Emmory said, and they followed Zin into the other room of the shop without argument. He turned his back on the door and studied me for several heartbeats before leaning in. "Hail, what is it?" His voice was soft in my ear.

"My gut," I whispered back. "This is wrong."

"Okay," he said, and nodded once before ushering me into the other room. "Zin, we're heading back—figure out a route."

"Yes, sir."

Cas was clearly still upset about not pushing forward, but he wasn't about to argue with either me or Emmory more than he already had.

Moments later we were back into the dark, silent streets hauling ass for the dubious safety of the headquarters.

"Your Majesty." Caspel took a deep breath.

Generals Vandi and Saito glowered at me, making me feel like I was seven years old and in serious trouble with my mother. That alone made the smile I was trying to keep off my face struggle even harder to break free.

"Our intelligence suggested it would be best to move right then, Director. Once we were able to observe the terrain we realized it was unwise to continue on and decided to come back here to regroup."

"Majesty, if something were to happen to you—"

"That's what Alice is here for," I said, cutting General Saito off. "We have a line of succession for a reason, people. I'm not the end-all-be-all of the Indranan Empire, and the sooner everyone in this room realizes that, the better off we're all going to be." I stood. "Wilson is mine and there isn't a force in the universe that is capable of stopping me from going after him."

The chorus of "Yes, Majesty," followed me out of the room.

"Nicely done," Hao said, falling into step with me. "You know, despite your reluctance you're very imperial at times."

I snorted and rolled my eyes at the ceiling.

"What was it about the conversation we overheard that set your gut off?"

It was a relief to not have to explain how I was feeling to

Hao. He just accepted it as fact after so many years of listening to my gut and trusting it to keep us all out of trouble. His question had everything to do with seeing if we could pick out the important piece from the mess that had set off my alarm bells.

"Wilson's been a step ahead of me since the beginning."

"More like a kilometer or so, *sha zhu*."

"Fine, whatever." I smacked him on the shoulder and kept walking. "Don't interrupt. He's been ahead. This is his plan and only his plan, as far as I can tell. He didn't trust anyone else enough to let them in on the secret."

"What about Leena?"

"What about her?" I hadn't thought about her since we'd realized her betrayal, but judging by Hao's frown that was a mistake.

"How long has she been involved in the plot? You don't really know, do you?"

"We don't," I admitted.

Hao huffed out an exasperated noise. "I taught you better. She's Indranan—do you really think she's content to just sit back and let Wilson be in charge?"

That brought me to a standstill. Zin narrowly managed to avoid crashing into me by twisting to the side, and his hand skimmed over my back as he slid past.

"You've been out in the real world for too long," Hao said with a smile.

"Apparently." I made a face. "Zin, who requested the match between my nephew and Leena? Was it Cire?"

"No ma'am. The Surakesh clan put forth the proposal. Your sister and mother both approved it."

"Bugger me," I muttered. "Zin—"

"I'm looking for connections between Leena and Wilson now, Majesty. I'll call Cas to come take my place."

"Tell him I'm going to see Fasé, he can meet me there." I started down the hallway again.

"I'll go with Zin," Hao said. "No offense, but your Farian gives me the willies." He shuddered.

"Baby," I teased.

As we rounded the corner to Fasé's quarters, the door to her room opened and Cas came out.

"Majesty," he said.

"That was quick."

"I'm sorry?" He frowned.

"Zin needs to take off, you're staying with me. You can hang out here while I see Fasé." I waved at Hao. "I'll talk to you later."

"We'll let you know when we've unraveled this puzzle," he said.

I nodded and pushed Fasé's door open. She looked up, the surprise on her face the first I'd seen since she'd brought Emmory back from the dead.

"Majesty." She quickly composed herself and gave me a tiny nod.

I closed the door behind me. "Something you want to share with me, Fasé?"

"No, Majesty."

I sat and crossed my legs. Fasé stared back at me and we stayed that way for a long while in an unspoken battle of patience. She caved first, shaking her head with a sigh.

"Did you have something to ask me, Majesty? Or did you just come to stare?" There was a curious bite in her voice, one I didn't blame her for. That happened even with the most even-tempered of people when they came up against me.

"What does it feel like?"

She blinked. "Excuse me?"

293

"I'm just curious and assuming it feels different when you heal someone versus bringing them back from the dead. How does it feel?"

"Wrong," she said.

There was a moment of silence. Fasé chewed on her bottom lip, her lashes a smudge of red against her pale cheeks. When she looked up at me again, her golden eyes were dark, the shimmer of galaxies reflected in their depths.

"Imagine taking the fabric of the universe and tearing it asunder, then painstakingly sewing one piece back in. Imagine that happening in the space between one heartbeat and the next.

"A heartbeat ceases and the universe continues. The universe doesn't care that some of us are shattered by it, it will continue on just the same. That is the way it is supposed to be. We are forbidden from altering that reality because it makes things wrong. I don't know yet the impact of doing that not only once but twice; however arrogant I am, I am not so much as to pretend there won't be fallout from this."

"So why did you do it?" I asked. "You already said Emmory was just a reaction to Zin's pain. But you didn't hesitate with Admiral Hassan either. You ripped the universe up and sewed it back together. You said to Dio that we needed her alive."

"We did." Fasé turned and looked at the far wall instead of at me when she answered. "The battle for Pashati would not have been won without Inana's expertise, Majesty. Your fleet would have been morally defeated because of her death even before the battle started. I saw that future very clearly. Saw how her death cascaded into a spiral that destroyed not only Indrana but a... much larger sphere." She trailed off and rubbed at her temple. "We would have all been dead, so in the end would it really have mattered? Maybe not, but I saw what I saw. I couldn't let her die. Not just because of Admiral Hassan, but because I couldn't allow all that would follow to happen; you should understand that better than anyone."

"I do."

Some of the tension leaked from Fasé's shoulders and she nodded once. "You need to get to the palace, Majesty."

"We're going to put a plan together and try again tomorrow." I arched an eyebrow at her. "What?"

"Nothing, Majesty." She pulled her knees into her chest and wrapped her arms around them, hiding her face from me.

I could have pushed, but I didn't. Instead, I got to my feet and shot Fasé one last look before I left the room.

Cas fell into step beside me. "Are you all right, Majesty?"

"Honestly?" I laughed. "I'm not sure things have been right since Emmory found me on the floor of my ship."

Cas smiled and reached a hand out, squeezing my forearm. "It's all going to be okay, ma'am. I promise."

I laid my hand over his with a halfhearted sound of agreement. I wasn't sure I believed him, but I could afford to hope.

29

There's nothing there," Hao said, shaking his head.

I crossed my arms when Zin nodded in agreement.

"I can't find a single thing tying Leena to Wilson, Majesty. Not until she decided to show her hand and take off for the palace. There's no bank records, no communication, no video evidence."

"She covered her tracks," I replied. "We basically let her do it. Bugger me." I slammed a hand down on the desk in front of me. Neither man jumped, though the Marine at the door jerked slightly. "We gave her access to it. I trusted her, and the whole time she was working for him."

"Why?" Hao asked. "It doesn't make any sense. Wilson killed her grandmother; he will kill her aunt and possibly her mother. The empire will still fall. What could she possibly stand to gain from backing him?"

"Maybe it's not about gain." Zin shook his head. "Maybe she's just crazy?"

"Everyone has a reason. It might not make sense to you or me, but it makes sense to them. Nobody does anything for free."

"I understand your view of the world might be a little jaded, Hao, but there are people who do things without thought of reward," Zin said.

"They are extremely few and far between," I said, putting a hand on Zin's arm before he could reply. "Hao's right. Leena got something out of this. We just don't know what it is yet."

The door burst open and Caspel skidded to a halt, his hand up.

"That's a good way to get shot, Director." I put my gun away.

"You need to see this," he said, and left the room.

I shared a look with Hao. He shrugged and followed Caspel. Zin and Jasa fell in behind me and we all headed down the corridor to the command center. Emmory was already there, and he shot me a grim look. The reason for it was clear when I spotted Leena's bright smile on the screen.

"People of Indrana, over a thousand years ago my ancestor attempted to right the wrongs of the Bristol family and depose her mad sister to bring a new era of peace and prosperity to our empire. She was betrayed and murdered, her family cast out of the capital and forever banished."

"Oh, bugger me," I muttered, rubbing a hand over my face as Leena's reason came crashing into place.

"But there were still some loyal to the cause, and Kastana's best friend took in her baby girl and hid her away, raising her as her own. She was given a place in the Surakesh line and over the years worked her family's way back to its rightful ruling spot."

Caspel's hissing exhale silenced the murmuring that rose on the air.

"My grandmother, my aunt, even my mother and sisters lost faith in our cause and were prepared to forsake everything Kastana had worked for—but I was not. I stand before you now as the rightful descendant of Kastana Ibiyah Helena Bristol, and I lay claim to the throne of Indrana." A smile spread across Leena's face. "Look around you for proof of how the Bristol name has fallen. An empire divided. The Saxons on our doorstep. You have accepted a lawless, arrogant, *barren* empress on the throne. She will bring us to ruin."

Oh, *bugger* me.

Emmory hadn't moved, but I could feel him coiled and ready to strike. I kept my face expressionless and my eyes locked on Leena's smug smile.

"I'm sorry, was that supposed to be a secret? How Hail got herself shot up on Candless and nearly died? She lived, but it cost her dearly. Nobody knew but her BodyGuard, and she thought he took that secret to the grave." She rubbed her fingers together. "Money talks, Hail dearie, and that doctor who kept you alive was more than willing to spill the story of your injuries.

"I can continue the Bristol line, the way it was meant to be! Think on that, citizens of Indrana, before you throw your lives away for that gunrunner criminal you call your empress."

The screen went black and an awful silence descended on the room.

Emmory and Zin moved in concert, stepping in front of me and shielding me from the rest of the room as my other Body-Guards formed up around me. Gita closed a hand around my arm. Hao hadn't moved, but his hands were on his guns.

"Majesty, she lies?" Alice approached with her hands up and hope etched onto her face.

"Why do you think I made you my heir?" I whispered, shaking my head with a weak smile. "You really are going to be empress, Alice. This wasn't just a temporary post."

"Now you tell me." Her muttered sarcasm broke the tension in the room.

"No time like the present."

"Your Majesty. It makes no difference." Alice cleared her throat and dropped to a knee. "You are the shining star of Indrana, and we will follow you to the end, be it bitter or sweet."

Everyone followed suit, echoing Alice's words, except for my BodyGuards, who were held in place by some invisible order from Emmory.

Hao wore a curious expression on his face, and when I met his eyes he gave me a nod of approval.

"Majesty." Caspel got to his feet. "We will need to answer her accusations. That broadcast went out to the whole empire. Even if we defeat them here, it could tip the balance on the outer planets."

I would have killed someone for Alba's comforting presence right that second. Instead, I nodded at him. "Start filming."

Emmory and the others moved out of the way. I took a deep breath, folded my hands, and exhaled until Caspel held up his hand.

"Citizens of Indrana, for months we have been under siege from traitors seeking to bring our empire to the ground. Now that we are on the verge of victory, you can see their desperation and their madness as they resurrect the ghosts of a millennium ago. When sister unlawfully took up arms against sister and challenged her right to rule.

"I am my mother's daughter, a Bristol. I came home to you when you needed me, and here I stay to lead Indrana into the light once more. I have acknowledged Alice Gohil as my rightful heir; her connection to the Bristol name may be through the paternal line, but it was approved by the Matriarch Council. My family ruled this empire for generations, but it is not my family that is sacred—it is the empire, and we will keep her safe at all costs. Even though it means my family's reign is done."

I kept my smile soft. "Never forget, this is your empire. It is your future that hangs in the balance. Do you want to leave that future in the hands of people who have repeatedly demonstrated how very little they care for your lives and the lives of your children? They have murdered, bombed, and waged war upon us all—not for your interests, but for their own. Do not let fear of the unknown drive you from the choices your heart knows is right. We are right here and we will continue to be the shining light of Indrana."

Caspel put his hand down.

"I want to send Wilson a message," I said. "Can we do that?"

"I can send it to the palace, Majesty. I'll have no way of knowing if he'll see it or not."

"That's fine." I jerked my chin up. "I'll know I sent it; that's all that matters."

The early light of dawn filtered down the streets of Krishan as we headed toward the palace. This time the stillness of the streets was broken by the echoing sounds of fighting as General Vandi's forces attacked Phanin's.

This time I had a damn sight more than just my Body-Guards, as a platoon of Marines cleared the streets in front and to each side of us. We'd given up stealth in favor of expediency, plus we were counting on the distraction of the attack to help at least a little.

My breath frosted on the air and my fingers were numb even within the gloves I'd yanked on just before we headed out. A dark cap covered most of my hair and the rest of it was tucked into the collar of my jacket. From a distance, you couldn't even tell the Empress of Indrana was skulking through the streets of her capital.

At least that was our hope.

Emmory stuck a hand out, stopping me in my tracks when Johar cut to the right and headed down the street. Moments later he nodded and we continued until we reached the far wall of the palace. Johar was in deep discussion with one of the Marines, and she looked away from him as we approached.

"What kind of countermeasures are we looking at here?" she asked Emmory with a gesture at the wall.

We knew this was an obstacle to overcome, but Emmory still hesitated for a second as he wrestled with telling a criminal about all the security for the palace.

Johar waited patiently, a tiny smile at the corner of her mouth, until my *Ekam* sighed.

"There's nothing on the wall itself; once you get over it and onto the palace grounds, there's a series of armaments programmed to fire at anyone without a royal *smati* ID."

"I'd bet Wilson shut that down, or they'd get shot at every time they stepped outside," Johar replied. "I'll watch for it, though."

"How are we getting over the wall in the first place?" Cas asked.

Johar and I both grinned. She hiked the bundle of rope slung crossways over her chest and winked at my *Dve*. "Like this." She took off at a jog away from us down a cross street. When she reached a distance that pleased her, Johar turned and sprinted back at the wall.

Johar hit the wall and ran straight up the fifteen-meter height, catching the lip and hauling herself up to lie flat against the edge.

"No fucking way," Cas breathed, cursing in front of me for the first time since I'd met him.

"I've seen her climb up twice that on a surface you would think was too smooth to find any holds," I said as she wiggled

301

out of the rope and dropped one end down to the Marines waiting on the ground. Jasa wrapped the end around her waist and gave Johar a nod once she was anchored. She returned it and rappelled down the other side.

"Johar says it's clear. Doesn't seem to be any active armament. I'm going first," Emmory said. "Then you, Majesty. Cas will follow and other BodyGuards after that."

One by one we scaled the wall and dropped to the other side. Emmory kept a hand on my neck as we scrambled across the grounds to the palace.

I ran my hand along the smooth wall. Now came the real test of whether Shanja Kaif had done what she promised Johar and left both doors cracked. My heart skipped when I skimmed over the surface and my fingers caught on the light irregularity.

"Cas, you and Kisah go in first. Gita next. Give me an all clear and set up a perimeter at the main door of the empress's quarters."

"Sir." Cas slung his weapon over his back and crawled into the opening. Kisah offered me up a smile before she followed and Gita went after, vanishing into the darkness without a word.

What seemed like an eternity passed before Emmory nodded and gestured at the tunnel. "Lantle, you and Ikeki are next."

"Yes, sir." The older BodyGuard crawled into the tunnel with his younger companion behind.

"Zin, Hao, go on. Majesty, you're after them. I'll be right behind you. Johar, you and the others stay here and keep an eye out. I want this as an option if we need to make a quick escape."

"Easy," Johar replied with a wink. "Ladies, let's set up shop in the trees; we'll be harder to spot there."

Her voice faded as I crawled into the tunnel and I dragged in a shaky breath when the light faded at the same time. Fasé's words about conquering my fear echoed in my head and I exhaled.

"You've got this, Hail," I muttered, and started crawling.

The darkness didn't last for long and soon I was grabbing Hao's and Zin's hands and sliding out of the tunnel into my closet.

"It's quiet," Zin said as he reached behind me for Emmory. I followed Hao out of the closet.

"It's too quiet." He patted me on the arm. "I'm going to go look around."

"Be careful."

"I'll take Gita." Hao grinned and slipped out of the room. I turned back to Emmory and Zin as they emerged from the closet.

"Hao's going to go look around. Said it's too quiet."

"I'm in agreement," Emmory replied. He put a hand on my back as we headed into the main room. Cas and Kisah stood by the door, their weapons in their hands. Lantle and Ikeki mirrored their posture by the windows.

"Not a sound," Cas said. "There's nothing on the scanners; the palace net seems to be completely down. I can't even bring up the cameras. The whole place is empty."

My stomach twisted unpleasantly. "You don't think he's killed everyone here?"

Emmory's expression was grim. "I'm not sure we can discount it, Majesty."

"We're not going to find anything out by staying here," Cas said. "Let's go take a look."

Emmory finally nodded after a long moment. "Cas, take point and move slow. Lantle and Ikeki will follow you. Kisah, you and I are with the empress. Zin—"

"Watching our backs." He finished Emmory's sentence with a nod.

We moved slowly into the corridor. I slipped my weapon from its holster and tried to ignore my unease, focusing on keeping my breathing slow and even.

My quarters had been undisturbed, but as we moved farther into the palace toward the throne room, the signs of fighting and destruction became more clear. Scorch marks decorated the walls and broken vases littered the floor.

"Hail, you need to see this. I'm in the throne room." Hao's voice was calm, with only the barest ripple of tension over the com link.

"I'm almost there," Cas said.

"We're on our way."

"This place is empty, you don't have to keep sneaking," he replied.

I shared a look with Emmory. "Thoughts?"

"If this were a trap, they'd have sprung it already," he said. "Kisah, throne room. Keep your eyes open."

Slipping through the door to the throne room behind Emmory, I whispered a curse at the sight that greeted us and the proximity alarms that suddenly took up residence in my head.

Phanin lay sprawled on the floor at the edge of the dais. My crown sat on the throne, the cushion beneath it stained with dried blood.

"Cas, damn it, don't—" Hao shouted.

Gita lunged for my *Dve*, but Hao caught her arm before she could follow Cas across the obsidian. I sprinted across the throne room as Cas crossed the jagged line and knelt by Phanin's body.

"He's dead." Cas's voice was even.

"He's wired to blow." Hao's mouth was drawn into a tight line. "The whole area is wired."

Everyone snapped to attention, Zin closing a hand around

my wrist and backing toward the door. "Kisah, Lantle, Ikeki, head for the bay entrance," he snapped the order. *"Johar, it's Zin. Clear the area, repeat, clear the area. We're exiting via another route."*

"Emmory." My *Ekam's* name was an exhalation of air from my lips.

"Is there a timer?"

"You've got seven minutes and forty-three seconds. Go now."

"Get away from him, Cas." I pulled on Zin's grip but my BodyGuard was relentless in his retreat. Gita was just ahead of him, gun out and eyes searching the throne room.

"I put my knee on a pressure plate. I can't move without setting the bomb off," Cas said. "Hao's right. Wilson wired the whole damn throne, not just Phanin's body. Get her out of here."

"No." I breathed the denial, unable to believe this was happening again. Zin's hand tightened on my wrist, in sympathy or to make sure I didn't try to break free, it was hard to tell. "Cas, no."

"It's all right, this has to happen." My *Dve* smiled over his shoulder. "It's been an honor, Your Majesty."

"We can—"

"Go, Emmory," Cas said. Then he said something else I couldn't hear. Emmory reached out, his hand hovering near Cas's head, anguish clear on his face. Cas said something else. Emmory nodded once, dropped his hand, and crossed to us with Hao right behind him.

"No, I won't leave him!"

Hao grabbed my free arm. "Not an option, Hail."

Zin and Hao dragged me toward the door. The last time I saw Cas he was kneeling in front of my throne with his head bowed.

305

30

The next seven minutes were a desperate run for our lives. I followed Emmory and Zin at a full sprint down the hallway they'd escorted me along only a few short months ago, and ran across the tarmac of the landing pad until the explosion caused the ground under our feet to roll. Several seconds later, the shock wave slammed into us. I tucked my chin and my arms into my chest as I fell forward. I hit the ground and rolled.

"Majesty?"

"I'm okay." I took Zin's hand and let him help me to my feet. "Shiva, preserve us," I whispered, staring at the destruction.

My palace and the streets around it were smoking rubble, flames peeking out from the dust cloud slowly settling back to ground. Gita whispered a litany of curses. They floated on the air with her frozen breath.

"We need to keep moving."

Fisting my shaking hands and blinking back tears, I nodded at Emmory and followed him across the tarmac.

Debris from the palace had taken down the fence around the landing pad, and we climbed over, jumping down to the other side. Tears streaked Kisah's face, but my BodyGuard's green eyes were hard with purpose as they scanned the streets around us.

"Majesty, down!" She shoved into me, grunting when the laser blast slammed into her side instead.

"Hostiles at our three o'clock."

"Johar, where are you?"

"Lantle's down!"

I grabbed for Kisah, dragging her behind a shattered wall and yanking my knife free. "Keep pressure on that," I ordered, shimmying out of my coat and my sweater.

Zin appeared at my side, taking the fabric as I finished cutting and jerking the long sleeves of my shirt free. "Put your clothes back on before you freeze, Majesty."

Kisah laughed and then winced. "Don't do that."

Zin gave her a crooked grin as he bandaged her wound. "Can you stand?"

"I'll be fine," she replied, leaning on him.

More sounds of fighting echoed in the air, but then it fell silent and Johar's voice rang out.

"All clear here."

I picked up my Hessian again and shared a look with Zin. Kisah's eyes had glassed over and our makeshift bandage was already red with blood. *"Emmory, we need to move. Kisah needs Fasé."*

"Johar's got transport," he replied. *"Can she move?"*

"We've got her."

"Majesty, you take her, I'll cover both of you."

I rolled my eyes at Zin and stepped out of cover. Johar and the Marines were guarding a truck and I led the way across the street toward them. Gita was already waiting for us and she slipped to Kisah's other side to keep her upright.

Emmory, Hao, and Ikeki emerged from my right and my already broken heart collapsed into smaller pieces.

I asked the question anyway. "Lantle?"

Emmory shook his head.

I crawled into the truck, taking Kisah from Zin and tucking her against my side. She was trembling, from grief, or shock, or a combination of both, and I pressed my cheek to her hair, murmuring useless words of comfort as the truck lurched forward.

"Where's Fasé?" I passed Kisah off to the medic.

"I don't know, Majesty. We'll take care of her. Major Morri is in the medical bay."

I nodded and watched as they helped my BodyGuard away. Chaos swirled around me and I swallowed down the grief still bubbling up in my throat as I sank down onto a nearby bench.

Cas was gone. Lantle was gone. I couldn't wrap my head around it.

I shivered against the sudden cold and pulled my robe tighter as I stared out through the windows into the darkness.

"Do you want something hot to drink, Highness?"

I turned with a smile in Cas's direction. "I'm all right, thank you for asking."

He returned the smile. My baby-faced Guard, still so uncertain but desperately trying to follow in Emmory's footsteps. It was clear he idolized my Ekam. *Clear he wasn't sure what to think of me.*

The feeling was mutual. I wasn't sure what had possessed Emmory to pick a kid barely old enough to shave for my BodyGuard roster, let alone for my first team. Though if I had to guess, he was probably hoping that Zin's and Jet's experience would help Cas.

"Are you from the capital?"

"Not originally, Highness. My grandmother and I moved here a few years ago when my mother went to temple."

"I'm sorry to hear that," I murmured, glancing at him over my shoulder.

"Thank you, Highness. She'd been ill for a while; it was very hard to lose her, but also a blessing. I'm glad she's no longer hurting."

"Hail." The warmth of a wet cloth on my blood-sticky hands and Emmory's smoky voice pulled me out of the memory. "Are you injured anywhere?"

"My heart is shattered into pieces."

He squeezed his fingers around mine, then set the cloth aside and grabbed a towel, rubbing my hands between his in what was a futile attempt to warm them.

I was never going to be warm again. I was going to lose them all, one after the other until I would be alone just like Wilson promised. The shudder ripped through me and Emmory jerked his head up, clearly expecting tears to fall from my eyes. His frown grew when they didn't and he rose up on his knees, pulling me into his arms via the blanket I hadn't even noticed was wrapped around me.

Pressing my forehead into his shoulder, I willed the tears to come, but they refused. There were only the tremors I couldn't seem to stop and I shook in Emmory's arms for what felt like an eternity.

"How can we go on like this? What is the point of fighting if we're just going to lose the best pieces of us?"

Emmory slid his hands up my back and into my hair, pulling me away just enough so he could touch his forehead to mine and look me in the eyes. "Because the alternative is to quit, and that's something you and I both know we're incapable of doing. It's something you and I both know Portis, and Jet, and Cas, and all the others wouldn't want from us. So we'll keep going—you'll keep going—to the end of this."

"I—"

The cursing in Cheng cut through the air like a knife. Emmory and I jerked apart.

"That's Hao."

"It's coming from the medical area."

We sprinted across the room and Emmory parted a path through the crowd with a booming "Move!" People scattered, revealing the scene on the far side of the room.

Hao had grabbed Fasé by the throat and had pinned her to the wall. He was swearing at her, his words made almost unintelligible by his rage.

"How could you? You have no right!"

Dailun grabbed Hao and tried to pull him off the Farian but only got a punch to the mouth for his trouble. He staggered into me. I grabbed him by the upper arms. Dailun shook his head and swore.

"Help Emmory clear the room," I said, passing him over to Gita.

"Hai, jiejie." Dailun wiped the blood from his mouth and nodded.

Hao had his gun out, but it wasn't pointed at Fasé—who was eerily calm—it was pointed at the room behind him. I'd never seen my mentor this angry, not in all the years we'd been together. Once or twice he'd come close, but his famous self-control had kicked in and taken over.

Not this time.

I shared a look with Johar, who was on the other side of the room. She was circling around to get a better angle of attack.

"Stay put," I said over the *smati*. *"If I can't get him to let her go, then move."*

She nodded and froze in the shadows.

"Hao, let her go." I closed my hand over the gun and his hand, felt his resistance.

"You don't understand, Hail. She killed him."

"You're going to kill her and I can't let you do that. Let her go." I reached across and put my other hand on his forearm. "Let her go," I whispered.

Hao squeezed his eyes shut and I watched in shock as a tear slid free. Fasé fell into me when he released her, coughing and choking as she slid to the floor.

"She killed him, Hail. She sent Cas to his death."

The words didn't register for several heartbeats, but when they sank into my thick skull they detonated with the same force as the bomb that had just reduced my palace to a pile of rubble.

"What?"

"She sent him to his death." Hao shook free of me, slamming his gun back into its holster. "Your *zhù* had to have gone nuts with the proximity warnings, Hail. You don't think *his* was doing the same thing?" He tapped himself in the temple, impatient with my incomprehension. "He didn't accidentally put his knee on that damn pressure plate. He knew it was there. She told him it was there!" Hao jabbed a finger at Fasé as she got to her feet.

My *smati* had done its job and registered the explosives. Cas's should have done the same. His words floated back to me: *It's all right, this has to happen.*

"Fasé?"

"It was necessary, Majesty." She was still so calm. Her wide golden eyes shone without a hint of the misery I was feeling. It was unnerving.

"Necessary?"

Fasé blinked at me, her lashes falling over her eyes, resting on her cheeks, and her face suddenly seemed very alien to me. "Yes, necessary. Cas's death was required."

"I hope you're going to be the one to tell his grandmother that."

"He already told her, before you left for the palace."

Her smile made my hand twitch toward my gun.

"After all that cowshit about rocks and rivers, you *told* him what would happen? You knew Wilson had wired the palace and you didn't warn *me*?"

"I took a chance and told him what needed to happen. He proved his loyalty and his devotion to you, to the empire—"

I slapped her without thinking. The blow sent Fasé spinning away from me. Before I could advance on her, Emmory had my arms locked up behind my back.

"Shiva damn you into a barren wasteland. How could you?" I yelled at her. "I should have let you shoot yourself! Cas would still be alive if you were dead!"

Fasé didn't react, but I felt Emmory flinch against my back at my cruel words.

"Did you know about this?" I demanded.

"No, Majesty. You know I never would have—but Cas told me in the throne room before he died. He said Fasé told him what would happen and that his sacrifice would keep us all safe."

I didn't try to stop the choked sob of relief at his words. I wasn't sure I could withstand a betrayal from him.

"He also told me to tell you not to blame Fasé."

"He died because she told him—" I couldn't even finish the

sentence. "How could you, Fasé? It makes no sense. You sent him to die—for nothing."

"I sent him to die for everything." Fasé folded her hands together and bowed. "Everything I have seen after today ended in disaster for us. This was a moment where the war was won or lost. Where we all lived or died.

"I know it makes no sense to you, Majesty, but that is what I saw. Cas survived the bomb in the palace and we all died, or he died and we all lived."

"You are the one who was cautioning us about changing things. This isn't even a boulder, Fasé, you dropped a mountain into the stream! And Cas is gone." I sagged in Emmory's grip, nearly dragging us both to the ground.

"It's not right." Hao snarled the words from behind us. "You've no right to do this. Use us up like chess pieces, sacrificing us as you please for whatever delusions you're having."

"It is not a delusion," Fasé replied.

Hao's response was a curse in Cheng that had even Johar inhaling in shock, and then he turned and stalked out of the room. Emmory lowered me the rest of the way to the floor and let me go. I dropped my head into my shaking hands. My shuddering breaths drowned out the murmuring of my *Ekam* and Johar.

The heavy weight of a blanket settled around me again, followed by Zin's hand on my shoulder. "Majesty, can you stand?"

I gave a jerky nod and Zin helped me to my feet.

I didn't look up as we navigated our way out of the room. Couldn't look into the faces of the people who were still lining the hallway as Zin ushered me past. I had sent a good man to his death—knowing or not, it was my responsibility and now Cas was gone.

We reached my quarters and I sank down into a chair, pulling my legs up against my chest and wrapping the blanket tighter. The silence was a strange blessing.

I rested my cheek on a knee, looking at Zin. He stood by the door, lost in his own thoughts.

"Thank you."

"Majesty?" He blinked.

I held a hand out. "Thank you. I don't say it enough. I should have told Cas . . . I don't know why all of you—"

"Stop." Zin crossed to me and sat in the chair next to me, taking my hand in his. "You don't have to say it, Hail. Cas knew. We know, it's why we're all here in the first place." He squeezed my fingers. "And I know what you're going to say. You don't have to understand it, you just need to trust in it. And in us."

31

The noises outside my door woke me from a fitful dream and I slid from my bed, rubbing at my eyes. Opening the door resulted in Hao falling into me and both of us ending up on the floor in a tangle of limbs.

"Are you *drunk*?"

"Are you *not*?"

"I'm sorry, Majesty." Gita apologized, making a grab for Hao as he rolled off me. "Damn it, Hao."

"It's fine. He's hard enough to manage when he's sober." I took advantage of Hao's distraction and stole the bottle out of his hand. "Leave him, Gita, it's fine."

"Majesty—"

"Go on," I said, waving a hand at the door. I kicked Hao as soon as the door had closed.

"Ow! What was that for?"

"A number of things." I took a drink from the bottle. "Starting with pretending to be drunker than you really are, which you don't have to do to come see me, you know. Secondly, I kicked you for giving Gita a hard time. And finally, for nearly getting yourself killed. Fasé could have snuffed you out like a candle."

Hao rolled upright and gave me a clear-eyed look that proved my first point. "I like giving Gita a hard time; she's like you and doesn't put up with it."

I held the bottle out of his reach until he sighed.

"I was angry. I'm sorry."

"To Caspian Yuri Kreskin, a man who was better than all of us." Taking another drink, I handed the bottle back to him.

"To my fellow stupid fool." Hao saluted the ceiling with it before he drank. "She's dangerous, Hail, and you know it. She doesn't know what *she's* doing or, even worse, she does know and is fucking with us."

"Are you saying I should have let Emmory die?"

"Of course not." He shook his head. "That was an accident, an aberration. It's what started this whole mess with Fasé in the first place. You couldn't have stopped her any more than I could have stopped Cas from stepping over that line.

"I'm saying that meddling in things like this has consequences. There's a natural order to life. We win some, we lose some. We don't know what kind of damage we're doing by changing things."

"So I should quit fighting?"

Hao reached out and smacked me in the back of the head. "Don't be a brat. I'm a big fan of the fight-to-the-death scenario, but I'm also a realist and I know one of these days I won't win."

"Liar. You're going to live forever."

"I hope not, that's a dreadful thought." He took a drink and held the bottle out. "What I'm saying is you can't rely on Fasé. It sets a dangerous precedent. You've got to commit to winning or losing this on your own."

"If I lose, you're all going down with me," I replied.

"I'm okay with that."

I set the bottle aside, my stomach suddenly rolling at the thought of Hao dead. "What have I done to inspire this loyalty from you?"

He started to say something, thought better of it, and rested his chin in his hand. "Putting it into words would ruin it, little sister. Just trust that I have always been and will always be your family."

I laughed, but the tears that followed caught me by surprise. Hao muttered several curses as he scrambled to my side and wrapped his arms around me.

The door opened and I peeked past Hao's shoulder at my *Ekam* standing in the entryway.

"Majesty."

Untangling himself from me and picking up his bottle, Hao got to his feet and offered it to Emmory. My *Ekam* took a drink and handed it back. Hao saluted us both and left the room, closing the door behind him.

"I have a message from Cas for you," Emmory said, helping me to my feet. The message passed to my *smati* with the contact. "I'll let you view it in private."

"No, stay." I tightened my hand around his. "I don't want to watch it alone."

When he nodded, I tossed the message up onto the wall.

"Your Majesty." Cas's smile was heartbreaking. "I left these messages so Emmory would find them and distribute them. Please do not be angry, especially with Fasé. She, like the rest of us, cares for you and wishes to keep you safe. I hope you can forgive her—forgive me—for this.

"Your road is not done and I regret I can't be there to walk it with you any longer. Please, do not forget: You are the Empress of Indrana, you are the legendary gunrunner, and there is nothing you cannot do." Cas folded his hands together and pressed them to his heart, lips, and head. "It has been the greatest honor of my life to have been your BodyGuard."

The message ended and I pinched the bridge of my nose. I was out of tears, the anger boiling and rolling through my gut. I was angry at Cas and at Fasé. How I was going to trust her again I didn't know.

I checked the date on my *smati*. "Emmory, I want that man dead before the bells for Vasant start to ring. Find him."

"Yes, Majesty." He bowed and left me alone. I curled into a chair, pulled up the information we had on Wilson in my *smati*, and began to read.

"We can be reasonably sure that the prisoners Wilson had in custody were not in the palace when the bomb exploded."

"Define 'reasonably sure,' Caspel," I said.

"We haven't found any remains."

Alice pressed her hand to her mouth as she turned her head toward Taz.

"And no response from their *smatis*?"

"No, Majesty."

We'd lost so many matriarchs already. I didn't want to think about how Indrana would suffer if I had to stock the council with third and fourth daughters. I studied the tabletop before looking back at Caspel. "He wouldn't have killed them. Not like that. Keep looking through the rubble and let me know if you find anything."

"We will, ma'am."

"What about Ambassador Toropov?"

Caspel shook his head. "Same, Majesty. We're not sure, but

our guess is that the palace was empty when you entered. Wilson could still think Jaden is on his side, or he could be holding him prisoner."

I ticked the item off my list. "General Triskan, your report on the status of the ground forces?"

"Cleanup continues, ma'am," he replied. "The bulk of Phanin's forces surrendered at the Surakesh port. There are some pockets of resistance, but we've got troops moving through the city. They're running out of places to run."

"Good. Continue to accept surrenders as they are offered. If they fight you, though—"

"Take no prisoners, yes ma'am." Aganey nodded.

The war was won. Phanin was dead, his forces defeated. Leena's betrayal stung, and I'd issued the controversial order to take no prisoners among those who decided to keep fighting instead of surrendering. There'd been few objections, and aside from a look from Emmory, none of my BodyGuards disagreed.

What was left of my BodyGuards, that was. As Aganey continued with his report on the ground fighting, I looked around the room. Emmory stood by my chair. Gita and Kisah were by the door inside the room. Ikeki and Zin were outside, guarding the hallway.

Emmory had received a message from Iza and Indula asking for permission to rejoin us for duty. Despite my promise to not interfere in his BodyGuard decisions, I'd refused, and Emmory hadn't taken it well. The resulting argument about the need for more security around me had been bitter.

We were down to five BodyGuards, but we also had our Marines as well as Johar, Hao, and Dailun. I wasn't ever alone.

Besides, I was in the mood for a fight and Dark Mother help anyone who decided to be stupid enough to tangle with me.

"We're searching what video feeds survived the palace explosion," General Saito said, dragging me back from my morose thoughts to the meeting in front of me. "There's no sign of Wilson leaving."

"Is there any reason we don't think he skipped the planet?" Johar asked. She sat in the corner with her feet kicked up on Bial's leg. "I wouldn't be hanging around here if I'd just gotten my ass handed to me."

"She's got a point; he's traditionally taken off after big events and this one didn't go as he'd planned." Bial pointed at the image of the smoking crater that used to be my palace still hanging in the air. "He's got to know we'll be combing the capital for him. I wouldn't stay. It's a death sentence."

Others around the table were nodding in agreement, but I shook my head. "No, he's still here. Maybe not in the capital but somewhere close."

"That goes against everything we've learned about the man," Hao said. "He's patient. He'll fall back and wait. It's what he's done every time."

"Not this time," I replied. "It's too late for him to disappear and start over. Where we are, ladies and gentlemen, is the culmination of decades of planning for this man. He has one thing left to accomplish and he's not going anywhere until he finishes it—finishes me."

"He can try," Hao snarled from his spot across the table.

"So when are we headed out?" Emmory asked.

I looked up at him with a strained laugh. "I think we should figure out where he is first, don't you?"

Emmory smiled one of his rare smiles. "You're the one who said she wanted him dead by Vasant."

"*Ekam*, you can't possibly think that it's a good idea to use the empress as bait." Caspel rubbed a hand over his face.

"It's not, but it's the best idea we've got and we all know that she'll do it regardless. I'd rather be at her Majesty's side when it happens than leave her to face this alone."

Warmth blossomed in my chest, but I contained my smile as I slapped my palms down on the table and got to my feet.

"General Saito, coordinate a few of your Tracker pairs with Hao and Johar. Let's start reviewing recordings from a week before the explosion at the palace. Flag any movement, no matter how inconsequential."

Hao and Johar both nodded.

"Is there anything else?" I looked around the room. Everyone shook their heads. "Meeting adjourned. Alice, Taz, if you'll stay?"

I settled back into my chair as the room cleared out. Alice watched me closely, Taz at her side.

"Alice, I want you to take the lead on reconstruction efforts."

"Majesty, that is—"

"Your job now," I interrupted her. "If you get pushback from the matriarchs, I want you to tell them to come to me. Our government is in disarray. Indrana is at war and the throne has the power. *You* are the throne. Never forget that.

"We have a chance here to change things for the better. I want you two to be the face of that change." I gave them a soft smile. "Start planning your wedding. The people will need something bright to focus on in the coming months."

Taz covered his face with his hands. Alice gave me a look I was all too familiar with and the sight of it had me laughing. "The empire appreciates your sacrifice."

"With all due respect, Majesty, I hate you."

Reaching out to pat her hand, I shook my head, still laughing. "I know, Alice, believe me, I know."

32

hit the ground hard, the air gushing out of me, and I tried to drag it back into my lungs as I rolled over, but they refused to cooperate.

It cost me precious seconds, and the kick that caught me in the ribs would bruise. I managed to swing my arm out and I wrapped it around Hao's ankle. Jerking him toward me, still gasping for air, I rolled into him.

Hao was forced to drop to the mat or suffer a broken leg. Spitting a curse at me that was tangled in his laughter, he let his head fall against the mat.

I flopped onto my back, still trying to force air into my lungs. Zin was there, grabbing my wrist and stretching me out until my diaphragm decided to start functioning again.

"I thought for a minute you hadn't learned anything new since I'd seen you last," Hao said, crawling over and patting my face.

"Still missed that sweep." I slapped his hand away.

"It happens." Hao caught my hand and pulled me upright. "You had the presence of mind to react to it. I remember the first time I did that to you, you just lay there flopping around like a fish."

"It took me forever to even see that coming." I laughed. "That was almost worse, to just watch it happen and not be able to avoid it."

"It was fun to watch your face when it happened."

Rolling my eyes at him, I took a deep breath, the expected pain of my ribs spiking. "You want to go again?"

Hao shook his head. "Zin will kick my ass." He touched my ribs, eyebrow rising when I shifted away. "You're going to need to see a Farian for that."

"I'll be fine." I hugged Hao, feeling him jerk in surprise. "Thank you," I whispered against his ear. "For everything."

"Of course, *sha zhu*. Always."

I took the towel Zin handed me, quirking an eyebrow at his frown. "What?"

Zin didn't reply right away, but merely fell into step with me as I left the room. We'd moved from the hidden intelligence headquarters into a hotel on the outskirts of the capital, and I was grateful for the hot water and other luxuries.

"What was that?"

I finished drying my face while we waited for the lift. "What was what?"

"Thanks for everything." He reached out and held the door, gesturing for me to go first.

"I can't thank people?"

"It sounded more like you were saying good-bye." Zin reached out and flipped the stop. The lift shuddered to a halt and I gripped the towel as the familiar panic sank its teeth into me. "You've been doing this all week, Hail. Putting Alice in charge of reconstruction efforts, putting her in front of the cameras, getting people used to her face. You've been going around saying good-bye to the people who matter to you. Most of them haven't noticed. I have."

"What's the reality here, Zin? I die trying to kill Wilson, or I win."

"And if you win?"

I brushed off his question as easily as he'd brushed off the idea that Wilson might kill me. "I am not the best option for the empire. We've all known that from the beginning, haven't we? The only reason I came home was that there was no other choice."

"Majesty." There was hurt in Zin's voice. "Your duty is to the empire—"

Anger snapped to life in my chest and I slammed a fist into the wall of the lift. "My duty was to my sisters! To my mother and father. I don't owe the empire anything. But I have gone above and beyond for it regardless. I have thrown body after body into the shredder, sacrificing everyone I love into the relentless gaping maw of the empire. What else do you want from me?"

"For you to be the empress," Zin replied. "Otherwise what was the point of all this?" He hit the button and the lift started moving again.

"The point was to save the empire," I whispered. "It was never about me being empress."

The door opened and I pushed by Zin into the hallway. As I passed I swore I heard him murmur, "It was always about you being empress."

My step faltered, but before I could ask Zin what he meant, Gita and Dailun rushed up.

"There you are, you need to see this." Dailun grabbed me by the arm and dragged me down the hall. "Sorry, *jiejie*," he said at Gita's growled warning.

"What's going on?"

"We think we've figured out where Wilson is," Gita said. "Or at the very least where Leena was when she transmitted that message."

"How?"

Dailun pushed open the door and gestured at the young man sitting at the table. "Lel here used to work at the Desai estate outside the capital." He pointed to the image on the wall. Leena dominated the screen, but there was a piece of the background showing and they'd sectioned out that chunk and enlarged it into a separate image.

"What am I looking at?"

"Flooring, Majesty."

I gave Gita a look but she was as confused as I was.

"The video search gave us some idea of when they left the palace. There were several trucks moving in and out in the weeks before. We suspect that's what Wilson used to move the prisoners and the bulk of the staff. The rest of the staff was fired the morning the palace exploded, including Lel."

"Phanin told us to go home, Your Majesty. Truthfully we were all relieved. We didn't want to stay after they took over the palace, but they threatened our families." The young man kept his dark eyes locked on the floor at my feet.

"We put out a call for anyone who might have any information about Wilson's and Leena's movements while in the palace or after," Gita said. "Lel answered us and mentioned that the flooring in Leena's broadcast looked like the Desai estate."

"How do you know?"

Lel glanced up at me. "I used to work for the Desai family, Your Majesty. All the noble families provided staff to the palace around the time the Lady Leena married the traitor."

"Both traitors now," I muttered, and Lel dipped his head.

"Yes, Your Majesty, my apologies."

"Are we sure about this?"

"As we can be, Majesty," Gita replied. "We did a news search and found some photos from an event held at the Desai estate last year." She brought those images up on the wall next to the others. "It's a match."

"It's a trap," Zin said.

"Probably. Wilson's not that sloppy." I didn't look back at Zin when I replied. "Have we checked on other possibilities for the floor?"

"It's custom-made, Majesty, installed when the main house was built."

"Okay, find Emmory, and get him up to speed." I made a face. "I need to clean up. We'll meet downstairs in half an hour."

"You need to see a Farian first, Majesty," Zin said, catching me by the arm. "Fasé's room is on the way—"

"No. Call Major Morri. Have her come up to my rooms." I hadn't spoken to Fasé since Cas's death. It was a rift I wasn't sure we could heal. As much as Cas might have wished that I not blame her for his death, I did—and I didn't see any way to forgive her for it.

"Jasa, take Henjai and circle around the west side with Johar and Bial. Gita and Zin, take Kisah up the north stairs. Everyone keep their coms open and their scanners up. At the first hint of explosives you stop your asses—is that clear?" Emmory's voice was hard and echoed in both my com link and my ear.

Their responses were swift and without hesitation.

I crouched by Emmory's side, my Hessian loose in my hand. Major Morri was on my left. Ikeki was at my back and Hao was down on one knee by the bumper of our vehicle.

"It's quiet, like the palace," Zin said. *"No movement, no life signs."*

"I'm not picking up any explosives," Kisah said. *"Not on this side."*

"Bial and I are in through the side door. Still no sign of explosives. I'm picking up a weird smell, but my sensors aren't reading it as poison or possible contagion." Johar's voice was calm and collected.

"The ballroom is where the flooring is," Gita said. *"Permission to head that direction, Ekam?"*

"Granted. Keep your eyes open." Emmory reached out and tapped my shoulder, pointing toward Hao and then the house. He tipped his head at Ikeki and made the same gesture.

I used the vehicle for cover, poking Hao on our way by and pausing for just a moment so he could get in front of me as we made our way toward the house.

"There's a tablet in the middle of the ballroom floor, Emmory," Zin said. *"Scans indicate it's not rigged with anything. Should we search the rest of the house?"*

We'd reached the servants' entrance. Hao pressed his hand to the door panel. "It's not locked," he whispered, and carefully eased it open.

"Wait," I said. "Johar said she picked up a weird smell?"

Emmory nodded. I reached down at the edge of the doorframe. The snow coating the ground was pockmarked with holes from the melting snow that dripped off the roof. I brought my hand to my face, grimacing at the smell on my fingers. Hao muttered a curse, grabbing my hand and inhaling.

"Accelerant. Something waterproof."

"Everyone out of the house now," Emmory ordered. "Why didn't our scanners pick it up?"

"It's not an explosive," Hao replied. "It's harmless unless—"

The ground at our feet erupted into flames. Hao pushed me back and I wrapped my hand in his jacket when I fell, jerking him with me away from the fire.

The flames spread, engulfing the house as we scrambled back to the vehicles. I slapped at Hao, burning my hands as I tried to put out the fire crawling across the sleeve of his jacket. He stripped it off with a curse and stomped the clothing into the dirt.

The others came running from the house, clothing singed and smoking, faces smeared with soot, but they were all uninjured and alive. I leaned against the vehicle, my arms wrapped around my waist, and released a shuddering breath as I slid to the ground.

Zin handed the tablet off to Emmory and crouched at my side. "Trap," he said.

"Yeah." My hands throbbed and I squeezed my eyes shut against the sudden pain. "Almost a good one."

"Are you hurt?"

"I was putting Hao out." Wincing, I uncurled my fingers. My left hand was merely red, but the right, the one I'd dipped into the accelerant by the door, was blistered from the tips of my fingers and down across my palm.

"Major," Zin said, waving Dio over.

She put a hand on my shoulder and a wave of relief washed over me. I was still shaky, so I didn't protest when Zin helped me to my feet. Emmory finished his orders to the Guards and they spread out in a defensive circle around the vehicle.

"Message for you, Majesty," he said, holding out the tablet.

I took it from him, trying to shake off the sense of dread that had appeared in my chest.

"Hail." Wilson's face appeared, and he smiled slowly. "So glad you could make it. I'm sorry that you were too late, though.

We've moved on, but I can't promise we'll stay here long. We might need to go where the air is easier to breathe. I don't want you to fool yourself into thinking we're on the run or you somehow have gained the upper hand here. I am smarter than you and I've been at this for far longer than you could imagine."

"That's what you think," I muttered. "I know who you are."

The recording shrugged as though he'd heard me, even though I knew he hadn't. "Since I can't see into the future, either you've watched this and are now trapped in a burning building, or you've somehow managed to escape and are watching it in safety. I suspect you're safe, Your Majesty." He gave a mocking bow. "You've proven damned difficult to kill despite my best efforts. I just hope your precious BodyGuards made it out alive also. You should keep an eye on them, you're starting to run out of bodies to throw at me."

I refused to let the anger out, and it hardened into a frozen lump in my stomach.

"I don't want you to think you've got all the time in the world, Hail. So don't wait. Time is ticking. Your aunt Loka seemed to think you'd win this, even as I put my gun to her head and pulled the trigger." Wilson wiggled his fingers at me. "I'll see you soon."

I handed the tablet back to Emmory before I gave in to the urge to smash it against the side of the vehicle. "Get in the car. I know where we're going next."

33

"ajesty, where are we going?" Emmory wasn't happy about me driving, but I'd gotten behind the wheel before he could stop me.

"The Naidu estate is just down the road," I said. "He wasn't at all subtle with the clues. Aunt Loka had an antique Earth clock in the hallway. This gigantic thing we could actually hide in as children."

"The clock is ticking," Zin murmured from the backseat.

"Most likely. He's also probably hinting at the fact that he still has four matriarchs in custody and if we don't play his little treasure hunt he's going to start executing them." I glanced away from the road at Emmory's muttered curse.

"There will be another trap," Hao said, and I nodded.

"He's been at work on this since they took over. We can't just rush in there, we'll have to try to figure out what the danger is."

"Or I could just go in," Johar said.

I glanced into the rearview mirror in time to see her shrug.

"Jo—"

"It takes a lot to kill me." She grinned and winked. "The next message will be in the clock, yes? I go in and get it and get back out before whatever trap Wilson's laid can spring shut. We can be reasonably sure he's not going to use explosives or fire."

"Why would you say that?" Zin asked.

"It's repetitive. He thinks he's smart, he'll want to do something new. That actually makes it easier. We can narrow down possible traps as we go."

"As long as they don't kill us first, we're golden." Hao pointed out the window. "Pull over there, Hail. We've got good cover coming up to the estate."

I nodded and steered the vehicle off the road, slowing to a stop behind a stand of trees. The Marines pulled in behind us and everyone piled out, checking weapons and moving into position in easy synchronicity.

"Be careful," I said to Johar. "Rai will never let me hear the end of it if you die."

"*He* won't?" She laughed. "Hell, I'm coming back to haunt your ass."

"Fair enough." I patted her back.

Johar nodded and tapped a hand on Bial's shoulder. He nodded, following her into the brush.

The Naidu estate was a sprawling affair. Building after building rose up from between the rolling snow-covered hills. The main house was at the center of it all, a massive mansion with graceful spires reaching for the blue sky.

"The clock was in the main entrance," I said over the com link. *"I doubt it's been moved, but that's always a possibility."*

"I've got a map," Johar replied. *"We're not going in through the front, though."*

"Probably a good choice," Emmory said. *"Bial, give me a visual."*

"Yes, sir."

"Coming up on perimeter. No alarm systems active. No life signs."

Zin elbowed me in the side. "Why did Wilson say they wouldn't stay long but would be moving to where the air was easier to breathe?"

"What?"

"He said they were moving on to where the air was easier to breathe. It doesn't make any sense. The Naidu estate is in a valley, but not particularly higher or lower than the Desai one. They're equal distances from the capital. Air quality would be the same."

"Coming up on the mansion," Johar said over the com link. *"Still no life signs. The air tastes funny, kind of like—Bial!"*

"What's going on?"

"Bial went down," Emmory said. "His readings are all over the place. *Johar, can he stand on his own?"*

"No. He's only barely conscious. I'm getting him back up now." She grunted over the com link as she lifted him. *"Come on, big guy, give me a little help, will you? You're the size of a damned Parsi elephant."*

"Zin, Jasa, go get him. Johar, keep going." Emmory pulled his gun free. *"Everyone else, keep your eyes open."*

I rubbed my sweaty palms on my thighs as I waited. Zin and Jasa came back a few moments later, dragging a semiconscious Bial with them. Major Morri rushed up to meet them, putting her hands on his chest. She frowned, slid her hands up to cup his face, and then looked at me.

"I don't know what this is, Majesty. There's no damage I can sense, but his lungs aren't functioning right."

"Wouldn't matter anyway," Bial said with a smile. "I'm not compatible."

Major Morri nodded in confirmation. "He's right, Majesty. I wouldn't be able to do anything even if I knew what was wrong."

"The air." Wilson's words snapped into me. "Bugger me. *Johar, what's the air quality? Are you in the house?"*

"Yes, I'm inside the house. That smell is getting worse. Let me run a scan."

The numbers appeared on my *smati* as Johar gathered them.

"There's a spike in several elements that's above normal range and something I can't find a match for. It doesn't seem to be an issue for me; Rai's filters are taking care of whatever this is."

"I don't want you in there any longer than necessary," I replied. *"Get to the clock and get out."*

"Yes, ma'am."

I kneeled at Bial's side, putting a hand on his shoulder when his eyes opened. "Don't talk, just focus on breathing."

He dragged in a breath and abruptly started coughing. I turned my head, too slow, and the blood spattered over my cheek.

"Emmory!"

Dio put her hands on Bial again. "I don't understand this. His lungs are—" She broke off and looked at me with a horrified expression. "We have to get him to a hospital, now."

"Johar, where are you?"

"Behind you," she replied, tossing a tablet in Zin's direction. Blood stained her lips and she gave me a wry smile. "Tell Rai he needs to upgrade his filters," she said, and collapsed.

It was a terrifying race back into the capital and the nearest hospital before both Johar and Bial drowned in their own blood. Zin and Jasa also started coughing up blood as we reached the hospital, but their exposure to the unknown toxin had been far less and the doctors were optimistic about their recovery chances.

Johar was slated to make a full recovery, thanks in part

to the filters Rai had installed and her own amazing body modifications.

Bial, on the other hand, was dying.

I pressed a hand to the glass separating us, watching the nurse slip the mask over his face. "Can I go in?"

Emmory knocked on the glass, catching the nurse's attention. He pointed at the door and she nodded, crossing the room to meet us.

"Majesty. I am so sorry. We've never seen anything like this." She bowed her head at me. "There's too much damage to his lungs. He doesn't have much time left. All we can really do is try to make him comfortable."

"I'd like to sit with him, if I can."

"I'll get you a chair."

"Thank you."

I moved to the bed, reaching out and wrapping my fingers around Bial's hand. His eyes flew open, met mine, and a slight smile appeared beneath the oxygen mask. Emmory circled around the bed, resting his hands on the edge. Bial reached up and tugged the mask down.

"Majesty." His voice was thready, the single word a clear effort.

"Bial." I smiled, surprised by the tears threatening at the backs of my eyes. The nurse brought a chair and I sank into it.

"I'm sorry, Your Majesty." He gasped the words out, his hand tightening around mine. "Sorry for doubting you. Sorry for failing your family."

"Stop," I whispered. "You did your best, Bial. I forgive you."

He smiled. "I hope the gods are as kind, Your Majesty." Turning his head to Emmory, he reached out his other hand to my *Ekam*. "Don't give up, Tresk. Don't let them win."

"I won't, I swear it to you."

Bial's breath rushed out, a jagged exhale that was followed only by the even tone of his heart monitor flatlining.

I squeezed his limp fingers one last time, murmuring a benediction as my tears fell onto our joined hands. "Go to temple, Bialriarn Plantage Malik, stand before the Dark Mother with your head held high. You were a loyal citizen of the empire and your name will never be forgotten."

"Jai maa." Emmory covered our hands with his as the doctors came into the room. "Come on, Majesty." He led me out and down the hall until he found an empty room, ushering me inside and closing the door behind us.

"He deserved better." I couldn't stop the sharp laugh and threw my hands up into the air. "I can't believe I'm saying that, Emmy."

"It's true. I know how you feel, Majesty, I know how conflicted it is to grieve for someone we were sure was an enemy. Bial proved his worth. It's cold comfort."

"It is." I sank down onto the bed and stared at my hands. "Even worse is I can't do anything for him right now. Maybe once this is all over, if any of us are left to remember the dead."

Emmory sat next to me and handed over the tablet. "There will be, and right now there are four women still alive who we need to find. Bial would want us to keep going."

I pressed the button on the tablet, and Wilson's face appeared.

"Found us! Well, almost, we've gone and abandoned you again. I hope you're not coughing your lungs out, Hail. That would be disappointing. I found an old stockpile of Mustard T-18 gas in an abandoned warehouse on Humlvid. Such nasty stuff, but outlawed for so long I'm pretty sure none of the modern scanner programs will recognize it. I'd say you've got about four minutes until you're spitting blood if you're watching this inside the house."

"Emmory," I said, but he was already on his feet.

"Gita, Mustard T-18, tell the doctors. Get everyone out of their gear and into the nearest decontamination showers. I've got the empress."

I headed for the door, shouting for a nurse as I opened it. "I need a decontamination shower, now."

The young man I grabbed gaped at me for a second, shook himself, and pointed. "Three doors and to the left, Your Majesty."

"Get me a pair of scissors and a saline wash," Emmory snapped as he grabbed my upper arm and propelled me down the hallway.

Mustard T-18 was a bastardized version of Earth-made mustard gas, a chemical weapon outlawed in the twentieth century. It had been revived and used in a civil war on Humlvid. By the time the Solarian Conglomerate had intervened, more than half the population of the planet had been killed or permanently crippled by the new gas.

"Rinse her eyes," Emmory ordered the nurse, taking the scissors and cutting through the neck of my shirt and down the sleeve. "Tip your head back, Majesty."

I tossed the tablet in my hand onto a nearby counter and complied as the nurse squeezed saline into first one eye and then the other.

"Your hair."

"Cut it," I said. It would take too long to wash and dry.

"I'm sorry." Emmory's voice was filled with surprising regret and I felt the separation as he sheared off my braid at the base of my neck. Fumbling with my belt and swearing when I realized my boots were going to be a problem, I took the saline from the nurse. "Cut my laces," I said, blinking to clear my vision. "Emmory, your eyes."

"One second, Majesty."

"Don't fucking argue with me."

Emmory stopped, arching an eyebrow, but tipped his head back so I could rinse his eyes out. I tossed the saline back to the nurse, kicked my boots off, and shimmied out of my pants as I headed for the shower.

I stripped the rest of the way, dousing my head under the spray pouring from the ceiling and pumping a generous amount of the cleanser into my palms. I smeared it over my face and into my hair, scrubbing as hard as I could before moving on to the rest of my body.

"Emmory, you have fifteen seconds to join me before I come out there and drag your ass into the shower."

"It's awkward enough as is, Majesty," he said. "Don't make it worse."

"Tell me about it." I snorted a laugh, keeping my eyes shut and my face turned toward the wall as I rinsed off. "Wash my damn back."

"Zin is never going to stop giving me shit about this," he muttered, taking the brush from me and scrubbing my back.

"We're never going to speak of it after this moment is over," I promised, opening my eyes and fixing them on the ceiling. Emmory turned his back on me after handing the brush over and lathered up his own face and head as I scrubbed at his back.

I rinsed off and took the towel the stoic yet blushing nurse handed me as I stepped from the shower. Several other nurses and a doctor skidded into the room and surrounded me, peppering me with orders.

"Open your mouth, Majesty." One sprayed a foul-tasting substance on my tongue. "Swallow."

I did, gagging a little as it went down. "Did someone get Johar cleaned off?"

Another pressed a mask to my face. "Inhale, ma'am."

I did, but raised an eyebrow, and the nurse's eyes went wide.

"They're tending to her now, Majesty, along with the others. Inhale again, please." We repeated the process five more times, interrupted only by an injection in my arm that made me yelp and Emmory's emergence from the decon shower.

I took the offered scrubs from a nurse and followed her behind a curtain, leaning heavily on her as I changed.

"The counteragent is going to leave you a little weak, Majesty; I'd recommend not moving without assistance," she said as she helped me back out into the room and lowered me into a chair.

"Hand me that, will you?" I gestured at the tablet. The nurse grabbed it and passed it over. As the doctor finished up with Emmory, I queued up the message again.

"...inside the house. I really hope that's not the case though, I'd hate to think I beat you that easily. After everything I've heard about the vaunted Cressen Stone, I expect a lot more from you.

"I'll bet you're wondering why I don't come out and fight you like a woman. There's a good reason for that." He grinned, but his eyes were filled with fury. "I want you to understand what it feels like to jump through hoops and then fail so utterly that nothing in your life has any meaning. I want you broken and hopeless and alone at my feet when this is all over." Wilson stopped as the anger Cas had pointed out almost overwhelmed him.

"There's no time to waste, Haili. If you totter around like an old lady, your matriarchs are going to die."

34

I knelt in the tiny hospital temple before a row of lit candles and prayed for the dead. Gita and Hao stood quietly off to one side, their hair still damp and their feet clad in hospital slippers. We were all dressed in scrubs as we waited for clothes to arrive and for the staff to finish decontaminating our boots.

Johar would make a full recovery. Her skin had started to welt from the gas when Emmory and I had gotten the message from Wilson, but the staff was able to clean her up and minimize any additional damage.

"Bial hated me when I first showed up," I said, pressing my folded hands to my heart, lips, and forehead. "Then we were convinced he was working with Ganda, so I counted him as an enemy. He saved my life during the coup and when we thought he'd run off he'd actually still been trying to save the empire."

"He was a good man, Majesty," Gita said. "He didn't have anything but his faith in the empire."

"Johar said his formality was a shield against the world. He opened up to her more than anyone, but I saw some flashes of a decent sense of humor. He will be missed." Hao held a hand out and helped me to my feet. "Where are we going next, *sha zhu*?"

"I don't want to risk your lives again."

"It's too late for that." Hao poked me in the side. "We all knew what we were getting into, even Bial. He could have lived his time out peacefully in a cell. He chose to fight for the empire instead. He'd make that choice again, even knowing what it cost him."

I gave him a wan smile. "That's not much comfort."

"I know." He exhaled, reached up, and patted my cheek, his fingers tangling briefly in my now chin-length hair. "Let's finish this."

Kisah came into the temple. "Clothes are here, Majesty."

"We're going to the Maxwell estate," I replied, and headed for the door. "Gita, find me something to tie my hair back with, will you?"

"Yes, Majesty."

The next fifteen minutes was a flurry of activity as we all got dressed and gathered our equipment.

"The Maxwell estate?" Emmory asked.

"He said tottering old lady." I checked over my gun, slid it into my holster, and finished lacing up my boots. The new laces were stiff and uncooperative. "Plus it makes sense— Clara Desai, Loka Naidu, and Ipsita Maxwell were the most respected members of the council."

Emmory nodded. "I called General Saito's people in to do a flyover, give us some imaging, since they would have time to scramble the flight. I don't want to go in there blind again."

"I'm not going to argue." I leaned back in my seat and put my foot up on the dash. "I want this over with, Emmory. I want him dead."

My *Ekam* didn't respond, but there were several murmurs of agreement from behind me as we pulled out onto the road and headed away from the capital.

The Maxwell estate was more than an hour away; it was smaller than the others and more utilitarian. I rubbed a hand over my heart, sadness for the elderly matriarch blossoming in my chest. We'd lost something amazing with each of the women who'd been killed, but Indrana would feel the loss of her wisdom very keenly.

"Wilson said he wanted me to jump through hoops so I could feel the same way he did," I said, staring out at the snow-covered landscape. "At first I thought he was just referring to courting Mother, but now I think that's the clue for whatever is waiting for us at Maxwell's."

"I'm going to agree with you." Emmory stepped on the brake, bringing the vehicle to a stop, and I looked back at the road as Hao muttered an ugly curse.

The bridge had been blown out, leaving a twelve-meter gap with a yawning canyon below.

Hao slid from the vehicle and I followed, joining him at the edge of the canyon. "What are you thinking?"

He scanned the landscape to our left, shook his head, and swept to the right. "There. There's a low spot about forty meters down."

"Can we make it in the vehicles?"

"Probably." Hao agreed. "But we can't get them across. We'll have to go the rest of the way on foot."

"It's not much farther to the house once we get across. Emmory?"

"We can try it, Majesty. The alternative is to wait for General Saito to scramble some air transport. The ships already did their scan and are back at base."

"We don't have time to waste." I rubbed at the back of my neck, uneasy without the comforting weight of my hair. "Wilson will start killing his hostages if we delay. Take it slow,

Emmory, we'll see how far we get. And call General Saito again, I want some air support for this. We're going to need a ride out of there anyway."

"Yes, ma'am," he replied, heading back to the vehicles. He bypassed our car and leaned in the window of the second one to relay the plan to Jasa and the other Marines.

"What's going on, Majesty?" Zin asked as I got back into the front seat.

"Bridge is out. Hao says there's a shallow spot that way. We should be able to off-road it and then hike the rest of the way." I turned and reached for his hand. "I'm considering having you and Jasa drive the vehicles back to the road after if we make it without ruining them."

"Our lungs are fine, Majesty," Zin replied with a shake of his head. "Major Morri was able to repair the damage."

I glanced in the Farian's direction and she nodded. "They didn't have the same amount of exposure as Johar, ma'am. It was an easy fix."

Easy or not, it had cost Dio. I could see that in the dark circles bruising the skin below her golden eyes. I'd tried to get Emmory to leave her behind at the hospital with Johar, but he'd overruled me.

Emmory got back in the vehicle and pulled us off the road. I braced myself as we jolted and crashed through the brush, making our way parallel to the canyon. I watched the gap fluctuate, growing wider as we worked our way away from the road until it eventually shrank down to a more manageable eight-meter separation with a slightly shorter drop.

"There," Hao said, pointing over Emmory's shoulder.

We piled out of the vehicles, shoulders tense as we looked over the area. The sun was setting, bathing everything in gold light and throwing shadows.

"We've got an hour of daylight left," Emmory said. "Jasa, Henjai, get a tether set up. Zin, Gita, do a perimeter sweep. The rest of you take a few minutes and check your gear."

Murmurs of assent answered him.

I joined Hao on the other side of the vehicle. "Thoughts?"

"If he wants you to jump through hoops this is one way to go about it."

"It's also effectively stranding us without backup and a way out when things go sideways."

"True." Hao squinted into the setting sun. "Hail—"

The pause was so uncharacteristic of him, but I stayed quiet, letting Hao wrestle with the phrasing of whatever it was he needed to say to me. Finally he leaned his shoulder into mine but didn't look away from the sunset.

"I know you have fond memories of this man. I wish you didn't. It would be easier if he were a stranger. However, he's not, and you—despite all that you've been through—are a good person." He reached across and put a hand over my heart. "Don't hesitate. When you have the chance to strike, I need you to do it. Be without mercy. Promise me?"

"I promise," I said, laying my hand over his.

The shadows were blending into the darkness as we approached the Maxwell estate. The lights were off across the compound and I switched my vision over to compensate for the failing light as we sprinted toward the main house.

Gita was on my left, Hao on my right. Kisah and Dio were each down on a knee at our backs, their guns trained on the empty dark as Emmory, Zin, and the Marines breached a side door and slipped into the house.

"Entryway clear," Emmory said over the com link. *"Gita, bring the empress in. Jasa, take your team and do a sweep of the*

lower level. Slow and careful. Use your scanners, use your common sense. Anything out of sync and you stop where you are and report. Henjai, same for you, upper level."

"Yes, sir."

The air inside the house was slightly warmer, but my breath still billowed up over my head as I exhaled. "Emmory, let me see the scans they did on their first run."

He yanked off a glove and reached behind me to touch his fingers to my exposed wrist. I shuddered a little at the information, closing my eyes and letting the images appear behind my eyelids. Flipping through them, I frowned when nothing obvious stood out to me. "Hao?"

He held his hand out and I shared the scans. "What's this?"

"Dining room," I replied.

"Look at the heat map," he said. "That looks like the kind of heat signature you'd get off an active piece of equipment."

When I overlapped the two, I saw the bright spot of red in the center of the room. "Emmory, dining room?"

"I see it. Down this hallway and around the corner to our left. Zin, Kisah, take the lead."

"ETA on the incoming bird is four minutes," Zin said.

We crept along the hallway; Zin and Kisah hit the doorway first and slipped into the dining room.

"I see it," Kisah said.

I peeked around the corner and frowned. "Kisah, stop. Nobody move."

The room was empty, with its wide windows and black granite fireplace on the far wall, but there was no massive table and ornate chairs that usually would have dominated the space.

A tablet lay in the middle of the floor.

"Jasa, Henjai, head for the door. We found it," Emmory ordered.

"Jump through hoops."

"What, Majesty?"

"He said he wanted to make me jump through hoops," I repeated, staring at the floor.

The faint crackling sound grew louder and I swore. "The floor. There's something wrong with the floor."

"I can get it, Majesty," Kisah said. "Just one more step."

"No, it's not worth it. You step back, Kisah. Very, very carefully."

She ignored me and instead slid one foot forward, stretching her arm out until her fingertips brushed the edge of the tablet.

The sharp snap echoed through the room. Kisah snagged the tablet as the floor crumbled around her, flinging it at the doorway. Hao caught it with one hand, snatching it out of the air.

Zin leapt forward, locking a hand around Kisah's forearm as he held his other out behind him. I grabbed onto it with both hands, hooking a foot around the doorframe, and jerked to a stop as Emmory got a hand around my belt.

"Pull!" I shouted. Emmory was already backpedaling, opening up enough room for Hao to reach through the doorway and add his hands to mine. Gita dropped to her stomach, Dio holding her legs, and reached down into the yawning pit. She was able to grab onto Kisah's vest and we hauled the pair onto the solid floor of the hallway.

"I owe you a thousand apologies, Emmory, for all the times I've ignored you," I said, leaning across Zin to punch Kisah in the arm several times before flopping over onto my back.

We untangled ourselves and I leaned my head back into the dining room. The floor was gone; a few jagged pieces around the edges remained, but what was left was a gaping hole and below I could see the gleam of sharp spikes jutting up out of the darkness.

Shiva, this man was terrifying.

I swallowed back the sick feeling and reached for Kisah again, this time pulling her into a tight hug. "You shouldn't have done that."

"You would have, Majesty," she whispered back.

She was right, so I squeezed her again and let her go, scrambling to my feet and taking the tablet from Hao with a nod.

We headed out of the Maxwell house into the transport waiting in the front yard. Jasa and the other Marines were arrayed around it, their eyes locked on the dark landscape of the estate around us.

Dropping into a seat, I leaned my head back and closed my eyes, letting the flurry of activity swirl around me. That had been too close. A shudder worked its way up my spine as I replayed the events from my *smati*. From the safety of the future I could watch and see just how close Zin had come to missing Kisah's arm, how if I'd moved a half second slower I'd have caught his fingers instead of his wrist. How dangerous it had been for us to go into the house at all.

Damn it, Hail, what are you doing? Throwing away people's lives playing this madman's game.

I flinched away from the sharp end of my conscience's demand.

What happens next time? What happens when you're not fast enough and Emmory dies, or Zin? Or Hao? Is your ego so frail you have to pursue this even knowing that Wilson has you so completely under his control? Kisah risked her life for that tablet because you *would have done it. Don't you see how badly this will end?*

"Majesty?" Emmory put a hand on my knee. "Where next?"

"Home," I said without really thinking about it. "The hotel, I mean."

"I knew what you meant." He frowned and gestured at the tablet in my lap. "What about Wilson?"

"I'm not going after him in the dark, Emmory. It's an awful chance but I don't think he'll start killing his hostages until he has a chance to scold me. We need a good night's sleep and an opportunity to regroup." I handed him the tablet. "Here, have Zin look over this and see what he can come up with."

"Did you watch it?"

"Yes," I lied, and closed my eyes again. "I've got my own ideas. I'll talk to him after he watches it."

"Yes, Majesty."

I cracked an eye open, watching Emmory leave, and spotted Hao on the far side of the transport. His eyes were half-closed, but I knew his gaze was fixed on me, so I let my eye flutter closed again, hoping it looked like me falling asleep at a distance.

While I wasn't one hundred percent sure I could lie to Emmory and get away with it, I was sure Hao could spot any lies I threw at him. He'd known me for far longer, after all. So the only way to avoid it was to avoid him.

The beginnings of a plan took shape in my mind. I was done with Wilson's games, done with my people dying. The empire would survive in Alice's hands; even if something happened to me, it could carry on. Trading my life for the lives of my people was an easy decision to make.

If Wilson wanted me, he was about to get me, and all the fury of Naraka I could bring along.

35

I lay in my bed, staring at the ceiling and watching the clock in the corner of my vision tick closer to zero one hundred. Shift change had happened a little under an hour ago and the two Marines on the door would start to settle into their posts at the door. They were good but lacked the BodyGuard training that kept them alert.

Sliding from the bed and onto the floor, I slipped my boots onto my feet and quickly laced them up. I reached under the bed for the bag I'd smuggled up after dinner and slung it across my back.

Keeping my breathing even and my heart rate steady, I eased the window open and stepped out onto the ledge. The cold air hit me in the throat, stinging and biting with a force that almost set me coughing. I stifled it, closing the window behind me so the cold didn't alert my guards, and grabbed for a hand-hold to my right.

We were on the second floor, thankfully; otherwise I would have had to steal a length of rope or figure out a way to knock out my Guards, neither of which was ideal, and likely would have led to Emmory showing up in short order.

The outside of the hotel was native rock, perfect for climbing, and I made it to the ground with little trouble. Slipping into the trees of a nearby parking lot, I scanned for an easy target with my *smati*, spotting an unlocked vehicle on the far side, and made my way through the shadows toward it.

My *smati* gave me all the specs on the vehicle, from the location of the overhead light switch to how to hotwire it. I popped the door, reaching in and quickly turning off the light. Tossing my bag into the backseat, I slid into the seat and reached under the column, ripping off the cover and pulling wires.

"You were never very good at that." Hao leaned on the door.

"Necessity is the mother," I replied. "What are you doing here?"

"I'm wondering the same thing about you, and without an answer I like, your *Ekam* is going to be asking you a similar question in about four minutes."

I glared at him for a long moment before sliding across the front seat. "Start the damn car. I'll explain on the way."

Hao complied and we pulled out of the parking lot, gliding silently onto the dark street. He waited until we were well away before he opened it up and we took off out of the capital.

"Where are we going?"

"The Surakesh estate." I pulled my bag out of the backseat and busied myself checking over my gear.

"Start talking, *sha zhu*, or I'll turn the car around. You didn't watch the message from Wilson."

I snorted on a laugh. "I'm done playing his game. He could have us running around for the next week for all we know. What happens next time? When you die, or Gita? Or Emmory?" I hated the catch in my voice and looked out the window, blinking away the tears with a muttered curse. "He wants to hurt me by killing all of you. He said as much. It was stupid to play his game, and the Surakesh estate would be the end point anyway because of Leena."

"So you figured you'd just go off by yourself instead?"

"Something like that." I untangled my holster and put it on, shoving my weapon into its spot with more force than was necessary. "He wants me, he can have me, but he doesn't get any more of my people."

"Do you know when I decided I was taking you with me?"

"When I asked you?"

Hao laughed, shaking his head, and threw something in Cheng skyward, too fast for me to catch it. "No, it was before that. When I watched you stand up to a man twice your size who was harassing one of your co-workers. It's impossible to fake that kind of loyalty, Hail, the automatic, bone-deep devotion to standing up for what's right."

I remembered the incident. A drunken idiot grabbed a girl barely older than me and refused to let her go. Portis had been on a break and the few patrons in the bar at that hour didn't seem inclined to intervene.

I resisted the urge to swallow as the man rose out of his seat. He was almost a third of a meter taller than me and built like a Kodan bear. Shoving Huia in the direction of the bar, I squared my shoulders and looked up at him. I'd been in charge of the night shift of the bar for a month and while I could call security, they'd wake up Binto and I really didn't want my boss to think I couldn't handle it on my own.

"Mind your own business."

"My waitresses are my business, sir. If you wish for more personal companionship, that's on deck eighteen."

"I'm not going to take orders from some piss-faced bitch," he snarled.

"You have two choices, sir: Pay your bill and leave, or I will make you leave."

I spotted movement out of the corner of my eye. The lean man who'd been sitting at the corner of the bar drinking tea every night for a week had shifted on his stool and was watching with half-closed golden eyes.

The giant laughed. "You're going to make me leave, sweetie? How's that going to work?"

I pressed the gun I'd slid from my pocket against the underside of his protruding belly. "A Jandar shotgun at this angle is going to rip through most of your intestines and take a decent chunk out of your stomach. It might not kill you in the process if you're lucky.

"The hospital facilities on this ship are very good, but the likelihood that you'll get sepsis is at least fifty-fifty." I smiled. "I'm okay if you want to chance it. It seems a hell of a way to spend a vacation, though."

He'd paled at my words, anger and terror at war on his ugly face. "Bitch." The epithet was ruined by the shaking of his voice.

"Bye."

He turned and fled. I slipped the shotgun back into the leg pocket of my cargo pants and returned to the bar.

"Jandar shotguns are illegal."

I looked up from my trembling hands to the stranger and offered up a cold smile. "You going to report me?"

He gave me a blinding grin, pushing his metallic-streaked hair out of his face and extending his hand, palm out in a traditional Indranan greeting I was surprised to see. "Hardly. That was nicely handled. We haven't properly introduced ourselves. I'm Cheng Hao."

"Cressen Stone." I pressed my palm to his. "It's nice to meet you."

Hao held a hand out to me and I took it, shuddering a little as the program passed to my *smati*. "With Johar's compliments," he said. "It's Rai's cloaking program. Should keep us hidden from anything they'll have hunting for us."

It would also keep me hidden from my BodyGuards. We'd been gone for over an hour. I figured I had maybe another hour before Emmory was awake and checking on me.

I got out of the car, tossed Hao a gun, and closed the door. "Ready?

He nodded. "Everything except for the east wind."

I smiled at the familiar proverb and ducked into the shadows, moving at a sprint toward the stone wall that ringed the outer perimeter of the Surakesh estate.

"There are lights on in the house, and I'm seeing three sets of patrols," Hao said, crouching at my side. "They're moving in a pretty standard pattern. If we hit the one at the back of the house, we'll have more time to get in before they find the bodies."

"Hao, if Wilson catches you he's going to kill you."

"I'll stay out of sight." He grinned.

"I know you will." I tossed the *sapne* powder into his face. It startled him and he inhaled before he could flinch away. "I'm sorry," I said, catching him when he slumped into me.

"Damn it, you brat," he wheezed, and passed out.

"You'll be fine." I eased him to the ground, making sure he was well hidden behind the wall. The *sapne* wouldn't keep him asleep long, but it was enough time for me to get away, and by the time Hao woke up I'd be long gone.

I vaulted over the wall and moved toward the back of the Surakesh main house.

The first guard had his back to me and I slid Johar's knife into his kidney as I covered his mouth with my other hand. He died before he realized I was there, sliding limply to the snow-covered ground.

I sprinted around the corner of the house, flattening myself into the darkness as the second guard passed me by. I grabbed him, dragging him into the shadows with my arm locked against his throat until he stopped moving. I finished him off with a knife to the heart.

Padding up the steps to the back entrance, I was unsurprised to find it unlocked and eased the door open just enough for me to slip inside.

The muffled sound of voices greeted me, becoming duller and indistinct as their owners moved farther into the house. I stripped out of my jacket and stashed it with the bulk of my gear behind the staircase. Holding my gun loosely in my hand, I crept around the corner and followed the sounds until I reached a door at the end of the hallway.

"There's no sign of them at the Zellin estate. I think Wilson was right and they went back to the capital."

"Maybe they realized the estates were under surveillance?"

"Doubtful, even our scanners won't pick up that equipment when it's off. And it's only coded to come on if we turn it on or if their *smatis* are within range."

"Yama is saying that Icho hasn't checked in. Go take a look."

I moved out of the way just as the door swung open, flattening myself against the wall and holding my breath. The two men who left the room didn't turn around and let the door swing closed on its own.

"Icho probably fell asleep again."

"That would be the third time this week," the other man replied. "Wilson's going to shoot him if he doesn't get his shit together."

The two men in the hallway were so distracted by their conversation they didn't hear me following them. I kicked the knee of the one on my left and he fell forward with a startled shout. I shot him in the back of the head.

His buddy died with Johar's knife in his throat.

I heard the door behind me open again and spun, shooting two of the three men who came into the hallway before they could even comprehend what was happening.

The third man scrambled for his weapon but I beat him to it and kicked it across the room. He backpedaled, tripping over a chair, and I caught him by the collar before he could make it out the door.

Clocking him hard enough to stun him, I pushed him into the same chair he'd just tripped over and kicked the door shut. "Hi," I said, pointing my gun at him. "Where's Wilson?"

"Not here."

"You want to elaborate, or should I just shoot you?"

"I don't know where he is. Lady Leena is here, but not Wilson. I haven't seen him for a few days." The words came out in a rush. "Please, Majesty—"

"Oh, you stop right there." I shoved my gun in his face. "The time for begging and pleading is over. You chose your side and I ran out of mercy long before I was dragged home."

I heard the sound of booted feet on the floor outside and moved to my left as the door came apart. The blasts that destroyed it slammed into the hapless guard.

I shot the first man through the door in the head.

"Put your gun down, Majesty," a hard voice ordered. "Wilson wants you alive, but we've got permission to do what's necessary if you won't cooperate."

"He's going to kill me anyway. No point in going down easy."

"You're surrounded and there's no way out of that room." The sound of a gun powering up was all the warning I had before the shots came through the wall. I dropped to the floor, one arm over my head as the splinters flew.

A foot drove into my back, pinning me down, and a second

354

crashed down on my wrist, grinding against the bones until my hand opened. Someone reached down and snatched my gun up.

"Hands behind your back, slowly."

I complied and the cold snap of cuffs around my wrists echoed in the silence. Someone grabbed my upper arms and hauled me upright.

My captors half dragged, half marched me into the main hall and up the wide staircase, stopping outside a door and knocking before opening it and shoving me through.

"Hail." Leena was at the head of the table, Toropov on her left. She put her knife and fork down and waved us in. "You are not supposed to be here yet."

"I can leave if you'd like."

Her smile was cold as she took my Hessian from one of the men and turned it over in her hands.

The disrupter shot from behind took me by surprise, the pain in my leg nothing compared to the shock of the electricity, and I dropped to my knees, gritting my teeth against the surge as my *smati* died.

Leena pushed out of her chair and looked down at me. "Such a waste; you have been an utter pain in my ass. You ruined everything. We had it all planned. I was going to be empress without any fuss whatsoever. Why didn't you just die in your shitty little smuggler's ship like you were supposed to?"

"Everyone keeps asking me that question," I said. "I guess I'm just lucky. You were involved with Wilson from the beginning."

She bobbed her head, curls bouncing with the movement. I glanced past her at the Saxon ambassador. Jaden hadn't moved, his face a perfect mask of disinterest that for just a second was broken when he blinked. I prayed he wouldn't put himself at risk in some foolish gesture.

"Even before Laabh, he didn't know I was involved. He

thought he was so smart. He never realized Wilson only approached him because I suggested it."

"Why? Your grandmother—"

"My grandmother was weak! So were my aunts and my mother and my sisters. They were content with what they had, were ready to betray everything Kastana had worked for just for their own comfort. They've deserved everything that has happened since for turning their backs on our family. If Wilson hadn't brought me my ancestor-grandmother's journals when he came to me, I'd never have known what they threw away." Leena's eyes burned with fanatical devotion.

"When he came to you?" I couldn't stop the laugh. "Oh, Leena, you have no idea who he is, do you?"

"He is devoted to tearing your family's empire to the ground, that's all I care about. We will build something better from the ashes."

"Your shortsightedness will be your downfall." I shook my head.

She leaned in and pressed my gun to my temple. "I should just pull the trigger and take your corpse to Wilson."

"Do it," I said, not taking my eyes off hers. "My only regret is I won't get to watch him peel your skin off while you scream."

Leena's face twisted into a snarl. Grinning, I surged forward and slammed my forehead into her nose. The crunching sound it made was worth the blow to my back that stole my breath.

Rough hands grabbed me and hauled me upright as Leena stumbled away from me with her hands pressed to her face. "That was probably unwise," the voice said in my ear, and the sharp sting at the side of my throat made the room spin around me.

36

I woke in the dark, in a box, and the panic immediately set its teeth into me. Razor sharp with fear, it gnawed through my brain, devouring anything resembling rational thought.

"No." I couldn't have stopped the sobbing exhale even if I'd tried. I had nothing. No weapons, no *smati*. It was pitch-black in the box. The only reason I knew there was something in front of my face was that I could lean my head forward a few centimeters and touch my nose to it.

Snap out of it, Hail. Concentrate on what you know; the rest will sort itself out, or it'll kill you.

Hao's words ricocheted through my brain, startling my fear enough to send it scrambling in the other direction.

You'll have to overcome this, Majesty. It was time for Fasé's earlier advice to echo in my head, and I swallowed as I realized she must have known this was coming.

Damn you, Fasé, why the vague pep talk?

Focus, Hail, what do you know?

I was standing upright, not lying down. The only reason I hadn't crumpled to the bottom of the box was the lack of space.

They'd taken my boots and my socks and I could feel the chill of the metal under my feet.

My hands were at my sides, no longer cuffed behind me, and I rubbed my fingertips against the rough material of my cargo pants. There was enough room to work my right hand across my chest and up so that my forearm rested against the metal in front of me.

I wiped the tears from my face as I worked my other arm free and ran my fingers up across the metal until I encountered the top. It was only a hand span above my head.

Box: unknown metal composite. Approximately two hundred twenty centimeters high, maybe twenty centimeters deep, and sixty wide.

The air tasted clean. There was probably a vent somewhere but I couldn't hear any sounds besides my own breathing.

An eternity passed. After I investigated every corner of the box I could reach, I inventoried my supplies—limited as they were. My pants, underwear, shirt, and tank top were all intact. I had my belt and the tie in my hair. Johar's knife was gone. She was going to kill me if that disappeared.

After that depressing thought there was nothing to do but wait.

The light in my face woke me from a doze. "Hail, are you sleeping?" Wilson's voice was equal parts gleeful and incredulous.

"What else am I supposed to do?"

"I honestly thought you'd be crying. I know how much you hate enclosed spaces. I had this made especially for you."

"It's a bit snug for my tastes. You should get a refund."

He laughed.

"I misjudge you time and again. Pampered princess. Uncouth

criminal. Uncertain empress. Every time I think I've gotten a handle on you, Hail, you surprise me."

"I'm good at that." I had to swallow back using Janesh's real name. I wanted to see his face when I said it.

"We will see how you handle this, then," he said. "And I feel it's only fair to mention that when I say 'we,' I mean your empire is watching. Have fun."

The light stayed on as water started to stream down the sides of the box, pooling at my feet. The only thing keeping the curses from escaping were Wilson's parting words.

Your empire is watching.

He wanted me to fall apart. He wanted the whole empire to watch me die utterly broken and hysterical. I would be Shiva-damned before I'd give him the satisfaction.

The water crawled over the tops of my feet and lapped at my ankles.

"If all I can do is refuse to give you the satisfaction, it will be enough."

The box filled with agonizing slowness. The water crept up my calves to my knees. I folded my hands together, pressing my lips to the tips of my fingers. *"Adhou karma prasangath kalay-athi kalusham."*

It had been years since I'd uttered the prayer of forgiveness, and yet the words rolled off my tongue as though I'd said them yesterday.

I lifted my eyes. There was no telling where the camera was focused, so I could only hope I was looking at the lens as I chanted.

I would not be afraid. I would be strong.

If I could give my people hope, it was worth it.

If I could show them a Bristol died with honor, it was worth it.

The water slid around my thighs as I continued my prayer. I tried to focus on the words, not the cold, not the way my shirt was soaking up the water, drawing it relentlessly upward.

I understood, with painful clarity, how Cas had been so calm in the palace. How the knowledge that facing your end with utter peace would bring comfort to those around you.

"Kim dhaanena dhanena—" My breath caught. The cold was a vise around my chest and I forced the rest of the line out, feeling the panic start to rise.

Not now, baby, not when you've gotten this far. Don't let him win. Portis's voice saved me, and the realization that I would see him again soon made my next words steady. I finished the prayer, tears in my eyes, and the water rising higher. As I reached the last line of the last verse, the water hit my chin.

"Citizens of the empire, it is *you*, not I, who are the shining light of Indrana, do not forget."

I sucked in my last breath as the water closed over my head.

Now you can let go. Just exhale and inhale and we'll be together again.

I couldn't. The darkness was closing in, the light fading as my oxygen-starved brain refused to let my mouth open, my lungs contract.

I held my breath for as long as I could. It felt like an eternity. It wasn't long enough. Until my brain, in desperation, forced the air out of my lungs and water flooded into the void.

The world went black.

I woke to the painful sensation of water gushing out of my lungs. Hands rolled me onto my side, holding me still when I tried to curl into a ball. My hacking coughs tore through me, but through it all I was listening for the comforting sound of Emmory's voice.

It never came.

"Well, that was close, Hail," Wilson said. "We lost you there for a minute."

"Breathe, Majesty." A mask was pressed to my face and I inhaled. The young woman who bent over me had soft brown eyes. She smiled when I coughed, rolling me to my side again as I retched. The pain from the disrupter shot to my left leg flared, wrapping around the fire in my chest in a vicious dance.

"I know it hurts, but keep breathing." She slid her left hand down, out of sight of Wilson, and squeezed my fingers.

The floor under my arm was dark wood, hand-cut and polished and brought over from the last forests of Pageron Ulysses. I glanced around me and the familiar surroundings brought with them a sense of peace.

I was home. Not the palace, of course, now lying in a smoking ruin, but the Bristol country estate at the base of Mount Rishabha. I knew without looking that a stone fireplace dominated the wall behind my head and a cozy set of ornate chairs held court around it.

I took the mask and inhaled again; this time the pain was less and the feeling of an elephant on my chest started to recede.

"I feel like I should applaud for that performance in the box. Here I was thinking you'd come apart at the seams and instead you turned into a damn Bodhisattva."

"I've always been good in a crisis," I said through the mask, and Wilson laughed.

"Funny, your mother wasn't."

I sat up, gripping the arm of my nurse for support. "You don't know a thing about my mother."

Wilson was in a chair about three meters away from me, a wineglass in his hand and a gun resting on his thigh. A wide window behind him showed the mountain looming in the light of the still-rising moon. Because I was watching for it I saw his fingers tighten on the stem and the way his jaw muscles twitched.

"Leave us," he said.

"But sir, she's not quite—"

He lifted the gun, his finger on the trigger. "Unless you want me to vent your skull, get the fuck out of here."

"Go," I whispered, giving her a little push. "I'm fine."

"Three more deep breaths, Majesty." She got to her feet, bowed in Wilson's direction, and hurried from the room.

I took a deep breath from the mask as Wilson watched the girl leave, and a second when he returned his gaze to me. He put the gun back on his leg and gestured at me with his glass. "Drink? The bottle's behind you, I promise it's not poisoned."

Inhale, exhale.

I set the mask down and climbed to my feet, spying the table and chair behind me. My pants squelched as I moved, hanging heavy and cold around my hips. Pouring a drink, I sat down and saluted Wilson with it. "To family and betrayal, Janesh."

His smile was a fraction too slow, preceded by narrowed eyes and a tightening of his lips. "To family and betrayal, Haili."

I drank, the wine sliding down my abused throat and giving me a false sense of warmth.

"It was Clara, wasn't it? I knew I should have muzzled her."

It was a pleasure to shake my head and watch him frown. "No. We heard her, but we didn't quite know what she meant. You picked the wrong mod shop to burn down. Not that you'll ever need mods again, but I recommend making sure that next time your black market contacts don't owe Bakara Rai money. He gets annoyed when he can't collect."

"Interesting." He tilted his head and took a sip of wine. "You are remarkably resourceful. I used to pretend you were my daughter."

I paused with the wineglass halfway to my lips. Wilson smirked.

"I will be eternally grateful my mother made the better choice." I kept my eyes on him as I raised my glass the rest of the way and took a drink.

Wilson whipped the gun up and fired at me, the blast zipping by my head and obliterating the back of the couch behind me.

"Temper," I murmured.

"Your mother disliked my temper also. And my laugh. And my hair. And apparently *everything* about me!"

"I can't imagine why."

This time the shot shattered my wineglass, leaving me holding nothing but the stem. I turned my head, the spraying glass cutting into my cheek, neck, and scalp.

"You mouth off to me again, child, and I'll put the next one between your ribs." Wilson drained his wineglass and dropped it to the floor.

"So this is it? You decided to destroy a whole empire because a woman told you no?"

"I should have been where your father was. I deserved it more. I could have done so much better." His reply was so deadly calm it chilled me worse than my damp clothes.

Wilson snapped his fingers and the doors at the other end of the library opened. Two men entered, dragging Hao's body between them.

I rose, but Wilson aimed his gun at me. "Stay there," he said.

"I am going to kill you." In the midst of my grief my voice was strangely even.

Wilson smiled as the men dropped Hao to the floor, and

then he waved them out. He crossed to Hao's body and pushed it over with his foot.

Hao groaned and I bit the inside of my cheek to stop myself from screaming his name.

"Hey! Not dead. Yet." Wilson beamed at me and knelt at Hao's side. "What do you think, Haili, should I just put him out of his misery? Or should we have some fun first?"

I brushed the shards off my shirt, the damp fabric glittering with pieces of glass, and weighed the odds of my next words qualifying as mouthing off before deciding it was worth it. Anything was worth it if it distracted Wilson from Hao.

"My mother chose my father because she loved him."

The shot didn't surprise me, and the force slammed me back down into the chair. I grunted in pain, pressing my left hand against the wound and feeling the sticky warmth of my own blood on my fingers. My right hand was still wrapped around the stem of the destroyed glass and I slipped it down between the arm of the chair and my leg.

"Is that what they told you?" He laughed and threw his hands up in the air before rising to his feet and pacing toward me. "Of course it is, not like they'd tell a child the truth." He leaned down and glanced at the wound. "You're going to want to keep pressure on that." This close to him I could now see the crows'-feet at the corners of his blue eyes and the madness lurking within. His mod had made him look younger. By my memory Janesh was in his sixties, but I was injured and it was obvious he wasn't a weak old man.

"Your mother hated your father. Well, perhaps *hate* is too strong a word. She didn't respect him. She thought he was weak, too quiet, and not royal enough. And then, all of a sudden, she names *him* instead of me.

"I asked for an explanation. Begged even. I should have been at her side. I should have been ruling Indrana with her."

I kept my mouth shut, letting him rant, and trying to breathe through the pain. The cough caught me by surprise and Wilson whistled at the bright red blood on my hand.

"That doesn't look good."

"Do you mind if I—" I broke off into another cough and gestured at the med kit still on the floor.

"Sure, you're only delaying the inevitable, but go ahead. We both knew this was going to end this way, Haili. I planned my revenge for too long to fail. I deserve this triumph after everything that was taken away from me. You never had a chance."

I slipped the wineglass stem behind the case as I went to a knee and fumbled through the contents for a patch. It wouldn't help with the blood filling up my lung, but it would at least help with the outside wound.

I could see Hao from where I was, but I couldn't reach him. His chest rose and fell in shallow movements. One eye was swollen shut, the other matted closed with dried blood. Beyond that I couldn't tell without my *smati* just how badly he was injured.

As I hiked my shirt up, movement in the corner of my eye distracted me. A shadow glided past the window, and then another. I glanced cautiously in Wilson's direction, but his back was to the window and he hadn't seen it.

I smoothed the patch on and continued rooting through the box until Wilson brought his gun down just behind my ear and I collapsed.

"Don't abuse my generosity, Hail."

"I was looking for pain meds," I wheezed, rolling over onto my back.

"Oh." He dropped the arm that was holding the gun to his side. "Sorry."

Swinging my leg out, I caught him in the ankles, knocking him to the ground, and I scrambled across the floor on my hands and knees trying to get to the gun as it went flying. Wilson slammed his elbow into my kidney and I dropped, face-first, to the floor.

I rolled, blocking his second swing and grabbing his shoulder as I brought my knee up into his face. But Wilson anticipated the move and leaned back, so my knee glanced off his chin. He rolled over, in the same movement grabbing the gun above his head.

Move, Hail, move.

I surged up onto a knee, using all my weight to slam Wilson's face into the floor. There was a crunch as his nose broke. I yanked the gun out of his grasp with my left hand, put it to his temple, and fired.

37

Nothing happened and my shock cost me. Wilson drove his elbow into my side, just under where he'd shot me. It was enough to loosen me up. The second elbow caught me as I fell forward and it hurt so much I saw stars.

I rolled over the top of him.

Wilson batted the gun out of my hand, sending it spinning off to the left of us as he punched me in the face. I heard the crack of my own nose and fumbled, somehow managing to lock my right hand around his face, pulling on his broken nose as he punched at me again.

Wilson howled in pain and rolled away from me.

I scrambled to my feet, grabbed the useless gun, and spat a mouthful of blood onto the floor. We stared at each other for several moments, each dragging in air.

Wilson had the better end of that deal. I could only manage half a breath before my left lung protested with violent spasms.

"What now, Haili? You can't shoot me and you're in no shape to keep fighting."

I smiled and backed away from him toward the fireplace. Saluting him with the gun, I tossed it in and hit the button to start the flames. The acrid smell of burning plastic billowed from the grate, tainting the air before the recyclers sucked it away.

"Now you can't shoot me either. As for the fight, I'm more than willing to give it a go."

Wilson threw a look at the doors and I wondered for a second if he was going to run or his men would come in and end this for him. Instead he heaved a sigh and charged.

I spun to the side, performing the move I'd seen so many times from Zin—though with far less grace—and bringing the side of my hand down on the back of Wilson's neck.

Wilson snarled and spun, kicking me in the leg right where the disrupter shot still oozed blood, and pain ripped through me as my leg gave out. I rolled away from him.

Get up, Hail. Shake the pain off. Portis and Hao were both screaming in my head and I somehow made it to my feet and punched Wilson in the back. I moved in as he spun to face me, blocking the punch to my side with my elbow and swinging it up to catch him under the chin.

Wilson staggered back and as I advanced I spotted the ruined wineglass I'd left by the med kit. I punched him twice in the face and deliberately missed the block on his wild retaliation, letting it spin me to the side.

I faked a stumble, dropped to my hands and knees, and snagged the stem as I scrambled away. "You know, now that I think of it Mother used to tell us girls she was glad you had died. She said you were a poor influence on my father. She'd only considered you out of respect for Matriarch Hassan, but you'd never really been in the running. You were far too ill-mannered and headstrong. She wanted someone who behaved like a proper man."

My words had the desired result. Wilson ran at me, fists flying. I blocked his punches with my right arm, holding my left tight against my side to conceal the wineglass stem and making it look like he had me on the defensive as I backed away from him.

Don't hesitate. When you have the chance to strike, I need you do to it. Hao's words came back to me and I chanted them in my head like a mantra.

Be without mercy.

Wilson was frothing at the mouth, screaming incoherently at me in his rage. I dodged his next punch, a wild haymaker with his right hand, and slid past him on his left.

I snapped my left hand out in a perfect arc.

The razor-sharp edge of the wineglass stem cut through flesh and artery.

Wilson staggered back a step, clutching at his throat in a futile attempt to stop the spray of blood. He went to a knee, eyes wide with confused denial.

I stepped away from the widening pool, the copper tang of it flooding my nose, but kept my eyes on Wilson.

"Haili," he gasped, reaching for me. "Please, your father would have—"

"Been proud of me for avenging my family. All that rage, all that time you wasted, all for nothing. You will be remembered only as the greatest traitor to this empire, nothing more."

I watched, dry-eyed and calm as stone while the man who murdered my family died.

I dropped the wineglass and stumbled back across the library to Hao, my fingers fumbling at his throat for a pulse. "Hao? Come on. Do not die on me, you stupid idiot."

The door opened behind me.

"Majesty?"

Turning at the sound of Emmory's voice, I exhaled a shuddering breath and somehow got to my feet. My *Ekam* and Zin came through the door, Johar and Dailun on their heels. They were all bloodied and bruised, though not nearly as badly as I was, and I limped toward them.

"Hao needs help. I don't know how badly he's hurt."

I fell into Emmory. He wrapped his arms around me as Zin murmured a litany of my injuries.

"Collapsed left lung. Gunshot wound left leg. Gunshot wound left side through fifth and sixth ribs. Body temp is at thirty-five degrees and dropping. She's going into shock soon if she's not already in it."

I started to shake.

"Find me a blanket, anything," Emmory ordered as he scooped me up and carried me to the fire. *"Gita, we found them. The empress is alive, repeat the empress is still alive. Send Major Morri my direction asap."*

Emmory lowered me to the floor, pulled a knife free from the sheath at his thigh, and sliced my long-sleeved shirt off. He stripped the still-soggy material away from my clammy skin, leaving me in the form-fitting tank underneath.

"What is that smell?"

"I tossed his gun in," I managed between my chattering teeth. "It was locked. Couldn't use it. Didn't think he should either."

He jerked his gloves off and rubbed at my arms.

"I'm sorry I didn't wait for you. Didn't—"

"I watched you die."

There was pain. Such a depth of pain in his words, and I squeezed my eyes shut but I couldn't force the apology out between my gasps.

Zin dropped to his knees at my side, wrapping a blanket

around my shoulders. "The house is secure. Major Morri is on her way." He threaded his fingers through mine.

"Killed him. He's dead. It's done." My laughter was sharp in my ears. "Told you a wineglass stem makes a great weapon in a pinch."

"Don't talk, Majesty. Save your strength."

I summoned up the last of my reserves and managed to stop shaking for a moment. "Hao needs Dio more than me. Don't let him argue. Don't let him die." My vision tunneled abruptly and I slumped forward as the exhaustion and pain took over.

"No, no. Stay with us, Hail. Get Dio in here now!" Emmory cupped the back of my head and I dropped into unconsciousness with the sound of my heart loud in my ears.

I awoke in the dark, heart still pounding as I replayed the fight with Wilson. Had I imagined the end? Emmory's and Zin's faces?

"Be at ease, Majesty."

The voice and sudden light sent me rolling from the bed and I felt ten times a fool as my knees gave out and I clung to the blanket to keep from falling to the floor.

Zin crossed the room and helped me upright. Emmory stayed where he was, leaning against the doorframe, dark eyes watching me closely.

"Careful," Zin said. "Major Morri healed the worst of it, but your lungs are tender, especially the one they reinflated. You've been out for a few days."

"What?" I blinked at him and realized at the same time that my *smati* was back up and running.

"The doctors installed a new *smati*; yours was pretty fried, but they salvaged a lot of information from the secondary memory and used the backup from when you last logged into the *Bristol*'s shipboard system. You lost any recent recordings."

"Well, that's lucky," I muttered. I was okay with relying on my imperfect organic memory of drowning and the fight with Wilson. "Why am I so sore?"

"Major Morri expended a lot of energy on Hao, and she thought it was best to let you heal naturally. You took a beating."

"I know, I was there when it happened." I leaned my head back against the pillow. "Wilson's dead."

"He is, Majesty." Zin tipped his head to the side. "You weren't making a lot of sense in the library, obviously. What did you cut his throat with?"

"A wineglass stem." I looked down at my hands. There wasn't any joy in it, only the weary knowledge that my revenge was done. A curious hollow-eyed beast had taken up residence where the fury used to live. "Is everyone okay? Hao?"

"A few minor injuries," Zin replied. "Hao's awake. He had a broken set of ribs and massive internal bleeding."

I slid a sideways look at Emmory, but his expression hadn't changed. "I had to go alone. It wasn't bravado or anger. I couldn't—"

"Let anyone else die for you," Emmory finished. "We know, Majesty."

Alba slipped in through the doorway before I could reply. "Majesty." She bowed low, hands folded together. "It is a great relief to see you alive."

"You are not supposed to be here," I said.

She smiled. "Jia sent me home along with Iza and Indula. She said we were needed here more than on Canafey now that the danger has passed."

"I am glad to see you." I held a hand out and she crossed the room to take it, squeezing my fingers as she blinked away tears.

"If you are feeling up to it, Majesty, there are a number of people who would like to see you."

I nodded, murmuring thanks to Zin when he tugged the blanket back up over my legs. When I looked back to the doorway, Emmory was gone and Alice had taken his place. My heir didn't bother to conceal her tears when she saw me, and she rushed in, leaning over the bed to hug me.

"Majesty, I cannot—" Alice stopped and swallowed, passing a hand over her face. She released a breath and managed a smile. "How are you feeling?"

"Sore," I replied. "And tired, which is strange considering I've been asleep for almost three days."

"The doctors said it was expected. It's a natural reaction to trauma." Alice sat on the side of the bed. "The last of the traitors have surrendered and normal operations in the capital have resumed, except for the area around the palace, of course.

"The four matriarchs and the other prisoners Wilson had in custody are safe, unharmed except for minor injuries from their captivity."

I nodded. "Good, I'm glad to hear it. Leena?"

Alice suddenly found the edge of the blanket very fascinating. "She was taken into custody when your forces raided the Bristol estate, Majesty. We had her in a GIS holding facility and I'm afraid the security wasn't up to the job."

"She escaped?"

"No, Majesty, she took her own life last night."

My heir was a horrible liar, but I didn't say so out loud. It was a conversation to have with Caspel, preferably somewhere a long way from any kind of surveillance.

"A pity," I said. "Inform Matriarch Surakesh of the throne's condolences and that I will call for her and expect a prompt appearance so we can discuss the issue of her family's treachery."

"Yes, Majesty." Alice nodded and rose. "I am under orders from your doctor and your *Ekam* not to stay too long, so I will go with your permission."

"We'll talk again soon."

"Yes, Majesty." Alice dropped a little curtsy and left the room.

That afternoon and the days after followed a similar pattern of visitors until I was released back into the wild by my doctors. I saw an almost endless parade of faces, but it was the absent faces that I noticed: Fasé, and Hao especially.

Dailun, however, visited me daily, and the pink-haired pilot sat across from me in my hotel room playing some strange game on his *smati* that caused him to flail his hands through the air at things only he could see.

I flipped through the news on my own *smati*, my hand freezing in the air when I was confronted with a video clip of me in the box.

The water covered my face and I could only stare in horror as I ran out of oxygen. The image was briefly obscured by bubbles, but it cleared in time to catch a glimpse of my face, eyes open, and the life gone.

I watched you die.

Emmory's words slammed back into me. I must have gasped, because Gita came away from her position at the door.

"Majesty? What is it?"

"Jiejie?"

"I—" I pressed a hand to my mouth to hold in the scream until I could swallow it back down. "I haven't seen the recording. Wilson said the whole empire was watching me?"

Gita nodded slowly. "He was broadcasting live, Majesty. Most of the galaxy saw you."

"Saw me die," I said, and she nodded again.

"It was—" Dailun paused, searching for the words as they escaped him. "Most unpleasant."

"We were gearing up and heading out the door as it happened. Hao had followed them to your estate and called it in to Emmory. We all saw it." She fisted her hands at her sides and looked away from me. "It was a moment of failure I hope to never repeat. We all thought you were dead until Emmory and Zin found you in the library."

"Failure is a good word. We were devastated, *jiejie*. My honored cousin took it especially hard," Dailun said. "I shouldn't speak of such things, but he would never be able to find the words to tell you that himself."

"I thought he was mad at me."

Gita's laughter startled me. "He was mad at *himself*, Majesty. Still is, I think, for letting you get so close to death."

"Wilson would have killed him if I'd let him come with me. He almost did kill him."

Gita dropped into a crouch at my side and put her hands over mine. "Majesty, have you not figured out that we are all right where we want to be? That dying is preferable to watching you die?"

"I don't deserve any of this."

"It doesn't make it any less real." She smiled. "Ah, speak of the devil."

The door opened and Hao came in. "Do you have a moment?" he asked.

I nodded, not trusting myself to speak as Dailun and Gita suddenly had a pressing need to be out of the room. The door closed behind Gita. Hao shoved his hands into his pockets and stared at the floor.

"Po-Sin is sending a ship for me," he said finally, and the words hurt worse than Wilson's shot to my chest had.

"Okay." My nod was stiff. "I'll get with Alba about transferring your payment. What would be a sufficient amount for your assistance and the loss of your ship?"

"I don't want your money."

"You don't get to make that choice. I'll owe you the favor we agreed upon originally, but I'm also paying you for your help and you don't get to argue with me."

He snapped his eyes up, gold and full of fury. "I'm not one of your subjects to order around, *Your Imperial Majesty*." He snarled my title.

I shot out of my seat, advancing on Hao, my own anger overriding Dailun's advice about my older brother's pain. "No, you're not, but you'll watch your tongue when you're speaking to me, Cheng Hao."

"Or you'll what?" he challenged.

"What do you want from me?" We were nose to nose as I shouted the question.

"I want to erase the memory of your lifeless eyes staring at me!" Hao grabbed me by the shoulders and shook me. "But they are seared into my brain! I swore to myself I'd keep you safe. That I wouldn't fail again like I had with Mei. But I did. You died and I couldn't stop it." He jerked me against him, his arms wrapping so tightly around me I could barely breathe.

"I'm not her. I'm not dead, brother," I whispered against his ear.

"For five minutes I thought you were," he whispered back. "And in that eternity my life was over."

"When Wilson's men dragged you into the room I thought you were dead and I—" I choked back the sob and fisted my hands in his shirt. "Please don't leave me."

"Someone has to stay and keep you out of trouble." He let me go and I turned away from him, wiping the tears from my face.

"Why you think you're at all qualified to do that is beyond me." I laughed and turned back to him. "However, I welcome your company, Cheng Hao, for as long as you'll give it."

"You have it for as long as you'd like it. I'll call Po-Sin and let him know I'm staying," he replied.

38

Your Majesty?" Kisah stuck her head around the door. "Fasé would like to know if you have a moment. There's someone she'd like you to meet."

I waved away the report on the palace compound and nodded. "Send her in."

Emmory stepped up behind my chair as Fasé and a Farian with piercing silver eyes came into the room.

"Your Majesty." Fasé dropped into a curtsy, her eyes on the floor at my feet. "I apologize for the informality. I know there are usually protocols to be followed, but if you would permit me to introduce Collector Ninz Terass, my father."

"Your Imperial Majesty." Fasé's father was taller than her by half a meter, his voice deep and like stone scraping on stone. It was a sound that was out of place against his Farian features.

"Father is a—" Fasé frowned as she searched for the word. "Librarian? *Professor* might work better."

"It's very nice to meet you."

Ninz nodded, his eyes flicking past me to Emmory, and

he studied my *Ekam* for a moment before responding. "I have come to take Fasé home."

"Very well. Have you done your outprocessing?" I hated how stiff my words were.

"Captain Gill has processed my discharge papers, Your Majesty," Fasé replied with a nod.

I wanted to grab her, shake her, hug her, scream at her again for sending Cas to his death. If we'd been alone, maybe I could have found the courage to do it, but as it stood I simply nodded back. "Very well. Have a safe trip home."

"We will, Majesty."

Ninz bowed sharply. "My daughter and I leave after your Vasant celebration. She expressed an interest in hearing the bells one last time."

"They are quite lovely. I hope you enjoy them." I stood and gave them both a nod. "Thank you for your service, Fasé."

"Majesty—"

"Good-bye." I turned to the windows. Emmory's voice was a low murmur as he walked Fasé and her father from the room. Only when the door closed did I let the tears fall.

"Good afternoon, Your Majesty." Toropov executed an elegant bow.

I held out a hand. "Ambassador, it is good to see you." I smiled when he took my hand and squeezed it before bringing it to his lips. "You are unharmed?"

"Quite. My part was the easy one." Jaden released me. "My replacement will be here in a few days. Then I will travel to Ashva and collect Trace."

"Tefiz said he survived the worst of the withdrawals, but he's having a hard time remembering who he is most days."

Toropov nodded. "He will abdicate the throne to his brother as soon as we are returned to Saxony. Off the record, you have done us a greater favor than I can repay you for," he said. "There will be no civil war for us. Thank you."

"Off the record, you're most welcome." I smiled. "On the record, I expect Saxony to uphold their end of the bargain we struck."

"We will, Majesty." Toropov bowed his head. "You have my word."

"Safe travels, Ambassador. I hope we see each other again."

"Me, too." Toropov turned on his heel and left the room. He exchanged greetings with Alice and Taz as they passed.

"Are you ready for tomorrow?" I laughed at the identical looks on their faces. "I'll take that as a yes." Crossing the room, I took Alice's hands in mine and pressed my cheek to hers. "The people need something to celebrate, something to look forward to beyond the end of this war. You are that light."

"I know, Majesty. It's just..."

"Sudden," Taz supplied when she trailed off.

I reached for his hand. "You two are the new faces of Indrana. You will usher in the change you've worked so hard for all these years. I know it feels a bit like a dream, but I promise you it is very real."

The plan that Alba and I had been working on for the past week was relatively simple in that I would take the brunt of any criticism directed at the new policies. The public loved me enough that I figured I could ride that currency for a while. And in the meantime, Alice and Taz would be showing the people how the change would bring Indrana up out of her economic troubles. Their faces were already widely known and the message of the *Upjas* on gender equality was closer to being legitimized in the eyes of the public thanks to their relationship.

The wedding would cement that and I was going to make sure it happened before the nobles had a chance to gather their defenses and protest.

"Come take a look at this." I led them over to the couches. "Alba and the others have done a great job getting things planned."

The meeting with Alice and Taz went well and an hour later I was walking along the beach with Emmory on one side of me and Zin on the other. The dolphins played in the frozen surf.

"How long are you planning to stay, Majesty?" Emmory's question was expected.

"I don't know what you're talking about."

He gave me the Look and Zin chuckled.

"You're setting Alice and Taz up very neatly to be your successors," Emmory replied. "Everything points to it from policy briefs to your carefully chosen speech yesterday."

I'd done a brief address to the empire yesterday. A brilliant speech written by Alba that talked about the new direction Indrana was moving in, the need for change, how stagnation had resulted in the horrific events that nearly toppled our empire and ended the lives of so many Indranans.

"I'll stay as long as they need me," I said as the dolphins leapt up into the sunbeams lancing across the water. "A few years, maybe more, I don't know. If I do this right, any objections to the changes will fall on my shoulders, not hers." I exhaled and smiled. "Alice is the heir and there will be a time when it's better for her to wear the crown. I don't know when that time will come. I just know it will."

Emmory nodded, surprising me. "All right, Majesty."

"Is he going to stop with the title once I'm not empress?" I asked Zin, and he grinned at me.

"I can't make any guarantees, ma'am."

"I hate you," I said to Emmory with a laugh.

"Liar."

I have flown through the outer edges of dying stars; walked into enemy strongholds with nothing more than my shirt on my back and come out with a deal that fed my crew for months. I have stared my own death in the face more times than I can now count. The knots of tension wrapped around my heart over the wedding threatened to put me on my knees. My hands were clammy and I tried not to fidget as Stasia finished fixing the drapes of the brilliant green sari I wore.

My amazing maid had gone above and beyond her duty in finding me an outfit for today's event. The golden edging was hand-done by a little old grandmother in a shop on the outer edge of the city not far from the hotel, who'd been more than happy to let me borrow the sari for the wedding. The jewelry I wore had been donated by all the matriarchs. I'd only drawn the line at having a new crown made; wasting money on such frivolous things when we were going to be paying to rebuild large parts of the capital made no sense to me.

I was the empress. I didn't need a piece of metal on my head to prove it.

Two weeks had passed since I'd awoke in the hospital, almost three weeks since I'd slit Wilson's throat with the stem of a wineglass—a fact that was going to turn me into even more of a legend than I already was, if Dailun was to be believed about it.

I'd used that notoriety to shut down the opposition that had surfaced over making the head of the *Upjas* the Prince Consort. Most of the protests had come from the older surviving members of the Matriarch Council during an exhausting meeting that detailed the benefits of the match for Indrana. I'd had the support of the newer members and all of the Ancillary Council, but even if I hadn't I'd have held fast to this wedding.

It was time to take that final step, and creating what amounted to a new royal family for the empire would set the stage for all the changes that were coming.

"Are you nearly finished?"

Stasia reached up to smooth back a twist of hair. "Yes, Majesty."

We hadn't talked about why she wasn't going with Fasé. All I knew was I'd tried to offer her a release from her position, and she'd refused it with a tiny smile and gone right back to fixing my hair.

I stared at myself in the mirror, hardly recognizing the woman looking back at me. Her short hair was pulled back and twisted up away from a sharp face dominated by weary eyes. The white *choli* she wore was cut from a material with a shadowed pattern that matched the petticoat. The sari itself was a sheer emerald green, edged in golden thread. She looked— regal, confident, like a damned empress.

It's you, Hail, get used to it. Portis's voice was edged with amusement.

Straightening my shoulders, I exhaled. "All right, let's do this."

My seven remaining BodyGuards were lined up in the hallway of the temple, dressed in the standard matte-black uniforms with crimson piping along their cuffs and worked into the detail of the intricate star pattern on their left breasts. They all came to attention as I stepped out of the room.

"*Dve,*" I said, cupping the newly promoted Gita by the back of the head and pressing my forehead to hers. She echoed the gesture, her fingers warm on the back of my neck.

I worked my way down the row: Ikeki, Iza, and Indula; Kisah, Zin, and finally my *Ekam*.

There were too many missing. Pezan and Rama. Willimet and Elizah. Jet and Cas. And all the others. I had to use my *smati* to call up their names and faces.

Those we'd lost were reflected from my eyes to Emmory's as I pressed my forehead to his and a tear leaked out, trailing down my cheek. Emmory flexed his fingers in my hair.

"Your Imperial Majesty," he said as he released me and then went to a knee. "Shining star of Indrana, we are forever your loyal BodyGuards."

The other Guards echoed him, their voices hanging in the air.

"We are grateful for your service." I pretended the words didn't stick in my throat with the tears that wanted to break free. I waited for them to stand and gestured at the stairs. "Shall we?"

The tiniest smile peeked out from the corner of Emmory's mouth and he tipped his head in a silent order for Zin and Kisah to take the lead.

Alba met us at the base of the stairs and gestured toward the main temple area. "Everything is ready, Majesty."

"Thank you." I crossed the empty entryway and stopped at the set of double doors. They were unassuming things, large brass handles curved over the dark wood.

The shattered court of Indrana lay behind those doors. The surviving remnants of the noble families, the councils, and the Assembly General were seated side by side with the *Upjas* and a good number of common people who'd fought bravely during the occupation.

Inhale, exhale. I blew out the breath I'd been holding and nodded to my Guards, letting them pull the doors open. I walked in, my back straight and my chin high, listening as the silence rolled over the crowd with each step I took toward the front of the room.

Taz waited by the blazing fire. The red-gold flames flickered off the embroidery of his cream jacket and left reddish highlights in his black hair. He smiled at me and bowed low. "Your Majesty."

I returned the bow with a nod and smile of my own. As I turned I spotted Johar and Hao sitting with Dailun in the front row, all three looking exceptionally uncomfortable. Fasé was several rows behind them, with Major Morri and her father flanking her.

Emmory stayed by my side, but the other BodyGuards peeled off, taking up station around the fire with a precision that must have stunned the crowd.

I folded my hands at my waist and smiled. "It has been a long, dark winter for Indrana. Today the bells of Vasant will usher in the spring and I hope with them a new dawn for the empire." I took a deep breath and looked at Alba, giving her a nod.

The doors opened again and Alice came in. I heard Taz's indrawn breath and bit the inside of my cheek.

Her silver-blue sari was done up with hundreds of tiny silver bells and their chiming echoed up to the ceiling of the temple, a precursor to the Vasant bells that would soon ring through the air. The shimmering material of her veil hung to her waist and spread out behind her in a train that looked like shattered ice.

She walked with her father, her arm looped through his, and even from the distance I could see the tears on both their faces.

The crowd held its breath as Alice walked up the aisle. She stopped, dropping into a graceful curtsy that made me a bit jealous. I reached out and took her hand from her father, smiling at him as I urged her to rise.

I put her hand in Taz's and took my seat off to the side.

"Children." Father Westinkar had been a controversial choice for the wedding. Mother Superior Benedine had protested the decision to remove her from the traditional spot, but I'd held fast to the order that my favorite priest from the family temple would be the one to marry Alice and Taz. Change would start now, or not at all.

He laid his hand over theirs. "Do you come here of your own free will to circle the fire and join two lives into one?"

"I do, Father," Alice replied.

Taz smiled, squeezing his hand around hers. "I do, Father."

Father Westinkar removed his hand and stepped around them to address the crowd. "This pair stands before us, before the sacred fire. Seven times they will circle so that they can see for a thousand years. Seven times they will promise so that happiness will follow them for a thousand years. Seven times they will sacrifice so they will love for a thousand years. This is the gods' will. Be this your will?"

If there was a negative response, it was lost to the roar of approval from the crowd. Another thread in the knot around my heart slipped free as he turned back to them.

"Proceed, children."

They headed around the fire. The ornate stone base would be warm under their feet, heated by the flames.

When they reached Father Westinkar again, Taz dropped to a knee in front of Alice, taking both of her hands in his.

"I would be worthy of you, Alice. In word and deed. With my heart and breath. Before the gods I vow."

"I'll be proud of you, Tazerion. In word and deed. With my heart and breath. Before the gods I vow," she answered.

Father Westinkar flicked them with rose-scented water, droplets hissing as they flew past and fell into the fire. Taz rose, and they took the little red packets from the basket, tossing them into the fire. Blue flame flared as the packets caught fire and burned.

They repeated the circle again with pledges to honor the gods. Then again, where Taz dropped and promised to give her daughters while she promised to raise them well. The fourth circle was for love.

"I'll protect you with my life. In word and deed. With my heart and breath. Before the gods I vow." Taz's heart was in his eyes and I had to swallow down the lump in my throat as the sight of it brought an aching reminder of Portis to life in my chest.

"I'll keep you safe. In word and deed. With my heart and breath. Before the gods I vow." Alice's voice was clear and firm.

More water. More red packets that hissed blue flame. Taz promised to be a shoulder to lean on. Alice promised to listen to his counsel. And on the final circle, they both knelt before me to pledge their allegiance to the empire.

"May your fealty serve you well," I said, flicking water over them.

They rose, and I watched Alice clutch the red packet in her hand for a brief moment, whispering a prayer for strength and peace before she tossed it into the fire. Taz followed with his packet and the pair of blue flames wrapped around each other for a second before they vanished into the reddish-gold.

"I love you," Taz murmured, lifting Alice's veil and kissing her. As she sank into him, the last unruly thread of painful fear twisted around my heart came loose. The empire would be safe in their hands when it was time for me to go.

The crowd greeted the happy couple with the stomping of

their feet, the sound threatening to shake the very foundations of the temple.

Alice stepped to the side as Taz took a knee before me. I reached out, putting a hand on his head.

"I, Hailimi Mercedes Jaya Bristol, with the best interests of the empire weighing on my mind, do formally acknowledge Tazerion Benton Shivan as Prince Consort to my rightfully named heir."

"I, Tazerion Benton Shivan, do hereby accept and take my rightful position as Prince Consort of the Empire of Indrana."

I stepped back and there were tears in Alice's eyes as she held a hand out to Taz and helped him to his feet.

"You two will lead this empire back to peace," I said, kissing first her forehead and then his. "And do it in a far more gracious manner than I could accomplish."

My BodyGuards formed up around me as I started back down the aisle. Alice and Taz were on my heels and we passed through the open doors, crossing the entryway and emerging into the sunlight.

The crowd outside was silent, breaths held in anticipation as I raised my hand to them. "To the new Indrana!"

The crowd took up the chant as Alice and Taz came out onto the steps of the temple and the bells began to ring. Their music filled the air, filled us all with hope, and I shared a look with my Trackers as Indrana took her first steps toward the future.

ACKNOWLEDGMENTS

My job is to write the words in my heart, to show you all the scenes in my head. It's a solitary pursuit, but not one I accomplish alone.

The first nod always goes to my family. To my husband, Don, who is a constant, steady presence in my life as comforting as the sea and as imposing as the mountains. Thank you, my love, for all you do.

To my brothers and sisters, you all know who you are and I could not do this without your love and support every single day. To my parents, thank you as always for everything you have given me; so much of what I am is because of you.

Thanks will never be enough for my agent, the indomitable Andy Zack, for all his hard work, and for his ability to see Hail as she needed to be when my vision hadn't cleared enough to recognize what needed to be done to the story I had in my hands.

To my editor, Sarah Guan, who stepped up to the plate of a daunting task of editing the third book in a series and owned it. Thank you for your wisdom, your support, your questions, and your presence. Thanks also to Ellen for your bright light and amazing support of my books, as well as to the rest of the Orbit team for all their hard work. And special thanks to Nazia and Jenni for all they do for Hail and Co. across the pond.

ACKNOWLEDGMENTS

Special thanks go to M. B. Boroson for recommending the Sirens Conference to me last year. The experience changed my life. Thanks to Amy Tenbrink for her kindness and support in the face of my anxiety, to my roommate Carolyn Grey for giving me that last little push I needed to go, and to my awesome fellow warriors: Cass, Jenny, Rook, Blair, Kallyn, Jessica, and too many others to mention. I was wounded when I arrived— thank you for the space to heal and for the companionship that was so desperately needed.

Additional thanks to Blair MacGregor for her fight expertise and being willing to give her input on the final showdown.

To CJ, Beena, Ana, and Lisa. These books would have been a sad shadow of themselves were it not for your input, your love, and your encouragement. Thank you for being there at the beginning and thank you for being here at the end.

Dear readers, to you all my thanks for letting me share this moment of time with you. This is all I have ever wanted to do with my life, and it's because of you I am afforded the opportunity. I will never forget that kindness—that when you had the choice to spend some of your precious time it was with my stories.

extras

orbit

meet the author

Photo Credit: Donald Branum

K. B. WAGERS has a bachelor's degree in Russian studies, and her nonfiction writing has earned her two Air Force Space Command Media Contest awards. A native of Colorado, she lives at the base of the Rocky Mountains with her husband and son. In between books, she can be found lifting heavy things, running on trails, dancing to music, and scribbling on spare bits of paper.

if you enjoyed
BEYOND THE EMPIRE

look out for

THERE BEFORE THE CHAOS

The Farian War: Book One

by

K. B. Wagers

*The battle for the throne is over. The war
for the galaxy is just beginning.*

*Hail Bristol, the infamous gunrunner-turned-empress
of Indrana, has avenged the murder of her family and, in a
bloody civil war, secured the throne she never expected to inherit.
She looks forward to fulfilling her duties to her people: retiring
her gun and throwing herself into the rebuilding of her empire.
Her hard-won peace, however, is short-lived.*

extras

When Indrana's closest ally asks her to intervene in an interstellar military crisis, Hail embarks on the most highest-stakes diplomatic mission the empire has ever faced. Caught between two alien civilizations at each other's throats, she must uncover each side's true intentions before all of humanity becomes collateral damage in a full-blown galactic war.

The sun was setting, streaking gold across the sky, when Emmory came through the door of my rooms. "Majesty, Major Morri is here with another Farian. She apologizes for not contacting Alba about your schedule and wonders if you have a few moments."

The request—and the fact they had circumvented my chamberlain—was curious enough to pull me away from the window. I smoothed both hands over the gray-and-black sari I'd worn to dinner with Alice and Taz and nodded to my *Ekam*.

He opened the door again, and Major Dio Morri came into the room, followed by an older woman in a pale green dress.

"I am sorry for the interruption, Majesty."

"It's fine, Dio." I waved off her apology.

"Your Majesty, may I present Ambassador Adora Notaras?"

I stayed where I was, with my hands folded together at my waist. Even were it appropriate for me to offer a proper Indranan greeting of a palm out, there was no way Emmory would let an unvetted Farian touch me. "It's a great pleasure to meet you," I said instead.

"Your Majesty." The elderly woman bowed low and I glanced past her to where Major Morri stood, tight-lipped, at her side.

"Welcome to Indrana, Ambassador. If I'd known you were coming, we would have been better prepared."

"It is quite fine as it is. There is no need for elaborate ceremony." Adora rose, her dark eyes serious. "Fasé sends her deepest regards."

"She's well?"

"As she can be. She's atoning for her crimes."

Whatever my issues with Fasé were, the edge to Adora's words made me uneasy. They carried a heavy weight, reminding me how much I owed her, how much Indrana owed her. She'd sacrificed everything for us and I'd repaid her with cold fury at the end of it.

I felt Emmory's fingers brush against my back, dragging me back to the Farians in front of me. I forced out a smile as I released the breath I was holding.

"What is it we can do for you, Ambassador?"

"I have come to extend an invitation to you, Your Majesty. The Pedalion would like to meet with you to discuss a stronger alliance between Faria and Indrana."

The shock that Major Morri failed to hide told me all I needed to know about this unprecedented offer, and I remembered Fasé's words about how the Pedalion had never met with a human in all the years they'd been in contact with us.

"I would be happy to talk with the Matriarch Council and put together a delegation. We would need to select an ambassador—"

"The Pedalion would like to meet with you, Majesty. No one else."

"Me? Why?" Something about this whole situation made the hairs stand up on the back of my neck, and I couldn't stop myself from shaking my head. "Indrana values our relationship with Faria, Ambassador. However, this is an incredibly difficult time for us. I'm sure the Pedalion can respect that there is no way for me to leave my empire. We've just finished a war, two really, when you get down to it. I have things that must be handled here at home."

It was surprising to know I meant those words. I didn't want to leave. Indrana was counting on me, trusting me to lead her back to stability and peace. I couldn't leave my people just because our alien allies had decided they wanted a chat.

There was so much work to still do and with Alice pregnant it wasn't fair to expect her to take up my job. I'd managed to whittle my duties down to almost nothing, but it was still a burden my heir didn't need.

"The Pedalion requested you, Your Majesty. If they had been willing to meet with anyone else they would have said so."

"I'm sure they will understand my position," I replied with a smile and watched as her eyes narrowed a fraction. This was a woman not used to being refused.

Not an ambassador then. Interesting.

I wondered if that was just an easy title for the Farians to convey their wishes or if there was some awkwardness in the translation from Farian to Indranan. *Smatis* weren't always perfect in deciphering the nuances between languages.

Major Morri's behavior was the most curious. Her tense shoulders and the barely controlled muscle twitching at her jawline screamed her unease. She kept her eyes glued to the floor rather than looking my way.

"I will send a message home and let the Pedalion know of your concerns," Adora said finally.

"That sounds like an excellent idea. I'll let Alba know you'll be contacting her for any future meetings. Do you need accommodations?"

"No, Your Majesty. Major Morri has already taken care of that for me." Adora's smile was tight, the woman so clearly perturbed by my refusal that I did all I could not to laugh out loud. "Thank you. Good night."

"Night." I waited for the door to close behind them before I turned to my BodyGuard. "That sounded an awful lot like a summons," I said.

"It did, Majesty. And one they weren't expecting you to refuse."

"You'd think Fasé would have warned them about me."

"You'd think they were paying attention over the last year."

I punched my *Ekam* in the arm with a laugh, but my amusement was fleeting and was soon replaced with a hissing curse. "Find Caspel, Emmory. Tell him I want to talk to him now."

My BodyGuard didn't argue and left me alone to find the director of my intelligence service. If anyone on Pashati knew what was up with the Farians, it would be Caspel Ganej.

By the time Caspel arrived, Hao was lounging on one of the couches in the main room of my hotel suite while Johar pillaged my bar. Alice and Taz occupied the other, my heir looking far more alert than she had a right to at six months pregnant.

Alba followed Caspel into the room, Emmory and Gita on their heels. Zin was already stationed by the door and the other three of my old BodyGuards were in the hallway.

Director Caspel Ganej of the Imperial Intelligence Service raised one eyebrow when he took in the assembled group but didn't say a word.

"A woman claiming to be an ambassador from the Pedalion visited me just a little over an hour ago," I said as I leaned a hip on my desk. "They want me to come visit to discuss strengthening our alliance."

"Claiming, Majesty?" Caspel asked.

"My gut," I replied. "And she was distinctly unhappy when I told her there was no possible way I could make such a trip."

"Could I see?"

I pushed away from the desk and touched the back of Caspel's hand, transferring the recording my *smati* had made over to his.

The head of my spy agency blinked in surprise. "I am impressed you stayed so calm, Majesty. That wasn't a request. It sounded like a—"

"Summons?" I laughed. "Yes, Emmory and I thought the same thing. What's going on in Farian space, Caspel? There's a reason for this beyond 'let's be better friends.'"

"I'm sure of it, Majesty." Caspel cleared his throat and looked around the room. "Let me look into things and I will get back to you?"

"Fine, make it quick though. I suspect I'll be hearing from Ambassador Notaras again very soon."

Caspel bowed in my direction and then Alice's and left the room.

"I'd have thought you would have jumped at the chance to leave the planet," Alice teased, and I laughed.

"Once upon a time, maybe. If I thought it was a simple diplomatic mission, I'd have agreed to take it to the council. But it's not; something else is at play there." I pushed Hao's feet off the couch and sat down next to him. "You're being awfully reticent."

He shrugged. "What can I say? You're in charge."

"Thank you for noticing."

Hao shrugged again. "You know I distrust the Farians on general principle, *sha zhu*. I'm not going to influence your decisions because of my bias, however justified it might be." Hao's words may have been casual, but his jaw was tight and he didn't look at me. Cas's death had hit us all hard, but something about the incident had shaken my mentor to the core. I knew better than to press him in front of the others and so I let his comment pass without a reply.

"We'll wait and see what they do," I said instead to Alice. "I suspect I'll hear something before the end of the day tomorrow."

"Keep me in the loop," she replied, and with Taz's help got herself off the couch after I stood.

"I will. Good night."

Johar handed me a glass and tapped hers to the rim, the crystal ringing in the silent room. "Sounds like interesting times ahead."

"Gods help us," I murmured. "I haven't recovered from the last round."